Praise for Anne Kelleher

"Anne Kelleher's engrossing fantasy, *Silver's Edge*...
weaves an enticing tale as Nessa braves unknown
dangers to find her father and bring him safely home
in this beguiling story of courage and adventure."
—*BookPage*

"Ms. Kelleher weaves another fantasy epic
of grand proportions, sweeping the reader
off into lands, legends and lore. Part Arthurian,
part Tolkien and part fairy tale, the mix creates
an incredible world for the reader's fertile mind
to take root. It starts off slowly, but then takes off
with a bang and never releases you from its grasp."
—*The Best Reviews,* on *Silver's Edge*

"The characters are complex and multifaceted, and the
writing is rich with colorful prose....Women control
their fates, and fear is not an option when it comes to
the tough decisions that must be made in a time when
all that is held sacred is facing destruction."
—*Romance Reviews Today* on *Silver's Edge*

"*Silver's Edge* is a first-class fantasy.
The characters are vivid, believable; they captured
this reader's heart, taking me on an unforgettable
journey as they confronted their fears, made
tough decisions and accepted the consequences of
those decisions, no matter what it cost them."
—*In the Library Reviews*

"…displays vivid imagination."
—*Publishers Weekly*

"Fascinating—
a most ingenious blend of science fiction and fantasy."
—*New York Times* bestselling author
Marion Zimmer Bradley on *Daughter of Prophecy*

SILVER'S BANE

ANNE KELLEHER

LUNA™

www.LUNA-Books.com

LUNA™

First edition June 2005

SILVER'S BANE

ISBN 0-373-80222-6

www.LUNA-Books.com

Printed in U.S.A.

This book is dedicated with love to all the women
in my life—friends, teachers, mentors, guides and
guardians who are far too many to list—and most
especially to my mother, Frances Kelly;
my stepmother, Alice Kelleher;
my grandmother Rose Castaldi;
my sisters, Sheila Kelly Bauer, DJ Kelleher and Pam Boyd;
my daughters, Kate, Meg and Libby; all those yet to
come and all those who have gone before.

Blessed be.

Glossary of People and Places

Faerie—the sidhe word for their own world. It includes the Wastelands

The Shadowlands—the sidhe word for the mortal world

The Wastelands—that part of Faerie to which the goblins have been banished

Lyonesse—legendary lost land that is said to have lain to the east of Faerie

Brynhyvar—the country that, in the mortal world, overlaps with Faerie

The Otherworld—the mortal name for Faerie

TirNa'lugh—the lands of light; the shining lands—mortal name for Faerie; becoming archaic

The Summerlands—place where mortals go at death

Humbria—mortal country across the Murhevnian Sea to the east of Brynhyvar

Lacquilea—mortal country lying to the south of Brynhyvar

Killcairn—Nessa's village

Killcrag—neighboring village to the south

Killcarrick—lake and the keep

Alemandine—Queen of sidhe

Xerruw—Goblin King

Vinaver—Alemandine's younger twin sister and the rightful Queen

Artimour—Alemandine's half-mortal half brother

Gloriana—mother of Vinaver, Alemandine and Artimour

Timias—Gloriana's chief councilor and the unacknowledged father of Alemandine and Vinaver

Eponea—Mistress of the Queen's Horses

Delphinea—Eponea's daughter

Finuviel—Vinaver's son by the god Herne; rightful King of Faerie

Hudibras—Alemandine's consort

Gorlias, Philomemnon, Berillian—councilors to the Queen

Petri—Delphinea's servant gremlin

Khouri—leader of the gremlin revolt and plot to steal the Caul

Nessa—nineteen-year-old daughter of Dougal, the blacksmith of Killcairn

Dougal—Nessa's father; Essa's husband; stolen into Faerie by Vinaver

Griffin—Dougal's eighteen-year-old apprentice

Donnor, Duke of Gar—overlord of Killcairn and surrounding country; uncle of the mad King and leader of the rebellion against him

Cadwyr, Duke of Allovale—Donnor's nephew and heir

Cecily of Mochmorna—Donnor's wife; heiress to the throne of Brynhyvar

Kian of Garn—Donnor's First Knight

Hoell—mad King of Brynhyvar

Merle—Queen of Brynhyvar; princess of Humbria

Renvahr, Duke of Longborth—brother of Queen Merle; elected Protector of the Realm of Brynhyvar

Granny Wren—wicce woman of Killcairn

Granny Molly—wicce woman of Killcrag

Engus—blacksmith of Killcarrick

Uwen—Kian's second in command

The Hag—immortal who dwells in the rocks and caves below Faerie; the moonstone globe was stolen from her when the Caul was forged

Herne—immortal who dwells within the Faerie forests, from which he rides out on Samhain night, leading the Wild Hunt across the worlds

Great Mother—mortal name for the Hag

The Horned One—mortal name for Herne

ACKNOWLEDGMENTS

Special thanks to Rosmari Roast, herbalist,
wise woman and friend, for eleventh-hour research;
to my agent, Jenn Jackson, and my editor
Mary-Theresa Hussey for seeing the potential before
I did; to Laura Rose and the rest of the Goddess Girls:
Anne Sheridan, Susan Grayson, Leslie Goodale,
Lisa Drew, Barbara Terry, Jamie King, Louise Rose,
Alicia Tremper, Judy Conrad—you guys are the best
midwives in the world; to Judy Charlton for reiki;
to all the folks in the CT over 40 chat room on AOL,
especially GtimeJoe; to all my fellow LUNA-tics in the
LUNA-sylum for cheerleading. But most of all, this
book would never have been written without the
unwavering love and unstinting support of one man:
Donny Goodman, I adore you.

BEFORE

It was the weight of the world above her that nearly drove Vinaver mad. The thought of it crept, unbidden and unsought, from the deep places of her mind, a fat white worm of fear threatening to suffocate her from within, even as she struggled through narrow fissures and sloping corridors of unyielding stone. The pressure bore down on her from all directions, and the fear rose, writhing and squirming, coiling and expanding, filling her lungs, constricting her throat, wetting her palms, so that the lych-light at the end of her slim hazel-wood staff dimmed to a pinprick until she felt she would be swallowed by the dark.

The solid rock surrounding her was nearly as foreign to the intrinsic nature of her kind as the deadly silver from the mortal Shadowlands, for the sidhe of Faerie were creatures of light and air. But Vinaver had been forced to learn the first time her journey had taken her into the places where sunlight was not even a legend, that when the longing for the light and airy open spaces threatened to overwhelm her, she should close her eyes, and breathe, and let the crushing sensation roll over and through her like an enormous wave, until her mind quieted, leaving her feeling as exhausted and battered as the sea after a storm. But at least she was able to grip her staff and go on.

This was the last place anyone would ever think to find a sidhe. Her kind were never cave dwellers, stone carvers or earth diggers. According to the Lorespinners, the Underlands had been the realm of the goblins once, in the earliest time before the great Goblin Wars, when the sidhe, led by Vinaver's mother, the great Queen Gloriana, had bound them into the Wastelands above. At least they'd still been bound in the Wastelands when Vinaver had started on this quest. She had no idea how long she'd been below the surface. There was no day or night, there was no sun or moon to mark the passage of hours, or the advance of seasons. She found the longer she was there, the less time had meaning.

But the domesticated trees within the Grove of the Palace of the Faerie Queen, as well as the wild ones of the Forest, had been adamant. Only the Hag—She who dwelled in the dark places below the surface world—could tell Vinaver why her sister, Alemandine, had failed to become pregnant with the heir of Faerie in her appointed time.

Now Vinaver followed the creature that slithered before her, a near-formless thing that gleamed wetly as it led her through granite canyons, leaving a trail of its own slime, its face perpetually turned away from the yellow glow of her lych-light.

Just beyond a jagged outcropping, her guide paused and

drew back, indicating a tunnel leading off to one side. Vinaver stopped. The thing wanted her to follow it. She crept cautiously forward, feeling her way down the rough walls with fingertips made exquisitely sensitive. She peered inside the black slit of the opening. Patches of lichen glowed as she extended the staff as far into the tunnel as she could, and frowned as she saw that the roof sloped away into a low opening that disappeared into deep and utter blackness. It appeared barely wide enough for her shoulders. She'd have to slither through it, wriggling like a worm. Her breath caught in her throat at the thought of the massive rock surrounding her on all sides, and she nearly turned, shrieking, maddened beyond reach, dashing back like a butterfly trapped in a net, frantic for the taste of sun and air. I cannot do this, the voice of her own panic screamed through her mind, as she gripped the hazel staff with wet, white-knuckled fingers. But you must do this, she thought immediately in response. And she forced herself to breathe.

The world above was sick. The trees whispered it in their branches, sighed it in the wind. What beauty Faerie possessed was illusory, fleeting, and fading even as she lingered. If she failed to find out what could be done to heal the land, everything and everyone in Faerie would be lost forever, dispersed into some chaotic void, forgotten and forsaken. Her son's image rose up unbidden, and her heart contracted that such grace and beauty as was his should be wasted. Finuviel. She saw his coal-black curls and long green eyes, high cheekbones and slanting brows and a smile that contained within it everything right and good and beautiful of Faerie. For him, she thought. For Finuviel, I will do what I must. She closed her eyes and concentrated on the air rushing in and out of her lungs, summoning up the strength to let herself be led into that dark and narrow passage. Finally she was able to nod.

Her guide had withdrawn, crouching in a formless lump. It had no eyes but she knew it watched her. So she nodded again and waved the lych-light. The creature shuddered away from the light, but gathered itself up into a sort of ball and slithered forward.

Disgust roiled through her but she tamped that down too. With a final breath, she entered the narrow tunnel. Almost immediately she was forced to bend, then to hunch, and finally, just as she feared, she was forced to crawl, first on all fours, and then, creeping and squirming like the thing before her. She found that she was grateful for the fluids the creature exuded, for they slicked the walls, easing her passage, even as she battled the panic that threatened to undo her completely when she felt the rock walls close in around her head.

She tumbled out at last, wet with sweat and slime, and she raised her face to the rush of cold still air and looked up into a vaulted cavern covered in tiny pinpricks that resembled infant stars. It was the lichen, she realized.

The thing quivered. The stone beneath her bare feet was smooth and very cold and white mist rose from the surface of a vast, still lake. Within it, patches of luminous phosphorescence lit the whole chamber with a pale greenish glow. An underground sea, she thought. But the thing at her feet was moving again, squirming down the sloping lip to the very edge of the water. It roiled and shuddered and a single arm formed out of the shapeless mass, and a rough approximation of a hand pointed a stubby finger. Vinaver squinted. In the middle of the water, behind the shifting mist, she saw a cluster of boulders that rose from the center of a small island some distance from the shore. "Is that where She lives?"

The words hung flat as if the water somehow absorbed the sound. A heavy stillness permeated the moist cold air, a silence so profound, she could feel the skin stretching over her sinews, the air moving in and out of her lungs, the pulse of her blood against the walls of her veins. Her tongue felt sharp as crystal against the dry leather of her mouth. That this could be the end of all her wanderings made her knees weak and her heart pound like a hammer against her breastbone.

But the wide water lay between her and the Hag, and there was no other way across as far as she could see. She would have to swim. Her breath hung like the mist over the sea. The thought of immersing herself in that cold bath made her bones ache. It had been so long since she'd been truly warm, she thought. She touched her face with one cold hand. She could scarcely remember a time when her muscles were not knotted and stiff, when her bones did not feel like flesh-covered lead. She did not want to bathe in that greenish glowing water. The great rocks themselves seemed to shift and groan and sigh all around her and the stone beneath her feet undulated as if a great beast stirred from some black unbroken sleep.

Vinaver looked down at the thing crouching at her feet, throbbing in time to a silent pulse, and she understood that it had brought her as far as it could. The rest was up to her. She removed her cloak and her gown—what was left of them—and placed them neatly on the stony shore beside her leather pack and the hazel rod. The lych-light faded to a faint twinkle. The gooseflesh prickled her skin and she crossed her arms over her breasts, then walked barefoot, naked but for the ragged chemise she wore, directly down to the water.

The first few strokes were a pleasant surprise. For far from being cold, the water was warm, welcoming as a hot salt sea under a summer sun. She stretched and relaxed into it, her strokes purposeful and sure, steady as the warmth that seeped into her legs and down her toes, caressing her with a deliberateness that was almost aware. Around her the white mist rose—not mist, she thought, but steam—drifting off the surface. She could see the island rising black and barren in the center. She swam on, the warmth bolstering her and sustaining her, trailing through the long locks of her coppery hair like a lover's fingers.

It was when the water began to thicken around her that she began to worry, that she realized that what she swam through was not water such as that which coursed through the rivers of Faerie, nor even the salt ocean that surrounded it on all sides, but some strange primal sea, and her heart clenched as she saw long, shadowy strands and huge clumps of glutinous fiber swirl through the depths, like shadowy leviathans roaming the deep. If one of those things takes me, I shall be lost, she thought, and she stroked harder, kicked faster, even as the water gathered around her, congealing into rubbery strands. Dismayed, she kicked harder as the stuff twined around her limbs, sapping her strength. But still she had hope, that here, at last she had come to where the Hag dwelled, and she whipped her hair out of her eyes, stroking desperately toward the savage-looking boulders rising tantalizingly, mercilessly, just out of reach.

At last, when finally she thought she could stand no more, her feet touched solid stone. Nearly weeping, she looked down at the thick gelatinous clots that swirled and clumped around her ankles and her calves. She wiped and kicked them away, shuddering with disgust at the way the stuff persistently slimed around her as she plowed up the steep slope. Her teeth began to chatter audibly even before her knees broke the surface of the sea and she clutched her arms close about herself, shivering in the cold, cold air, even as she scraped the thick slime off her chemise and her skin, raking it out of her hair. At last she stood on the shore. She turned and looked back. In the dim greenish light, she could barely make out the white spot of her clothes, the round, black shape of her guide crouching patiently beside it. The water pushed up against the shore, as if searching for her, and she stepped farther away from it, warily peering in the dim light for some sign of the Hag.

She thought she heard a chuckle, and she whipped around, but it was only the insistent lap of the water against the stone. She drew herself up, and opened her arms as wide as her shaking body would let her. "Great Herne," she whispered, "if ever you were with me, be with me now." She drew a deep breath and cried, into the thick and chilly air, "Great Hag! Great Hag, come forth upon my call." The rock was slick beneath her soles, and she felt something slice through her feet as she took a single step forward. She cried out and nearly lost her balance. She looked down and saw that unlike the opposite shore, these boulders were punctuated by shards of what looked like glass. She squatted down, watching her pale blood roll down the slope into the sea, carefully feeling all around her for smooth places between the razor-edged outcroppings. She edged forward, feeling her way with questing hands and careful feet. But for all her care, the jagged edges sliced unmercifully and she nearly fell more than once. At last she reached a relatively smooth plateau, beside the cluster of boulders that rose from the center of the island like the throne of the Goblin King in his stinking hall.

"Great Hag," she whispered, scarcely daring to give the words voice. "Great Hag, come forth and heed your child's plea." Her voice echoed up and around and down the vault of the ceiling, sighing and rippling across the water, and she saw the depths dull to dark green as the drifting shadows within it seemed to thicken in response. It was as if everything about her in some way was so intimately connected to the place that every move she made, every breath she drew, every thought, even, had some effect. "Great Hag," she whispered, this time pouring every ounce of need, of desire, of hope she possessed into the words. "Come forth."

But the boulders were silent and the sea was still.

Vinaver sank shaking to her haunches, her arms wrapped around her knees. Her guide was wrong, so obviously wrong. And she was so stupid, so obviously stupid to have trusted him—it. What could she have expected from a blind, deaf, voiceless, practically senseless creature? What could she have expected from the foul misshapen things that led her to it? Tears filled her eyes and spilled down her cheeks, seeping down her fingers, rolling down her arms unheeded. Was all of this for naught? Had she truly come here to the underbelly of the world to find nothing? She would not survive another swim back across that swarming sea. She had failed. Faerie would disintegrate, Finuviel, her fair son, so bright with promise, would die the true death, and all the great and shining beauty that was Faerie would go down into nothingness. Down here, she thought, into this primal soup. There was nothing else to do but wait for it.

She rested her cheek on her knees, and in the soft and swirling mist, wooing as a lover's whisper, she thought she heard a snatch of music, clear and airy and piping as any ever drifted across a Faerie meadow. A woman's voice danced through her mind, low and mocking. "A queen who's never a queen to be—is that who comes to call on me?"

Slowly Vinaver rose to her feet, forcing herself to straighten, as a sudden fear greater than any she had yet known gripped her like a vise. "Great Hag?" she whispered, for the voice was not that of an old woman. Scarcely daring to believe that here, at last, was the end of all her striving, she peered into the darkness, gaping in astonishment as the boulders lifted and shifted and finally resolved themselves into the hideous visage of an old woman hunching over a great black cauldron. The cauldron was balanced over a firepit by a curious arrangement of two polished crystal globes, and a makeshift tripod of iron legs beneath a flat disk where a third globe should have been.

As Vinaver stared in horror, steam spiraled up from the depths of the cauldron, half obscuring the grinning, toothless rictus on the Hag's gray-blue face, which was striated with wrinkled folds carved like channels into the bedrock of her sunken eyes and cheeks. She gripped what looked like a thick branch—for a few dead leaves still clung to it—in two clawlike hands as she stirred her brew.

The Hag's bright eyes fixed on her, and Vinaver gasped. Like Herne's, glowing red then green, they pierced her with a force that made her stagger. She regained her footing and took a single step forward, forgetful of the sharp crystals that slashed her feet to the bones, and cried out as the pain lanced up her leg. As more of her pale blood leaked into the rock, it shuddered beneath her feet, smoothing itself beneath her bleeding soles. And she understood she was to draw closer.

Each step was agony but she refused to flinch. She had come so far. She could go a little farther, after all. There was neither kindness nor cruelty in that glittering green gaze, just a hungry interest. The Hag's gray tongue flicked over her yellowed and blackened teeth and for a moment her eyes turned red.

Suddenly more frightened than ever, Vinaver paused. Such was the nature of the Hag, Vinaver understood with sudden insight, she who destroys that all might be made new. Everything was fodder for her cauldron, grist for her mill, silt for her sea. Vinaver wanted to speak, but something that felt like her heart blocked her throat. She saw more clearly the improvised contrivance that supported the cauldron in place of a third globe. It was of iron—three cast-iron legs bound into a tripod, a small disk placed on top. And suddenly, with cold and certain knowing, she knew exactly where the third globe was.

"The moonstone," she whispered, daring to meet the Hag's eyes. "The moonstone globe—the one that wears the Caul within my sister's Palace—that moonstone globe is yours."

The Hag hissed, her rheumy eyes darting from side to side. She gave a great turn to the stick and the steam rose and swirled and in the depths, Vinaver thought she saw a familiar face—a furtive face that turned his back and threw a robe over his head before the image dissipated into nothing.

"Timias," Vinaver whispered, recognizing her mother's Chief Councilor and perpetual thorn in her side. "'Twas Timias who took your globe?" Another hiss was the only sound the Hag made as she swung her shoulders in a mighty arc as she gave the cauldron another stir. A shiver ran through Vinaver. She looked down at the other two globes, this time more carefully, and saw that one gleamed black as pitch in the bluish glow of the unnatural fire that burned within the stone pit beneath the cauldron, and that the other was flecked with specks of black, white, green and red. And suddenly, in a flash of insight, Vinaver understood something of the nature of the problem. The black globe—the goblins, perhaps. The other, the mortals, most like. And the missing moonstone that Timias had apparently stolen in some way represented Faerie. It WAS Faerie, Vinaver realized. And Timias had taken it from the Hag. She had always wondered why the stories were so vague about the origination of the globe. "The trees have told me that Faerie is dying. I see that your globe is—is missing." These two were connected in some way, she was sure of it. She hesitated, attempting to gauge the thoughts behind the creature's burning eyes. And then she gathered her courage and spoke quickly, lest she lose her resolve. "I know there's something terribly wrong for Alemandine is unable to conceive her Heir. And the trees told me to come to you, Great Hag, that you would know how to save Faerie." Vinaver finished quickly, for there was something in the Hag's eyes that made her want to run into the water, to give herself up to those sultry depths, to the peace the green sea promised.

The steam rose up in a high cloud as the Hag stirred the cauldron. She said nothing, but the same mocking voice Vinaver heard before swirled out of the steam, the words carried on the vapor. "Round about the circle goes, dark to light and back it flows—world without end can never be, so says every prophecy."

"But what do you say?" asked Vinaver, suddenly brave with the courage of desperation. What, after all, did she have to lose? She had no chance of going back without the Hag's help. If she were only fodder for the Hag's eternal soup, so be it. "What do you say, Great Mother?" Something made the Hag look up. She fixed Vinaver with that cold unforgiving stare, but Vinaver refused to shrink. She took one step forward. "Must it end now?"

The rocks groaned, as though shuddering beneath the weight of some eternal sorrow, and the Hag's appearance rippled, shifting from the hungry visage of She Who Destroys to the drawn and ravaged face of She Who Mourns. Suddenly she did not seem at all malevolent. Her shoulders collapsed, leaving her stooped and frail, and her face thinned and the reddish light in the green depths died. Her lipless mouth twisted and a tear seeped down one ruined cheek.

Time hung, suspended, the moment prolonged beyond all reality. The darkness seemed to shrink, expand, then retreat once more, as a light, white and clean as springtime sun leaped up from the cauldron's depths. And in that radiant flash, Vinaver thought she saw the Hag transformed, her craggy features melting, dissolving, her flesh rounding and firming and lifting, flushing to a gentle shade of pink, and her eyes faded to violet. The Maiden, she thought. But even as Vinaver recognized the transformation, it faded away, dispersing into the air like one of the squirming things roaming the water's depths. Finally it was Vinaver who broke the spell. "I think I understand," she whispered. "You can't change. Something's happened. And you can't change." The rage that flared from the Hag's red eyes gave Vinaver her first real thread of hope. "Tell me," she whispered. "Make me understand. If I should be the Queen, why am I not? Why can you not become the Maiden, and why did Timias take your globe? What is it that's killing Faerie, and how do I make it stop?"

Vinaver thought at first the Hag would not answer her at all, for the creature only shifted from side to side, and she wondered if the Hag was incapable of speech. After all, Herne had never spoken to her, in their encounter. But in a smooth motion that belied the image of the ancient crone, the Hag suddenly turned to face Vinaver and shrieked, in a voice that echoed across the vaulted space like the harsh cry of a crow, "Why? Why? Why?"

Perplexed, Vinaver stared. "Why what?"

With another shriek, the Hag went back to her stirring and the steam billowed up in great white clouds, wreathing and obscuring her face. For a moment, Vinaver was afraid the Hag would disappear. But as the steam cleared, she was still there, bright green eyes fixed on Vinaver. "Why should I help you?"

It was not a question Vinaver expected and the Hag's voice alone unsettled her, grating on her ears like a blade scraped over stone. She cast about, taken aback, momentarily confused. What could she possibly say that would convince the Hag that Faerie should be saved? What part was more beautiful than the rest? Where to even begin?

And then Finuviel's face rose before her, his form danced out of her memory, the tiny infant, delicately made, but sturdy, so fair and strong and merry as he grew, the epitome of what a prince of the sidhe should be. She remembered the first time she'd heard his laugh. A butterfly had landed on his toes. Her eyes clouded with tears and her throat thickened. "Well," she said at last. "I have a son."

"Ah," sighed the Hag, and with a stir of her stick, the great cauldron released another cloud of steam. This time it resolved itself into the angular, antlered face of Herne, the Lord of the Forest and the Wild Hunt.

"You know—you know about my son?" Vinaver said. For the appearance of Herne's image implied that the Hag knew he'd fathered Finuviel. No one else had ever believed Vinaver. Everyone accused her of using the claim of Herne as a way of concealing Finuviel's true parentage. The enormity of the Hag's knowledge burst like a sunrise into her mind and suddenly Vinaver believed that not only was there hope, but that the Hag would help her.

Without another sound, the Hag beckoned. Vinaver crept forward, wincing on her ruined feet, her heart pounding audibly. At the edge of the firepit, just before it was possible for Vinaver to see inside the cauldron, she held up her hand. "Yes," the Hag whispered, a long, low croon that tickled the back of Vinaver's neck like the barest stroke of her long sharp claws. "Yes, I know about your son. I know all about your son. And yes, for his sake, and for his father's, I shall help you. But there is always a price, and so I ask you, Vinaver Tree-speaker, the would-be, should-be Queen—tell me, what will you pay for the knowledge of the Hag?"

"What would you have of me?" The water was still dripping off her hair. It ran in chilly rivulets down her back, between the cleft of her buttocks, trickling down her legs to
drip off the two swollen lumps of throbbing flesh that were
her bloodied feet. She felt as if she stood in a pool of her own
congealing blood. The cold air raised gooseflesh on her entire body, but an act of will greater than any she had ever
known she was capable of kept her upright and still. She had
come so far and searched for so long that she had nothing
left but the rags on her back. What could the Hag possibly
want of her?

"There are three things." The whisper rasped down her
spine like a fingernail across granite. "For the first, I want my
globe back. For the second, I want the head of him that took
it from me."

At that, Vinaver's head snapped up. "Timias?"

This time she was standing far too close when the angry
light flared in the Hag's eyes. A searing pain lanced up her
leg as she involuntarily stepped back onto a sharp edge,
while an image blazed clearly in her mind, the image of
Timias creeping away from the cavern, bearing the moonstone globe. "You want me to kill Timias?"

"His life is mine, and my cauldron wants his head." The
Hag's hiss, her narrowed eyes, reminded Vinaver of a snake.
"Cut off his head with a silvered edge, and give it to me for
my cauldron. So those are the first two things I want of you.
Will you agree?"

The depth of the hatred in the Hag's voice frightened
Vinaver. "All right." She had no idea how she would actually fulfill the second requirement—for to do what the Hag
asked required some forethought. And it had not occurred

to her that murder would be involved. Vinaver swallowed hard. "What's the third?"

This time the Hag's response was a sinister chuckle. She leaned forward, even as Vinaver instinctively shrank back. "The third is the most important and the most necessary. I want your womb."

At first Vinaver was sure she had not heard correctly, even as her hands clasped her belly. So she could only stare while the Hag chuckled with anticipatory glee. "What?"

"I need your womb."

Vinaver looked at the scaly gray claws that gripped the stick, recoiling at the idea of those twisted, thickened digits anywhere near her flesh. "Why?" she whispered, horrified.

The Hag's laugh was like the rumble of rocks down a hill-side. "Ah, little queen. Already the circle widens into a spiral. The spiral turns, the center loosens, and soon all will spin away, down, into my cauldron. And my cauldron must not be cheated. If you would undo what has been done, you must feed it. And that's what it wants. That's what it needs. That's what it craves." She drew out the last long syllable, beckoning Vinaver closer with a crooked, yellow claw. "Come, if you will, and look within—but feed the cauldron to stop the spin." She stirred the stick, swaying a little, eyes closed as she chanted. Suddenly she stopped and opened her eyes. "You want your sister pregnant with Faerie's heir? Give me your womb. That's how it has to work, I'm afraid."

Vinaver swallowed hard, trying to control the beating of her heart. The monstrous thing muttered as she stirred, her lumpen shape rolling in slow motion in a large, left-turning spiral. Left-turning, Vinaver thought, the direction of breakdown, banishment and change, and in that moment she understood. As the Hag stirred the cauldron, so the tide of Faerie swung. Turning it to the left meant the undoing of the world. "Stop that!" cried Vinaver. "You're doing it—stop it—"

The Hag jerked around, the hairs on the end of her nose twitching, as if she smelled Vinaver's desperation. "Round about the circle goes, dark to light and back it flows," she chanted, as if Vinaver had not spoken. "She that dares to stop my spin, had better put a tidbit in. Feed my cauldron, pay the price, lest all be lost when light turns dark and dark turns light."

Vinaver's stomach clenched and her gut heaved at the thought that that creature might touch her. But she had come all this way, and what need had she of a womb, after all? She'd borne a son in her appointed time, such as it was. What did it matter whether or not she gave up her womb? "But—but if I give you my womb," she whispered, "will it not mean I can never be Queen?" The Hag threw back her head and howled as if at some unwitting joke, but Vinaver would not be dissuaded. "Tell me—tell me what I shall become—if I give you this—this part of me. If I shall not be Queen, what then?"

"She who comes with bitter need, had better then my cauldron feed."

But suddenly, Vinaver understood something that had eluded her for a long time. She had never understood why the god had come to her that Beltane night when Finuviel was conceived. No one had believed her. But the Hag knew. Her womb had served its purpose. "All right," she shrugged. "Done."

The Hag cackled. Vinaver's mouth dried up like a desert,

and she thought she might faint as nausea flopped in her gut like a dying fish. The Hag's claws closed around her wrist, drawing her closer, and the Hag's face seemed to fill her entire field of vision. The Hag's eyes glittered red, then green in the leaping blue flames, and her craggy face dissolved into unrecognizable chaos. Vinaver collapsed, crying out as she felt the scratch of the Hag's cold fingers, pulling at her clothing, kneading at her flesh, creeping between her legs, probing for the opening to the very center of her self, seeking, separating, pushing in with sharp, grasping claws.

Vinaver cried out at the first stab of blinding pain, and she pushed away, but the Hag held her hard. She shut her eyes as the pain flamed through her, and a kaleidoscope of voices and faces exploded in her mind, uncurling like ribbons, in long slow swirls of scarlet agony. She heard the wet, sucking rent, as her flesh ripped, but she didn't care, because she understood at last that it was in the pain that the Hag imparted her knowledge. As her body broke and bled, her mind opened, and a torrent of images cascaded in. She saw her mother, Timias and the mortal by whose hand the Caul was forged. She saw the moment of its making, when the three called down the magic and bound the two worlds— Shadow and Faerie—inextricably together, tightening the normal bonds between them tight as a noose.

In some detached corner of her mind, she felt the Hag tear away her womb, felt the hot gush of blood between her thighs, and she lay flat, legs thrown open, dazed and helpless as a newborn child. The pictures shuddered, swirled, spun and split into a double set of likenesses—somehow at once both that which was, and that which should have been. She saw herself born the sole daughter of Gloriana,

Faerie's great Queen, named her Heir, and made Queen when Gloriana went into the West. She saw a Faerie green and flourishing, Finuviel born in the fullness of time, welcomed as the new King of Faerie, even while, running concurrently, like the overlay of the Shadowlands on Faerie, she saw what had really happened since the forging of the Caul. And then, as the pain settled into a slow throb, she saw faint and pale the images of what might be. She lay back, eyes open, staring into the vaulted ceiling as the ghostly outlines formed and reformed, and the world slowly dissolved into nothingness.

When next she opened her eyes, she was lying flat on her back still, staring up at what she first thought to be pinpoints of twinkling lichen. Then a warm wind rustled through the branches of the trees above her, and she realized that the soft grass beneath her was slick with morning dew. And as she watched through eyes suddenly flooded with tears, the black sky above her brightened to gray as the first light of a Faerie dawn broke the horizon at last.

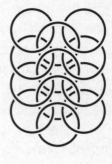

1

The gremlin's howls filled the forest. Like an avalanche, like a tidal wave, the sounds of rage and anguish and despair too long checked, exploded through the silent Samhain night, unleashed in earsplitting shrieks that continued unabated far beyond the physical capacity of such a small being to sustain such unbroken cacophony. Delphinea crumpled to her knees, crumbling like a dam against a sudden thaw, and pressed her head against the horse's side, trying to stifle the wails that wrapped themselves around her, first like water, then like wool, nearly choking her, crushing her with their weight of unadulterated sorrow, anger and need. The moon was hidden and the still sky was only illuminated by silver starlight. The night condensed into nothing but the blood-wrenching screams and the slick salt smell of the horse's coarse hair beneath her cheek. She felt subtle tremors beneath the surface of the leaf-strewn ground as if the great trees all around them shuddered to their roots. The horse trembled and shook, and Delphinea wrapped her arms as best she could around the animal's neck, murmuring a gentle croon more felt than heard, trying to create a subtle vibration to act as the only shield she could think of under such an onslaught of sound. But there was nothing, ultimately, that could stand against it, and finally, she collapsed against the horse's side, the mare's great beating heart her only anchor.

It was thus, curled and quivering, that Vinaver's house guards found her shortly before dawn, palms plastered against her ears, the horse only semi-aware, its eyes rolled back, its ears flattened against its head. Petri's cries showed no signs of diminishing. The orange torchlight revealed the gremlin flopping on the forest floor like a fish caught in a net. *As he is,* mused Delphinea, *within a net of Samhain madness.* Every Samhain the gremlins all went mad, and usually they were confined. But nothing seemed to be happening quite the way it usually did.

It took all six guards to overpower him, despite the fact that he was less than half the size of Delphinea. Even the thick gag they improvised from a strip of hastily cutoff doublet sleeve barely stifled Petri's cries. When at last Petri was subdued, his howling reduced to smothered moans, they turned their attention to Delphinea, sitting quiet and disheveled beside the near-insensible horse.

"My lady?" The dark-haired sidhe who bent over her wore a gold breastplate emblazoned with the Queen's crest, and for a moment, Delphinea was afraid the soldiers had been sent out by the Queen and Timias to drag both of them back to the palace under arrest. She scrambled backward, as the flickering torchlight gleamed on the officer's insignia embroidered on his sleeves. But his next words made her nearly weep with relief. "The Lady Vinaver sent us out to find you. I am Ethoniel, a captain in the Third Company of Her Majesty's Knights. If you would be so kind as to come with us, we will escort you to her Forest House."

"How'd that thing get out?" asked one of the other soldiers, with a jerk of his thumb over his shoulder in Petri's direction.

"Petri is not a thing," she sputtered, even as the captain extended his hand and helped her to stand. Two of the others coaxed her mare onto her feet.

"We'll take you both." The captain spoke firmly. "It doesn't look as if it'll give us any trouble now. We can't leave it here." Indeed, Petri lay in a forlorn little heap, his arms bound to his sides, one leathery little cheek pressed to the pine needles and leaves that carpeted the forest floor, eyes closed, breathing hard, but every other muscle relaxed. "Forgive me for taking the time to ask you, lady, but how *did* this happen? Did it follow you, my lady? How did it get past the gates?"

She knew that for any other sidhe, the presence of a gremlin leagues away from the palace of the Queen of Faerie, the one place to which they were forever bound, at least according to all the lore, was surprising to the point of shocking. But how to explain to them that despite his incipient madness, it was Petri who'd guided her through the maze of the ancient forest, close enough to Vinaver's house that they could be rescued? Surely Vinaver, herself outcast by the Court, would understand that Delphinea could not leave the loyal little gremlin behind, for it was abundantly clear that Timias and the Queen intended to lay at least part of the responsibility for the missing Caul on the entire gremlin population. But now was not the time to explain how or why the gremlin was with her. For, if it were possible, there was something even more unnatural within the forest, something she knew these soldiers must see for themselves to believe.

The torchlight illuminated the clearing, but it was not just the broken branches and torn undergrowth alone that made her certain of the direction in which to lead the guards. "The magic weakens as the Queen's pregnancy advances, Captain." Surely that explanation would have to suffice. "But I have to show you something," she said. "Please come?" She gathered up her riding skirts and set off, without waiting to see if they followed or not. It was like a smell, she thought, a foul, ripe rot that led her with unerring instinct back through the thick wood. Once, she put her hand on a trunk to steady herself and was disturbed to feel a tremor beneath the bark, and a sharp sting shot up her arm. The branches dipped low, with a little moaning sigh, and for a moment, Delphinea thought she heard a whispered voice. She startled back, but the captain was at her elbow, the torch sending long shadows across his face.

"Where are we going, lady?"

For a moment, she was too puzzled by this sense of communication with the trees to answer the question, for she had never before felt any particular connection to the trees of Faerie. Indeed, in the high mountains of her homeland, trees such as these primeval oaks and ashes were rare. "This way," was all she could say. And with a sense as certain as it was unexplainable, she led the grim-faced guards through the forest, to where the slaughtered host of the sidhe lay in heaps beside their dead horses and golden arms that gleamed like water in the gray dawn.

The guards gathered around Delphinea in shocked and silent horror, surveying the carnage. The corpses lay like discarded mannequins after a masque, armor all askew, swords and spears and broken arrows sticking up in all directions like bent matchsticks, impotent as mortal weapons. A mist floated over all, and from far away Delphinea could hear the rush of water. Without warning, a banner stirred and flapped on its staff, blown by a ghostly breeze that whispered through the trees, and as the mist moved over the remains, it seemed for one moment, the host might rise, laughing and whole. The captain raised his torch and Alemandine's colors—indigo and violet and blue on gold-edged white—flashed against the backdrop of the black trees.

They spoke behind her, in hushed and disbelieving whispers. "Can this be the—"

"Are they the—"

"Is this really our—"

"These are our comrades," interrupted the captain, answering all. There was a long silence, then he continued, in a voice heavy with loss, "You see, my lady, we, too, should have been among their company. But Prince Finuviel ordered us to stay and guard his mother's house."

"What could have done this?" another murmured.

"Who could have done this?" put in a third.

Delphinea could feel them tensing all around her, shuffling their feet, skittish as horses at the smell of blood. The captain bent down, holding his flaming torch a scant foot or so above the nearest corpse. He turned the body over. The face

of the dead sidhe was calm, pale, and it crumpled into powder, finer than sand, as the light fell upon it. He ran the torch
down the armor, to the insignia, the sword, and spurs the
knight wore. A dark slash ran diagonally across the golden
breastplate, where the metal itself was scarred and shriveled,
as if burnt away to ash. "Silver," he said after a long pause.
He shut the empty helm and rose to his feet. "They've died
the true death. They'll be gone when the sunlight hits them."

"So this is the host, then, that was called up to reinforce
our borders? The host the minstrels sing of, in Alemandine's
Court?" She had missed the glorious parade by scant hours,
arriving from the mountains too late. A chill ran through
her that had nothing to do with the temperature of the air.
She wrapped her arms around herself, feeling cold all over.
Now she would remember all too well forever this last sight
of them.

"That's exactly who they appear to be, my lady." The
captain handed his torch to one of the others and gestured
at his men. "Fan out. We'll have to come back when it's light,
but let's see as much as we can now."

While the bodies are still intact. The chilling thought ran
through her mind. But she said nothing, and he continued,
"Look for His Grace. Look for the Prince. It's the first question the Lady Vinaver will ask." His voice faltered and broke,
and Delphinea was struck once again by how much Finuviel seemed to be loved by everyone who knew him. She
had begun to suspect that his was the face that haunted the
visions that came to her while she slept—the visions mortals called "dreams." The sidhe didn't dream. At least, all the
others didn't. But lately the phantoms that haunted her sleep
came more frequently, and she was no longer able to ignore

them. She had come to Court hoping that someone there could explain them to her, and reassure her, perhaps, that this was not as unheard of as she was afraid it was. She had been afraid to mention them to anyone at all, but she had resolved to tell Vinaver, if she ever had the chance. She didn't want to think how Vinaver would react to the news that the army her son led had been slaughtered and that her son himself was missing.

For if the minstrels sang sweetly of the hosting of the sidhe, it was nothing to the songs they sang about Finuviel. Finuviel was the "shining one," loved by all who knew him, claimed by his mother to have been fathered by the great god Herne himself one Beltane. Although everyone dismissed Vinaver's claim as a pathetic attempt to gain some place for herself at the Court, it was universally acknowledged that Finuviel, whoever his father had been, was the epitome of every grace, and the master of every art. Even those who scorned Vinaver publicly spoke highly of Finuviel, and it was Finuviel that Vinaver and a small group of councilors conspired to place upon the throne of Faerie in the sick Queen's stead. What would they do, if Finuviel were lost?

But he's not. The knowledge rose from someplace deep inside her, a small voice that spoke with such silent authority, she felt immediately calmed, although she did not understand either how she knew such a thing, or why she should trust such knowledge. All she knew was that she did. She watched the torches bob up and down across the field as the soldiers wove through the heaps of the dead. At last the captain waved them all back. "Well?"

"We don't see him, sir," answered the first to reach the perimeter.

"But it appears that every last one of them was slain. There's no one of the entire host left, except for us?" The second soldier's brow was drawn, his mouth tight and grim.

"We should take the lady to Her Grace," interjected a third. "She has done her duty by bringing us to this terrible place, and we have not yet discharged ours to her."

There was a murmur of general agreement. Delphinea met the captain's eyes. They were gray in the shadows, lighter than the gray of his doublet, gray as the pale faces of the dead sidhe beneath the graying sky. "Who could've done this, Captain?"

"Mortals." He shrugged and looked around with a deep sigh. "From what I can tell, they were all killed with silver blades. Who else can wield silver in such fashion?" In the orange torchlight, his face was yellowish and gaunt.

"But why—"

He shrugged and turned away before she could finish her sentence. The sight alone defied reason. *We are all sickening,* she thought. *The Caul must be undone or we shall all sicken and die.* She turned away silently, gathering up her riding skirts, the men following. That so many should die the true death, the final death, was terrible enough. But was it really possible that *mortals*—mere mortals, as the lorespinners dismissed them—could have armed themselves with silver and attacked an entire host?

So much was happening, so much was changing. *Round about the circle goes, dark to light and back it flows.* The old nursery song spooled out of her memory. But for the first time, she had the sense that the turning wheel of time was in danger of spinning violently out of control.

By the time they reached Petri, the dawn light had

strengthened enough to show him lying curled into a heavy sleep. He had stopped making any noise at all except for long shuddering snores and his mouth hung slack over the gag. She wondered how long it would take to convince Vinaver that Finuviel did not lie dead beneath the ancient trees with the others.

For Finuviel was not dead, she was quite sure of that, in an odd way she could not at all explain. Something had happened to her last night, something had changed within her, awakened in her, in some way she did not yet fully understand but knew with absolute certainty she should trust. And she knew that Finuviel was not dead. *Not yet.*

But these grim guards would have to see for themselves—Vinaver would require as much proof as could be had that Finuviel was not here. She would not take Delphinea's word for it; why should she? So Delphinea said nothing as they marched back beneath the trees and it struck her that the sound of the wind in the branches was like the lowing of the cattle on the hillsides of her homeland. *What* wind? Her head jerked up and around, as she realized that the air was still. The captain, ever alert, held up his hand.

"Are you all right, lady?"

The curious sound stopped. She shook her head, feeling foolish. She was only overwrought, and succumbing to the rigors of the night. Best not to call attention to it. What would her mother say to do? *Smile.* "I but found last night somewhat taxing."

It was as brave an attempt as she could muster at the polished language of the Court, and no lady with a lifetime's experience at Court could have phrased it better. Half smiles bent their mouths, but melted like spring snow. How meaningless the words sounded, brittle as the drying leaves gusting at their feet, swirling at their ankles in deepening drifts. There was simply no etiquette to deal with such a loss, which must affect the soldiers doubly hard. What stroke of chance had led Finuviel to send these six back to guard his mother's house? But why did he think it needed special guarding? How vulnerable could it be so deep within the Old Forest of Faerie? It was leagues and leagues from the goblin-infested Wastelands. Had he suspected something? Had he known that mortals armed with silver might attack?

She felt, rather than heard, a deep throbbing moan as she passed beneath the branches of a nearly leafless giant. Its great trunk divided into two armlike branches that ended in countless outstretched skeletal hands. The Wild Hunt had swept many of the trees bare. Yet the trees of Faerie had never before been bare. Their leaves turned from gold to red to russet to brown to green in one eternal round of color, and if a few fell, new ones grew to take their place, in an endless cycle of regeneration. She thought of the dust on the floor of the Caul chamber, the rust on the hinges of the huge brass doors, of the rotting bodies of her cattle and the foals, the fouled streams. Was this just another piece of evidence that Faerie was truly dying? But she was silent as she allowed the guards to help her onto her saddle. The mare seemed fully recuperated, and tossed her head and whickered a greeting as Delphinea gathered up the reins.

Petri was slung over the back of another horse like a sack of meal. Though Delphinea protested his treatment, the horse shied and whinnied and finally a blanket had to be placed beneath the gremlin and the animal before the horse could be induced to carry him.

"I cannot imagine what circumstances brought you here on such a strange, sad night, my lady." The captain swung into his saddle, and raised his arm in the signal for the company to ride. He rode past, stern-faced and tensed, and she realized he did not expect an answer. The milk-white horses moved like wraiths beneath the black leafless branches, as a red sun rose higher in a violet-cerulean sky. Even now, stark as it was, it was beautiful, beautiful in the intensity of its pulsing radiance. The air was crisp, but heavy, charged with portent.

They rode in grim silence another half turn of a glass. The light grew stronger and suddenly, the thick wood parted, and a most extraordinary sight rose up. Like a living wall, a latticework of high hedge grew laced between the trees, and just beyond, high above the ground, within what appeared to be a grove of ancient oaks and sturdy ashes, Delphinea saw a house that looked as if it had grown out of the trees, not been built into them.

The reins slackened in her hands as she gaped, open-mouthed, at the peaked roofs, all covered in shingled bark, windows laced like spiderwebs strung between the branches. Winding stairs curved up and around the thick trunks, and tiny lanterns twinkled in and among the leaf-laden branches. *There is magic yet in Faerie,* she thought, and was a little comforted. Her mother's house of light and stone was nothing like this living wonder, and even Alemandine's palace, as beautiful as its turrets of ivory and crystal were, could not compare to this house of trees.

As if he'd heard her thoughts, Ethoniel smiled. "Indeed,

my lady. The Forest House of the Lady Vinaver is a wonder in which all Faerie should delight, not shun." He held up his hand and the company slowed their mounts to a walk all around her. He leaned over and touched her forearm. "Slowly, lady. Do you not see the danger that grows within the hedge?"

As they came closer, she saw that the hedge was full of jagged thorns, skinny as needles, some as long as her fingers, with tiny barbs at their ends which would make them doubly difficult to remove, all twined about with pale white flowers that put out such a delicate scent that Delphinea had to force herself not to push her nose into the hedge's depths, to drink more deeply of it. She realized that the plant was nourished by the blood of things that impaled themselves upon the thorns, and from the profusion of flowers, the thickness of the vines, and the lushness of the scent, there were plenty of creatures that did. She shuddered as she rode through the narrow archway that formed the only gate, shrinking away from what was at once so beautiful, and so deadly, so tempting, and so dangerous.

Only one leather-clad attendant came forward, slipping out from a set of doors within the great trunk of an enormous tree, and Delphinea wondered once again why Finuviel had diverted any number of his host at all to guard Vinaver's house. Secluded as it was within the heart of the Great Forest, and surrounded by the high hedge of blood-thirsty thorns, it appeared not at all vulnerable, except perhaps to a direct goblin attack. But was such a thing likely? From the talk of the Court, she had surmised that the war was expected to be fought on the borders of the Wastelands, not within the very heart of Faerie itself.

But the fact that Finuviel had regard for his mother's safety made her like him, too, and she wondered if she was falling under the spell of his reputation. She followed the captain of the guard inside the house, trying not to gawk at the golden grace of the polished staircase that flowed seamlessly around the giant central oak forming the main pillar of this part of the house. From certain angles, the staircase was invisible; from others, it was the focal point that drew the eye up and into the leafy canopy forming the roof. She kilted up her skirts and followed the men up the steps, trying not to trip as the golden radiance filtered down, soothing and nourishing as new milk. She closed her eyes, her feet moving in some unconscious synchrony, bathing in the incandescence, forgetting for a moment the dire news they bore. There was only the warmth and the light. On and on, up and up, she climbed, and the face that filled her vision against the backdrop of rosy light was framed with coal-black curls. But instead of smiling, the face contorted in agony and Delphinea gasped, opened her eyes and tripped.

"Watch your step, my lady," growled the guard who had Petri, by this time in a dead stupor, slung across his back.

Still groggy from the vision, Delphinea could only murmur. It was bad enough that the dreams came while she slept. If she was going to start having them while she was awake, she would have to talk to someone about them. Vinaver, hopefully.

But as they reached an upper landing, Ethoniel paused before a door and turned to Delphinea. "You've had a harrowing night, my lady. This may be somewhat difficult. I don't expect Lady Vinaver will welcome this news."

"But I want her to know I'm here—maybe there's something I can do—" *Maybe she will believe me if I tell her Finuviel is alive.* But she left the last unspoken, and looked at him with mute appeal.

He looked dubious, but shrugged. "As you wish, my lady. The Lady Vinaver is given to some unexpected reactions on occasion. Beware." He knocked on the door, and opening it, stepped inside an antechamber. He motioned Delphinea, and the guard carrying Petri inside, then knocked on the inner door. Vinaver herself opened the door.

All potential greetings died in Delphinea's throat as the expression on Vinaver's face changed from one of welcome to one of horrified disbelief at Ethoniel's quick report. She had only stared at him, her eyes glowing with a terrible green fire in her suddenly white and flame-red face. Delphinea thought Vinaver might faint, and she wondered if it was that for which Ethoniel had sought to prepare her.

But nothing could've prepared Delphinea for the sight of Vinaver's collapse, for she fell to her knees in a brittle crunch of bone, as the framework of her wings splintered like icicles. And as Delphinea watched in horror, the wings sheared away completely, the tissues tearing with the wet sound of splitting skin, leaving twin fountains of pale blood arcing from Vinaver's shoulder blades.

She could think of nothing to say or do, for nothing but intuition made her sure that Finuviel was not dead. *Not yet.* And in that moment Delphinea understood that if anything really did happen to Finuviel, the consequences would be far more terrible than anything she had yet imagined.

As if from very far away, Delphinea heard Ethoniel bellow for Vinaver's attendants, saw a very dark and burly stranger rise from a chair beside the fireplace and point in her direction. She felt the room suddenly grow very hot and very crowded, as more guards and attendants rushed in. Vinaver's blood was flowing over her shoulders like a cloak, running in great waves down her arms, dripping off her fingers, soaking the fabric of the back of her gown. The captain turned on his heel, brushing past her, and she felt strong arms ease her off her feet, as the world finally, mercifully, went dark.

When next she opened her eyes, she was lying on a low couch in the little antechamber of Vinaver's bower. The door to the inner room was closed. The couch had been placed next to a polished hearth in which a small fire burned. A basket of bread and cheese and apples had been placed beside her, and a tall goblet, filled with something clear that smelled sweet, stood beside a covered posset-cup on a wooden tray. A drone worthy of a beehive rose from the floor beside her. She looked down. It was Petri, lying curled up on a red hearth rug, in a round patch of sunlight, his head on a small pillow, sound asleep. *Poor little thing,* she thought. If her ordeal had been bad, his was surely worse.

"How d'you feel?"

She bolted straight up at the unexpected voice. It belonged to the big dark stranger she'd noticed in Vinaver's bower before. He was sitting on the opposite side of the hearth, and she knew instantly what had drawn her attention, even amidst those few terrible moments in Vinaver's presence. He was mortal.

It was so obviously apparent she did not question how she knew. He looked faintly ridiculous, for the stool on which he hunched was much too low for his long legs. He wore a simple fir-green robe of fine-spun wool, over a pair of baggy trews which from their rough and ragged appearance she assumed were of mortal make. The skin of his bare legs and feet poking out from the bottoms of the trews was bluish white, covered by a sparser pelt of the same coarse black hair that curled across his face. She wondered, with a little shock, if it were possible that Vinaver kept the mortal as a pet, just as in the songs the milkmaids sang, of moon-mazed mortals lost in Faerie, willing slaves to the sidhe. Her mother did not consider such tales seemly and scorned all talk of mortals. Delphinea had never imagined she would meet one, so she examined him with unabashed curiosity.

It was midmorning or later, and the light streamed down through windows set within the upper branches of the trees, filling the room with a brittle brilliance, casting strong shadows on the mortal's dark face. He must be old, she thought, very old, even as mortals counted years, for his dark hair was shot through in most places with broad swaths of gray and white and his skin was grayish and hung off his face. Deep lines ran from the inner corners of his eyes, all the way past the outer corners of his mouth. His eyes burned with such intensity there was no other color they could be but black.

A tremor ran through her as her eyes locked with his, for it seemed that within those depths lay some knowledge that she not even yet imagined, coupled with pain, a lot of pain. His forehead gleamed with sweat, and as he raised his arm to mop his brow with a linen kerchief, she caught a glimpse of a white bandage, stark against his skin, beneath the vivid green. But his eyes were like twin beacons burning through a storm, and she realized that whatever the source of his pain, he wasn't afraid of it.

She felt drawn to his solid strength, sensing that he was strong in a way that nothing of Faerie could ever be. His essence was all earth and water, unlike the sidhe, who were manifestations of light and air. One corner of his mouth lifted in the slightest hint of a smile. "You put me in mind of my daughter, sidhe-leen. All big eyes and innocence." He closed his eyes, and winced as if in pain, then opened them. "I'm Dougal," he said. "What do they call you?"

Delphinea paused, uncertain how to address him. Meeting a mortal was one of the many recent events her mother had failed to foresee. But the way he looked at her, as if she were a skittish filly, calmed her for some reason she did not understand, and for a moment, at least, she felt comforted. The Samhain sun had risen on a world utterly different from the one on which it had set, and in this upside-down, topsy-turvy world, time suddenly had new meaning. Was it only yesterday that Delphinea had awakened in her bed within the palace of the Faerie Queen? So much had happened—the complete control of the Queen Timias had been able to achieve, and subsequent arrest of all the Queen's Council, her own escape with Petri, their flight into the ancient Forest and the Wild Hunt that had nearly overrun them, even Petri's madness, was yet nothing compared to the discovery of the decimated host and the sight of Vinaver's collapse. Nothing and no one were quite what they appeared; no one and nothing were what she had been prepared to expect. Was it possible this mortal was involved in the whole confused plot? She wasn't at all sure how to answer the question. "My name is Delphinea," she said at last. "Will the Lady Vinaver be all right?"

He shrugged and folded his arms across his chest carefully. "Don't know yet. No one's come out of there—" he bent his head forward to indicate the closed bower door, then jerked it backward, toward the outer door "—and no one's come through there since the guard went out to see what's what."

She cocked her head, considering. He didn't sound quite the way she'd imagined a moon-mazed mortal would, and his weary, battered appearance certainly didn't fit the flowery descriptions of them, either. "May I—may I be so curious as to inquire exactly how it happens that you have come to be here, Sir Dougal?"

At that his smile reached his eyes. "Pretty speech, sidheleen. I'm no one's sir. In my world, I'm a blacksmith. And in this one, too, more's the pity." He broke off and the smile was gone. Far from being enchanted, he seemed quite vexed.

"You don't seem very happy to be here."

He laughed so hard his shoulders shook, and a whiplash of pain made him clutch his arm. "And that surprises you, does it?" What amazed her more was that he could laugh in spite of everything. But maybe, being mortal, he didn't really understand what was happening. He sagged, sighed and shook his head. "You're right, though. There're many, many places I would much rather be. But that doesn't answer your question, does it?" He indicated his arm with another jerk of his head. "Met up with a goblin. Woke up on this side of the border. She found me, brought me here. Here I am."

"The Lady Vinaver healed you?"

"For a price, of course she did." His mouth turned down in a bitter twist and for a moment, she thought he might say something more. But he only drew a long, careful breath and let it out slowly. Finally he looked at her. "What sort of sidhe are you, anyway?"

There was a long silence while Delphinea, completely taken aback, cast about for some sort of appropriate response. Surely he wasn't inquiring about her ancestry? He seemed to imply there was something different about her, and she raised her chin, determined not to let a mortal get the best of her, when he leaned forward and caught her gaze with a twinkle. "But the world's full of surprises, isn't it? So now you tell me—what's a small sidhe-leen like you doing traveling alone on Samhain of all nights? We heard the Wild Hunt ride past—I heard the noise that—that—thing made—"

"Petri is not a thing. He's a gremlin."

"Oh, is that what you call it?"

"What would you call him?"

"Hmm." Dougal cocked his head and cradled his injured arm across his chest, as if it pained him. "Looks more like what the old stories say a trixie looks like. Brownie's another name in some parts and my gram called them sprites. Never saw one myself. Some say they all got themselves banished from the mortal world long ago for their mischief. I say it's a damn convenient explanation for why no one ever sees them. But whatever it is, why do you keep it naked?"

"Naked?" Delphinea blinked. She flicked her eyes over to Petri. He wore the same court livery he always wore. It was, as always, perfectly clean, although somewhat rumpled. She would have said more, but the inner door opened, and Leonine, one of Vinaver's attendants, beckoned.

"Lady Vinaver requests you both." The lady was gowned

in a plain russet smock, and her long yellow curls were held back by a simple gold chaplet. "If you will, my lady?" She dropped a small curtsy, then rose, and indicated the open door. "Sir mortal, if you please?"

Dougal made a sound almost like a growl, and again Delphinea had the distinct impression that unlike the mortals she'd heard of, he hated everything about Faerie. But why, when everything she'd seen of Shadow—the dust, the rust, even the clothes he wore—was so coarse, so crude? He needed one hand on the mantel to pull himself up. Delphinea followed Leonine through the door and hesitated, just inside the threshold. Another attendant, this one clothed in the color of autumn wheat, slipped past them, carrying a large willow basket of stained linen.

Vinaver lay on the edge of a great bed, which incorporated a natural hollow within the tree. It was lined with silk velvet that resembled moss, draped with filmy curtains. Her usually vivid color had drained away, leaving her coppery hair dull as the rust that marred the hinges of the Caul Chamber, her narrow cheeks and shriveled lips chalky. For the first time, Delphinea saw the resemblance she bore to Alemandine. And to Timias. *Great Herne, he's her father, too.* And didn't she say he wanted her drowned at birth? She had no memory of her own father—he had gone into the West a long time ago, but her mother never failed to speak of him with anything but bemused anticipation of seeing him again.

"Leonine, bring her closer. Come here, child." Vinaver's voice was faint, but still sharp with innate command, and Delphinea was glad to hear Vinaver yet retained something of her determined spirit. But as the attendant gently propelled her across the polished floor, Delphinea's eyes filled with tears when she saw Vinaver's face more closely. "Don't weep for me," Vinaver said. "There's not enough time." Her hand plucked at Delphinea's sleeve until she slid her warm hand into Vinaver's cold one. Vinaver tugged weakly and Delphinea leaned over, until her face hung only a scant handspan above the older sidhe's. It occurred to her that Vinaver appeared only marginally more lifelike than the pale faces of the dead sidhe in the starlight. "I hated those wings. I was a fool to suggest them and a fool to grow them." She paused, as if gathering her strength, and tugged again once more, until Delphinea's ear was practically right against her lips. Her breath was like the flutter of a butterfly's wings. "I want you to tell me, quickly, don't think about it, just tell me—is Finuviel dead—truly dead?"

Not yet. "Not yet." The words rose automatically to Delphinea's lips. All she had to do was open her mouth.

"Not yet," Vinaver breathed. She closed her eyes, then opened them. "*He* didn't come, but *you* did. With a gremlin of all things. Whatever possessed you?" She gripped Delphinea's hand so tightly, Delphinea was forced to bite back a yelp of pain. "How was it ever possible you were able to bring the gremlin? And why? What on earth made you do it?"

"He saved me, my lady. He led me here. But for Petri, I might have met whatever killed that host, myself. But, m-my lady—" she faltered. Where to even begin? She didn't understand any of it. She blurted out the first question that occurred to her. "Why do you ask me if your son still lives? I've never even met him. And why are you surprised that I should come? You told me yourself that my life's in danger, and you turned out to be right. Which is why I brought Petri, for he helped me to escape." Delphinea turned, following the movement of Vinaver's eyes, to see Petri crouching in the doorway. "Timias intended to sequester them early. It seemed so cruel—so meaningless—"

"Timias has his reasons, child, don't ever doubt that Timias does anything without a reason." An ugly look flashed across Vinaver's face. "This should not be."

Delphinea collapsed to her knees, so that she was level with Vinaver's face. "It seems that there are many things that should not be, my lady. Perhaps you'd better tell me what's going on. Where's the Caul, and where's Finuviel, and who's responsible for that horror in the Forest?"

But Vinaver only closed her eyes and sighed. "So many questions all at once." She tried to shake her head a little but winced.

"I have more."

"Tell her the truth, Vinaver." Dougal spoke from the door. Petri sniffed at his leg like a hound at a scent, and Dougal swatted him away. "Tell her the whole truth."

"We took the Caul," Vinaver answered wearily, her eyes closed, her cheek flat against her pillow. "Finuviel and I, and we gave it to a mortal."

"But why?" Delphinea rocked back on her heels in horror.

"It's as you guessed, child. The Silver Caul is poisoning Faerie. I couldn't tell you the truth in the palace. How was I to know you'd not go running to Timias the moment I'd left your room? We took the Caul, Finuviel and I, and he gave it to a mortal to hold in surety of the bargain."

"What bargain?" Delphinea drew back, staring down at Vinaver in horror.

"We needed a silver dagger. Where else to get it but from the mortals?"

"You mean to kill the Queen?"

"No." Vinaver shut her eyes once more. "I could never kill my sister." She opened her eyes. "But, she's not really—she's not really my sister." Delphinea cocked her head and sank down once more onto a low stool that Leonine had drawn up to the bed, as Vinaver continued. "Alemandine isn't really anything at all—she's neither sidhe nor mortal. She's a—a residue of all the energy that was left over when the Caul was created. The male and female energy mingling in my mother's womb was enough to create her out of ungrounded magic, magic from her union with Timias and the mortal. They didn't consider what would happen—they didn't understand the energies they were working with. No one ever really does, you know. If I learned nothing else from the Hag, I learned that." She broke off and with a shaking hand pushed back a loose lock of Delphinea's hair. "There was nothing to say that Alemandine should not be Queen. After all, she was born first. And whatever else Alemandine is, she is a part of me. So no, the intention was never to kill the Queen. Timias is the one meant to die. Timias must die, Timias will die when the Caul is destroyed. For as long as the Caul endures, so will Timias. He will never choose to go into the West. He'll never have to."

Delphinea glanced over her shoulder. Dougal stood in the doorway still, his arms crossed over his chest. "Philomemnon said Alemandine would die when the Caul was destroyed. Is that true?"

"I doubt she has much longer to live as it is, though yes, that is a consequence. But what would you have us do? There is no way to save both the Queen and Faerie—and to save the Queen is to ensure that we all die. What choice was there really?"

"So you made a bargain with a mortal—for the dagger. And what was your part?"

"In exchange for the dagger we promised the host—"

"The host in the Forest."

"We knew the mortal world was in chaos. A mad king sits on the throne, the people chafe beneath the rule of his foreign Queen. The events of the Shadowlands echo Faerie and those in Faerie, Shadow. It was in our best interests to resolve the strife there—"

"Why, that's exactly what Timias said to the Council," Delphinea blurted. "That day in the Council—the day he came back—"

"Whatever I say of him, he's not a fool. He understands better than anyone how tightly the worlds are bound." Vinaver plucked restlessly at the linen pillow. "But now—" She raised her head and looked directly at Petri. "Now—"

But before she could finish, the door opened and Ethoniel hesitated on the threshold, with a flushed face, breathing hard. From somewhere far below, Delphinea heard distant shouts. They all turned and looked at him, and Vinaver moved her head weakly on the pillow, beckoning Ethoniel with a feeble wave. "What news, Captain?"

At once, Ethoniel crossed the room and went down on one knee beside the bed. "I bring both good and bad news, my lady," he hesitated. "We found no sign of Prince Finuviel, no sign at all. We found nothing of his—neither armor, nor standard, nor horse—and all of us combed the sad remains as carefully as we could. But there is a company of knights, at least ten thirteens or more, marching on the Forest House. They are coming to arrest both you and the Lady

Delphinea—" here, he turned to look at Delphinea over his shoulder "—yes, my lady, you, too, on charges of high treason and the theft of the Silver Caul. They are more than a hundred against my one squad, my lady. What would you have me do?"

Even Delphinea understood his dilemma. He likely was outranked by whoever led the guards. To defy to open the gates was treason. To disobey Finuviel's orders to defend his mother offended honor.

For a long moment no one spoke. Then Petri hissed from the door and he scrabbled forward, his eyes cast low, his tail tucked under in perfect obeisance. In a series of quick gestures, accompanied by a few stifled hisses, he motioned, *I can help you find him, great lady.*

Vinaver's eyes narrowed and she looked down at the cringing gremlin, and then up at Delphinea. "The removal of the Caul from the moonstone must've made it possible for him to leave."

Petri's eyes were huge, and he looked up at Delphinea with flared nostrils. *I can help you find him, lady. I know the way through Shadow. I can find him. And the Caul.*

"Petri says he can help me find Finuviel." Delphinea clasped his hand in both of hers. The thought that she should be the one to look for Finuviel jolted her into the realization of exactly how dire the situation was.

At once Dougal shifted on his feet, crossing and uncrossing his arms. "I don't like that idea. There's a saying, never a trust a trixie."

"What about the knights, my lady? They've orders to burn the Forest House if we don't open the gates." Ethoniel broke in, desperation clear.

Vinaver moved her head restlessly on the pillow. "We have to find Finuviel. We're running out of time. The Caul must be unMade before Mid-Winter."

"I suppose I'm the one that's seen him last," said Dougal. "With Cadwyr. That night at my forge."

Beside Delphinea, Petri tugged on her hand. *I can help you, lady. Please, lady, I can help you find the Caul. I can find the mortal Duke. I can find the Caul. I brought you here.* He stepped in front of Vinaver and groveled before her. *Please, great lady. You know how we, too, are bound to the Caul. It calls to me from Shadow, even now.*

"Let me go find him," Dougal said suddenly.

Vinaver replied with an arch look, "That's not exactly our bargain, is it, Master Smith?"

"Do you want your son and the Caul found or not? I'm the last who saw him, I know who he was with. Who else do you have who knows Brynhyvar the way I do?"

I know it better than any mortal—I know the Underneath and the In-between. I can take her through the Mother-Wood. Petri quivered, his hands knotted tightly together. "Forgive me, gentle folk, if my unkind voice offends," he said in his high-pitched strangled shriek. "But I remember—I can lead—let me—let me—"

"Be quiet," interrupted Vinaver. "Be still, *khouri-kan.*"

"Delphinea can't go," broke in Ethoniel. "They're here to take her as well."

"But I'm the one who discovered the Caul was missing," Delphinea exclaimed. "But for me—"

"But for you, the plan might have proceeded apace, without anyone at Court ever knowing," Vinaver cut her off with a savagery belied by her appearance.

"Then let me go," said Delphinea, looking down at Petri, who squeezed her hand and bowed gravely.

"I should be the one to go," insisted Dougal.

"You cannot go, Master Dougal. You've a bargain to fulfill. Don't you?"

Dougal shut his mouth and crossed his arms over his chest. "What exactly are you thinking, Vinaver? Surely this child isn't—"

"I am not a child," said Delphinea. "I may appear young in mortal years, but I have known far more seasons than you, Master Smith. I can find him. I know I can. Petri will help." She squeezed his shoulder and Petri bowed.

"There you are, Master Dougal. Delphinea has certain advantages—"

"She may have certain advantages from your point of view, but—"

"My lady Vinaver, master mortal, with all due respect, you've no time to continue to debate this," interrupted Ethoniel. "I need an answer, my lady. What shall I do?"

"Open the gates, Captain. I'm in no condition to travel. They may see for themselves if they wish. And no one can make me leave until I am satisfied my son does not lie among that host. Is that acceptable? Does it satisfy both the bonds of honor and command? All I ask is a delay—long enough for Delphinea to cross into Shadow—Leonine, fetch my cloak of shadows."

As the attendant left the room, Ethoniel hesitated. "There's nothing more I'd like to do, my lady. But they'll expect to see the two—"

"Then give them me as well," said Dougal.

Ethoniel covered his mouth and coughed, then smiled as

one might at a well-trained hound. "Unfortunately, master mortal, you and the lady Delphinea bear only the slightest resemblance to each other. Unless you've not noticed."

"Put a cloak on me and let me pretend to be Vinaver. They expect Vinaver to be tall—they don't know she lost the wings. She's a tiny thing now—let her lie on her bed and pretend to be the sidhe-leen. What do you say, Captain? Demand they search the field for Finuviel. And unless you've a better idea as to how to rig some on that maid there—" He jerked his head as Leonine stepped into the room, carrying a thick, dark cloak. "I'm about as tall as Vinaver's wings were. Unless you've not noticed."

I shall lead you, lady. Petri smiled up at her and stroked Delphinea's hand. He rubbed his cheek against the back of it as Dougal frowned.

"Is there no one else to take her?" asked Dougal. "I don't like the thought of that at all."

"Why not?" asked Delphinea. "Petri's been my friend."

But Vinaver was looking up at Dougal with weary acknowledgment. "You're right, Master Dougal, there are reasons not to trust the *khouri,* or trixie, as you call him. But the *khouri's* correct. He *is* bound to the Caul. And Shadow is his native element. So long as the Caul lasts, his power is largely bound to it. I believe him when he says he can find it."

"And what if Finuviel and the Caul aren't in the same place?"

But cries echoing up the great stair forestalled Vinaver's answer.

"Captain Ethoniel, you must come!"

"Are we to open the gates, Captain?"

"Captain, come now!"

The voices were closer now, accompanied by the patter of booted feet on the polished stair.

"Open the gates, Captain. But hold them in the court-yard," said Vinaver. "Come, child, let Leonine put the cloak on you."

Before Delphinea could agree, the other woman settled the dark cloak over her shoulders. It was a color between dark purple and black, the color of the indigo night sky, and it was soft and thick and silky all at once. "What stuff is this cloak made of?" she asked as she spread it wide. It fell in rich dark ripples, as if it absorbed the light, rather than re-flected it.

"Faerie silk, and the shadows of Shadow," said Vinaver. "There are only two, and how they came to be, I don't have time to tell you. Finuviel had one. Now you have the other."

"What does it do?" asked Delphinea, turning this way and that. It had a damp feeling to it that was not completely pleasant.

"It will make you invisible in the eyes of mortals, if you draw it over yourself completely." Vinaver took a deep breath and closed her eyes. "We've not much time, so lis-ten carefully, Delphinea, and I will tell you what I can. Mor-tals are highly susceptible and suggestible but you must not underestimate the effect they shall have upon you. A fresh mortal intoxicates like nothing else—"

"What in the name of Herne do you mean by a fresh mor-tal?" asked Dougal. "And do you mind not referring to my people as if we were a race of animals that happen to walk and talk?"

But Vinaver ignored the interruption. "Like nothing you can even imagine. For some it's the way they smell, or taste, for others, the way they look. Whatever it is, and however it strikes you, beware of it. Keep your wits about you, for mortals are perverse, and when you expect them to do one thing, they will do the opposite. Don't try to understand it, but seek to use it, if needs must. Keep close to the trixie, and don't let him from your sight. Keep him tethered to you if you sleep. Water is one sure way back to Faerie, the other is through the trees of a deep forest. For the trees of Faerie and Shadow are linked. Some even say they are the same." She shut her eyes and took another audible breath. "Listen as you pass below them. Listen and see if you hear them talking." Her eyes fluttered open. "They will help you. I have no doubt."

"Why are you so sure?" asked Delphinea. "Is it only the way I look? There are visions that come to me in my sleep—"

"What do you see?"

"I see Finuviel. I hear his name."

Vinaver reached out once more and touched Delphinea's cheek with a shaking hand. "I understand why you've come. Bring my son and the Caul back to Faerie. You were meant to find them. I'm sure of it." She closed her eyes.

Delphinea hesitated, wondering if Vinaver truly knew, or if she only wanted to know, and she wondered how much Vinaver really did know, and how much *she* actually did. But before she could speak, Dougal stopped her with a hand on her arm. "I've a word of advice. Don't go directly to Cadwyr of Allovale. Go instead to his uncle Donnor, the Duke of Gar. He's the only one with any influence over Cadwyr. Donnor's an honorable man, whereas Cadwyr's like a blade too well oiled. He shines pretty, but he turns too

easily in your hand. Find the Duke of Gar, and tell him—"
He paused, then shrugged. "I suppose under the circum-
stances it doesn't much matter what anyone thinks. Tell
Donnor that Dougal of Killcairn sent you, and if possible, ask
him to get word to my daughter—my girl, Nessa—back in
Killcairn. Tell her I'm alive. All right?"

As Delphinea nodded, Leonine stuck her head around the
door. "I think, my lady, that you must leave now, if you're
to leave at all. The company from the palace is within the
courtyard, and the commander is demanding to be let in."

"Go, child," said Vinaver. "And, *khouri-kan,* remember
that I know the secret of your unMaking. Betray me, and I
might forget it."

Petri hissed and bowed and rubbed his hands, and Leonine led Delphinea toward to the door. As she stepped out
into the hall, she turned back to Vinaver. "My lady?"

Vinaver's pain-dulled eyes flickered muddy green in the
gloom. "Yes, child?"

"Talking to the trees—understanding the trees—isn't
that a gift reserved for the Queen of the sidhe?"

Vinaver smiled then, but her face was sad. "Child, don't
you understand? You *are* the next Queen of Faerie. That is,
if Faerie survives at all."

There was the faintest smell of rot in the air. Like the
warm tap of a random spring raindrop, the odor drifted,
now here, now there, never so much that one was ever quite
sure what one smelled. But it was enough to make one
pause, turn one's head, wrinkle one's nose and sniff again.
It had first been detected after Samhain, and it was becoming noticeable enough that a fashion for wearing perfumed

lace face masks was spreading rapidly throughout the ladies of the Court.

And it was noticeable enough that Timias had been forced to listen, a prisoner in his chambers, to Her Majesty's Master of the House, Lord Rimbaud, and her Chatelaine, Lady Evardine, while they lamented the situation for nearly a full turn of the glass, before a summons from Alemandine's Consort, Hudibras, interrupted their torrent of complaint. Now Timias tightened his grip on his oak staff, and pressed his mouth into a thin line as he hurried through the palace of the Faerie Queen as quickly as his aged legs would allow. A small puff of stink through the lemon-scented air was enough to make him furrow his already wrinkled brow as he scurried through the arching marble corridors, hung with tapestries and mosaics so intricately and perfectly executed, some were known to move. He passed the image of a stag brought down by a huntsman's bow, the great antlered head lifted in eternal agony, and something made Timias pause, transfixed, before it. The crimson blood flowing from the stag's side shone with a curious rippling gleam, as if the blood that flowed from the wound was real.

Timias stepped closer, narrowing his eyes. As another trace of putrid odor filled his nostrils, he reached out and touched the gleaming rivulet. For a moment his finger registered the cold pressure of the stone as wetness and he started back, peering closely at his finger, half expecting to see a smear of blood. But his fingertip was clear, without a hint of moisture. Of course there wasn't any blood, he told himself, there was no blood. How could there be blood? It was only a picture. There was no blood. It was but a trick of his overwrought senses, a consequence of his agonized mind. He had enough to occupy a dozen councilors. His discovery with Delphinea of the missing Caul led to the disclosure of the plot against the Queen, and allowed him to once again assert his position and authority as the oldest of all the Council. The stupid girl had not waited long enough to allow him to thank her properly before she'd run off. The first thing he'd done had been to order the arrests of every one of the Queen's councilors in residence at the Court. This meant that, while the immediate threat was contained until he could determine who was to be trusted, he alone remained to steer Alemandine through the task of holding her realm together both under the strain engendered by her pregnancy and the inevitable attack by the Goblin King. But the calamity of the missing Caul, coupled with the revelation of Vinaver's treachery, made what would have been a heavy burden especially weighty. A lesser sidhe, one without so many years and experience as his, would surely not be equal to the task. He touched the wall again, just to make sure. "No blood," he whispered aloud. "No blood." He realized he was still muttering as he stalked through the halls to Alemandine's chambers.

There was certainly enough to mutter about. Vinaver, that foul abomination, had seized the opportunity afforded by his absence in the Shadowlands to hatch some horrific plot against her sister, Alemandine, the details of which he did not yet understand. It was her cronies on the Council he'd had arrested, all of them—all of them save Vinaver herself, who'd prudently retired to her Forest House. Well, he'd not let that stop him. The very hour he'd discovered Lady Delphinea gone missing, he'd sent a company of the Queen's Guard out to drag both her and Vinaver back to the palace.

He'd find out what had happened to the missing Caul and then turn his attention to the defense of Faerie. The calculated way in which Vinaver had so coldly plotted against her sister when the pregnant Queen was at her most vulnerable intrigued him and made him admire her in a way he refused to contemplate.

He'd already decided that it had been a mistake to allow Finuviel to take over Artimour's command, and the sooner Artimour was restored to his proper place, and Finuviel recalled, the easier they could all rest. After all, it was only logical to assume that Finuviel was an integral part of Vinaver's scheme to make herself Queen in her sister's stead, and so the sooner Artimour resumed command, the better. After all, Artimour would be so pathetically grateful to have his place back, Timias knew he'd be able to trust him. And maybe not just trust him, thought Timias as he considered new and different roles for Artimour to play. He was always something of a misfit around the Court. He couldn't have been happy about the revocation of his command. He'd owe tremendous loyalty to the person—or group of persons—who restored it.

It was time to recall Artimour, decided Timias, time to assure the dear boy of their continued support and offer apologies for the terrible mistake they'd made in replacing him with Finuviel, the spawn of that foul abomination, Vinaver. If necessary, Artimour could be dispatched to the mortal world with an offer of assistance. And wasn't that what should've been done in the first place? Timias's head ached. There was simply too much to think about all at once. He came to himself with a little shake and realized he'd been talking to himself the entire length of the corridor.

The two guards standing watch over Alemandine's private rooms gave him a curious glance but said nothing, as together they opened the great doors that led into the reception room of Alemandine's suite.

There, Timias found Hudibras, looking distracted, even as he berated two bedraggled ladies-in-waiting huddled in the window seat. They all looked up, their expressions an odd mixture of both relief and fear, as Timias entered. He pinned the ladies with a ferocious stare, and their wings, fragile and pink as rose petals, trembled above their heads. But why were they both wearing crowns of oak and holly leaves? Oak for summer, holly for winter—why both at once? He peered more closely at them, and realized to his relief the illusion was nothing but a trick of the light and that their small veils were held in place, as usual, by the customary ribboned wreaths that all Alemandine's ladies wore. "What's going on? Where's the Queen?" He addressed Hudibras, but it was one of the ladies-in-waiting who answered.

"She will not unlock the door, most exalted lord," she replied, olive-green eyes huge in her angular face so that she resembled a frightened doe. Honey-colored hair spilled over her shoulders and across her rose-colored gown, partially obscuring her fichu of ivory lace. It matched the lace of her face mask, Timias saw, as another foul whiff momentarily distracted him. This time the seed pearls in her wreath looked like writhing white worms. He started back and she gave him another questioning look, as he realized that that was exactly the effect the pearls were meant to have. It struck him that this was a bizarre conceit for an adornment for one's hair, but then, he never paid attention to the fashions of the Court. Since Alemandine was crowned Queen, they changed with such dizzying frequency, he could not keep up.

He really had to get control of himself, he thought. He tightened his grip on his staff and the wood felt dry as a petrified bone in his palm. He must not succumb to the pressure. Surely that's what Vinaver hoped for, and it occurred to him that indeed, the success of the very plot itself might hinge on his ability to single-handedly uphold the Queen through this hour of her greatest need. He would show Vinaver that while he wore an old man's face, he yet possessed a young man's vigor.

Hudibras was wringing his hands in a manner most unseemly and his tone was peevish and demanding. "Whatever you have in mind, Timias, you better get to it, for she refuses to come out. You've got the entire Council under arrest, Vinaver's gone flitting off Herne alone knows where, that wild young thing's gone running off with that gremlin—" Hudibras marched across the room, struck a mannered pose worthy of a masque beside the empty grate, and, to Timias's astonishment, removed a peacock-plume fan from the scabbard at his belt. With a zeal that the temperature of the room in no way warranted, he snapped it open with an expert flick of his wrist and began to fan himself. "What's to be done, Timias? What's to be done?"

What was wrong with the man? wondered Timias. Since when was there a fashion for wearing peacock-plume fans like daggers? Or white worms in one's hair? Could it be that something was affecting the entire Court? It was as if they were all going mad. But it was that last piece of information that made him pause. A gremlin with Delphinea? How was such a thing even possible? "Why was I not informed?"

Timias asked, gaze darting from the overwrought Hudibras to the stricken ladies.

At that, the ladies and Hudibras stared at each other, and then at Timias. "But you were, my lord," said Hudibras.

"Every hour on the hour since the clock struck thirteen," said the second lady, and he realized with another start that her gown was nearly an exact duplicate of the first's, except that the shade was slightly lighter. When had Alemandine begin to insist that her ladies-in-waiting dress alike?

Timias shoved that superfluous question away, and pulled himself upright, wondering if he himself were not suffering from some malady. There'd been no disturbances on his door—he'd heard no knocking all night at all. But then of course there'd been no gremlin to answer it. All the gremlins were sequestered in the Caul Chamber. Their shrieking on Samhain had been enough to sour cream. No wonder Alemandine was feeling so poorly. In her delicate condition, her strength already taxed, she must've suffered the gremlins' annual bout of madness dreadfully. No wonder she didn't want to come out of her room. She probably wasn't recovered yet.

Another trace of rot swirled delicately past his nose and he blinked, momentarily dizzy. These fools were only trying to make him look as if he was the foolish one. They were trying to blame him for their inability to understand and care for the Queen as if he were the one ultimately responsible for her. "I'm here now," he snapped.

Hudibras pointed the fan at Timias, as if it were indeed a dagger. "There's been no word from Artimour, or Finuviel. We don't know what's happening on the border, Timias. Alemandine won't even speak to me except to tell me to go away. She's placed a spell of binding on the door, and refuses to leave her bed."

"But that's not all, most ancient and honorable lord." The darker, more assertive lady glanced first at him, then over her shoulder, out the window. "The moonflowers are blooming." For a moment, he was so completely taken aback he could think of nothing to say, and the lady hastened to explain further. "The Queen's moonflowers. They shouldn't be blooming while she's pregnant."

There was a surreal quality to the whole scene that made Timias pause, just as he had before the stag. It was as if the world around him was ever so slightly...off. But what was it? he wondered. Hudibras and his fan? Rimbaud and his stink? The lady and her moonflowers? Again he felt slightly dizzy as if the very floor on which he stood suddenly swayed. "I must speak to the Queen."

"She won't let anyone in, Timias," said Hudibras, with a twitch of his cheek. "That's what we've been trying to tell you. She's put a spell on the doors and won't leave her bed."

To that, Timias raised his chin. "We'll see about that." He strode through the doors that led into the antechamber of the Queen's bedroom. The twilight filtering into the darkened chambers lent a purple blush to the marble walls, deepened to indigo the pale green upholstery and silken hangings. A profound hush hung over all. He pounded so hard on the ornately carved oak door with his staff that splinters flew in all directions. "Your Majesty!" he cried. "Your Majesty?"

But there was no answer.

He waited, fuming quietly under his breath, and again his nostrils were assailed by the faintest whiff of something foul, something that dissipated even as he turned his head to trace the source of the odor. "Alemandine?" He tried again, rattling the knob, knocking with a hard fist. "Alemandine? Let me in. I command you in the name of your mother, open this door and let me in!"

For a single moment, he thought he would have to blast the doors apart. But then he heard the lock click, and the two doors slipped open as the spell of binding came undone. That was easy, he thought. The doors stood as meekly open as a lamb to the slaughter. He threw a look of triumph over his shoulder at the cowering ladies and an extremely discomfited Hudibras hovering in the doorway. Then he pushed open the doors.

It was like stepping into a wall of rot. The odor made him stagger on his feet, so that he was forced to hang on to his staff to remain upright. The heavy draperies of Alemandine's favorite pale green silk were drawn, and what light there was slashed through the dark cavern of the room like gold blades. Only once before had Timias ever smelled anything so foul, and that was during a plague year in the Shadowlands, when the whole countryside had reeked like a charnel house. "Alemandine?" he managed to gasp out, before he was forced to cover his mouth and nose against the heavy reek. "Your Majesty? My Queen?"

The bed was empty. The sheets hung over the side of the bed, and were marked by foul greenish stains. A damp trail led across the marble floor to the open floor-length windows.

"My Queen?" he whispered. But nothing answered, and nothing moved. Terrified of what he might find, he stepped out of the ghastly silent chamber, into the grove where one of each of the thirteen sacred trees of Faerie grew in two concentric rings.

A silence even more profound hung over the enclosure and he looked up. The sky above was a dull leaden color, as if something had sucked the blue away. And the trees—at the base of each tree, a perfect circle of leaves lay crisped and sere, their branches partially denuded. Even the holly's needlelike leaves were tinged brown and yellow and an ankle-deep pile lay around the base of the tree. So many leaves were falling it was like a steady, downward curtain, of mingled yellow, gold and russet. He heard a soft sound from the center of the inner circle, a sound something between a moan and a sigh.

"Alemandine?"

Creeping closer, clutching the staff, shoulders hunched against the weight of that horrific stench, Timias saw that the thing which lay upon the ground was only a fragile approximation of the Queen. Her entire body had shrunk, as if it was collapsing in on itself, as if the muscles and sinews and organs were diminishing, leaving only skin and bones. Only her bloated abdomen rose roundly, like an obscene fruit hidden beneath her white gown.

But nothing could have prepared him for the horror as the Queen turned her tortured face to his. He gasped and stumbled back. Her white hair streamed about her vulpine face, the lips drawn back so tightly her mouth was nothing but a black slash. Her eyes popped from their sockets, as if squeezed outward by the pressure of whatever foul liquid it was that seeped from every orifice.

Amazingly, horribly, beyond all reason, the thing that he had called his Queen spoke. "Timias?" Her voice was less than a sigh, less than a whisper. "Timias? Timias, what's happening to me?" She twisted her head back and forth and even as he realized she was blind, he heard the wet rent of tearing flesh. "Where is my sister? Why does she not come?"

He stumbled back, not daring to come any closer lest the thing touch him. Nausea rose in his throat as disgust warred with pity. The creature held out her hand and tried to speak again, but this time the words were lost in a gurgle of green slime that spooled down her chin.

Her form seemed to collapse in and upon itself, her very bones cracking and splintering like rotting wood. A quiver ran through her, and fluids gushed from every pore, bubbling up and out through the stretched skin, which withered as Timias watched.

The earth itself shuddered, the great trees groaned, and the wind made a low mourning keen as it whined around the crystal-paned turrets. With a whimper and a sigh, Alemandine bubbled away, leaving a froth of scum, the filthy remnants of her tattered gown and the long strands of her white, spun-silk hair.

"Great Gloriana," Timias muttered. His eyes glazed over as, in one horrific moment of insight, he understood that the remains of the creature lying before him was not at all one of the sidhe, but instead something else—something strange and monstrous, a true aberration and abomination that he had not only called into being, but had seen placed upon the throne of Faerie. This was what he and Gloriana had wrought. This was the ultimate consequence of what they had created the night the Caul was made. Even half-human Artimour might've been a better choice. But it was the final realization that sent him spiraling down into the well of madness. Vinaver—may she burn in the belly of the Hag— had been right all along.

2

You didn't think to ask? You didn't think to ask? Artimour's accusation slammed like a hammer through her head as Nessa fled down the stairs, out of the keep and into the inner courtyard, blindly heading toward the first sanctuary that occurred to her. She stopped up short before she reached the gates. Molly's lean-to by the river was most likely destroyed, or so befouled by the shredded goblin carcasses the screaming spirits of the naked dead had left in their wake, it would have to be shoveled away.

As it was, once outside, the stench was so overwhelming she felt nausea rise at the back of her throat, and she stumbled into the forge, where the fire had been left to die. Broken swords and spears, shields, and even bows lay in haphazard piles, hastily dumped by the teams of just about every able-bodied person in the keep as part of the cleanup the harried Sheriff was directing even now. Through the open door, Nessa caught a glimpse of him striding, fat and red-faced, through the courtyard in the direction of the gates, bawling orders right and left, surrounded by harried-looking guards, grooms and a motley assortment of refugees young and old, male and female, who hastened to do his bidding. She peered inside the huge iron cauldron they'd used to melt the silver in. Dull and black and coated with ash on the outside, the inside shimmered, pearly and opalescent in the shifting streams of light that poured in through the shutters. Nessa wiped the tears off her cheeks and sniffed. She *had* made the dagger.

But she'd no choice. When the Duke of Allovale and the sidhe had appeared at her door, they expected a dagger. Once the Duke decided she was capable of making one, he hadn't offered her a choice. How was she to know the sidhe intended to use it against Artimour, as part of the plot against his half-sister, the Queen of the OtherWorld?

More tears filled her eyes and she tried to blink them away. Artimour had promised to help her find her father, and after last night's realization that her mother must be somewhere in the OtherWorld, too, held captive, perhaps, she had intended to ask him if he'd help find her mother, as well. But now, it seemed unlikely he'd even continue to look for her father, angry as he was. Not that she blamed him. It was by her hand, if indirectly, he'd been injured. She should find a way to make it right with him. Wasn't that what her father would tell her to do? With a sigh, she wiped away the tears with the back of her grimy sleeve, got to her feet, tied a leather apron around her neck and waist and began to sort the piled weapons into some semblance of order. Work was always her father's refuge, too.

She shut her eyes at a wave of loss and grief, remembering with bitter clarity that unseasonably hot autumn night just after the harvest was celebrated, when those two cloaked and hooded figures had come knocking on the door of Dougal's forge. He'd have been better off if he'd just sent the unlikely pair on their way. *That's what put this whole thing in motion,* she thought. *The moment he opened the door, it all changed.* And that's exactly how he'd vanished. One moment, Dougal was there, the rock at the center of her world. And the next, he was gone. It was worse than if he'd died and gone to the Summerlands, for at least then she could take comfort in the thought he walked among his ancestors. She could come to terms with his death.

But she would never come to terms with her father lost, like her mother, forever in thrall to the sidhe. And so, armed only with determination and that first goblin's head, she had gone to look for Dougal in the land beyond the mists that the old stories called TirNa'lugh. The sidhe soldiers who'd found her stumbling over the border had taken her to Artimour, who was different enough from all the other sidhe that she had been able to recognize his mortal blood at once. Different enough to agree to help her.

It was more than that, she knew, for Artimour affected her in a way no one—not even Griffin—ever had. All the village girls older than twelve twittered over this shepherd's boy or that farmer's son like a gaggle of broody hens, but she'd never understood what the fuss was all about. She thought of Griffin, of his clumsy kiss goodbye, the way he'd taken her amulet and left his for her to wear, even as her father's voice echoed out of her memory. *This is what they do to you with their OtherWorldly charms. It's why you stay away from them. Always. And never take off your silver. Never.* It was what he'd say if he were here.

But Artimour wasn't quite like the other sidhe, she was sure of it. His half-mortal blood made him different, much as he might want to deny it, and it was his half-mortal blood that had saved him from the silver's deadly poison—that and her own work boot.

Nessa fumbled beneath the apron and withdrew Dougal's amulet. Maybe it only proved Dougal was dead. *And maybe I am just a "lovesick, moon-mazed maiden"* like all the songs say, she told herself as she dragged three battered shields to the scrap pile she was building on the other side of the forge.

"Nessa?" Molly's soft voice broke through the smoky gloom, and Nessa looked up to see the corn granny from Killcrag hesitating at the door. "Is that you? Are you in here?"

"It's me." She was surprised it had taken Molly this long to find her. She dropped the shields and they fell with a clatter onto the pile. "I don't want to go to Gar, Molly. Let Uwen tell the Duke what happened with Cadwyr, let Artimour explain how—how he came to be stabbed. Why do I need to be there? Can't I stay here with you? I can help—"

She heard Molly's long indrawn breath, heard her soft sigh. "Ah, Nessa."

Before Nessa could speak, Molly crossed the space between them and drew Nessa into the strong circle of her arms. She felt her throat thicken and her mouth work, and the tears she'd been swallowing spilled down her cheeks. "I don't know what to say to him, Molly. I did make the dagger. It was my fault he was stabbed—"

Molly gently tucked one errant curl behind Nessa's ear. "You could tell him you're sorry."

"I don't think he wants an apology."

"Well, there's not much more he's likely to get. What's done is done, child. It's the past, it's over. Yes, perhaps you should've asked a few more questions, but Cadwyr is a Duke, a noble Duke. You'd no choice, really. He'll come around to seeing that."

"Shouldn't I do something—something to make it right?"

"Make it right? If he were a mortal, perhaps the druid court would set a penalty, but, Nessa, don't forget. They would also take into account that you are still a child, in the eyes of the law, still beneath your father's roof, and Cadwyr of such high rank. What choice did you have? No court would judge you half so harsh." Molly drew back, holding Nessa at arm's length. "You listen to me, girl. Your father would be proud—"

"That's exactly it," Nessa said, her face crumpling. "Artimour promised to help me—but I had this horrible thought last night when I thought about what my—my grandmother's ghost said to me. What happens if my parents die in the OtherWorld?"

"But no one dies in TirNa'lugh, child. Should you ever find her, your mother will be as young and as fair as the day she was lost to it. That's what your grammies meant—"

"Molly, I remember one of Granny Wren's stories, about Vain Thomas who goes to TirNa'lugh and loses his head and his soul is swept up by Herne into the Wild Hunt. Don't you see, Molly? And Granny Wren said that's where most of the souls in the Wild Hunt come from, the ones who're truly lost forever. That's what I'm afraid of, Molly. I don't want them lost forever—"

"Well," said Molly, "you can't worry about that right

now. The lord's still healing. But I do think if you apologize, Lord Artimour will come around. And besides..." She paused and nodded at the bulky bandage Nessa wore around her left hand to conceal the ring Artimour had given her in token of his promise to look for Dougal in the OtherWorld. "Won't he want that back?"

"My father always said that honor meant nothing to the sidhe." Nessa fingered the awkward bump. The central stone was round and hard and felt big as a robin's egg beneath the linen wrapping.

A stir outside interrupted Molly, and Nessa looked over her shoulder. She heard men calling for the Sheriff, and then Sir Uwen. She glanced at Molly. "Someone's come."

Molly nodded. "Nessa," she said slowly. "Am I wrong to think you've never been to the greenwood, as they say, with any man, even the 'prentice lad? Griffin?"

Mortified, Nessa shook her head, wondering how to explain to this kind-eyed woman how Dougal had communicated without words that he both desired and condoned distance between himself and Nessa, and the rest of the village. From memory's dark well, she heard Dougal's voice, deep and halting. *Your mother was the sort of girl the lads all liked.* As long as Nessa could remember, it seemed that there was something about this aspect of her mother that was irrevocably tied to her susceptibility to the sidhe. Which was why the goodwives all watched her. "My—my mother— my father said my mother was the girl the lads all liked."

"And he warned you away from the lads altogether?"

"Well, no. Not really." She hesitated. "He said that the reason the goodwives watched me so hard was to see if I was going to be like my mother that way. Because that's what

drew the sidhe, they all thought. That she was...like that."
And the easiest way to avoid their eyes and their whispers
and their questions was to avoid all the men as much as possible, as well, thus earning for herself a reputation for being
more taciturn than even Dougal.

Molly was silent for a moment, and then spoke slowly.
"Well, then. I suppose that explains that." Again she hesitated. "But tomorrow you're about to go off—" And again
she broke off, and Nessa wondered what the wicce-woman
wanted to say.

"What are you worried about?"

Molly's brows shot up and she laughed. "*Worried* isn't exactly the word I'd use. Your father wanted to protect you,
but there are things a woman must know, things only a
woman can know, and only a woman can teach. You're far
too innocent and unaware of the effect you have on the
young men around you." Once more she paused, and in the
gloom, her eyes twinkled. "There's an old saying that's
proven true more often than not in my experience. The
apple doesn't fall far from the tree."

Flustered, Nessa stared at the weapons lying in half-sorted
heaps. "What do you mean?"

Molly smiled gently. "Griffin's in love with you, did you
know that?"

"Griffin?" echoed Nessa. She did not like thinking about
Griffin, she realized, especially with Artimour so close. She'd
known intuitively, from the moment she had first contemplated Artimour's arrival in Killcairn, that it would upset
Griffin to know how Artimour made her feel. Griffin's
clumsy farewell kiss, the amulet he'd left behind for her,
even the pack of food he'd hastily thrust into her hands be-

fore she'd crossed over into the OtherWorld—each memory sent a guilty pang through her, even as they bore silent testimony to the truth of Molly's assertion.

Molly looked at her with one raised brow.

"He took my amulet," Nessa said, knowing that Molly had already talked to Griffin himself. "And left his for me. Is that why? You really think he loves me?"

Dust motes danced in the shaft of sunlight filtering through a loose shingle on the roof, and Molly's brown eyes twinkled. "What do you think?"

In colored fragments of sight and sound, images of suddenly remembered snippets twisted themselves around Molly's sentences, weaving a coherence and a meaning into the fabric of her memories that she only now understood: Griffin watching from the other side of the yard as she shoveled coal; blushing suddenly as she reached for a pitcher and the neck of her summer tunic dipped low; splashing water on her late last summer, then backing away, with a face reddened by what she'd assumed was exertion when the entire bucket upended over her breasts, flattening the thin summer linen against the round curves so that her dark nipples were as perfectly visible as if she were naked, even as Dougal immediately barked, "Cover yourself, girl," and tossed her a cloak. How long had Griffin's feelings been growing, while she, all the while, was unaware? "You think I should marry Griffin?"

Molly looked completely taken aback. "Goodness, girl, what gave you thought of that?" She reached out and touched Nessa's cheek, then her hair. "Your father was right in a way. You're not like the others—to be honest, I suspect you're Beltane-made, much as he denies it for some reason.

But like your mother, the lads like you, too. Though unlike
her, I don't think you know what you do to the lads. So you
trust your heart and mind that birch staff of yourn. That tree
has a powerful, protecting spirit to it, and she's sent a piece
of herself out into the world with you. I think if your father'd
had his way, he'd've built a wall higher than hedgerow and
thicker than an oak around the forge, to keep you safe
within." She touched Nessa's hair again, smoothing it back
from her burning face. "But now you're about to go off with
two men—two men, either one of which would set any
maid's heart aflutter."

"Even Uwen?" Nessa wrinkled her nose. She thought of
Uwen's crooked grin and offset jaw and bony frame. He might
be one of the Duke of Gar's own Company, but she could not
imagine anyone finding Uwen the least bit attractive.

But Molly smiled. "Ah, child. I've seen a few make it very
obvious that they'd happily join Sir Uwen on a trip to the
greenwood, and one or two who have. You've not been
paying attention. Sooner or later, whether it's Griffin or
Uwen, or this sidhe-lord himself, don't be afraid to lie with
any man you truly desire, for what happens between a man
and a woman is the root of every kind of magic worked in
this world, and the Other, too, I imagine."

Nessa closed her eyes as she remembered riding through
the forest of the OtherWorld, sharing Artimour's saddle. She
remembered the pungent resin rising from the dark green
pines, the slow flutter of gold leaves, the feeling of his velvety hose against the backs of her legs as they dangled awkwardly off the horse, the solidity of his chest against her
back, the smooth satiny feeling of the saddle between her
thighs. A part of her understood that Molly had imparted

knowledge of much importance—that had something to do with why the wicce-women were said to be had for a silver coin and what they did to make the fields fertile and the corn grow—but all that really seemed to matter right now was that she somehow make peace with Artimour.

"Granny Molly? Nessa?" Uwen's voice sounded so different, that for a moment, Nessa wasn't sure who stood starkly silhouetted at the threshold. It was Uwen's familiar bony form, but it was hardly Uwen's voice, for it fell hollow and flat, totally devoid of his usual light, teasing lilt. "There may be a change in plans. A band of Cecily's clansmen from Mochmorna came in just now. They took refuge last night in an abandoned dovecote somewhere in the hills. But they'd a druid with them who'd an idea of what to do and he summoned up the dead. Seems Donnor's ghost was seen among them."

The Duke of Gar was dead, the castle was in shambles, and Cecily, his widow, did not feel at all the way she imagined a widow was supposed to feel. If Donnor was dead, it was his own fault. She'd tried to warn him not to trust Cadwyr, his nephew and his heir, begged him to wait until at least half his Company could be assembled. But no, he insisted on riding out on some trumped-up excuse a blind mule could see through. She had thought, at first, that only she and Kian had seen Donnor's gray ghost as it picked its way across the carcass-littered field, fading into the blessed Samhain dawn. But everyone on the walls had seen it, and rumor ran rampant as a ram in rut through every level of the castle, leaving even the most hardened of the warriors looking stricken as an orphaned lamb.

Now she picked her way across what yesterday had been the outermost ward, flanked on one side by Kestrel, the ArchDruid of Gar, and at least six of his highest-ranking fellows, and on the other by Mag, the chief still-wife, and as many wicce-women as could be coaxed away from the nursing and the grieving. They would never survive another night if the goblins came back. But if there was a way to prevent them, both druids and corn grannies were conspicuously silent. Her thoughts chased each other like a dog its tail.

A silence as leaden as the lowering sky hung heavy over all, deadening the slap of her boots, muffling the sobs of those few strong-stomached souls who came forward to press a kiss on her hand as they searched amidst the rubble for possessions abandoned and befouled. On the walls, the engineers and stonemasons directed teams in the critical repairs of the curtain wall. On command, the men bent and with a mighty heave, lifted the great stone block on a huge wooden lever as another team swung it into position. The dull thud of stone, punctuated by the creak of timber and the shouted directions of the men echoed flatly across the yard, as if the sounds were swallowed by the huge holes the goblins had torn in the walls, soaked up by the deep gashes of bloodied earth. She pressed the linen square soaked in peppermint oil more tightly to her nostrils and swallowed hard as she realized she had nearly stepped on a foot. "Be careful."

She held out an arm to prevent anyone else from stepping on the remains, and signaled to a team of stable hands who, with linen kerchiefs wrapped across the lower half of their faces, armed with a shovel, a pick and a wheelbarrow, gathered up remains as carefully as they could.

Smoke from the midden-fires stung her eyes, and on the high tor behind the castle, a slow procession wound up the steps carved into the hill, carrying the bodies to the funeral pyre the druids of lower degree were building. Swarming on the standing stones, others set up the iron frames to hold the plates of glass that, when properly positioned, would focus the rays of the setting sun so as to bring about the spontaneous combustion of the bodies. At least, it was supposed to bring about the spontaneous combustion of the bodies. Kestrel and the other druids had emerged from their hiding place in the wine cellars and announced that all who'd died on Samhain would be given nothing less than a full druid funeral. As if that would bring the dead back. As if that would protect the living when the goblins returned.

A couple of the corn grannies paused and spat thick greenish wads of cud-wort on the ground, aiming expertly between two stones. Cecily hoped her lip hadn't curled automatically. Cud-wort was considered a low habit, but many of the corn grannies were addicted to it. It was said to give one clearer dreams.

She looked around the ruined ward. All her dreams were nightmares. Now they stood vulnerable, not just to goblins, but to Cadwyr. Cadwyr, who'd murdered Donnor. Cadwyr, who was in league with the sidhe. Before Samhain, she and Kian had told Kestrel their suspicions, but the druid had listened skeptically, clearly unconvinced that either goblins or sidhe existed, except in the mind of a moon-mazed girl. She hoped that last night had made believers of everyone.

But she was even more afraid of Cadwyr, if that were possible, than the goblins, for Cadwyr had made it clear before he left with Donnor that he considered Cecily part of Donnor's bequest. And for all she knew, she thought with weary realization, maybe she had been. Maybe that's how Donnor had rationalized taking her for himself, if he had in fact done as Cadwyr charged, and offered himself to her parents rather than Cadwyr as a suitor for her hand. Maybe he considered her as much a part of the holdings of Gar as Cadwyr did. What would they all say if they knew she was too angry at Donnor to care that he was dead?

She caught sight of Kian, Donnor's First Knight, working with the other men on the walls, stripped down to his shirt despite the cold wind. The strip of linen bound around his face could not disguise his flaxen braids, nor the familiar lines of his body beneath the sweaty, dirty clothes. As she watched, Kian squatted down and gripped one end of the long wooden pole, and, at a signal, pressed down on it with all his weight. His arms and back bulged with the knotted cords of his muscles. At the other end of the lever, a team grabbed the ropes around the block and wrestled it into place. Kian set the lever down, stripped his mask off and used it to mop his face. As exhausted and as frightened as she was, her own body stirred in response.

For Kian was the man she loved. She loved his strength, she loved his smile, she loved the way the other knights loved him. He had the gift of making people like him, for he led with smiles and faultless courtesy. Donnor had loved him, too, until last Beltane, when the goddess had led her to choose Kian to take her to his Beltane bower. From that day, Donnor had been deaf to all but the angry mutterings of his thwarted heart. But Donnor was dead.

"We'll measure the angles from the top of the tor itself—take them at sunset and dawn, as well," Kestrel was saying.

The ornately embroidered lining of his wide sleeve flashed a startling green against the outer white as he pointed first at the sun, then at the tor, the vivid color at stark odds to the stained gray drab and homespun everyone else, even Cecily, wore.

"We'll need measurements from the towers, too, won't we?" put in another.

"But what about the goblins?" Cecily asked. All the druids wanted to talk about were the funeral plans, which would have been understandable, even expected, perhaps, under any other sort of circumstances. "Can any of you tell me if they'll come back tonight? Or if there's a way to stop them? If the dead will rise and fight?"

The wicce-women exchanged surreptitious glances with each other and looked pointedly at the druids. Kestrel cleared his throat and the others flapped their robes and shifted from foot to foot. They'd all failed miserably last night, and they knew it. Shouts from above momentarily distracted her, and she peered through one of the huge holes in the outer curtain wall to see a speck of dust emerge from the eastern road leading out of the forest. A rider, she thought, coming fast. Someone else had survived Samhain. She saw that Kian noticed as well, but he went on with the task at hand. There were not many hours of daylight left. So she too turned back to Kestrel. "Well?"

Kestrel linked his hands together beneath his capacious white sleeves and cleared his throat again before he answered. "The bards are studying the druidic verses, my lady, and the elder brethren have been in the groves since early this morning, interpreting the trees. To be sure, however, these are arcane matters, the learning encoded so as not to be easily understood by the uninitiated."

"I'm not asking to understand, Master Druid. I just want to know how to protect us. Can we count on the dead?" But the only answer was the flap of the mourning banners from the towers. Someone—probably Mag, or maybe even Kian—had seen to that.

"They came because it was Samhain and they could," whispered a corn granny. "We can't count on them again, til next Samhain."

Cecily immediately looked at the women, but it was impossible to know who had spoken. "Will they come back?"

The painful silence was broken by Kestrel's snort. "They don't know any more than anyone else."

"What about the goblins?" Cecily asked again. "Will they come back tonight?"

"At Imbolc," blurted Mag this time.

"The blood of the new lambs will bring them. Our magic can hold them back til then, but come Imbolc, 'tis druid magic that's needed." Another granny spoke up, from somewhere behind Mag. The words were followed by a hawking cough, and a green gob shot through the air, landing with a loud smack right in front of Kestrel. He startled back, and Cecily caught the flash of red Lacquilean leather under his heavy woolen robes. Serves him right, she thought. *What sort of fool would wear such finery in a mess like this?* An answer ran through her mind unbidden: *One who thought it easily replaced.* But they're not likely to be readily replaced, thought Cecily, even as she dismissed all thoughts of Kestrel and his boots.

Kestrel's lips quirked down as his eyebrows arched up.

"There you are, ask the wicce-women," Kestrel sniffed. "They seem to know all about it." He turned away, waving a hand back and forth in front of his face, as if the very smell of them offended him. Cecily looked down at the bubbled green slime glistening in the sunlight and felt nauseous herself.

But she couldn't let that deter her. "Please tell me what you can. Anyone. Please."

It was the women's turn to exchange glances, to shuffle restlessly beneath shawls and skirts, like a motley flock of roosting broody hens. They ranged in age from women who looked no older than the oldest of her foster sisters, to the most wizened of crones.

"Please," Cecily said again. "Whatever you think might help."

Kestrel coughed.

It was the druids, Cecily knew. The druids looked down on the wicce-women, and their magic was considered something less, because, as the grannies said, they carried their magic in their hearts and not their heads, and certainly not in arcane verses in half-forgotten languages, or obscure symbols slashed on the limbs of trees.

"They're laughing at us, Your Grace," Mag sniffed back and folded her arms across her ample bosom. Kestrel claimed that she had sabotaged a Mid-Winter ritual one year by deliberately adding dream-bane to the required mix of herbs. Unable to achieve the necessary trance, the druids had stormed off in a huff, and the rite itself disintegrated into a riotous festival, which culminated in a fight in which several of Donnor's knights had nearly died. This alone was not so unusual, but the druids were expected to help keep the order, and so Donnor had blamed the druids. And thus the druids, never among the most favored of the inhabitants of Gar, for even the lowest considered himself the equal of the Duke, fell a few more points in Donnor's grace.

But Donnor was dead. "I don't think there's much to laugh about," replied Cecily.

The speck on the horizon had resolved itself into a rider, who entered the ruined gates with a look of glazed exhaustion. He barely cleared the wrecked gatehouse when he slid to the ground, even as his horse collapsed. Cecily saw guards and two women scavenging amidst the rubble run to his side, even as Kian leaped off the walls and hurried over, calling for water. *Let it be from Donnor himself,* she thought. *Let that shade have been nothing but a trick of the light. Let us all have been wrong.*

But she knew in her heart such hope was only futile. She saw Kian glance at her over his shoulder as he swung the rider up into his arms, and understood he'd seek her out as soon as he could. Followed by the women, he took off in the direction of the summer kitchens.

"Please," she said again.

There was a long silence and another gust of wind brought a blast of reek. "They come three times a year," said a low, hoarse voice. "Three times...three times...three times, the gates between the worlds swing wide." The voice quivered, as if some tremendous amount of energy was being repressed. The women parted, and a small, pudgy granny with hair like dandelion wisps stood rocking on her feet, as her hands twitched up and down before her. "Three nights... three times...three nights...our magic cannot hold. Three times our magic cannot hold."

"Three times? And when—what three times are those?" Cecily prodded. She glanced at Kestrel and the other druids, hoping they had the sense to hold their tongues. They appeared to be paying close attention. The druids were all trained to remember. Many of them could repeat, word for word, conversations that had taken place before them decades past.

But the granny shook her head with closed eyes.

"At Samhain, Imbolc and Lughnasa." It was another voice, softer this time. A woman with the face of a turtle-dove and a shawl the color of a robin's breast eased around Mag. She was chewing a wad of cud-wort that she shifted from cheek to cheek as she spoke. "At Beltane, the sun's too strong and the light holds them back. But at the other three—only druid magic can hold them back."

Cecily glanced at the druids. That was the problem. The druids didn't seem to know what exactly their magic was. "What about the other times? The rest of the year?" The granny visibly quailed, and even Mag wouldn't meet Cecily's eyes. "Mag, please."

Mag huffed. "Do you have any idea what they say about us?"

Cecily drew a deep breath. She looked at the women's worn, guarded faces, their shoulders broadened and bent, their hands rough and callused. She knew what was said about the wicce-women—that they wanted men for only one thing, that at the dark of the moon, they did unspeakable things to make the corn grow. "You don't have to reveal anything. Just tell me if you think there's something you can do."

Mag nodded shortly. "We think there is."

"Can you be sure?"

"Our hearts tell us to be sure." She met Cecily's eyes steadily.

"Do you really think it will work?"

"We believe that it will."

"They don't have any idea it will work at all," interrupted Kestrel. "Whatever 'it' is. That's the whole point, my lady, and that's what makes corn magic such a lot of nonsense. They don't know—they base their knowing, such as it is, on no authority. No verse or rune guides them, no teacher even teaches. It all just comes to them in a flight of fancy. Or in a puddle of that weed they chew." He sniffed, and immediately pressed his own oil-soaked wad of linen to his nostrils. "The corn grows. The sun shines, and the rain falls. There's nothing to say their rituals work."

Cecily drew a deep breath. This was an old, old argument and one that she had largely been able to ignore her entire life, for what the druids, the masters of ancient wisdom, poetry and law, thought of the wicce-women, the healers, the corn grannies who worked the corn magic in the fields, and vice versa, had never affected her in any meaningful way. As the daughter of two of the greatest Houses in Brynhyvar, with a potential role to play in the governing of the land, it was a forgone conclusion that she would study with the druids. And as a woman, her duties required her to have a knowledge of herbs and simples, and that brought her in close contact with Mag, a corn granny longer than Cecily had been at Gar. Both necessary, both separate. But now...

She rubbed her forehead, as if to clear away the flinty edge of desperation and exhaustion that threatened to cloud her mind completely. "There's nothing to say that it doesn't.

We have to try anything. We can't waste time arguing who has the greater magic and the truer understanding, for the goblins surely won't wait for us to decide."

"Grannies'll have us all tuppin' in the fields tonight, you wait," said a druid from the depths of his hood. A snicker went through the druids like wind through wheat. The women exchanged glances.

Cecily raised her chin. "I'd rather tup out there than die in here." She met their eyes and tossed her hair back in a gesture she was quite sure was the last one a widow was expected to make, and winked. She turned back to the women, and met the eyes of each in turn. "Say what you will."

"We've no wish to be laughed at."

"No one will laugh," said Cecily. She held up her hand. "And if anyone thinks he might," she paused and looked over the druids. "Think on this first. In five hundred years, since these walls were built, no enemy's stood where we're standing now. The walls have never been breached. But the goblins tore these walls apart like they were made of sticks." She looked Kestrel square in the eyes. "I'll tup in the fields myself if that's what it takes." *And expect you there alongside me,* she nearly said, but that thought was nearly as horrifying as another goblin attack.

The hint of a smile lifted Mag's mouth, but she still sounded hesitant. "We must...we'll begin at sunset, isn't that right, Granny Lyss? When the sun slips below the trees, below the tor, beside the river, the oldest granny, Granny Lyss, here—" she stepped back and indicated a tiny, wizened, birdlike woman, who was working on such an enormous piece of cud-wort, it slipped in and out between her lips with the motion of her jaw "—will work the rite. We need a volunteer, of course. A man. In his prime, or near approaching it."

"Nah, the younger the better—fourteen, fifteen." The old woman spoke in a quavering voice and tapped Mag's arm with a curved finger that ended in a thick yellowed nail.

"That's disgusting," muttered Kestrel. "Completely and totally disgusting."

"Can *you* think of anything else?" asked Cecily. The greasy smoke made her eyes burn. Fire, she thought. Perhaps a ring of fire would deter them. She made a mental note to suggest that to Kian.

"Would be better magic if one of them would do it," said the old woman, and Cecily saw she had no teeth and her lips were drawn into her mouth, like those of the corpses who'd gone with Herne. What lad would volunteer? she wondered. And she wondered if even Kian could be induced to lie with such a woman.

"I'll do it." The voice resonated like a born bard's, but the tall boy who pushed through the druids was slight of build, his skin pimpled patchy red.

"What are you doing here?" demanded Kestrel. "I thought you were gathering up the dead—"

"I was," he answered. "I overheard." He gestured to his stained white robes. "What do you need me to do?"

"What's your name, young druid?" asked Cecily, bemused.

"He's not a druid." Kestrel rolled his eyes. "He's naught but a third-degree bard and he's always where he's not needed and never where he is."

"Well, then, young third-degree bard, what's your name?" Cecily motioned to Granny Lyss to stop cackling.

"I'm Jammor, Your Grace. Jammor of the Rill, they call

me." He bowed and handed Kestrel his shovel with such a flourish, she nearly laughed aloud despite the situation.

"Oh, indeed, he'll do right fine," cackled Granny Lyss. "Come over here, boy, and let me feel your arm."

"Tell him, first, what he's in for, and see if he's still interested." Kestrel stepped forward and pushed the shovel back into Jammor's hands. "Get back to work."

"Now, just you wait, young man," cried Granny Lyss. "I want a look at you—"

The boy hesitated, even as Kestrel opened his mouth to protest, and the impasse was broken by Kian, who came striding over the rubble, picking his way with the grace of a mountain cat, despite his size. But his expression was grim. At once Cecily asked, "What word, Sir Kian?"

"A sad word, that we expected," answered Kian. He paused on the periphery of the group and sought her eyes with his. "It's just as we feared, my lady. Great Gar is dead." He glanced at Kestrel, then at Mag. "If you'd be so kind as to step aside a moment with me, my lord druid? Still-wife? Your Grace?"

"Shall we talk about the funeral?" Kestrel asked as Kian shepherded the three of them behind a pile of rubble. Blood stained the stones, and goblin gore clung here and there to the ruined wall, but at least the worst had been removed, thought Cecily as she carefully stepped over a suspicious pile of cloth.

"Funeral?" said Kian. He had removed his mask, and his face was furrowed with worry and exhaustion, and grime and sweat streaked his skin. "There's no time to talk of funerals, my lord. Donnor's death isn't the only news the scout brought. Cadwyr of Allovale has raised his colors over

Ardagh, and ten thousand mercenaries from Lacquilea are marching up from the south, led by one of Cadwyr's foster brothers."

They all gasped. Kestrel glanced around, white robes bluish in the shadows, so that his garments seemed to blend in with the stone. "Surely the messenger's mistaken? What about the King? What about the Court?"

Kian shook his head, grim-faced. "He never got that close. He was sent back ahead of the rest. He did flank Cadwyr's army. There's at least two thousand horse, four thousand foot. Between them and the mercenaries, Cadwyr's got nearly three times what we could muster ourselves."

"Where did he get all those men?"

Kian shook his head slowly. "The lad didn't get close enough to see if they were men, my lady. And if they are—" He broke off and put his hands on his hips. "Who knows what promises Cadwyr has made to others?"

"Do you really think Cadwyr is leading an army of the sidhe?" Cecily asked.

"You can't seriously believe—" began Kestrel.

"How can you have seen those monsters last night, and Great Herne, too, and not believe what we tell you?" interrupted Cecily. "None of us want to believe it, my lord. None of us wanted to believe it before." Kestrel had refused from the first to believe Kian's tale of the blacksmith's daughter and the sidhe.

"But this was what Donnor meant when he told me an opportunity had arisen suddenly, one that wouldn't wait. Donnor knew about Cadwyr's plan to use the sidhe."

"And now he's marching on Gar," said Kian.

"Well, did this scout see any sign of any—any Other?" asked Kestrel. "What other evidence is there, really?"

"Other than Cadwyr's colors over a castle that's built on a rock over a whirlpool? What other evidence do you need, you old goat?" asked Mag with such derision that Cecily raised her brow. Mag was, after all, but the still-wife.

"They came upon a squadron or so of archers, who looked to be butchered where they stood," answered Kian. "Most of them didn't even have time to draw their sidearms."

"So no one's actually seen any—" said Kestrel.

"We've a witness," said Kian. "The blacksmith's daughter from Killcairn. Don't you recall?"

"Have you any better explanation, Lord Druid?" asked Mag.

"I don't want to believe it, either, my lord," Cecily repeated. "But for all we know, Cadwyr may have a bargain with the goblins as well. I don't think we can discount any possibility."

"Cadwyr would not dare—" exploded Kestrel.

"He's already dared to make himself master of Ardagh. I think we may well believe Cadwyr's capable of anything," said Cecily. "How soon will he be here?"

"We must call for an Assembly at once, obviously," said Kestrel. "Donnor's funeral will give us our perfect—"

"Oh, will you stop blathering about funerals?" interrupted Mag. "Cadwyr's loosed both sidhe and goblin on us—how soon will he be here?"

"But I'm the one he wants," said Cecily, thinking fast. "With Donnor dead, he considers Gar already his. I doubt he'll attack the castle. Especially if I'm not here." She looked at Kian, and was grateful to see him nod.

"Not here? Your Grace, you can't leave—" began Kestrel. "Think of your duty—think of the people— Where would you go?" The color drained from his face and suddenly he looked sick. "And besides, what makes you think Duke Cadwyr would harm you? It has ever been my observation that the Duke cherishes you—" He broke off and glanced away, refusing to meet Cecily's eyes.

"Cecily has a better claim to the throne." Despite the situation, Cecily looked up, for it was the first time Kian had used her name in public. *Donnor's dead, and I am free.* "She has to leave, my lord," Kian continued. "We don't know what Cadwyr's bringing with him. Obviously he must've used the sidhe against Ardagh. There was no damage to the castle, do you understand? Whatever he brought against Hoell was awful enough that they opened the doors and let him walk in. I've but a quarter of the men I had yesterday. And I had less than half a full garrison to begin with. "

He used my name, Cecily thought again, and a part of her that was so long buried she had nearly forgotten it ever existed within her stirred to new life. Her heart skipped a beat. *Donnor is dead,* she thought with a little burst of the most unseemly happiness. *Donnor's dead and I'm free. We are free.*

"But you've no reason to think—"

"I have every reason to think that Cadwyr intends to force himself upon me, my lord druid," Cecily snapped. He'd been like this before Samhain, too, insisting on questioning everything.

The druid shut his mouth with an audible pop as a shadow crossed his face, and bitter shrieks made Cecily turn her head to see a flock of ravens rise and wheel off the roof of the Great Hall. *The ravens are the Marrihugh's birds,* she thought, and she is marching across this land in her crow-feathered boots. She must've been well pleased last night.

"Then where will you go?" asked Kestrel.

"North, of course," Kian answered. "The scout said Cad-wyr's army was still at least a day and a half out. Sheer size is slowing him down, thank the Marrihugh for some luck."

"And what about the rest of us?" demanded Mag. "Cad-wyr's coming, and who knows what he's leading. To go or stay—'tis a choice that must be put to one and all."

But the druid was shaking his head. "Bah, woman, what're you suggesting? There're no guarantees that your magic will work. Her Grace, the knights, they at least have fast horses—they may have a chance of outriding the goblins. But to take wounded women and children on some mad dash 'twould be the death of most of them." He looked at Kian and pushed his hood off his face, so that it fell back over his shoulders in graceful, fluid folds. He was shorter than Kian, but he drew himself up. "You go, Sir Knight. I'll stay—we'll all stay, my brother druids and I. We'll do what we can to protect the people here. By every means we can contrive."

Cecily glanced around, assessing the progress of the re-pairs. Whole sections of the outer wall were missing. The second wall appeared sound, but it had not been built to withstand the brunt of an attack, especially not such a one as last night's, and she remembered her idea. "What about fire?" asked Cecily. "A ring of fire around the castle?"

"That's a thought," said Kian. "Hard to maintain, perhaps. I'm not sure we've that much fuel—but still, it might be a way to block those holes. I'll go and speak to the captain of the watch. We leave—" He broke off and looked up. The sun was still high above the tor. "Can you be ready to leave at dusk?"

"Dusk?" echoed Mag and Cecily as one. Cecily nodded at Mag and she went on, "Begging your pardon, my lord knight, but we need Her Grace."

"Me?" Cecily blinked.

"For what?" asked Kian.

"She—she should be there. We're going to need her—her—her presence," Mag answered. "For the ritual. She'll bring a certain...energy...that the granny will need. Oh, I'm quite sure she should be there."

"And for how long?"

"Most of the night." Mag ducked her head apologetically. "You do want us to try all we can, right?"

Kian ran a hand over his eyes, and Cecily felt a wave of exhaustion sweep over her. And how much worse could it be for him? He'd fought most of the night, snatching only a few hours' rest between sunrise and midmorning. "We'll go at dawn, then. We should reach the Daraghduin by midnight tomorrow, if we're lucky."

If we're lucky. The little phrase echoed over and over in Cecily's mind like a death knell. But Kian was continuing. "You're the ArchDruid of Gar, my lord, is that not so?" asked Kian. When Kestrel nodded, he went on, "And as such, it's your role to hold disputed property until such time as an heir can be determined?"

"Yes..." answered Kestrel slowly, as an odd expression crossed his face. "But only with good reason. And Cadwyr is the son of Donnor's oldest sister. Only a child of his own loins, or a child of that child, has a stronger claim." He turned to Cecily with an incredulous look. "Is it your intention to also dispute Cadwyr for the duchy of Gar, my lady?"

"Donnor came to me the night before he left," Cecily said. She could pretend to be pregnant if she had to.

"I see," the druid said. There was an aloofness in his tone that made Cecily look more closely at him. Was it only the druid's surprise that there might be yet another claimant for the duchy of Gar? she wondered. Suddenly the walls didn't feel so much safe as suffocating. But it was Kian's next words that took her off guard.

"And a child of a child has an equal claim, as well?"

"Well, not as equal as a child—" Kestrel broke off. "What are you saying, Sir Kian? Donnor had a grandchild?"

Shocked, Cecily's mouth dropped open and she exchanged a wide-eyed look with Mag as Kian answered, "Aye. Donnor had a daughter, got off one of his father's women when he was very young. She was fostered out on the Isles, and when it came time to marry her off, she refused the man he'd chosen. So he disavowed her—"

"In a court? Before an ArchDruid?" Kestrel was frowning now, twisting his linked hands together beneath the wide sleeves of his robes.

"I don't know the particulars of all the circumstances, my lord," began Kian.

"Well, you'd better be quite sure of them if you mean to raise—"

"Lord Kestrel," interrupted Kian gently. "It's not me."

"Then, who—" put in Cecily. This was totally unexpected. She wondered why Kian hadn't mentioned it to her before.

"It's not for me to say. He'll reveal himself when he's

ready. If he were here, he'd have come to you himself," Kian said as he turned back to Kestrel. "So you'll do what must be done, to call the Assembly? That's your duty, no?"

"But—"

Her thoughts drifted as Kestrel continued to sputter questions, all to which she wanted answers as well. "I trust you to keep this information to yourselves, Your Grace, still-wife," Kian continued. "I only bring this up now because— well, because I suppose there's a possibility he's no longer even alive. But he should be given the chance to make his claim, don't you agree?"

So this was someone they all knew? Someone who lived here? Donnor had an heir he'd known nothing of? She had a feeling that Kian would tell her no more than he was telling Kestrel. "If that's what it comes to, my lord, yes," Kian was saying, and she realized the conversation had taken another turn. "It's not my wish to fight Cadwyr, but what choice has he given us? I'll be happy to meet Cadwyr in lawful Assembly, as will Her Grace, but we'd rather have an army of our own kin at our backs and know what exactly we're to face."

"Come, my lady, there're things to be done before the ritual," said Mag. "A bath and such. I'll explain it to you as we go."

"Make it up as you go, don't you mean?" put in Kestrel. "Don't forget to pack, Your Grace."

For some reason, that struck her as an odd thing for him to say, odd enough that she paused, even as Mag tugged at her arm. It was like a false note in an otherwise well-tuned harp. She opened her mouth, then shut it, and Mag looked at Kestrel. "What about the lad? Will you let him join us?"

"Absolutely not," Kestrel said with a dismissive wave.

An image of Kestrel's red boots of Lacquilean leather jumped into Cecily's mind, and she glanced down, to see one tip peeking out from beneath the hem of Kestrel's robe. There was something about those boots that pricked her like a pin lost in a seam. Maybe it was just the way he treated the wicce-women that bothered her. *Everyone knows the druids like their comforts. But so does Cadwyr.* She remembered the rose he'd brought her the night before he and Donnor had left on that ill-fated journey, the way it had reeked of the OtherWorld. She wondered if Kestrel's boots were really made of Lacquilean leather, and then the rest of the messenger's news echoed in her mind. *Ten thousand Lacquilean mercenaries are marching this way, as well—he well may think them easily replaced.* Could it be he knew they were coming?

"What do you need, still-wife?" asked Kian. "Is there anything I can do to help?"

At that, Cecily's brow shot up, but before she could speak, Mag answered as she nodded slowly with a speculative look. "You're not as young as you might be, Sir Kian, but come with me to Granny Lyss. We'll ask her if she thinks you'll do."

Cecily noticed that Kestrel went in the direction of the summer kitchens. *He's going to speak to the scout himself,* she thought. Donnor was not quite as universally loved as he had liked to believe. His own heir hated him, and there was another now, another who had not even made himself known while Donnor lived. "Kian," she asked, speaking softly under her breath as he guided her and Mag around the rubble. "Is it possible that Kestrel and Cadwyr—" She broke off, and their eyes met. He didn't answer, but she saw him watch Kestrel until he rounded a corner and they could see him no more.

Nessa did not even look up when the long shadow fell across the forge. Once the Sheriff noticed her, and remembered her, he'd summoned the four scullions assigned to help her yesterday, and put them all back to work, this time repairing the endless mound of weapons and other implements the goblins had nearly destroyed. Thus, Uwen startled her as she was hanging the heavy leather apron on a hook. "I need a word with you, lass."

There was something distinctly different about him, Nessa thought as she stifled a gasp, then bundled her tumbled hair off her face. He looked as if a great weight had suddenly fallen on top of him, and stern, as if he had set himself to do a great task. He leaned against the wall and glanced around the forge. "You've been busy today." His watery eyes were bloodshot and he looked tired. They were all tired, she thought. Up all night, a few hours of wretched sleep snatched at dawn. Now it was late, the scullions long since gone to answer the dinner bell's summons.

"What's wrong?" Her wound itched, her shoulders ached, but Uwen looked worse than she felt.

"I need to get to Gar. We've been dithering about it all day, but I need to find out what's going on there—if Donnor's really dead, what's happened to Kian and the Duchess and the rest of the Company. I need to speak to the ArchDruid." He hesitated, as if considering what to say next. "I want you to come with me. You're the only one who saw Cadwyr with the sidhe, you're the witness to at least part of the bargain. I don't know what Cadwyr's planning, or how things stand, but I don't want to wait for the upland chiefs to decide who should go and who should come. This is what he's counting on. There're more arriving every hour now, and that's only going to create more confusion. So I'm planning to slip away before first light tomorrow, lass, and I'd like you to come with me. Which is another reason we'll have to slip away. You're the last person the Sheriff will want to let leave. He may be as soft in the head as he is in the belly, but he knows enough to know he needs a smith." He paused once more, then said, "I'm sorry that I caused trouble between you and the sidhe lord."

"You weren't to know," she replied with a shrug. She had for the most part successfully avoided thinking about Artimour for most of the day, but Uwen's apology brought it all back. "I *did* make the dagger."

"You did, but you had no choice. I spent all day with him—he's not an unreasonable sort. Decent, really, for a sidhe. Or a half-sidhe, which is what Molly says he is. Go talk to him. But go soon—he says he's leaving tomorrow."

"So soon?" Her head snapped up. She wanted to talk to Artimour, to make sure that all was right between them before she mentioned her mother. She'd dared to hope that perhaps he'd take her with him. But she knew what her father would expect her to do and she knew he'd be angry if he thought she was moping after a sidhe. The more she thought about it, the more it seemed like the one thing guaranteed to make him the angriest. But she *had* made the dagger. Dismayed, she stared at Uwen as she automatically bent to retrieve a hammer bumped off the wall, set upright an overturned basket of nails.

"There's been talk, mutters, rumors. The sidhe are being blamed for the goblins' attack—"

"But that's not fair," she cried. "Artimour had nothing to do with it—"

"Of course you and I know that. But not all these dunderheads do. And he has questions, too, the answers for which are only in the OtherWorld, not here. Nessa, will you come? The longer we wait, the more who will insist on riding with us, and we can only go as fast as the slowest horse. By the time a whole troop gets there, who knows what Cadwyr will have done next? I can carry you on Buttercup if need be. We can be there by noon of the day after tomorrow."

His voice had a flat desperate edge that she'd never heard before, even on Samhain when he faced the goblin horde. *What's changed?* she wanted to ask. But she knew how her father would expect her to answer his question. She glanced around the forge, fingering the amulet. There was plenty of work to be done here. But all she said was, "All right. All right, I'll come. I guess I better go talk to Artimour."

"Molly said to suggest bringing him dinner. You'll find her in the kitchens."

She heard him sigh as he stood aside to let her pass and she was tempted once more to turn and ask him what was wrong, even as she wondered exactly how much about her Molly had discussed with him. In the doorway she remembered something, and turned to see him looking at something that appeared to be a flat disk that hung around his neck on a metal chain that glinted gold. She was about to ask him what it was, when he thrust it into his shirt, out of sight. "Your sword's over there—I banged out the rust that had started to eat the blade, and sharpened up the edge."

She heard him call a startled thanks but did not pause as she trudged on. She had faced the goblins. She had faced Great Herne. Surely she could face Artimour. In the kitchens, she found Molly, looking distracted, but sharp-eyed as ever. She beckoned Nessa and thrust a tray of food into her hands, then pointed upward. She leaned over and spoke directly into Nessa's ear. "I've borrowed your birch staff, lass, but don't you worry—I'll see that Uwen has it for you on the 'morrow."

Surprised, Nessa drew back and opened her mouth to ask why Molly needed the staff, and how would it be that Uwen of all people might have occasion to return it to her. But Molly forestalled her questions with a smile and a firm turn of her shoulders in the direction of the narrow staircase that led to the cramped chambers that normally served as the Sheriff of Killcarrick's private quarters. "There'll be time for explanations later, child."

Nessa glanced down at Molly as she trudged up the stone steps crowded with children and dogs. She was carrying a basketful of bright red cord, cord similar to that which Nessa had been unable to pry out of Granny Wren's rigid hands back in Killcairn. Whatever magic the granny had worked had held, as she'd said, til Samhain. Were the grannies here about to attempt another such ritual tonight? Was that why Molly wanted the staff? A burning wish to know stabbed briefly through Nessa, then disappeared in a flood of panic as she reached the top of the steps. Suddenly she wished she'd done more than taken the time to wash her hands and rake back her hair. Her shoulders ached, her legs felt like lumps, and she almost stumbled more than once over hounds or children.

The tray of food Molly had given her to carry up felt like lead in her arms, but at least it gave her an excuse to knock on Artimour's door. From the other side of the door, she heard him call, "Enter."

She pushed it open, and stepped into what felt like a cool bath of still water, after the heat of the forge and the chaos of the kitchen and the keep. He looked tired. She stepped over the threshold, and saw that his eyes were like smudges of ash in a face as gray and drawn as her father's after a long day or sleepless night. Only the luster of his hair and the slightly pointed tips of his ears betrayed his mixed blood. In the dull light filtering through the horn pane, even his skin had lost that velvety sheen. It was difficult to restrain her apology. "I brought your dinner."

He was standing by the open casement, one foot on the window seat, watching the activity below. He glanced over his shoulder, then straightened, obviously surprised to see her. "Put it there." He shifted from foot to foot. "You don't have to wait on me—I told Granny Molly that I was well enough to come down."

"They think it's better you stay out of sight. They say there's talk against the sidhe." She'd seen for herself that grief and shock were giving way to rage. She'd seen two brothers come to blows today over who had retrieved a third brother's sword, but rumors she'd overheard were so ridiculous she'd dismissed them out of hand until Uwen had mentioned them: the sidhe were coming to save them; the sidhe themselves had been overrun by the goblins at last. The Duke of Gar was at fault for rebelling against the King; the King's madness was to blame. The Duke of Gar had struck a secret alliance with the sidhe, the Humbrians had struck an alliance with the goblins. The Duke of Gar was dead. The Mad King Hoell was dead. But it was the muttered curses, the furtive looks cast upward as she carried the tray up the stairs that convinced Nessa that Uwen was right. "The people are looking for someone to blame."

She placed the tray on the low table beside the hearth, then turned, her hands clasped before her, eyes fastened fixedly on the leaping flames. The aroma of toasted bread and warm cheese tickled her nostrils, and she wondered what the food smelled like to him. She flipped aside the napkin to reveal crusty brown bread with a light smear of pale cheese on top, then took a deep breath. The words burst out of her like tumbling stones plunging pell-mell down a hill. "I'm so sorry. I didn't mean to hurt you, truly I didn't. I'm sorry—I just never thought—there was nothing that made me think—and Uwen says we're to leave tomorrow—and that you're going back to Faerie—" Her eyes filled with tears and she blinked them back.

He cut her off with a wave of his hand. "Nessa, it's all right. I understand. I understand you had no choice." He ran a hand through his hair and sighed. "I was wrong to speak to you so. If you'll accept my apology, we need speak of it no more."

Surprised, she stared at him, and then realized that whatever troubled him was so much greater that any wrong she'd done him was insignificant in comparison. What would happen to him if the world to which he intended to return did not expect to welcome him back? What was he walking into? She eyed his straight back, his broad shoulders that looked broader than she'd expected beneath his borrowed clothes. The skin on his hands was paler and finer than most men's, without any of the coarse curling hair that covered the backs of Dougal's. But they were large, the palms broad, the fingers square.

Blacksmith's hands. She shoved the absurdity of that thought away. Artimour was a prince of the sidhe, not a simple mortal smith. But she couldn't help wondering what he'd look like, stripped to the waist like her father, only a leather apron and vambraces to protect his chest and forearms, and a sudden flush suffused her whole body that had nothing to do with the warmth of the flames. "Can you tell me where you found this?" She fumbled at her neck and pulled out Dougal's amulet.

"Ah, there it is. I thought it'd been lost in the water. Do you recognize it?"

"I made it for my father when I was thirteen. I'd know it anywhere. Where'd you find it?"

"In the river, on a rock. It looked as if someone had tossed it into the water to try to negate its poison. Running water does, to some extent."

"But you saw no one about?"

Artimour shook his head. "No one until I met Finuviel. And he was alone, as he should not have been." He drew a deep breath. "There are many great houses along the river. Your father may have found his way to one, but any sidhe would've expected him to remove the amulet before they took him in. I found the amulet a league or two from where you and I parted company, but it may have drifted downriver somewhat." He hesitated. "I don't think there's any way to be sure of anything—"

"But that he's there," finished Nessa. She took a single step forward with a raised chin. "Don't you see? Everyone said

I was wrong to be so sure he'd fallen into the OtherWorld. But now you found his amulet. Surely that shows he's there." She took another step, her heart beginning to pound. "And last night—last night I realized my mother must be in Faerie, too."

A shadow crossed his face, and he indicated one of the wooden chairs in front of the fire. "Please sit. I must talk to you."

He still moved like a sidhe, she thought as she perched on the chair's hard edge, but she noticed that a furrow had appeared between his brows.

"Nessa," he said gently. "I'm not sure what's happening right now in Faerie, but nothing I can imagine is good. Finuviel—the one who stabbed me, who came to your forge with Cadwyr—Finuviel is Vinaver's son, my own sister's son. It wouldn't surprise me if the two of them have been planning this for a very long time, and saw Alemandine's pregnancy as an opportunity to strike while the Queen was at her weakest. I don't think he only intended the dagger for me. I think it's clear he made a bargain with this Cadwyr that Sir Uwen speaks of with such dislike—the dagger, in exchange for the host that Finuviel was supposed to lead to the border. After I found that amulet, before I met Finuviel, I came to a place beside the river where it appeared a great army had ridden across. It didn't occur to me then they might have ridden into the water and come out in the same way you did, here in Shadow. So the questions have become, where's Finuviel, where's the host, and where's the Caul, for Finuviel must've taken it in order to bring the silver dagger into Faerie. For all I know, Alemandine may be dead, and Finuviel already King. And as you say, it's better that I leave.

I'll go at dawn. It's at dusk the goblins hunt." For a split second, he smiled, but then his face darkened, and he looked old, careworn and tired. He paused, drew a deep breath, then continued. "I'll do what I can to find your parents, Nessa, but you must understand that I don't know what's waiting for me. Those goblins that came last night, Nessa, I've never seen anything like them. Oh yes, I saw them. I went to the top of the tower. There were so many. I'm not sure there's magic enough in Faerie to stand against them."

But silver still works, she thought, fingering Dougal's amulet as an idea occurred to her. There wasn't much time, and she was tired, but if she used a sword that only needed repair—she'd have to see what she could find. She leaped to her feet and headed for the door. "Do you know where to find the forge?" She'd have to satisfy her curiosity about the corn grannies and their rituals another night.

He looked startled. "The forge? Where the blacksmiths work?"

"Stop there before you leave? Please?" She only waited long enough to ensure that he nodded, and then she skipped down the steps, curiously more lighthearted than she had felt in days.

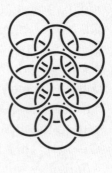

3

The afternoon was fading into twilight, when Merle paused on the threshold of the tower room overlooking the western sea. A storm was brewing, and the sound of the surf as it pounded against the rocks that formed the foundation of the house her father had so graciously provided was louder up here for some reason than in her own solar on the floor below. Then a wet breeze licked her cheek and she turned to see her husband's outline, black against the garish lines of red and violet light flooding through the gray-streaked clouds. "Hoell? My love?" She spoke tentatively, for ever since their perilous escape from the horrible things that had driven them from Brynhyvar, she could not quite believe that not only had they both escaped the fiends, but that Hoell, her one true love and anointed King of Brynhyvar, had come back to himself. He was no longer the meek and gentle creature he'd become as a result of their child's death.

Their *first* child's death, she thought, placing her hand on her swelling abdomen. *It could happen to anyone,* she thought. *Lots of people lost children.* She felt a feeble flutter against the thick silk of her new *chemista* and she smiled. *Swim, little fish, swim.*

But it worried her more than she wanted to admit to find him sitting alone in the dark, leaning so far out the open casement that his hair was damp with spray. But his expression reassured her, as did his words of sweetly accented Humbrian, "Ah, here you are, Merle. Come sit a moment. The sunset's splendid, don't you think?"

"My love, aren't you cold?" But she edged closer, curling her cold fingers around his surprisingly hot hand.

"Come, I'll warm you." He folded her against his chest, snuggling her against him so that she felt the beating of his heart against her shoulder. The sea looked angry as it lashed against the rocks and the sky was streaked with red. It reminded her of the blood dripping down the gray stone walls of Ardagh. She still heard the screaming of the dying and the screeching of the sidhe in her dreams. It was one of the reasons her father had given them this house. Only the insistent rhythm of the waves washing over the rocks soothed her. She closed her eyes and turned her face away, willing herself to relax into the circle of his embrace.

"I don't know what you like to look at up here," she said. "There's nothing to see but the water and the sky."

"Maybe you're right." She could feel his breath through the linen of her veil, hot against her scalp. It reminded her of all the nights they'd lain in her bed during his madness, when he'd clutched her to his chest like a little boy. "But when I sit here, and the light is right, I think I see Brynhyvar, sitting out there like a purple jewel, right across—" he extended their arms, folding his hand over hers, pointing with his index finger "—there."

He sounded sane. Too sane to spend all his time up here staring out across the ocean at a land she knew perfectly well he could not see, no matter how strong the light. It was too far. "You *are* happy here, aren't you?" Brynhyvar was so filthy and foul, full of savages whose language was as coarse as the barking of a dog, and who lived like dogs, too, in straw-strewn hovels they considered castles, their sad-eyed droop-eared hounds haunting every filthy corner. It had begun to occur to her that perhaps poor lost Renvahr— her younger brother who'd given his life for theirs—was right, when he'd argued, just before the disastrous hostage exchange, that they should leave Brynhyvar to the Brynnish.

How easy it would be to stay here, at the Chadurie d'Amarea. Let the Brynnish squabble it out for themselves, or let her father appoint someone else to go conquer the country. She and Hoell could stay here and raise their babies in peace. What need to ever return to the dirt and the dung and the straw?

He sighed against her hair, rocking her gently, but when he spoke, his choice of words alarmed every instinct she possessed. "I'm happy to be with you. I'm happy to have escaped the wrath of the sidhe—"

"I thought those creatures weren't real."

Again he drew a deep measuring breath and let it out in a long sigh before he answered. "I don't think you're the first to think so. But despite that attack, or maybe because of it, I'm unhappy because I'm not *there*."

Matra mea, what does *that* mean? It vexed her that she'd

understood him so much better when he was mad. He was gazing out over the water again, and the gulls were shrieking as they wheeled so dangerously close beneath the eaves, she was sure one might fly in. "Can't we close that window?"

At that, he turned her to face him, smiling down at her with gentle good humor. "What's wrong, Merle? You sound crankish tonight as my last milk-nurse used to say."

You had a milk-nurse long enough to remember her? Proper Humbrian children were weaned long before their first birthdays. She pulled herself out of the warm circle of his arms as the disgusting idea ran unbidden through her mind, and stalked away to the cold hearth, where a discarded shawl lay over a chair. She snatched it up and wrapped it around herself. "I thought you were happy here."

He shrugged. "I'm happy to *be* here. I'm happy for this asylum, for this chance to recoup and recover over the winter, and of course, I'm happy for such a faithful ally as your father. But, my darling, you must see that Brynhyvar is my home. I am its King. To be away from it, to be exiled from it, feels unnatural—as unnatural as the attack of the sidhe. I don't understand why they did that, and now I must wait until the winter passes, to see what's become of my country."

The words sounded like madness but he spoke them in such a calm and measured way, his look so steady, she knew he was not mad. "So you intend to return?"

"I thought we both did. It is, after all, what your father wants." He turned to close the casement, and stopped, cocked his head and frowned, holding up his hand to his ear, indicating that he wanted her to listen. He pressed one finger against his lips when he saw her open her mouth.

But hard as Merle strained, she heard nothing, and at last she stamped her foot in frustration. "Please close that. I'm cold."

He did as she asked with a question that surprised her. "Did you hear that?"

"Hear what?" She looked at him warily. Was this a sign that a fit was coming on him, brought on by a reaction to the very stress that had snapped him out of the last bout?

"Those voices—that singing."

A chill went down her spine. It was said that those with the blood of the Old Ones could hear the songs of the mermaids who sang off the coasts of Humbria, singing the songs of a lost land called Lyonesse in some ancient language no one understood anymore. But Hoell had no blood of Humbrian Old Ones. How could he have heard the songs of the Old Ones, assuming, of course, there was anything to hear. Her overwrought imagination was getting the better of her. "Perhaps the unholy noise of those monsters awakened more than your wits, my lord. They do say that mermaids sing off these shores. There're lots of old stories—I can arrange a *recitareo* for this evening, if you like. Rowend will be more than happy to stand and recite as long as you can bear to listen."

"So you don't—" He broke off, looking embarrassed. "So you don't think I'm mad?"

Only for wanting to go back to that pigsty of a country. But she only shrugged and said, "I don't doubt you heard something. I heard the awful sounds those monstrous sidhe creatures made. I can believe anything now."

"But you can't believe I want to go home?" He sat down on the window seat and beckoned her. "I understand if you don't. This is a pleasant place—although why I always seem to live in houses perched out over water, I don't quite understand." He gave a sad little chuckle. "But Brynhyvar— the land itself—" He broke off, as if searching for words. "You did not go through the King-making with me, for I was already King when we were married." His eyes found hers. She loved his eyes. Even in his madness, they were soft and dark and kind. But now he was making her uncomfortable, for there was something wild and strange in their depths, something she had only glimpsed by candlelight in bed. "It is a great ritual." He gave a rueful smile. "I have no doubt you would find it quite upsetting and barbarian."

"Why?" she blurted, wondering what on earth this had to do with why he wanted to return.

"It's made up of several parts—most of which are similar enough to yours—the bathing and the anointing and the crowning. But at the end of the ritual, you see, the King goes up to the top of the tor, and, well, he mounts what we call the LandStone and he joins with the land, in the way of a man with a wo—"

To her utter dismay, she understood at once what he was talking about and she interrupted, for she did not want to hear him speak the words that would conjure an image already too real. "You actually—" She broke off, horrified, at the image of a naked, painted Hoell bucking against a rock in some unnatural congress. Perhaps all the Humbrians who regarded the Brynnish as animals weren't wrong. Her stomach heaved and she looked at him with new eyes.

"It isn't foul or profane or any of the things you're thinking, Merle. It's a powerful, amazing thing—you feel connected and a part of everything on and under and of that land. It is a profound experience that changed me. And so now, much as part of me would like to stay here with you, in this beautiful house beside this beautiful sea, I feel as if a part of my very flesh has been torn away, and I am broken and bleeding until I return."

She actually thought she might faint. It was all more than she had ever anticipated. Maybe an evening of oration would distract him. If she could convince him to stay, together they could convince her father that Hoell was the wrong one to lead an invasion of Brynhyvar. He wasn't really one of those savages. She thought of his tender lovemaking and she knew he wasn't like that. There were no plans of an invasion until the spring, anyway. There was more than enough time to change his mind. As if in agreement, the child within somersaulted like a mermaid, reminding her that by that time her belly would be hugely swollen. She was certain she could parley the imminent birth into another delay. If she delayed long enough, maybe Hoell would forget. She would consult her scrying cards, or maybe even send to Court for one of her father's oracles. "I'll go see if Rowend would be prepared to recite the First and Second cantos of the Lyonessian Cycle at dinner this evening. You'll like that. Please don't be late." She shut the door with a firm click, leaving him standing in a halo of reddish light, staring out the closed window, listening to the muted screech of the gulls.

"Here you go, lad. Have a bowl of this—it'll put some meat on those big long bones of yourn." A friendly voice and a pair of rough hands thrust a wooden bowl full of mutton stew beneath Griffin's nose and he was forced to accept it, or drop it down his chest. The smell disgusted him for some reason, and he'd hoped to avoid taking any. But the smile on the cook's face precluded any refusal. And he was right, Griffin supposed. His clothes were hanging off his shoulders suddenly. He hadn't joined the dinner line for food, however. He'd been hoping to get a glimpse of where the barrels full of the strange brew he and the rest of the blacksmiths had been fed in the smithy camp might have disappeared to. The stuff had enabled them to work day and night, with no more than an hour or two's rest, burning through their veins with tangible force, endowing them with superhuman endurance. It also ignited a fire that had to be fed, or the lack of it, as he'd discovered, made one feel as if the weight of the world itself would feel like less of a burden than the sheer effort of holding up one's head.

Poor Gareth's flask hung on his hip, snug in his belt, too light for his liking. Poor dead Gareth, barely old enough to be apprenticed, had saved Griffin's life by sharing the contents of the flask he'd stolen from only Great Herne himself knew where. That was the only reason Griffin had been alert enough to drive the lance into the goblin's chest. It had died immediately, collapsing on him in such a way that he alone, of all the nearly two hundred blacksmiths and soldiers in the wagon train, survived.

But there wasn't much more than a slug or two left in the flask, and that was hardly enough to get him through the day tomorrow. The soldiers had carried off everything that could be salvaged from the ill-fated camp, and he was sure that had to include the barrels of brew. As Gareth had said, you felt like day-old scat when the effect wore off, so the key was to keep it from ever wearing off. And that required a sip from the flask now and again. But where could the barrels have gone?

He tried to scrutinize the supply wagons as he stumbled down the line, trying not to trip over the men clustered around their campfires. The wagons were arranged in tight circles, the perimeters protected by some kind of thinly beaten silver netting strung between high poles. Maybe in one of the other circles? He scanned the wagons heaped with soft bundles and copper-bound barrels, leather-strapped chests and wooden crates of every size, full of weapons and provisions and all the other necessities of war. He'd at first surmised this to be the main body of Cadwyr's army, but then he'd learned that this was but a core force. Another five hundred had joined them that day, and supposedly an even larger contingent, marching from somewhere unspecified, was expected to meet them near Castle Gar. But he paid the soldiers clustered around the fires scarcely any heed, for he was too busy trying to understand how the wagons were grouped.

The torches were arranged so that the supply wagons were mostly in the shadows. He edged down the narrow path between the campfires, trying to get as close as possible without attracting too much attention.

"Hey, be careful there!" A gruff voice snarled a warning as Griffin tripped and nearly sprawled flat over a bent knee.

He muttered an automatic apology, as another, kinder voice addressed him on his immediate left. "Come, boy, sit here."

More by reflex than any real wish to take a seat, Griffin squatted down, recognizing one of the men who'd found him beneath the goblin yesterday. He dipped his spoon into his stew and shoveled some of it into his mouth, nodding at Griffin, indicating he should do the same. "How you holding up, lad?"

It took Griffin a few moments to realize that the man was expecting an answer. "Oh," he said, taking a bite of stew. He regretted it the moment the stringy, salty meat touched his tongue. "I'm all right."

"Good lad." He turned back to his companions, indicating Griffin with a wave of his hand. "This one'll make a fine soldier if he decides to give up smithing. You should've seen the size of the thing we pulled off him. Killed it with one blow, didn't you, lad?"

Griffin acknowledged the polite acclaim with a modest shrug and a wave of his fork. "'Twas luck, just luck." He was glad when they turned back to each other, leaving him to realize that the drumming he heard at the back of his head was coming from inside his skull. He shut his eyes and pressed his thumb and forefinger tightly against his closed lids, trying to banish the pounding. He was conscious of the flask at his hip, imagined the last few drops rolling down the smooth sides. He wondered if it would be all right to dilute it with a bit of ale. That might give him more time to find out what had happened to the barrels. He knew intuitively that the barrels would only have been left behind if they'd been smashed. He was sure they were here, somewhere. It was just a question of finding where. His hands trembled and his mouth filled with saliva. The stringy lump he'd managed to swallow wasn't sitting too well. The smell of the stew curdled beneath his nose and his gut contracted. He wished he could pull the flask out, let the sweet soothing brew, whatever it was, roll down his throat. A drop of it would relieve the pain in his stomach, would make palatable the coarse slop. He had to find where the rest of it had gone tonight, he knew, even if it required a few extra of the precious drops.

"Ever been to Gar, lad?" His rescuer was back, leaning in with friendly interest.

Griffin met the man's weathered pug face with a short nod and what he hoped was a smile. He wanted to make friends with this man, wanted to ask him where they were bound, and what the new Duke's plans were. For Duke Cadwyr was Gar's heir, all knew that. He wanted to ask if they had any ideas about what use all the silvered weapons and silver chains and silver armor he and all the other smiths had made in Ardagh Vale might have been put. But right now, all he wanted to do was get rid of the pounding in his head, the queasiness in his stomach, the shaking in his hands. And then learn as quickly as possible where those barrels went.

"And that's not all I heard them say. The orders were to kill every one of them. Did you know that? Every last shrieking one of them." The man on the other side of Griffin leaned into the circle and spoke in a conspiratorial whisper. "I overheard him to say they hissed when they stuck the silver in them. And that's all I have to say about that." He shoveled a huge spoonful of stew into his mouth and sat back with a satisfied slurp.

Griffin saw the other men exchange dark looks before he was forced to squeeze his eyes shut tight. He pressed the heels of his palms into his eyes as tight as he could, trying to force the pain from his head. He was shaking in his bones, deep sinews trembling. Sweat was oozing from his pores and seeping into the crevices of his tunic and trews. He could feel the coarse linen of his shirt sticking to his back. He cared nothing for whatever secrets they thought to guard. "I'm sorry," he mumbled, staggering to his feet, his bowl spilling out unheeded into the firepit, where the fatty meat hissed and sizzled and spat great burning gobs in all directions.

In a daze he lurched away from the sudden angry chorus, nausea clouding his vision, bile burning his throat. He staggered generally in the direction of the latrines, hoping that once he was safely out of view he could uncork the flask and let just one drop of the stuff roll down the back of his throat like a balm. But he collapsed just outside the perimeter of the wagons, dragged to his knees by violent heaves and a hot spurt of vomit as his body rejected the stew.

"Ah, by the Mother, what have we here? Drunk already, are we? I didn't even think the ration had been put out yet."

It was one of the guards, come to find the latrine, the tramp of his heavy boots echoing through Griffin's skull like sledgehammers. Torchlight fell across his closed eyelids, and he felt a heavy hand gather up the fabric at the back of his neck and literally lift him off the ground, away from the smell of the vomit and the dirt. He tried to open his eyes and wondered if by any possible chance at all the ration the man referred to meant that drink. But somehow, he didn't think so. Light stung the back of his eyelids like a whip.

"Sweet Mother, what ails ye, lad?"

He was shaken, slapped, the torch thrust into his face so that he smelled his eyebrows singe. He turned his face away, wishing he could scuttle back into the dark just long enough to get one small drop of the brew into his mouth, but knowing it was futile. So all he could do was shake his head and mutter, "Not drunk."

"Lad!" The voice was harsher this time, like Dougal's when he was concerned.

He heard a muffled curse. The footsteps disappeared into the latrines. As if from very far away, he heard the gush of water as the man relieved himself. The footsteps resumed, louder this time, and the sledgehammers inside his head pounded on the top of his spine. He felt himself lifted again, then slung over a strong back with a muttered curse. The world twisted, dipped and spun.

"Hang on, laddie, I'll get you to old Janet in a trice. You look like you've had a touch of that tainted bacon that downland blackguard sold us."

He was dumped unceremoniously beside another fire. The heat of the flames licked the outside of his head, in excruciating counterpoint to the sledgehammers inside. A rough hand grabbed his chin, felt underneath his neck. He heard a few muttered words he did not understand. He felt a cold cloth on his forehead and a sharp smell jabbed like a needle up his nostril. He jerked away, and opened his eyes to the wrinkled, nut-brown face of an old woman in a red shawl and white kerchief.

"Whud'ya et, lad?"

He blinked, scarcely understanding the thick Ardagh accent. She sounded as if her mouth were full of marbles.

The old woman slapped his cheek gently with a rough hand. "Stay with me, lad, I got to know if I need to give ya the purge. Did ya et yesterday's bacon?"

He knew enough to shake his head. "No," he managed. His mouth was like cotton, his tongue soft and sticky. If they'd just leave him alone long enough to get his hands around the flask he'd be fine. "No, I wasn't here for breakfast yesterday."

"Ah." She sank back on her haunches with a little exhale. "You're the one they found."

He nodded, turned his face away from the fire, into the soft fur that he realized he was lying on, but she rolled it back with a firm hand under his chin.

She seemed to be studying him. Abruptly she leaned forward, touched his forehead and his cheeks with the back of her hand. She stretched both his eyes wide open and pulled his lips apart. She smelled his breath, looked at his tongue. She picked up a thick clay goblet. "Water?"

He turned his face away from the grainy, metallic odor. If she'd just let him have a taste of the brew, he knew he'd be fine.

"Don't even like that, do we?" The water sloshed unbearably loudly as she set the cup down beside his ear. The greater the need for the drink burned in his veins, the less he wanted anything else. He could practically smell it in the flask, where it nestled now against his flank like a whore's hand. At last he heard her get heavily to her feet. "All right, laddie. You just rest there. Here's a basin in case there's more that wants to come up. I'll be right back. Sleep, if you can."

He heard the rustle of her skirts, then the slap of a leather flap. He realized he was inside a small, snug tent. Corn granny, he thought. She must travel with the army, tending to the wounded and the sick. Like Molly, like Wren. He waited a few moments then rolled onto his side, loosening the flask with frantic fingers. He wondered briefly what had happened to Granny Wren, so old, so frail, so naked. He had left her squatting at the water's edge, her belly bulging, her legs wide and splayed, as if she would birth some enormous magic right into the water. He wondered what had happened to the rest of the villagers who'd fled with him from Killcairn through Killcrag, all the way to Killcarrick Keep. Had they survived Samhain? Had Killcarrick stood against the goblin onslaught? He remembered the size and the ferocity of the goblins that came roaring out of the trees on Samhain night, and hoped that it had.

With trembling fingers he uncorked the flask. The scent that bloomed beneath his nose was surely sweeter than any flower that ever blossomed in Brynhyvar. He hesitated a moment, then lifted the flask in a solitary salute, thinking of Gareth, and Engus, the master smith of Killcarrick, and all the others who'd lost their lives to the goblins. "May we all meet again in the Summerlands." He took a quick swig, not daring to take too much.

The taste sang on his tongue, seeped as slowly and deliberately as every kiss he'd ever imagined giving Nessa, down the back of his throat, soothing and sustaining as liquid light.

He felt it flood through his veins, a glow that spread outward from his center, infusing him with that marvelous energy. He threw back the worn woolen cloak and leaped to his feet, tugging his doublet into place. He dumped the contents of the goblet over his head, rinsing the stink of the vomit and the stew out of his hair, off his skin. He carefully eased back the entrance flap and peered outside.

He had survived two goblin attacks, by the luck of the goddess and maybe Nessa's amulet. He fingered her round silver disk on its skinny leather cord, and remembered the determination in Nessa's eyes when she'd handed it to him, just before she'd gone marching into the OtherWorld. Nessa never failed when she set out to do something. Nessa, he thought with a sudden pang. Nessa, his secret love. Well, maybe not so secret now, since he'd kissed her goodbye before she'd disappeared into the woods. He was glad he'd done that now. He'd taken her amulet and left her his to wear. Surely she would see the message in that? If she'd ever come back to find it, that is.

The camp was quiet, wagons gathered in close circles, the orange flicker of campfires glowing low. It was getting late, the first watch already standing. He wondered where the old woman had gone.

He took a deep breath. The night air was clear and crisp, all traces of the previously unseasonable humidity gone. The sip of the drink had done more than calm his stomach and revive his spirits. It had enhanced his senses, too, it seemed, for faint on the river of air flowing gently past his cheek, he was sure he smelled the barrels filled with brew. They had a distinctive aroma, a combination of oak and copper soaked in the honey-sweet liquid.

He drew another deep breath, closing his eyes, drawing the air up his nostrils, deep into his lungs, into his head, so that the cool moisture soothed his feverish brain. Yes, he was sure he could smell it now, beckoning across the silent night. The corn granny's tent was set a little apart and away from the others. He heard distant coughs, the smack of spit, the scrape of leather soles over gravel. A stronger puff of breeze brought another blast of scent. *That way,* he thought, turning his head.

"Ya looking fur the granny?" The voice startled him. Griffin looked around. A grizzled face peered at him from beside a fire, two eyes burning with fever beneath a blood-stained bandage. "She went that way, to the Duke's tent. Said she had to speak to him if it's the last thing she did."

The Duke's tent. Of course. Suddenly Griffin had a very good idea where the barrels might be found. "Which way's the pit?" Griffin used the term of Cadwyr's men for the latrine.

"Just over yonder."

"Thanks." He took off in the direction the man indicated. He certainly didn't seem likely to follow, but one could never be sure. He took another deep breath, veering away from the latrines as soon as he was certain he was out of the wounded man's eyeshot, following the thread of scent that twined like a fine line of molten metal through the air. It led him around and under and through the largest of the enclosures. He snuck up as close as he could to the largest tent he'd seen in the camp. Smoke billowed from a central vent, and light glowed in thin lines beneath the bottom edges. He crept up behind a wagon loaded with chests, and recognized them at once as the silver-filled coffers his ill-fated troop had been carrying. The barrels were somewhere nearby, he was sure of it. He closed his eyes and took a deep breath, concentrating on the cool rush of air, and in that moment, heard Granny Janet's voice rise clearly in the night.

"Huh'll no live without the brew. Ya mun gie m'some for'm, or huh'll no live."

Immediately, Griffin froze. He knew intuitively, beyond any shadow of doubt, that the granny referred to him. He licked his lips. Surely she was mistaken. Griffin flattened his ear to the canvas. The night was not completely quiet, but he could hear old Janet's voice clearly now, through the hide. "Ya feed that stuff t'anyone, including yourself, and they'll turn out just like him."

Griffin glanced quickly over his shoulder. Wagons were positioned along two sides of the tent. He could hear the measured paces of the guards around the perimeter. Keeping his ear as close to the tent as possible, he crawled beneath the wagons, scuttling on all fours, weaving through the round forest of spoked wheels, following the voices.

"I appreciate your concern for my men, Granny Janet, but whether or not—"

"Ya canna use the brew on any more of our lads. It's poison, can ya no see that?"

There was a rustle of fabric and Griffin wondered if Janet had dared to grab the Duke's arm. He sniffed and looked up and his knees went weak when he not so much saw as smelled a spreading stain above his head. *It's the brew,* he thought. *The brew.* He took another, deeper breath and tried to control the sudden urge to press his tongue flat against the splintered wood. He should listen to what they were saying. For Janet refused to give up.

"Ya'll no win this war if ya poison our own lads. The blacksmith boy is sick to death, I see it in his eyes, if not his face. He needs the brew but it's the brew that's killing him. Now let him have it, for I'll no take his blood onto my hands." There was a long pause and then a woman's muffled squeal. "Don't ya dare to lay a finger on me."

Griffin heard a sound like a snarl. "You hush your mouth, old woman, or I hush it forever for you."

"Ya're drinking it yourself, aren't ya? By all that's good, I see ya're. Don't ya threaten me, my lord Cadwyr Who-Would-Be-King. Ya won't live to be King long if ya drink too much of that brew." She was brave, he thought, brave or foolish, he wasn't sure which. Then her voice ended abruptly in a loud smack, and Griffin froze, but he could not stifle his own gasp.

There was a long silence during which Griffin did not dare to breathe. He began to wonder if, in fact, the old woman was still alive. He crouched beneath the wagon, the brew filling his nostrils. It was making him lightheaded, he realized, and he bit down on his lip, but even the taste of his own blood didn't steady him. He eased his hand down, and his fingers moved with lightning speed as he retrieved the flask. He touched the cork, hesitated. How loud would it pop when he pulled it? he wondered. But the aroma was driving him mad, making him faint with need, with desire so real it was beginning to pound in the back of his head. He pulled the cork, and with one swift motion, touched it to his mouth and took one slow sweet drop, just as the hide beside him split open with a savage rip. He turned, to see what looked like an angry giant looming out of the bright light of the lanterns hanging from the interior supports. Before he could react, he was hauled up and into the center of the tent, where Granny Janet stood, eyes narrowed, dagger drawn.

"I knew I heard something. You're the one she's talking about, aren't you?"

Terrified beyond all reason, sure that he lived only because of the shot of brew now boiling in his veins, Griffin could only nod. At that, Cadwyr sank into the fur-draped chair pulled up beside the brazier that served as his hearth. He extended his long legs to the warmth. "All right, Granny. Your job is done. I'll not let the boy die. Stand up, and try not to piss yourself. He did good work for me, him and his fellows—won me a great victory and will win me an even greater victory soon. So let's drink to him, shall we?" Cadwyr raised his goblet and nodded to more clustered on a tray beside the brazier. "Help yourself, Granny."

"My work's done." She sheathed the dagger and stalked out of the tent, mouth grim, and Griffin wondered why the granny obviously disliked Cadwyr so. For Cadwyr was smiling at him, nodding at the goblets. "She said you needed the brew. She said without it you would die. Please, take as much as you wish. The Marrihugh knows you deserve it."

Dazed, Griffin stared at Cadwyr, thinking surely he'd misheard. Rationed in the camp, guarded by the soldiers, held back from them on Samhain until he himself had demanded it be shared, he'd imagined the brew to be the most precious drink in the world And now he was told he could have as much as he wanted? His senses felt inflamed, overloaded. He took a deep breath and knew at once that was a mistake, for his mind was assaulted with a monstrous blend of brew and blood, tallow and sweat, and the rank raw stench of urine and feces. *The brew,* he thought, his mind latching onto the only pleasurable thing in the whole wretched mix. *The brew.*

He looked over his shoulder. A large square wooden crate stood next to a hidebound trunk, and on it stood a large flagon that looked as if it might really be gold. It shone with an unearthly gleam, a soft glow in the lantern light that had a quality to it Griffin could not define. He knew his nostrils flared. Griffin could feel Cadwyr's eyes fastened on him, as if Cadwyr fed somehow on his palpable need.

"Drink," said Cadwyr again.

Griffin looked back at Cadwyr, sprawled across his chair,

his hair shining gold in the reddish brazier light, and a single silent word sounded in his head. *Don't.*

No, he thought. Surely a little more wouldn't hurt him. It was when you stopped you felt awful. But as long as he could have what he needed... Griffin squared his shoulders. He might not be a knight or a duke or even a petty chieftain squatting in some miserable hollow, but he was, yet for another year of 'prenticeship, a free man of Brynhyvar. Already he had the skill to earn his living anywhere he went, if not the master's marque to prove it, and he need bow his head to no one.

As if he'd read his mind, Cadwyr chuckled. "Proud boy, aren't you? Your father taught you to stand tall, didn't he?"

"Aye," answered Griffin.

But Cadwyr only smiled into his goblet. "Help yourself, boy. Go on."

The reek in the air was thickening by the moment. Griffin opened the flagon and, unable to control himself, tipped his head back and drank his fill. It swirled down his throat, all the way to his toes, it seemed, in a buttery river of richness that revived him utterly. He downed half the flagon in one hungry gulp, all the while feeling the weight of Cadwyr's stare. He glanced at him, then drank again, helpless as a hungry nursling to resist its mother's teat. Another drink had him feeling as if he could run the distance between here and Gar by morning. He set the flagon down deliberately, and pulled the flask out of his belt, noticing the way Cadwyr's gaze lingered on his thighs. He felt himself harden in unexpected response as a thrill of desire sparked through him, fleeting, but intense. His fingers fumbled as he filled the flask.

"Go back to your billet, boy, and get your things. Stay

here with me. The drink will be there—in that barrel. Take it as often as you need it."

Griffin looked up at Cadwyr. He had not moved a muscle. There was something animal and wild about Cadwyr, but something calculated, too, in his look. Griffin knew what both Dougal and his father would tell him to do. He could practically hear both men saying the same words, in the same tone of voice. *He's already used you enough, don't you think? Stay away from him.* But the full flask settled so snugly into the hollow of his hip. It reassured him and calmed him. "All right," Griffin said.

"Good," said Cadwyr. "I'll alert my guard. Come back whenever you feel the need." And he smiled.

"I say you've made a mistake to trust that thing."

Iruk's voice was like the scrape of metal on bone. It brought Xerruw, the Goblin King, out of the reverie into which he'd slipped, lulled by the moan of the cold wind through the upper reaches of his rock-hewn halls, and the heavy lump of human meat in his overly full belly. The chilly breeze stirred up the straw in the nests of the hags, whined through the new skulls, gleaming in niches, white against the dark gray granite, made the thin human skins curing upon the walls and the bloodstained piles of human clothing flap weakly. It teased the huge fire roaring in the firepit, engulfing the smoking sides of human meat in sheets of blue and orange flame. Xerruw slowly uncoiled his monstrous frame and sat up, gazing down at Iruk from his boulder throne, even as he raised the round half of a human skull to his lips and drank deeply of raw blood-blend, a mixture of semifermented blood and water that had not been brewed in ages beyond remembering.

The creature that called itself Khouri and claimed to be bound into its stunted, vaguely goblin-shaped form by the magic of both mortal and sidhe, roused itself from its own drowse and hissed at Iruk, while Xerruw stared at his lieutenant with unblinking eyes.

Xerruw silenced Khouri with a low growl. Iruk could be trusted to lead the hordes in and out of battle without giving in to any goblin appetite. But he was developing a habit of questioning his king, which was beginning to grate on Xerruw, and he was staring back at Khouri with obvious dislike.

Xerruw took another long slow drink. The hall was unusually silent, even at this hour. This Samhain had seen the greatest hunt in ages, and, satiated at last on human blood and human meat, even the hags slept under the weight of the noon sun now filtering down from the upper reaches of the roof in pale shafts of watery light. His guards snored where they stood. It was a point of pride with him that while all around him slept, he, great Xerruw the Goblin King, would not.

He drank more of the tangy blood, licking the inside of the rough bone with his forked tongue. He could smell the aroma of wet clay and rock emanating off Iruk. He was in charge of the goblins working to widen the narrow tunnel built by Khouri and his fellow slaves. Iruk distrusted him because Khouri came from the palace of the sidhe witch. But Khouri claimed no love for either sidhe or mortal, and all he had asked in exchange for access to the very center of the sidhe witch's palace was the Silver Caul, in order to release themselves from the bondage of the magic of the sidhe. It seemed a small enough price to pay. Xerruw glanced at a shelf near his throne, where a row of tiny human heads gaped blindly. They were the heads of human children—some only infants—with which he would reward his captains in the next victorious battle.

For the next battle would be the last battle—the battle he and his kind would wage against the sidhe Queen. The dying sun gave less and less light every day—the longest night of the year, the Longest Dark, was drawing close. He could sense the collapsing magic, feel the Queen weakening with the light, even as the tunnel beneath his fortress was growing ever wider, ever deeper. Soon all that would separate his minions from the halls of the Queen of the sidhe would be a few yards of dirt and rock. The thought made his maw broaden in what on a mortal face would be a smile, and it occurred to him that there was no reason to wait for the solstice.

It was estimated that in two nights or less, they would reach the very underbelly of the palace itself. Why wait for the solstice? Why not strike? It would catch the sidhe wholly unaware, for Xerruw knew exactly what they expected. And they certainly did not expect the goblins to emerge from the very rocks below the foundations of their palace.

Rock had stood his kind well for centuries. It was an ally the sidhe had overlooked. And that brought his thoughts back to Iruk, and the blank expression his captain wore as he stood before the base of the boulder with clasped hands and coiled tail. It was impossible for Xerruw to read his flat eyes. The Goblin King hauled himself to his full height, which was nearly twice that of a grown mortal male, but before he could speak, the huge doors at the far end of the hall swung open, and the first surge of the changing watch marched into the hall. Wave upon wave, line upon line, tails twitching, maws slavering in anticipation of the feast that awaited them in the kitchens below, they marched, and as they passed the raised dais on which the throne-rock rested, they raised one fist in a salute and beat their chests with the other, while bellowing roars of allegiance. How proud he would be when he could lead them up from the bowels of the palace itself. More and more, he liked the idea of attacking before the solstice.

But the impressive display did not seem to have cowered Iruk. As the thunder of goblin feet died away, Xerruw said, "Why don't you trust this creature?"

"There is no reason to trust it," replied Iruk with a raised chin, not taking his eyes off Khouri, who quivered beside Xerruw. "What do we know of this thing that claims to be from the Shadowlands, and yet has no smell of man on it at all? That's the story *it* tells, but how do we know it speaks the truth?"

With a screech of rage, the gremlin launched itself at Iruk. Xerruw snagged him with a quick snap of his tail, dragging Khouri back. "I have no reason not to believe him." Xerruw sniffed. Khouri smelled not in the least appetizing, and Iruk was right in that it reeked of the sidhe, but yet, there was another odor, persistent and strong, earthy and sour, that told him the thing didn't lie. Xerruw looked down at the creature, then back at Iruk. "If there's something you haven't told me, speak now, before I begin to think that maybe it's you and not this creature I should not trust."

"The goblings are disappearing."

"How many? Why was I not told of this? When did it

start?" Xerruw's tail snapped out reflexively and he coiled it slowly back under his haunches. Khouri only hissed.

Iruk's eyes were fixed on his. They gleamed like the flat eyes of dead humans in the watery light. "Too many to count. For every thirteen that are sent into the tunnels, fewer than half come back."

Xerruw sat down to consider. "So what are you suggesting? That the sidhe are snatching at our goblings? Does not the digging progress?"

"I'm suggesting that it's foolish to risk our own goblings on the word of a thing that reeks of the sidhe. How can you believe that witch would allow one of her minions to escape?"

"Her magic grows weak." Xerruw looked beyond Iruk, as if he could see through the walls of solid rock. The web of magic was winking out, as if, with Samhain's passing, the Queen's strength was dissipating like the light. The more he thought about it, the more he liked the idea of a surprise attack before the solstice, not at it, when the sidhe expected it. They would never expect it to come from within, either. A slow smile spread across his face by degrees as he contemplated the perfection of his new plan. He imagined the walls and floors running slick with pale sidhe blood. The goblins didn't eat the sidhe, not as a rule, but this time they would, he knew. They would gorge themselves on the meat, drink the blood, and decorate themselves with entrails. It would be a glorious sight when he seated himself on the sidhe witch's throne. His tail curled up and down his legs in anticipation. All it required was that the tunnels be made bigger. "Send the nearly grown into the tunnels, with the smaller hatchlings. I want to attack before Mid-Winter, while our power is growing."

Iruk made a noise that might have been a growl. "Think." A swagger raised the thick roll of leathery skin beneath the crest of his skull. "They send to us an emissary, something we've never seen before, and arm it with some outlandish tale. Thus we begin to dig—thinking we dig into their castle, when all the time we make it possible for the sidhe to come straight into the very heart of *our* defenses. Is that not how a sidhe would think? What say you to that, Goblin King? Great Xerruw?"

With a growl, Xerruw lunged at Iruk before he'd finished speaking. As the last few words choked and died on his lips, the astonishment in his eyes gave way to fear. With one arm, Xerruw lifted Iruk straight into the air, muscles turgid, his tail whipping out so fast it whistled. With a single swipe, Xerruw ripped out Iruk's throat. As a trumpeting arc of purple blood painted a broad swath across this throne, Xerruw tossed the body into the firepit, where it landed with a mighty crash and a burst of orange fire. "I say you think too much and dig too slow."

It made Khouri curl into a nearly invisible ball, and roused the hags drowsing in the crevices of his throne, snapping the guards around the perimeter of the Hall to attention. The hags raised their heads experimentally, sniffed the air, and settled down with a few whining snarls when they realized it wasn't human. But the guards exchanged hungry, nervous looks of anticipation mixed with fear. They shook themselves and straightened at their posts.

Even Khouri, who'd up to now exhibited no fear of any of them at all, for he was not in the least appetizing and he seemed to know it, crept back to his nest with only a whispered, "Great Xerruw."

Xerruw flung the flesh away and licked the blood off his hand, settling down once more into the rounded bowl of his seat. A possibility such as Iruk had just outlined had already occurred to him, and tormented him on occasion. But something told Xerruw that the thing which called itself Khouri could be trusted. He could sense the growing instability in the sidhe magic, could feel its coming collapse. The sidhe witch was weakening, he felt it in his bones, in the ground beneath his feet, in the ancient rocks rising all around him. The arrival of Khouri, the thing bound in Faerie, was but the first crack in the heretofore unbreakable magic of the sidhe.

"Great Xerruw!" The pounding of the guards' feet brought him to his feet again. "The magic is broken—the way is clear. The border is open and we can attack any time!"

The two guards stared up at him, eager, hungry. Their expressions pleased him, and so did their news. Below him, a hag erupted in sudden squawks, and he peered down to see one rip another's head off her shoulders. The first hissed up at Xerruw, as if daring him to intervene. With a warning snarl, he retreated to the center of his throne. Nothing was more predatory, more unpredictable than a hag in human meat-induced heat. They'd even been known to eat their own eggs if frustrated in their hungers too long. He sank down slowly, and reached into a basket for a knuckle-bone to crunch, and suddenly he realized the reason for the goblings' disappearances. He would have to increase the amount of food sent below. They were eating each other. And the more human meat the goblings were fed, the bigger they'd grow. This Samhain-bred crop might start feeding on their older siblings as soon as their eggs cracked open. Of course, he thought. Iruk was an idiot, a fool. He'd been right to kill him. Xerruw crunched on another knucklebone, and the gelatinous marrow exploded in his mouth. He could feel the victory in the rocks beneath his feet, in the scent of human meat now flooding his awareness, lulling him once more into a light drowse, taste it in the ripe rich sweetness of the inner bone-meat. He waved an arm at the nearest guard, intent on giving him the orders to increase the rations to the goblings below.

"Prepare the armies, increase the rations, and send me the captains of the watch," Xerruw barked.

"When will we attack?" the one guard asked, cringing even as he spoke.

"We will attack," replied Xerruw, with a snap of his tail. "But we will not do what they expect."

The guards looked at each other, apprehension obvious in the rigid knots of their tails.

"We will attack when we reach the cellars."

"But, great Xerruw," said the guard, "is it not easier to simply walk across the border?"

"That's what they expect us to do." Xerruw paused and looked around. From the sides, from the passages and the dens below, the goblin hordes came creeping, drawn by the unfamiliar smell of burning goblin flesh. Xerruw gave a mighty bellow and this time, even Khouri threw back his small head and joined in the rising chorus as he howled: "But we will not do what they expect! We will not jump at the first bait they offer. For we grow strong! We grow strong! We all grow strong on human meat!"

Delphinea had never imagined what the border between Faerie and Shadow must be like, but the closer she and Petri approached, the more clearly she saw its elusive edges shimmering distinctly through the sentinel trees. It lent a subtle murkiness to the shadows on the ground, a definite weight to the light filtering down between the branches, even as the air itself gathered substance and texture. Filmy tendrils, vague as impersonal fingers, brushed against her cheeks, her arms, her breasts, and back, lightly as feathers, sending a chill down her spine. It was almost as if she was about to immerse herself in water, she thought, for the ground squished beneath her boots, and the rock-ribbed tree trunks were covered in thick green moss. Beside her, she felt Petri quiver. "Can you feel it, Petri?" she whispered. "Can you feel the border?"

The gremlin looked up at her with round eyes, but his only answer was a low, soft hiss. The light was fading, the shadows darkening, and she realized she had lost all sense of time. *It's at dusk the goblins hunt.* The ancient warning ran through her mind, but she shook it off. It was nowhere near dusk. Was it?

She tightened her grip on Petri's paw. Resolutely she plunged forward, holding her breath as she stepped over and through and into a world she had once thought as far away as the moon.

It was like stepping into a bath of cold ink. She gasped as the air hit her full in the face, and immediately stumbled over a tree root. "Oh!" she cried as she fell on all fours, her hands and knees feeling as if they were pricked by a thousand needles. She stumbled quickly to her feet and as her eyes adjusted to the dark, realized they stood within a grove of holly trees, grown huge and sprawling. Even the trees in Shadow grow wild, she thought as she looked up at the muddy stars twinkling in unfamiliar patterns.

The low-hanging branches of the nearest holly shivered and shook as Petri fell to his knees beside her, and with a squeal, plunged his hands into the spongy loam.

"Petri," she whispered. "Have you any idea at all where we are?"

"We're in the wood, lady." His voice was different—hollow—but not nearly as unpleasant as before. "We're very deep within the wood. We're almost still inside the Mother-Wood."

"What's the Mother-Wood?"

"The place between the worlds." He scooped up fistfuls of dirt and smeared it all over his face, washing in it, she thought, the way the sidhe washed their faces in dew. He sniffed it, licked it, rubbed it on his arms and legs and head. She realized why his voice sounded so different. The denser air of Shadow muffled the piercing shrillness that so discomfited the delicate ears of the sidhe. His stunted tail wriggled, dirt crusted his lips, and bits of leaves clung to his clothes. Tiny twigs stuck to his head, and he looked for all the world like a miniature version of Herne in his guise as the Lord of the Forests. "Even the In-between place is a place, my lady."

Wherever they were, it was night, and they were alone in the middle of a very dark wood. The whole world felt heavier—she had sensed it in Dougal and now she felt it pressing, dense and solid, from both above and below, within and without. From very far away, she heard a high, keening howl rising out of the wind, whining through the branches, at once a warning and a call. The shadows beneath the trees deepened and she felt very cold and very small. "Petri," she whispered. "What made that noise?"

"That sounded like a wolf, my lady."

"Are there really wolves in Shadow, Petri?"

In the dark, his eyes gleamed green. "Of course there are, my lady." He took a great sniff. "But they're not too close, not yet."

All she could smell was water, as if the whole world were wet right through. "Then maybe we'd better move on, Petri. Do you have any idea which way we should go?"

For answer he wriggled all over as he planted his feet even more deeply into the forest floor. He worked his toes through layers of needle-edged leaves, then dropped from the waist and pawed through the mud, sniffing as he unearthed twigs and stones and even the many-legged creatures that scuttled up out of the earth and swarmed over her boots. Startled, she danced back, tripped again, and landed this time sitting. The palms of her hands slammed down, and something sharp stuck her forefinger, and she cried out, even louder than before. Her finger gleamed wet in the moonlight, and she realized she was bleeding.

"Be careful, my lady," Petri hissed. "These woods are full of many things."

She sucked her finger, and struggled to her feet, feeling slightly foolish, until another howl and an answering wail made her freeze. "Does that sound as if they're coming closer?"

But for answer, he only dug deeper, sniffing first one paw and then the other. "Ah," he said at last. "Just as I feared."

Was the rustling in the branches overhead, or in the underbrush behind them? Delphinea jumped, reached for the tree trunk to steady herself, and another holly leaf pricked a third finger. "Oh!" she cried again. The leaf clung to her finger, stuck there by its needle-sharp tips. She shook it away, flinging it away with a few tiny drops of blood, and stuck her bleeding finger in her mouth. And immediately removed it, for the fat berries clustered among the waxy leaves at the base of the tree were beginning to glow a soft red, haloed in dark green. "What magic is this, Petri?"

The howling came again, unmistakably closer, and was answered by another call. "We have no time for magic of any sort, lady. We must be off, for the goblins hunted last night—this earth is saturated with blood, and all things that eat flesh are in a frenzy so even things that normally might leave us alone may not."

But even as he spoke, the glow was spreading, creeping up the branch, over the entire tree. Delphinea stared, open-mouthed, as the berries on the next tree began to blush a delicate pink at the bottom, where its leaves brushed the ground. "Look at them, Petri," she whispered. "All of them—they're glowing." All around the holly grove, the berries on every tree were beginning to gleam, a soft, pale pink, which blushed to bright red, so that the berries twinkled like tiny red stars, as the light rolled like a wave up and through the trees. Despite her fear, she gazed up, open-mouthed, spellbound by the sight.

"Come, lady." Petri tugged at her hand. She let him take her hand, for the howls were both louder and more frequent, but still she lingered, stunned as the red berries began to light. A soft gleam at her feet caught her eye as Petri yanked even harder, and she reached down and picked up a slender stick, about as long as her forearm, with a cluster of berries still attached to one end. They were surrounded by three dark green leaves and they were glowing. "Come, now!"

She tucked the glowing stick inside her cloak, and allowed him to lead her out of the glowing grove, into the thick woods, where here and there, one could spot a holly begin to shine. Maybe the trees of Faerie and of Shadow were one and the same, but she had never seen a tree shine like this in Faerie. And then a snippet of a rhyme ran through her head, and she remembered her mother singing in the sun-scented clover on the hill above their house, "The holly bears the berry as red as mortal blood."

Petri was pointing straight ahead. "There's only one way to get to Gar from here—the shortest road, anyway—"

"Are you sure it's this way, Petri?" She stumbled over a tree root into the tangled underbrush, and the slender holly stick slipped out of her cloak. She groped anxiously for it, then stifled a cry as a low-hanging branch tangled in her braids, nearly pulling a lock of her long black hair out by the roots. The trees were even denser here, thick-trunked and rock-ribbed, hoary with moss and mistletoe, or twined so thick with vines no bark at all was visible. And so deep the leaves, Petri plowed through in places nearly up to his waist. Above their heads, an owl hooted, and she jumped again, her heart beginning to pound uncomfortably. Perhaps it was just this suffocating air that made her feel as if her lungs were slowly filling up with water. Last night spent with a Samhain-mad gremlin looked like nothing next to this.

"We can cross through the Mother-Wood." He glanced at her, and his eyes reflected a swift bright green once more. "But I don't want to go that way."

"Why not? If it's the fastest way?"

He swung round to face her and spoke with such unexpected savagery that she gasped and nearly stumbled again. "It's the lair of the foul witch that sent us all to Faerie and got banished here for her troubles. But it's the only way to get to Gar—or anywhere else, for that matter, as quickly as we must."

"Witch? But those are just stories, aren't they?" But Petri wasn't waiting. He scampered off through the trees, and she kilted her skirts above her knees and wrapped the extra length of fabric around one arm. Her legs were beginning to feel wooden with exhaustion, but Petri showed no signs at all of slowing down. "Can the wolves follow us there?"

"No. The wolves of Shadow cannot cross. We'll lose them there." He turned to look at her over his shoulder. "Hurry, lady, hurry. We'll be safe there, as long as we avoid the witch."

Delphinea stumbled after him, determined to keep up. She was growing more used to the denser air, but the howls were definitely on one side of them now, to the side and to the rear. As if they were being herded. "Petri," she managed, "are we anywhere near the Mother-Wood yet?"

"We're there." The words floated over his shoulder like the mistletoe that draped the low-hanging branches of ancient oaks. "We're well within it. I don't know why—"

"Why can we still hear the wolves?" Something crashed down behind them and they didn't wait to see what it was. Galvanized, they bolted, dashing through the dark forest, as if pulled in one inevitable direction.

"There should not be wolves within the Mother-Wood," gasped Petri as another wolf cry came again, followed by a rising chorus that echoed from all sides. It was them, Delphinea realized. They were the prey; they weren't being herded. They were being hunted.

They stumbled out of the trees, into a small clearing, in the middle of which was a small stone cottage. White smoke spiraled lazily from a chimney in the middle of the roof, and the windows glowed a promising yellow. "Look, Petri, shelter." Delphinea pulled the gremlin in the direction of the cottage, just as he tugged nearly equally hard away from it.

"We can't go in there," he said. "That's the witch's lair, don't you see?"

But at that moment, seven wolves emerged from the trees on the opposite side of the clearing, huge and gray and menacing. Saliva drooled from their jaws, and their lips were drawn back to show their gleaming white fangs. The largest in the center took a single step forward, then sat down, threw back his head and howled. "I don't think we have a choice, Petri."

As if on cue, the door opened, and the crooked figure of an aged woman peered out into the night. She leaned upon a staff, and turned her head first one way and then the other, almost as if trying to sniff out the intruder. "Who's there?" she asked. "Who's there?" She turned her head this way and that, and Delphinea realized she was blind. She sniffed, as if trying to scent them out, then sagged against the door frame. "Vinaver, is that you? Are you come at last?"

Again, the wolf threw back its head and let out a long, mournful howl. The woman leaned against the frame and beckoned, a wide sweeping gesture that ended in a frantic wave. "Come, now, quickly, whoever you are. The wolves will give you one more chance. Then they tear you to pieces." She stamped her foot. "You've waited too long already."

The old woman turned and Delphinea saw that what she had first taken to be a cloak was in fact the witch's hair. It shone white in the silvery light, puddling at her feet, and trailed behind her in rich waves as she disappeared into the cottage, shutting the door with a firm slam.

"Petri," Delphinea whispered. The wolves were beginning to paw the ground restlessly, their reddish eyes fixed on them both. As Delphinea grabbed Petri, the biggest threw back his head and howled one more time.

The rest joined in an eerie baying chorus, and Delphinea bolted across the clearing, heading for the door, even as Petri slithered from out of her grasp. Just outside the door, she paused, openmouthed with shock, as he disappeared into the underbrush. In that same moment, the wolves vaulted after him, crashing and snarling, leaving Delphinea holding on to the door latch in shock. "Petri," she whispered. The wolves had gone silent, and her heart stopped in her throat. What was so terrible about the witch that he'd rather face the wolves?

Delphinea turned slowly as the witch gave a low cough, one foot on either side of the threshold. The witch leaned on her staff beside her hearth. She raised her blind face. "Shut the door. Did you bring a spell to release those wolves, or did you have to kill them?"

Shocked, Delphinea blinked. "Good dame," she began experimentally. "I—I'm not sure how many of us you think there should be, but I assure you, there is only me. M-my companion has—chosen to brave the wolves." She glanced outside, but the night was still. What had happened to Petri?

But the witch was speaking, frowning, advancing so that in the flickering firelight, Delphinea had a better look at her face. "Who're you? You sound like a girl, but you're not Vinaver. And why did she only send just one?" She broke off, and turned away, her lips pressed together, brows knit. She looked at once angry and bewildered, and Delphinea peered more closely, trying to read the complex play of emotions shifting across the witch's face.

A web of delicate wrinkles, gossamer as lace, crisscrossed the witch's cheeks, and her eyes were hooded in the shadows, their color impossible to see. But her hair fell to the floor in wavy strands of pure spun white gold, gleamed like a pale copper cloak in the reddish firelight, rippled like a waterfall over her shoulders as she cocked her head, and Delphinea gazed more closely, watching what the shifting play of shadows revealed across her fine-boned face. "Who are you, really?" she whispered.

There was something terribly familiar about the way the witch tilted back her head. The firelight fell on the opaque white circles of her eyes, and Delphinea knew that her guess that the witch was blind was correct. But there was something even more familiar about the way those ruined eyes were set within the narrow sockets, about the shape of her mouth as she pressed her pale lips together, in the regal set of her shoulders, despite her bowed back. She turned her head as a slow tear leaked from under her lids, and both the stark silhouette of her profile and the glorious shimmering cloud of her pale golden hair told Delphinea exactly who the witch within the Mother-Wood was. "By Herne and the Hag," she whispered, sinking to her knees in the most polished curtsy she could summon before the great Queen Gloriana herself. "I am Your Glorious Majesty's most unworthy servant."

* * *

There was fire and there was pain. Deep in the mines of Allovale, the air itself was thick with silver. It stung the back of Finuviel's mouth and tongue with every breath he drew, pricked every exposed surface like a thousand needles boring into his flesh. In the first hours of his torment it had become immediately apparent that the only way he could breathe at all was to filter the air through a layer of fabric against his mouth. The air was burning a hole through the fabric, and he wondered what would happen when his clothes disintegrated and the thin mortal blanket was all that protected him from the tainted earth. No shadows moved to mark the passing of the hours, no sunlight softened the impenetrable night, but even a torch to illuminate the shadows wouldn't have mattered, for his eyelids crusted over with the thick liquid that began to ooze from his pores.

And in his agony, he dreamed. Against the back of his eyelids, he saw the face of the Goblin King rise up to taunt him, black maw open to show rows of yellow, serrated teeth. Xerruw roared with laughter, and pointed, and Finuviel found that he was bound, like a stag, to a spit, over a great open firepit. The flames licked his face, seared his hair, burned away his eyelids and his eyelashes.

Xerruw's face faded from view, and was replaced by that of an old woman, an old woman who poked at his chest with a crooked finger, pinched his tortured cheek, then sniffed her fingers and licked her lips. "Give him another turn, Father, he's not quite cooked."

Finuviel struggled in his bonds helplessly. A silent scream ripped from his throat and was stifled by his gag as Xerruw gave the spit another turn and a vast sheet of flame enveloped Finuviel in its agonizing embrace. The flames died down and he felt the old woman force one of his ruined eyelids open. He struggled once more, pouring every drop of rage and pain and sheer stubborn determination to survive.

"He hates us, Father," said the old woman with a satisfied cackle and she let Finuviel's eyelid drop. But in the dream, he could still see her, still see them both and he felt the Goblin King flick his black forked tongue down his naked, open spine.

"Our children never understand why we do what we do. Why should this one be any different?"

Finuviel felt the spit move a quarter turn, and he braced himself for another dose of agony. But instead, he felt the old woman's breath next to his ear, and her words wove a balm around him, cold and sweet and soothing as snow. "As above, so below, boy, as below, so above. How else will you know how the land suffers? How else will we know when the land begins to heal?"

Will the land heal? he wanted to shout. Was this what his suffering was for? He was being poisoned in the same way as the land? But the dream was fading and now all he saw was blue, as clear as the skies of Faerie, cold as the shadows rising jagged and snow-peaked in the distance. Snow, he thought. As above, so below. Snow. His mind drifted and another dream began. This time he walked among the mountains, and his feet were bare but the snow felt good. Far ahead, he saw a girl turn and beckon. "Finuviel!" she cried. "Finuviel?"

I'm here, he wanted to cry, but the tainted air burned his lungs and he could only claw the thin blanket with blackened fingertips. Then this dream began to pass in its turn, leaving him with only one impression. *Blue,* he thought, as every shade imaginable, from palest cornflower to deepest indigo, swirled through his head. *Blue is the color of surcease.*

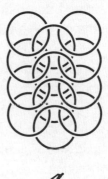

4

It was long past sunset when Mag, and another granny, so cloaked and veiled they nearly blended into the gray shadows, came for Cecily. She had bathed with the herbs they had left her, and dressed in the loose smock of bleached homespun wool. It would be cold near the water at night, she thought, and considered disobeying their injunction to wear anything else either over it or underneath. As it was, they made her remove the smock and turn it so the opening, which came nearly to her waist, gaped open below the knotted cord that held the neckline closed, exposing the goose-pimpled flesh between her breasts.

"She looks ripe." The other granny spoke to Mag as if Cecily weren't there, and she felt herself flush. She had some idea of what happened at the corn rituals, but she'd never before been invited to participate, and she was not quite sure what her role would require.

"Aye," said Mag. Cecily gasped as the older woman slipped one hand through the opening of her gown and cupped one breast, as if testing its weight. "She's full."

The woman shot Cecily a questioning look and she remembered Mag's suggestion she was pregnant. *But that's not possible,* she thought, mentally counting back days. *I've not lain...* And then she remembered. She had lain with Kian. *Before Samhain. Before Donnor died.* She tossed her head and Mag picked up the loose braid she wore over one shoulder.

"You'll want to let this loose before we begin, but it'll do for now." She handed Cecily a red cord. "Here, put this round your waist. 'Twill hold it closed. And here, wear this." She held out a cloak of the same rough-spun wool as the ones they wore, such as a simple peasant woman might wear.

"But what about—" began the second granny. She placed her hand on Cecily's plaid. "Should we not bring this?"

Mag nodded. "Why not? Anything that might help."

"Help to do what?" asked Cecily as they bundled the cloak around her shoulders. But they did not answer her as they pulled the deep hood over her face so that she could scarcely see where they led her out of the castle into the night, past the great bonfires set within the gaping holes in the outer walls. The blue-and-orange flames threw up huge shadows that leaped upon the walls like demented dancers. At the gatehouse, three saddled horses awaited, along with a troop of two dozen mounted guards in full battle dress. Which seemed to make sense until they were joined by six knights of the Company who fell in alongside them, and Cecily recognized Sir Maddig and Sir Ciariag, close friends of Kian both among them. When they questioned the sergeant of the guards, they received only a gruff "On the order of Lord Kestrel. He sent us to guard the rite."

"About time the druid lent some support to our rituals," said Mag.

It seemed an odd sort of support for a druid to lend, thought Cecily. But the knights just nodded and shrugged, and Mag and the other granny were galloping down the long causeway, even as it occurred to Cecily to ask if so many men should really be spared from the defense of the castle. But they were sweeping her away, riding past her, and Cecily had no more time to ponder. The night air was cold and the damp air seeped into the folds of the rough wool, making her aware of what seemed like every square of prickled flesh on her entire body, from the back of her neck to the small of her back, to her buttocks down the inside of her legs, where her knee itched just above her boot. When they reached the trail that led down to the river, Mag and the other granny reined their horses, and Mag turned to the men and said, "You can come no farther."

A low murmur rose from the ranks, and in the orange torchlight, a sergeant rode forward. "Our orders from Lord Kestrel—"

"This rite mustn't be disturbed," said Mag. "Unless you've all a mind to face more of what you faced last night?"

An owl cried out from somewhere in the trees, and below, Cecily thought she heard the muffled beat of soft drums. Mag shook her head. "You men must wait up here."

"But the lord said—" another began, leaning over his saddle, and the first swatted him on the shoulder.

"We're to stay with the lady," a third finished.

"Sir Kian's below," said Mag. "Shall we fetch him?"

"Aye," Sir Maddig answered, nosing his big warhorse to the fore. "Fetch Kian, why not?"

"Aye," said Mag. "Let's call for him. Of course, he probably won't appreciate being brought up here naked and painted blue, but you'll answer to him, not me. But best to get this all settled before we begin."

Naked, thought Cecily. Her nipples shriveled into hard peaks as a shiver went through her that had nothing to do with the cold night air.

At that, the sergeant looked startled and another guard nudged him in the ribs. "N-no, that won't be necessary." The sergeant subsided. "Pray don't disturb him. We'll wait up here, all right."

"All right."

And then Mag motioned her down the trail, which led to a shallow flight of steps carved along the rock wall. At the bottom was a sandy beach, where Cecily and her ladies frequently picnicked and swam on sunny summer afternoons, where Donnor's knights had sometimes joined them. The shallow caves a bit farther upriver were a popular trysting spot for the knights and Cecily's ladies.

Someone had been here today, she realized. Someone had prepared the torches burning in metal brackets set in ledges above the steps, and little bursts of bright yellow flame jumped and sparked in the sporadic gusts blowing off the water. The wind tugged at her braid, sending wild tendrils around her face. Her palms were slick with sweat but her fingertips felt like cubes of ice.

"Careful," said Mag over her shoulder. "The steps are slippery the lower you go."

The sand was swept and clean, and eight fires burned at

equal intervals around a roughly delineated circle about thirty paces in diameter. A five-pointed star had been traced within the circle, creating a smaller circle within the larger one, and now it lay like an open eye, staring back at the stars. A shiver ran down her spine. Most amulets were made in the shape of a pentacle, for its association with the element of Earth was said to strengthen the metal's effect. But the pentacle meant more than that—each of its five points was associated with each of the four Elements that made up the world, as well as the fifth one, the one unseen, the one some called Spirit, and others the goddess and the god. And some said the pentacle had other meanings too, that it was associated with chaos, with breakdown and change.

It was the Hag's symbol, some said, and encompassing her symbol with a circle meant that her power was controlled and confined. But Cecily, who had felt Her presence keenly at each miscarried birth, doubted that anything could really control Her. But the circle, too, had other meanings, including the endless cycle of life itself. It was said that the highest levels of the druids all understood the meanings, but she'd never met one who had. Beyond the circle, under a row of shoulder-high torches, ten or twelve men sat drumming on hide-skin drums of different sizes and shapes.

In the center of the inner circle lay a half-round plaid, a man's cloak, thick white candles pinning down the edges. Mag and her companion laid the cloak they'd taken from her room opposite the man's cloak, completing the inner circle, and a third granny stepped forward with more white candles. Together, they pinned the edges of Cecily's cloak in place, and used a long switch lighted from one of the bonfires to light the candles.

Again Cecily wondered how exactly she was expected to participate. Was that why they wanted her? The idea of her with Kian on those plaids, in the center of the circle, in plain view of everyone, at once ignited and terrified her. She did not want to reveal so much of herself to anyone, except to him. What they shared together was more than this—this—ritualized coupling, this animalistic display. It was difficult to get past the inculcation of her druid masters that corn magic was somehow debased magic. And yet, the thought of Kian, of his hair spilling down over her breasts, his chin rough against her cheeks, the musky scent of horse and grass rising off his skin as his rutting raised his sweat, the way his mouth tasted like peppermint—her senses spiraled in a heady rush and she quivered at the memory of that most recent night they'd found their separate ways to meet beside their Beltane bower. Donnor had still been alive, she reckoned, so technically, it was adultery. But it wasn't as if they'd planned it, Cecily thought. It had just...just happened. She'd no idea Kian had gone out to the wood. She'd just seen the flicker of his lantern and thought him some corn granny out to harvest herbs. Almost the way it had been at Beltane.

From somewhere within the row of drummers, a lone piper raised an experimental melody. The drums were louder here on the beach, a soft and insistent throb that she felt through the thick soles of her boots. She was conscious of the way the rude robe fit over her body, its homespun wool coarser than anything she normally wore next to her skin. It made her flesh tingle all over, not quite an itch, just enough to make her aware of places of which she was normally not aware—under her arms and down her sides, the backs of her thighs, the small of her back. Beneath the drums she heard the river gurgling over the stones as if in counterpoint. She smelled the mossy water, punctuated by burning wood. The women moved to take places within the circle of fires, and Mag beckoned to Cecily to join them. She found herself positioned at one tip of the pentacle.

"We are thirteen," said Mag.

"The circle is not yet complete." Granny Lyss hobbled into the center and stood on the plaids, her back humped beneath her robe, and Cecily saw that like her own, Granny Lyss's was open at the front as well. But hers was not bound by any rope, and through the gaping opening, Cecily could see the old woman's drooping kettle of a belly. Her breasts drooped like udders, shriveled nipples pointing straight down, and she wondered how the grannies could even imagine Kian could couple with such a woman.

On some indeterminate cue, the pipe began again, this time with slow deliberation. The grannies began to sway in place, and Mag thrust a small, round drum in one of Cecily's hands, and a short thick stick in the other. As the other grannies picked up the beat of the drum, Mag leaned over and whispered quickly in Cecily's ear. "Just follow along now. Remember to stay well away from the fires. When we remove our cords, you do, too, all right? But when Granny Lyss reaches for it, you give it to her." She smiled at Cecily and gave her a kiss on the cheek. "And loose your hair!"

With a start, Cecily pulled out the leather cord around the braid. She raised her arms and raked her fingers through her scalp, startled at the prickle of energy she felt sweep from the crown of her head and down her like a cloak.

Mag smiled and nodded and turned into the dance, leaving Cecily to raise the stick and join the dance. The music was sweeping through her now, like the wind sweeping through the bending willows along the shore. Most of the grannies had started to hum. Granny Lyss raised her arms, and the firelight illuminated the stringy strands of long gray hair still clinging to her nearly bald and spotted scalp. She looked at Cecily and smiled. "The circle is not yet complete. Let the Horned One be brought to join us."

The melody rose and the drums picked up the beat. It was a bridal dance, Cecily saw, of the sort normally performed to welcome the bride, but this time it was groom being brought forward. The circle parted, and Kian was led to the center of the plaids, blindfolded, wrists bound behind his back, long hair free and unbound around his shoulders. He was naked but for a strip of linen knotted loosely at his loins. On his bare chest, his nipples were surrounded by short strokes, like the rays of the sun, and a thick blue line capped with a triangle rose suggestively from the base of his belly, to just below his breastbone. The tattoos he'd earned in battle emphasized the curves of his arms, the planes of his chest. He was perfect, Cecily thought, the image of the Horned One himself, and desire rolled through her inexorably as a tide.

"We are thirteen," said Mag once more.

"We are complete," whispered Granny Lyss. "Let the circle be made unbroken."

From somewhere inside their robes, the grannies withdrew pouches, and as Granny Lyss began to chant, in a low, singsong voice that might have belonged to a woman of almost any age, they began to dance, sprinkling the salt onto the ground, between and through the bonfires.

"One for sun that burns so bright,
Two for moon that shines at night,
Three completes a sacred vow,
Let three begin what we do now—
Four for four directions green,
Five the center still unseen,
Six for balance, seven the test,
Eight the challenge, nine for rest
Ten when we begin again.
Round about the circle goes
Dark to light and back it flows
Now the sacred rite begins,
Round about the dancers spin
I call the Quarters Four to me
I call the sacred Two to me
Lord and Lady of the Law
Be here now, and heed my call
Round about and three times three,
The power raised I draw to me!"

She moved around Kian as she chanted, raising her arms, whispering, touching him now and then with fingers as light and feathery as wings, heedless of how her robe fell open. Her body hung like an old sack on her knobby, shriveled frame. She pinned Cecily with her toothless smile, singling Cecily out, watching every move Cecily made with hand or dress or drum.

The rhythm was picking up now, the other grannies all singing and humming, moving in and out of patterns apparently as random as they were complex. Within the circle, the air was warm, and the sweat began to trickle down

Cecily's sides, forming wet crescents under her breasts. The breeze felt good as it lifted her hair, ruffled her robe, raised her nipples to hard peaks. Suddenly the soft white powdery sand seemed to invite her to curl her toes into it, and as she bent to unlace her boots, she saw that she was already barefoot. When did I take them off? she wondered.

Cecily raised her eyes to Granny Lyss, who only smiled from behind Kian. He was standing completely still, his head raised. She could see a pulse beating under his chin. His erection bulged beneath the loincloth. Granny Lyss was touching his arms and legs now, letting her sparse hair flick over his torso and shoulders as she drew him down to his knees, stroking him all over, moving with the sinuous ease of a woman half her age. There was steam now, flowing from the cauldrons set over the fires. It blended with the smoke from the fire and the mist off the river, texturing the air. The resinous scent of pine and sage and cedar hit the center of her head like a burst of fire. Her senses seemed to enlarge and heighten, and suddenly she could smell the acrid odor of masculine sweat drifting off Kian, she could feel the fine grains of sand on the soles of her feet and between her toes. She could hear the subtle harmonies in the grannies' singing, and she dipped and spun and turned as she moved with the grannies in a dance she somehow knew. She could see the shifting patterns of steam and mist and smoke intermingling in the air, within and around the wind-whipped flames.

Granny Lyss cupped Kian's face, her feet planted a shoulder span apart, her robe falling off her upper arms. Her twisted body glowed in the firelight as she rained light kisses on his face, his nose, his lips, dodging back when he would have responded. She ran her hands lightly over his chest, rolling the nubs of his nipples between her fingertips, and he groaned and arched his back, the muscles of his thighs and buttocks straining for release. The loincloth slipped a little as his muscles tightened.

She could feel Kian's need, Kian's ache, as if it were her own, thought Cecily, at the same time, both acutely aware of her own desire and somehow removed from it, caught up in the dance, and yet separate from it, too. In the same way she both wanted to be there on that blanket, and was glad that she was not. But she was not prepared for the stab of blinding anger that lanced through her as Granny Lyss gathered his face once more and kissed his mouth, a lover's kiss, deliberate and hard. She raised her eyes and looked directly at Cecily.

It felt like a physical wound, directly into her heart, and Cecily sagged, as if against some invisible spear. But she couldn't turn her eyes away, and she watched, at once repelled and rapt, as the old woman drew her hands over Kian's face and neck and throat, so that he arched his back against her, and turned his face, blindly seeking her mouth as they moved in time to the music. The old woman's hands ranged lower on his belly, tickling in the tuft of hair that ran from his navel to his groin. Her fingers danced lower, moving in time to the drumming and the humming and the undulating women who moved all around them, even as Cecily herself was still.

She shouldn't be able to move like that, thought Cecily as Granny Lyss sank down on her own splayed knees beyond Kian, and reached all the way around him. She tugged at the loincloth, and it fell away, so that his sex sprang free. It rose above his navel, a fat drop of moisture pearled on the tip.

The grannies sighed and murmured and hummed approval. Desire exploded through her, a combination of the music and the smoke and the fire and Kian's nakedness, and the awareness of his own need, her own inflamed body. Despite herself, she began to move once more, giving in to the raw state of primal emotion that swept through her as her whole body traced out a pattern of long-thwarted want.

The other grannies were removing their cords now, slipping them over and away and up, holding them above their heads, twisting and weaving them in complex patterns. She quickly unknotted hers, and her robe gaped open nearly to her hips, so that her breasts hung bare above her softly rounded belly. The breeze washed over her feverish body like rain. Without knowing why, she tossed hers to Granny Lyss, who caught it with a smile. Unable to look away, caught up in the flow of her own unleashed emotion, Cecily watched as Granny Lyss dragged her age-thickened nails one by one down the shaft of Kian's member. The twisting pattern of the dance interfered and Cecily peered through the dancers, frantic to see. The old woman's fingers were pinkening and plumping, and right before their eyes, through the weaving dancers, Cecily stumbled in shocked disbelief as Granny Lyss transformed into a near mirror image of herself, dark blond hair flowing unbound around her haunted face, long throat over breasts striated with the marks of more than a dozen pregnancies. But it was the sight of the transformation of her hands, from the arthritic claws of a peasant hag into the smooth white fingers and pink nails of a young noblewoman that rooted Cecily in place, unable to look away.

Kian was on her now, moving with precision born of

need, but though the bonds around his wrists were off, his blindfold was still in place as he lay Granny Lyss tenderly on her back and covered her with his big body. Horrified but fascinated, Cecily could not take her eyes away, even as the dancers drove her on, twining around her as insistently as the drums that now pulsed to the rhythm of Kian's buttocks as he pumped between the granny's thighs so that she was forced into their moving midst.

Kian ripped off the blindfold and stared down at Granny Lyss, and Cecily was sure the name she heard him mutter was hers. In a swift motion, he brought her mouth up to his, as if he would draw her into himself, as his body shuddered in its final release. From very far away, Cecily thought she heard the clash of steel on steel and wondered what sort of instruments might make that noise.

The drumming slowed, the grannies surged forward, and as Kian rose on his elbows, struggling up from the tangle of plaid and limbs, armed guards rushed out of the night and tore a dazed Kian off Granny Lyss. As Cecily and the grannies staggered backward, dispersed by surprise, one guard threw the woman over his shoulder and started for the steps.

With the loud clatter of overturned instruments, the drummers charged forward and Cecily realized they were dressed in the plaids of Donnor's First Company. *That's why there were only six to escort us. But the others,* she thought, scrambling back, nearly over the back of a fallen woman. *What's happened to the other knights?*

Someone handed Kian a sword, and, naked but for the blindfold around his neck, he vaulted after Granny Lyss, whose belly was now beginning to swell like a pregnant woman's. "Cecily!" he cried, just as a guard brought his blade crashing down on Kian's upper arm, as another guard swiped at his unshielded thigh. Kian collapsed, bleeding, as they ran up the steps after the one carrying a half-conscious Granny Lyss over his shoulder. The rest sheathed their weapons and followed them into the night.

"Go after her," howled Mag, who had to be restrained from rushing after them herself. Through the haze of smoke and wind-thrown flame, Cecily heard the whicker and the neigh of horses. "You've got to go after her," pleaded Mag, throwing herself at the nearest knight. She was joined in her plea by the other grannies. "You have to go after her. The magic's not set, the magic's not made—" But the man only turned and shouted something that Cecily didn't bother to understand as she rushed to Kian's side.

His face was pale, blood flowed sluggishly down his side. Just let him live, she thought. Just let him live. She fell to her knees in the soft sand and slapped his woad-streaked face gently. "Kian? Kian?"

"Come, Your Grace."

She looked up into the steady eyes and sweat-streaked face of Sir Tuavhal. "We're not leaving him—"

"Of course not. But we're leaving here now. Kian expected something like this from that druid."

"But Granny Lyss," cried a granny, grabbing Cecily's arm. "She's got to birth that magic, or it'll kill her, don't you understand?"

Cecily turned to the knight, ready to plead the grannies' cause, when he cut her off. "Begging your pardon, Your Grace, we can't return to Gar. I'm sorry about the granny—

sorry about the magic. But there's nothing more we can do this night."

Torn, Cecily saw them lift a plaid-wrapped Kian into the waiting arms of a knight who drew him back against his chest. Another knight settled a cloak around her shoulders, and she saw it was her own plaid, swept up from the circle. It smelled like damp sand and sweat and sex. "Please," she began. But Sir Tuavhal caught her up and lifted her onto his own saddle, then swung up behind her. She held a hand out to the weeping women, but the knight put the spurs to his horse's sides and galloped off after Kian's mount, heading down along the water's edge where their scent would be harder to trace. "We'll come back," she cried, but her words were drowned by the wailing screams and the steady splashes as they galloped away.

Artimour was surprised by his strong urge to follow Nessa back to the forge. He watched the heel of her boot and the hem of her tunic disappear around the corner, and was tempted to go after her at once, but Nessa's warning held him back. He stared out the window, watching the milling crowds thronging the inner ward, the long lines snaking toward the kitchens. *The people are looking for someone to blame.* He had no wish to confront anyone, but he could not deny Nessa intrigued him. He had smelled the burning metal in her hair, on her clothes, seen the dark crescents of soot embedded in her fingernails and streaked across her cheeks, and again he wondered about the mysterious mortal who'd been his father. Maybe that was why Nessa unsettled him in a way no lady of the sidhe, no matter how skilled in the arts of love or courtship, ever had before. Or maybe it was simply that she was a mortal.

At last the keep settled down. He wrapped himself in the dun-colored cloak of mortal make that they'd given him since his own had been reduced to shreds by the rough rocks on the shore, and slipped out, careful to keep his face covered. Across the courtyard, the watch bawled the changing of the guard, and the campfires sprinkled like stars on the paving stones below began to flare out and die. Above, on the walls, the long orange flames whipped out like goblin tails in the chilly dusk. The wind licked at his face, acrid with the odor of burning metal. Nessa, he thought, with a pang. What had kept her up so late? A belch of white smoke over the long low roofs beckoned.

The smithy was nearly pitch-black, but for a lone lantern set just above a large anvil, and the red glow of embers in the forge. He hesitated just outside the door and peered inside, and as his eyes adjusted, he saw Nessa's bare white back rising out of the tunic she had bunched around her hips. She was standing in the opposite corner, using what looked like a small rag to splash water from a bucket under her arms. She bent and wrung out the rag, then twisted her neck this way and that, scrubbing at the lines of grime. Mesmerized, he stared at the way the muscles flowed beneath the milk-white skin of her broad shoulders.

There was an entrancing contrast between the strength implicit in her upper body and the delicate arch of her back as it curved from her waist to her round, full hips. She raised one arm and he caught a glimpse of a white breast, full as a ripe peach, the nipple pale pink in the reddish light. She put down her rag and swung low, upper arm flexing as she grasped another bucket. Her body looked strong and solid, round and ripe. As she bent over, the heavy black mass of her hair tumbled free from the rag turbaned around her head, and in one smooth motion, she set the second bucket beside the first, and caught her hair up in her left hand. A sudden pulse of desire made him step forward, and the sole of his boot scraped on the floor.

She turned her head in the act of twisting the springy curls into one mass again, and gasped when she glimpsed him standing in the door. Immediately she pulled up the front of her tunic to cover her breasts with one hand, but with the other, she reached for a dagger. "Who's there?" Her chin was high, her shoulders were back and the muscles in her arms and upper chest tightened menacingly.

She's brave, he thought as the ruddy shadows fell across her face. *No wonder Uwen wants to take her to Gar. With her by his side, how could he fail?*

"Who's there?" she repeated, and he heard the quiver of fear in her voice. He took a single step forward, so that the light fell across his face. As she recognized him, the dagger faltered and her face paled. The skin of her throat looked soft and very tender. How vulnerable she is, he thought as an urge to warn her not to leave the four high walls of the keep, urge to stay and protect her, swept through him. More than anything, he suddenly wanted to touch that tumbled mass of black curls now toppling over her face, to kiss her pale pink lips, run his hands along the curves of her arms and breasts and waist, and take possession of her firm, ripe body. "Great Herne," she whispered as she tossed back her hair and lowered the dagger.

"Not exactly." For the first time in his life, he had no idea what to say or how to say it. There had been times when he'd come upon a half-dressed lady in the moonlight, whether by chance or plan, but the feelings Nessa roused were so complex, he didn't know where to begin. "I'm so sorry. I didn't mean to startle you."

"How long have you been here? I told you to stay out of sight."

"No, oh, no. I came in—just now. I couldn't sleep. I had no idea you'd keep working so late."

"Ah, 'twas easier, really." She turned her back and struggled into her tunic, pulling the rough fabric up over her shoulders so hard he heard a seam give way. "Smiths do a lot of work at night—the black part of the day, my father called—calls it." As she turned back to face him, he saw that the neckline's seam gaped raggedly. He could see the fresh scar, long and thin and red, running vertically between the shadowed curves of her breasts.

"Why at night?"

"Slag—the scrap part, the part you don't want in the pure metal—shows up dark when the metal's molten. That's the part you beat out, you know. You see it better in the dark." She cocked her head. "Have you no smiths in Faerie?"

He shrugged, dragging the tip of one finger down a sooty anvil. "It's different, what they do. It's not the same at all."

"Well, what is it that they do then? How do things get made?"

"Things get made by willing them to be made."

"You mean, in Faerie, one has only to think about making something, and it appears?"

He shrugged. "Well, that's something like the way it

works, yes. In the same way you were able to cross the border. First you willed it to be so. And then you made it happen."

"But crossing a border and making a sword are two different things." She gestured to the array of implements and tools and weapons stacked high within the forge, hung on hooks and rails from every surface. "Aren't they?"

Artimour shook his head, entranced by the subtle play of candlelight on her bare arms and throat. "Not in Faerie. The stuff of Faerie is different. It's another kind of world altogether, really."

"And you can do this?" She was looking at him with a mixture of awe and disbelief.

At that, he flushed and skipped his fingers down the variously sized hammers hanging on the wall beside him, the physical evidence of his need stirring in his trews, but the memories she roused were like a sudden blast of ice water. "Well, to tell you the truth, I can't. It's a bit of a secret, actually. My mother at one point thought perhaps I'd do better with my father's tools. But I wasn't much good with those, either. The stuff of Faerie can't be worked with mortal tools, I guess. And there wasn't anyone to show me exactly how to use them. Fortunately I did well enough at swordplay and riding and archery that she was able to find something to do with me."

"That's how you came to command the outpost on the border?"

"Until Finuviel arranged to replace me." Resentment stabbed through him. What sort of influence had Vinaver been able to wield over both Queen and Council?

As if she read his mind, she said, "Are you frightened?"

He didn't like to think that he was frightened. But if he were honest with himself, fear was only the tip of the complex kaleidoscope of emotion that swirled through him. It enraged him that Finuviel should betray the Queen, it sickened him that Alemandine had been so easily duped. And it angered him that Nessa and her father should have been brought into this. But Nessa was continuing, her eyes darting from fire to anvil to door—anywhere but at him. "What will you do and where will you go?"

"After I cross the border, I'll go at once to the Queen." He was conscious of the smell of her still-damp flesh. The odor of burning metal emanated from her clothing, from her hair, but he did not find it at all unpleasant. In fact, he wanted to bury his nose in the wild tangle, to discover for himself where that acrid aroma ended and her mossy scent began.

Suddenly she said, "I made you something."

"You did?"

She picked up a stubby candle and darted to the other side of the forge, still refusing to meet his eyes. She held the candle up to the lantern and was forced to stand on tiptoe. The ripped neckline of her tunic fell off the opposite shoulder, and he watched her nipples harden beneath the coarse fabric as she raised her eyes to his. And he knew she wanted him, then, in the way he wanted her. But Nessa was no light-shod lady of the Faerie Court. Nessa had a substance to her that none of them possessed, a substance that at once made her stronger, and yet more vulnerable.

She beckoned, holding her sputtering candle over a long table, where various implements, presumably her night's labor, lay in neat rows. Set apart, on a frayed piece of plaid, a simple sword with a narrow, diamond-shaped blade had been placed. It might even be a practice sword, he thought as he picked up the weapon and took a closer look at the blade. It was about as long as his arm, and the pommel was a simple piece of leather-covered wood. He extended it, flexed his arm, tried an attack. Even the light weight pulled at the wound in his chest, but considering how much he didn't know, better to be armed than not. Then he noticed that the metal itself shone not only with the unmistakable shimmer of newly sharpened steel, but that its lower edge had a curious gleam. "What's this?"

She lowered the candle, and in the brighter light, he saw that one side of the blade had a distinctly silvery cast over the darker steel. "I coated the tip and one edge with silver. If you meet Finuviel and his dagger again—well, this time you'll be prepared."

For a moment, he stared down at her, speechless at the realization of the gift she'd given him. Neither goblin nor sidhe would expect him to carry a mortal weapon coated in silver. She handed him a scabbard. It was made of light strips of wood covered in leather, crude by Faerie standards, but necessary. "Here, you'll need this. And you'll want this, too, I think." A folded linen cloth materialized in her hands. "You'll want to wipe off goblin blood as quick as you can. It eats through the metal if you let it stay there." She gestured awkwardly at the long rows of implements on the table.

"Where did you find the silver?" Silver, or the lack of it, was one of the main topics of conversation that day. Gingerly, he ran the tip of his finger down the center of the blade, carefully skirting the silvered edge.

"I melted down my father's amulet. I—I know he'd want

me to do that. Especially after—well, since I was the one who—" She broke off and bit her lip, then said, "It was by my hand and my father's skill you were injured."

A pang went through him. She had taken something of her father's—her lost father's, that she herself had made for him, besides—and melted it down, so that honor might be satisfied, and he, Artimour, might be armed in this strange new world in which they found themselves. It was clearer to him than ever what her father meant to her, but he hesitated to accept her offering. Silver was dangerous, silver was poison. Bringing more of the stuff into Faerie could only hasten its breakdown, surely. He took a deep breath, then picked up her hand. "Nessa—" Her eyes were huge in the dim light. "Nessa, I don't think I should take this."

"B-but why not?" she stammered. "I know it isn't beautiful, it's just a common—"

"Stop." He placed a finger against her lips. "Listen to me. I appreciate this—your work, your gesture, the amulet you melted down. But you know that silver is poison to Faerie. I'm not sure it's good to take more into it. The amulet didn't belong there, that's why they made your father take it off." He broke off, floundering for words. Her reluctance to meet his eyes, coupled with an awkwardness in her stance, made him sure he'd hurt her in some way he didn't understand. "Nessa, you should keep this with you. There was much talk today about how depleted the silver stores are—there's none in the entire keep." But even this line of reasoning didn't seem to erase her bereft look. At a complete loss, he picked up her hand and brought it to his lips, and as he did so, he noticed the network of scars that crisscrossed her skin. Not easily at all was the stuff of Shadow wrought. This wasn't something she'd done on a moment's whim, formed with a careless thought and a heedless wish. It required even greater will and determined purpose to wrestle this reality into other forms and he saw that the lore spinners had it wrong. Mortals weren't fools at all, he realized.

She saw him examining her hand, and she started to pull it back, but he caught both of them together and brought them to his lips, pressing a kiss on each hand in turn. She gasped a little, and swayed forward, so that the hard tips of her breasts just touched the fabric over his chest. She looked at him with an intensity that at once took his breath away, and ignited a flame of need for her hotter than the last coals still glowing in the forge, insistent and demanding and diminishing his ability to think. But he struggled to put his feelings into words, for somehow he understood that mortal words and mortal feelings were inextricably linked in a way that the feelings and the words of the sidhe were not. "No, don't pull away, maiden. Think you one woman of the sidhe ever had a hand as strong as yours? Think you one woman of the sidhe could do as you? I see these marks, these scars, and I see that the stuff of Shadow is not so easily wrought as that of Faerie, but you—you can bend it to your will in a way that not one of the sidhe could."

"The sidhe work magic," she whispered, her eyes heavy-lidded and half-closed.

"That's what they would say you do."

The kiss took them both by surprise. It was not that he leaned in to kiss her, or that she leaned forward to kiss him. Rather it was a simultaneous motion that simply resulted in their mouths meeting as easily as if they had been drawn together by some outside force over which neither had any control. Her mouth opened to his and her tongue slipped along the satin inside edge of his lower lip. And all at once he was exquisitely aware of her pebbled nipples, of the weight of her breasts pushing up beneath her shift, of the pressure building in his groin. As his arms went around her, her head nestled into the hollow of his chest as if it belonged there.

Her fingers crept up his arm, to the warm damp skin of his own neck, making him aware of his flesh. She reached up to touch his rough, unshaven cheek, and the unexpected rasp of her fingertips took him unawares, and he broke away, leaving her gasping, even as he was enveloped by the damp, salt smell rising from the neckline of her tunic. She drew back, breathing hard, and he saw the question in her eyes.

"I—I've never needed to shave before," he said.

"I've never kissed anyone like that before." She stared at him, blinked, then said, "Molly shaved you. She noticed that your beard was growing."

He ran a hand over his chin. *What in the name of Herne is happening to me?* he wondered. And then, he cocked his head at her. *I've never kissed anyone like that before.* With sudden insight, he understood the source of her reticence. He pressed another kiss into the palm of her hand. Her fingers closed around his and in that gesture, he read her need. "Nessa," he whispered. "Do you want this?"

She hesitated again, the space of a heartbeat, and when she answered, he saw that her lips were soft and swollen as ripe plums ready to fall. "Yes. Oh, yes."

For another long moment, he wondered if he should, for to join with this mortal girl meant something more than an afternoon's delight or midnight pleasure, more than the game that lovemaking was to the sidhe, to be practiced and played in all its infinite varieties and variations, but ultimately, with no more aim or purpose than the satisfaction of its own pursuit of excellence. And with a sudden flash of insight, he understood that this was part of whatever it was that caused mortals to bind themselves to each other. It was something else, too. Something he wasn't sure Nessa was even aware of, or understood. This passion, this intensity now sweeping him up and over the brink of any rational thought—this was the energy of magic in its rawest state.

The need to plunge himself into her was overtaking him, demanding that he reach for her with a hunger he'd never felt for even the most accomplished of his previous lovers. As if by agreement, they reached for each other, mouths locking, and it seemed that every hour ever spent beneath overhanging branch or silken canopy, on dappled moss or cushioned chaise, was but child's play compared to the firestorm now unleashed.

He twined his hand in her hair and her neck fell back into his shoulder once more, exposing the long white arch of her throat, and the black curls cascaded over his arm, releasing a scent that was woodsy and warm, like that of the trees that had permeated his dreams the night they'd slept within the forest. He was getting dizzy, for the blood was beginning to throb in his groin, his thoughts clouded over with a bright red haze. His hand went to her breast, brushed gently against the hard tip, and when she groaned and leaned against him, he cupped his hand around its round weight. He could feel the heat rising from her damp skin through the rough-spun linen. She was not like any of the women of the sidhe, for it seemed that there was nothing about her that wasn't heavy and warm and wet and soft.

"Artimour," she breathed. She pulled back, and this time, he saw something serious in her black eyes, something that could be fear.

"Don't be afraid," he whispered. He drew one finger down the side of her face, tucking the black springy curls gently behind her ears. "I—" He broke off. How to put into words that what he felt was more than some simple enchantment, that the feelings she roused were so much more complex than anything he'd ever felt before? It was all part of this deep dark world, and in a flash of insight, he realized that the world the sidhe called Shadow and its inhabitants were all utterly more complex than any of the sidhe understood. It was only his dose of mortal blood—heretofore denied and despised—that enabled him to know that it was there, let alone to comprehend it. He cast about, seeking words, abandoning every one.

As if she sensed his struggle, she touched one fingertip to his lips. "I won't be afraid," she whispered. She wrapped her arms around his neck and pressed her body to his, so that he felt the inviting curve of her lower belly, soft against the hard ridge of his erection, saw his own face looking back at him in the depths of her dark eyes. "I won't be afraid. Not if you won't."

But she was afraid, for more than just a moment, as she led him behind the smithy, to the blacksmith's quarters on the other side of the stone forge, where the orange torchlight from the outer walls fell in checkered patches through the open windows across the blue wool blanket flecked with bits of straw. *I don't know what I'm supposed to do,* she wanted to say, but he was drawing her to him, wrapping his arms around her, easing their bodies together and down so effortlessly, she felt as if she floated. He might not look like a sidhe, nor sound like a sidhe, but Artimour moved with all the grace and delicate deftness of the OtherWorldly being he was.

He pushed the edges of her tunic off her breasts, and as the tips of his fingers brushed over the full round flesh, her back arched of its own volition, as if something in her of which she was only half-aware stirred and invited him to take her breasts in his hands. As if in answer to her body's offer, he leaned over her and gently brought the pebbled tip to his mouth, his palm like hot silk against her chilly flesh. The sensation that sparked through her as the heat of his mouth closed over her nipple and sucked shot straight to the swollen flesh between her legs. She gasped, and her hips rolled up and around, as if within the very core of her, some need, at once new in awareness but ancient with knowing, awoke to roaring life. He raised his head. "You like that?"

The absurdity of the question made her smile weakly. This is what Molly was trying to tell her, she thought. She felt as if she stood on the bank of some great river, and that but one or two more steps would sweep her away and into a darker and deeper and stronger current that was every bit as captivating as anything of Faerie, though far more fleeting. *This is what the sidhe want of us,* she thought in the small rational corner of her mind. She wet her lips and touched his mouth, his cheek, outlining the bare trace of beard on his chin with the tip of one finger, her body shifting restlessly. The flesh between her legs felt amazingly wet. "Oh, please," she managed. "Don't stop."

He smiled and bent his head once more, suckling harder,

drawing her deeper, and she closed her eyes, and breathed in time to the surge of desire that was turning her very center to fiery liquid. In the yellow-tinged light that fell through the horned windows, his skin had the texture and the color of honied cream. He gathered her up in his arms, teasing her with kisses and lifting the hem of her tunic, felt between her thighs for the sopping strip of underlinen now bunched between her legs. His fingers pushed the fabric aside, tangled in the slick curls, stroking and smoothing, twisting and pulling, working his way ever so gently but surely up and in, until her thighs spread wide and she was forced to stifle a moan against his lips. He pushed the pillow away so that her head fell back flat, and with his other hand swept down her belly, over the curve of her rump, making her aware as never before of the smooth sweep of her own skin over strongly knit sinew and bone. He lifted her leg and eased it gently onto his hip, so that the hard bulge of his erection pressed insistently into her belly. Their eyes met and held. He picked up one hand, raised it to his mouth and kissed each finger deliberately. "Now," he said. "Touch."

He guided her fingers to the head, easing her palm up and down its length. She looked down, where he rose red from the tangled mass of their hair. "See?" he whispered, suckling on her earlobe. "See how beautiful you are?"

She could only cling to him, helpless in the grip of conflicting sensations. The fear that her body could not possibly accommodate such an erection clutched at her like a claw, but he was kissing her, calling up an ancient craving. Her senses swam with his scent as he pressed her flat on her back, then ran his hands and his tongue and the feathery tips of his black hair up and over and down her body, awakening every part of her, so that she felt herself possessed of her body's power and beauty and strength in a way she had not even known she could.

Somehow, the blanket and his doublet and his shirt disappeared into the tangle of her tunic, her underlinen and his hose. He pushed the pile of fabric off the bed and stretched out beside her naked body, the thin red line of the dagger scar beside her cheek. He smiled at her as he traced the back of his hand over and into every curve and crevice, from ear to neck to waist to inner thigh, from knee to belly to breast. She gasped, as with the gentlest pressure of his thumb he probed her navel, pushing in just a little, then pulling away, then pushing in again, as if to suggest another penetration. As she raised her hips in response, he dragged his hand down to the swollen lips between her legs. He rubbed his fingers in the slippery spilling moisture, exploring with excruciating gentleness the entrance of her core. "Do you want this, Nessa?" His voice was a hoarse rasp.

Don't be afraid to lie with any man if your heart tells you it's good, for what happens between a man and a woman is the greatest magic that there is. Molly's voice echoed through her mind as she trembled all over. "Yes," she breathed. She lay back, fear overcome by need, as he gently rubbed the head of his penis up and down, all the way from the top of her cleft to the base, so that she drew her legs up and back, hips rising in an awkward spiral.

It made her cry out with frustration when he stopped, and withdrew, and she shut her eyes, telling herself to bite her tongue in half if she had to, but to do anything but scream. But a new touch made her sigh with delight instead. She opened her eyes wide as her legs and gaped down at him, speechless. He was crouching between her legs, tongue poised, just above the glistening cluster of curls. "Lie back," he whispered.

The texture of his tongue was like warm satin gliding over silk, and the feathery tips of his eyelashes, soft as finest down, tickled her inner thighs. She could do nothing but lie back, for the pleasure he brought her with tongue and lips and teeth carried her away so completely, that when at last he positioned himself with that hard knob pushing against her cleft, she found herself arching up to meet his thrust, so that the pierce of pleasure through the pain was like a stab of light into the very center of her being. He caught her up, wrapped her in his arms and cradled her to his chest, holding them both still until the worst of the throbbing eased. Her face was pressed against his wound, and she felt its rough scabbed edge against her smooth cheek. And even as she lay tense, ruptured membrane burning, that wanton pulse beat an insistent counterpoint, until the passion grew so intense it overwhelmed the pain, pushing her toward the brink of something she could still only sense. She turned her face and found his mouth.

It was when he began to move, gently at first, coaxing her body with effortless grace into a matching rhythm, tireless as steady rain, or the pounding of surf upon the shore, that she understood at last what Molly meant when she said this was the basis for every kind of magic ever worked. For in the relentless thrusting of his hips, she sensed a roiling mass of energy building to the point of bursting, until her muscles loosened, her bones liquefied and her body shuddered as the whole world dissolved into something that felt like warm flashes of gold light.

The wind sighing in the trees woke her later. She opened her eyes to a tangle of limbs and sheets and for a moment wondered where she was. And then the tenderness between her legs reminded her and she looked at Artimour on the pillow beside her. He opened his eyes and smiled. "Nessa. Are you all right?"

She nodded, but turned her face to the window. It was coming up to dawn. The shadows were fading to blue already and the scent of morning was in the air. The smell of baking bread wafted through the window. Uwen would be coming for her soon. Her body felt stretched and strained and spongy, and the last thing she wanted was for him to get up and leave her. But a terrible thought had occurred to her. "Artimour," she whispered. "What would happen to you—to my parents—if Faerie—if Faerie dies?"

For a long moment he looked at her. "To tell you the truth, Nessa, I don't know."

"The corn grannies say that mortals who die in the OtherWorld are doomed to follow Herne's Wild Hunt forever. I don't want that to happen to them. I'll never have a chance to be with them—not even on Samhain, not even when I cross back to the Summerlands, myself. They'll be lost forever. Do you see?"

She could not read his expression. "I'll do my best, Nessa." He leaned over and coaxed her mouth to his. The kiss was gentle, sweet, without last night's insistence. "I swear."

Her eyes filled with tears, but she blinked the tears away. No matter what happened, the memory of last night would remain, bright and shiny and etched forever in the fabric of herself. But she was no fool, and she had to know if what her instincts told her was true. So she swallowed down her tears and leaned into his kiss with everything she had.

Without another word, he swung his long legs over the edge of the bed and began to pull on the clothes he'd discarded so carelessly. When he was dressed, he knelt beside her and cupped her face between his hands, as if committing her features to memory. "Come back to me," she whispered. "Come back, and bring my parents home."

"I'll try," was all he said. And then he was gone.

She dragged herself out of bed and dabbed at the moisture seeping between her thighs. As she slowly dressed, she knew she not only understood more of what Molly had tried to tell her, she knew what she wanted more than she had ever wanted anything, more than she'd ever wanted her mother or father or Griffin, what she wanted with a fierce and desperate ache. She wanted Artimour to come back.

Sunlight tickled the back of Cecily's lids as she stirred, sniffed, then sneezed so violently it brought her upright. A fresh breeze blew a carrion stench full in her face as she looked around what appeared to be a clearing in a blackthorn thicket for fat purple sloes nestled among the dark green clumps of dew-laced leaves. And then she remembered where she was.

Kian lay beside her on an improvised pine-bough bed, his face pale, his flesh still damp to the touch. She pulled away the cloak and saw that he was still naked, and that the hastily applied bandages were dark with crusted blood. The slash to his upper right back was fortunately not much more than a flesh wound, but the injury to his thigh was more serious. The sword had bit deep into the meaty part of his thigh, slicing all the way to the bone. He'd lost a lot of blood and that was the wound which worried her. She replaced the bandages and closed the edges of his cloak together, then rose to her feet, dragging her plaid around her, following the smell of a fire and the snap of burning wood. When she peered around the thicket, she saw that it was part of a low dell, surrounded by oaks and ashes. Their low branches formed a shelter over the clearing, and two knights tended a small fire, over which a small iron cauldron steamed. The day was cold but clear, and the fire beckoned as a draft rushed up her bare legs. She shivered as she held her plaid closer to her throat and stepped around the thicket into view.

At once, the two knights, Tuavhal and Neven, whose name she always remembered because of the lush black mustaches he cultivated so lovingly, were on their feet. "Your Grace, how fares Kian?" asked Neven.

"He lives," she replied. He had to live. The possibility that she could lose him now, just at the very beginning of things, seemed like the ultimate injustice. But it was more than that. Kian was a natural leader, an able and respected warrior whose very presence by her side addressed what would surely be the most obvious objection to her claim. Without Kian, who would ride into battle in her stead, and who would direct her strategy? Without Kian, her kin would jockey among themselves for the privilege. That alone could cause enough infighting to destroy whatever alliance she was able to build. "Where are we? How far from some sort of shelter?"

The knight exchanged a glance with his companion, then nodded into the distance where the purplish hills lay behind the white veil of morning mist. "There's no way to say for sure. The bridge across the river's destroyed. We have to go farther upstream to find a way across, so if we're lucky, we'll reach Killcarrick tomorrow. If not, we'll try and find another place to shelter. But the horses were spent after last night—"

"Wait a minute," Cecily said. "Are you telling me there's only the four of us?"

Again the two men exchanged glances. "There were more of the ArchDruid's men waiting for us at the top of the trail, Your Grace."

Tuavhal continued in a low voice. "There may be some that lost us in the dark. They know to look for us, to rally with us at Killcarrick."

"Assuming we reach there ourselves," Neven finished.

"What do you mean?" she asked sharply.

"We don't know how long that enchantment on the granny lasted, Your Grace. We don't know what Kestrel might send after us once he realizes he doesn't have you. We probably pushed it a bit far last night. But we wanted to get as much distance as we could."

Again, a gust of wind blew a foul odor into her face, and unbelievably, the sound of a child crying. "What's that?" asked Cecily. "Is that a baby I hear? And that smell—"

"That smell is the garrison," Neven replied. "Or what's left of it."

"It's that bad?" She tried not to breathe through her nose as she held her cold hands over the fire.

"It's that bad," Tuavhal said. "As for the baby, yes, there's a band of refugees, mostly children, just around the bend of that thicket."

Curious and concerned, Cecily marched around the huge blackthorn thicket, and stopped, shocked, at the sight. In the center of the blackthorn thicket, a ragged group of mostly children, none, as far as she could tell older than twelve or thirteen, crouched around two carts, in which two harried and bedraggled women nursed four infants, and a tired granny offered a bowl to each of the older children in turn. "Granny?" Cecily tried.

"Your Grace?" The granny turned, spat a wad of cud-wort on the ground and wrapped an arm around a smudge-faced child who startled and screamed at Cecily's appearance.

At once Cecily knelt down among the children. "Yes. I'm Cecily. And you, Granny? And all you children—where are you from and where are you going?"

"M'name's Sorsha, my lady. As for where we're from, all over these parts, really. My girls and I—we took the carts yesterday morning and have been picking up babies and young ones too small for the goblins to want. There's a couple wounded in the other cart, there, but I don't think they're likely to live. We stopped here the night. I gathered the sloes and have made up a brew. You're welcome to some for the knight." She held out a crude clay pot.

"Thank you, Granny," Cecily said, wondering at the generosity. She could not abandon these kind women to their fate—nor the children, who stared up at her with huge hungry eyes and pale frightened faces. "Wait here." Once back at their own camp, Cecily said, "Cadwyr's still another day away. We'd better press on, for we surely can't stay here and neither can those poor people."

The knights exchanged glances and Neven said, "I'm not sure that's a good idea, my lady. We can travel faster on our own."

"But they have carts. Kian cannot travel on a horse, and we cannot leave those people to whatever fate awaits them. Besides—" A flash of metal and movement along the opposite shore caught her eye. "What's that?" she asked softly, pointing.

Tuavhal looked around as Neven half rose. "It's a company riding along the opposite shore—heading for the bridge, no doubt. They don't know it's no longer there."

"Whose boys are they, Nev?" asked Tuavhal as he peered across the river.

"Uplanders, from the coast, I think—don't know the plaids, but see the horses? Those shaggy ponies? Keep the horses quiet, Tully," said Neven as he doused the fire and gestured for Cecily to retreat into the blackthorn thicket. There were about fifty riders, she saw, surrounding eight wagons that were covered in bleached canvas, lashed down with thick ropes.

"What do you suppose they've got?" asked Neven. The riders were in tight formation, along both sides of the wagon train, clearly protecting the contents.

"I don't know," said Tuavhal.

"Look at their armor," whispered Cecily. There was no mistaking silver's white gleam in the morning sun. "Their mail, their spurs, even—look at the edge of that ax as it gleams—"

"Those are all Cadwyr's kin up that way, you know," said Neven. "All Cadwyr's kin."

As Cecily watched, she could hear the distant rumble of the wagons, the pounding of the hoofbeats. "What do you suppose they'll do when they realize the bridge is destroyed?"

The knights exchanged glances. "Depending on where they're headed ultimately, they may turn right around and try to cross at the very place we will."

"Then we'd better get moving, don't you think?" Cecily asked.

"Any kin of Cadwyr is likely on the way to Gar—"

"But we can't be sure of that." Cecily got to her feet. "We'd better get on our way."

As the two men dispersed to get the horses, Cecily bent over Kian and touched his forehead. The glistening sloes caught her eye again, and she picked a few of the fattest. Mag made brews of these to stop internal bleeding. Kian's nostrils looked pinched and gray, a look she had become all too familiar with in the last few weeks, the look men wore when the Marrihugh laid her staff upon them and marked them for her own. Another stab of fear went through her. *No, you won't have him yet, you black-hearted bitch-hound,* she whispered to herself. *No, and no and no. All I say three times shall be, as I will so let it be. So no and no and no again.*

But nothing answered her.

Then she realized that one of the knights had asked her a question, and both stood waiting her reply.

"Will moving kill him, do you think?" Tuavhal repeated.

"The granny shared some tonic with me. That and letting him lie in the cart is about as much as we can do right now. The leg wound's deep. But he's not feverish and that's a good sign." She touched Kian's forehead. Still cool, still damp. "Not yet," she whispered. *Not yet,* the alien voice echoed. And again, Cecily felt a ripple of cold run down her spine as the same words echoed once more through her mind, reverberating like the peal of a great bell all the way to the marrow of her bones. *Not yet.*

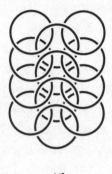

5

"**Y**ou *are* Gloriana, are you not?" Delphinea repeated as she rose unsteadily to her feet. Every sidhe-child knew the stories of the Witch within the Wood. But to discover that the so-called witch was really Gloriana and that the tales, which were presented as ancient and enduring, were relatively recent inventions, rocked the foundations on which her perception of reality was based. Of course Petri hated her. No wonder he'd bolted. But now what? *Never trust a trixie.* Dougal's words echoed in her mind and she felt a pang of disquiet.

"Who sent you?" the Queen demanded, her tone at once imperious and suspicious. "It wasn't Timias, was it? Or was it the Council? Was it Vinaver? He hasn't killed her, has he? How many soldiers did you bring? Are they out killing the wolves?"

"There are no soldiers," Delphinea said. The Queen's questions flooded over her, leaving her feeling uneasy and adrift. "There's only me." There's only me now, she thought. There was simply no way Petri could've survived that wolf pack. She swallowed back the tears that threatened to spill down her face. There would be plenty of time to grieve later. *Assuming you can keep your wits about you now and get out of here alive.*

"Only you?" echoed the blind Queen, bewilderment replacing frustration on her face. "And *who* exactly are you?"

"M-my name is Delphinea of the House of Light and Stone, and my mother is Eponea, Lady of the High Mountains, Hereditary HorseMis—"

"Hereditary HorseMistress to the Queen—I know exactly who she is. 'Twas I who gave her that title. 'Twas I who named you, Delphinea. Delphinea, I called you, because your eyes were the color of the delphiniums that were blooming in my bower. I told her to keep you away from Court, but she sent you, anyway, did she? So go on, girl. What's happened in Faerie that Eponea has sent you away?"

"I—I haven't been sent away. I've been sent to fetch Finuviel from the Shadowlands—"

"Fetch who?"

She doesn't know who Finuviel is, realized Delphinea. She looked over her shoulder. There was nothing she could do to help Petri, but perhaps, there might be something Gloriana could do to help her. "This is a long story, Your Majesty."

"Well, child." The Queen rapped her staff on the flagstone floor and pointed to a chair beside the hearth. "Sit down. The one thing Timias left me with was time. I'll make you a bargain. Tell me all I wish to know, and then I will tell you who you are."

"What do you mean, who I am?" Delphinea sank down into the chair, gripping the arms warily.

"My turn first," said the Queen. She turned her head and Delphinea had the eerie sensation that Gloriana could really see her. "What made your mother bring you to Court?"

"How did you know something happened?" Delphinea asked.

"Because she swore to me she would never let you come to Court. Your eyes made it clear you weren't like the others."

"Not like what others?" asked Delphinea, completely bewildered.

"The other sidhe, of course. There are none with eyes like yours. Are there?"

Delphinea could only shake her head as Gloriana beckoned. With a tentative hand, Gloriana felt her way across Delphinea's face, over the bridge of her nose, up the arch of her brow, over her forehead, down and around the curve of her chin. Her fingers danced lightly through Delphinea's hair, felt the knotted, tangled lengths, caressed her smooth cheek with the back of her brittle hand. "Begin at the beginning."

Haltingly, Delphinea described the discoveries of the rotting calves and foals that had spread to the wild animal, her arrival at Court and introduction to the Council and finally, the last frenetic days since the discovery that the Caul was missing, leading up to the desperate decision that she should go to find Finuviel. The Queen interrupted her a few times, interjecting a question, adding a comment, dismissing a conclusion. At last Delphinea paused and said, "And that's the last I saw of Petri, when half the pack took off after him." She blinked away a tear and Gloriana gave a snort.

"Don't fret yourself about that one. The *khouri-keen* are

ever more clever than mortals and go to ground very quickly. He may well have led you here in order to rid himself of *you*."

"Petri would not do—"

Gloriana leaned forward. "You don't know what he'd do. Mortals despise them, you know. Never trust a trixie, they say. Shouldn't they be the ones to know?"

"But—but he took me to the Forest House—"

Gloriana shook her head. "What was my daughter thinking to send a lamb like you? She's got it wrong—I thought I could trust her to hear the trees—"

"She can't hear the trees. She says that since the Hag took her womb, she can't hear them as well—"

"What?" Gloriana raised her face. "You did not tell me that."

"I—I didn't think it necessary to tell you—"

"Spare me nothing, child. Now more of it makes sense." She took a deep breath and buried her face in her hands and Delphinea could feel nothing but pity for the ancient Queen. At last she raised her face. "Now I see what's happening. Vinaver has it wrong. Well, we'll have to do what we can to make it right, won't we? I have something I must give you—something Vinaver doesn't even know exists, clearly. And Timias—you must tell her—he has the oak staff—the staff from which the fire to unMake the Caul must be kindled—together with the holly wand—the holly wand—" She broke off, and leaned on her staff. "There is no holly wand. The holly wand is dead."

"Alemandine has a wand—"

"Yes, of course she does, but it's just a dead stick—the berries don't glow. They stopped glowing when we made the Caul."

"Glowing like this?" asked Delphinea as she removed the stick, the berries glowing a soft pink.

"What do you have there, child?" asked the Queen sharply. She cocked her head and wrinkled her nose and beckoned with a frantic hand. "Wh-what are you holding?"

"A holly stick. I found it in the wood. The berries began to glow—" And even as she spoke the words, the end of the old song ran through her mind, lines that had never made the slightest bit of sense before: *When the berry glows, the holly knows the Queen of Faerie comes.* "It began to glow as soon as I touched a tree, and pricked my finger on the leaves and—the hollies all began to glow."

There was a long silence, and in the firelight, a tear crept down Gloriana's cheek. "Well, child. Maybe there's hope, after all. I did not expect to hear you say that. Come, now, I'll honor my part of the bargain. Your mother never told you, did she? That she's not your mother at all?"

Delphinea sank back onto her knees, feeling as if the old Queen had punched her in the chest. "What do you mean, she's not my mother? What—what are you talking about? Of course she's my mother—I—"

Somewhere outside the window, a lone wolf howled. "If I'd known then what I know now, I like to think I would've recognized what was happening. But that's the way it is, you see. No one had the wit to notice. Vinaver might've—if she'd been there. But she was young in those days, and I kept her at the Forest House, for no one would listen to her. Timias saw to that." Her eyelids fluttered over her sightless eyes.

"But if my mother isn't my mother, who is?"

"Well, we don't know. Not even Eponea knows. I'll tell you what I know, and then you're free to make up your mind."

"About what?"

"About who your mother is, child. Who your mother is, really. There's no one who can really say. It happened just after Beltane one year that Eponea came to Court. That alone was quite extraordinary, for we never saw her from Imbolc to Samhain. But what was more extraordinary is that she brought you. And you were unquestionably one of the most beautiful infants I'd ever seen, except of course for the fact your eyes were blue. And then she told the most extraordinary tale.

"It seemed that at Beltane the year before, an old woman had come to her door, just after twilight, and asked her for the service of her herd's best bull. And Eponea at first refused, of course, for the Beltane fires were just lit and the cattle had yet to be led between them—her attendants were all busy with the preparations. There was no one to see such a thing. But the old woman insisted, and at last she promised that if the offspring should be a heifer, she would bring her back next year for Eponea's herd. And so at last, weary of arguing, Eponea agreed that the old woman should have use of the bull immediately after he'd been led between the fires. And so the old woman and she were waiting when they led the bull to her, in the stable yard, for the mating. But it confused the attendants greatly that there didn't seem to be any evidence of a cow. The old woman shooed them away and of course they immediately told Eponea, who dismissed it as Beltane 'mazement. But the old woman had come back, just as she'd promised. But she left no heifer. She left you. Don't you understand? Your mother was the goddess herself."

Delphinea sat back, her hands clasped in her lap. And

Finuviel was the son of the god. Got on Vinaver. But her father? A bull? "My father—is a bull?"

"Foolish child. No one understands anymore. In the old days the god and goddess wandered freely through the land, choosing guises as they would. The bull, the old woman, were merely the guises they chose to wear."

"But—but for what purpose?"

The Queen leaned down and touched her hair, running her fingers through the dark silky strands. "To bind you to the earth, child, to connect you to the ever-flowing source of richness and abundance. No matter what we did, Timias and I, foolish, vain sidhe that we were. The great wheel turns no matter which way we think to will it. That's what we did not see. So blind we were, so blind. As Vinaver, apparently, is deaf." Gloriana shook her head. "All right, child. I've told you what I know about who you are. Now, let me tell you what I know about how the Caul was made. Three made it, three must unMake it— and those three must be the opposite of those that made it." The Queen leaned forward and tilted Delphinea's face to hers, and she had the uncanny sense the Queen could really see her. She wondered how the Queen had lost her sight. "I've waited all this time, hoping the trees would tell her, hoping she would understand, and send someone at last—"

"Why couldn't you talk to the trees yourself? Why did they have to talk to Vinaver?"

"Don't you understand, child? That's what I gave to the Making of the Caul. From the moment of its Making, I could no longer speak to the trees." She sagged back against the chair, a faraway look on her face. "We did something no one had ever dared. And we were so terribly wrong. It seemed like such a wonderful idea."

"Tell me what I need to know," Delphinea whispered. "Please?"

"I can tell you this much—a mortal male will not unbind the magic. She needs a mortal *woman* with the skill of a smith—the opposite of what was used to bind the magic—do you see?"

"A mortal woman with the skill of a blacksmith? Where are we supposed to find that?"

"I can't tell you everything, child, but I will tell you what I can. Listen carefully, for Vinaver has it wrong. On the night the Caul was made, three energies were bound into the Caul. An opposite configuration of the energies must be present to unMake it, but that's not all. The crystals of the *khouri-keen*—their eggs, their essences—which have been held within the marble pillar on which the moonstone rests—" The Queen broke off as Delphinea shook her arm to slow the torrent of information.

"The crystals which bind the gremlins are stored within that column?"

"They must be returned—" Gloriana continued. Delphinea remembered the crack within the column, the brown, seeping stain that indicated rot. *Never trust a trixie.*

"They—these crystals—they contain something of the gremlins' essential nature?"

"Child, what are you implying?"

"When I noticed the Caul was missing, Your Majesty, I saw something—poisonous seeping from the column. Something rotten."

"That's why the Caul must be destroyed, child. It taints

everything it touches. Here. You'll need this. Timias did not take as much from me as he thought he did." She fumbled beneath her chair, and her pale golden hair spilled like foam on the flagstones, whispered like a mantle of leaves over the floor. So perfectly ethereal still, she was, thought Delphinea, even blind and old and sick. She held out a bag. It was covered in black feathers. "Take it," she whispered. "Take it." As Delphinea reached for it, she said, "Wash this in the spring that comes up from the rock beneath the Caul Chamber, and the spell of masking shall be unbound."

"What is it really?" asked Delphinea. It felt like the loose skin of a bird, and she realized that that was exactly what it was, a bag, apparently made out of raven's hide.

"It's a cauldron Timias dipped in the Hag's brew when he took the moonstone," Gloriana whispered. "It's the only thing in all of Faerie that can hold the silver as it melts. You'll need it." She leaned forward. "But it belongs to the Hag. She'll be wanting it back. Remember that Timias will do whatever he can to stop you." She drew a deep breath. "But now we come to our more immediate problem. The wolves are still out there. Timias set them there, to make sure I never leave. I cannot go beyond the clearing. Nor can you."

"But I must," said Delphinea. "You know I must."

"Yes, child. Of course you do. But there's only one way to do that." She looked outside, where the first rays of the dawn were flooding through the russet canopy onto the leaf-littered clearing. A raven shrieked and a flock alighted as the light strengthened. "It's morning now. By day they'd see us both. So we'll wait til dusk."

"For what?" asked Delphinea slowly, warily.

"For an opportunity for you to escape. At dusk, when the

shadows are thickening, and the clearing is dark, I'll go first, and at my signal, you will run in the direction which I will tell you, while I—"

"But you could be torn to pieces," said Delphinea, horrified. "No, surely there's another way—Vinaver's cloak of shadows—" She fell on her knees beside Gloriana and picked up the old Queen's hand. It was like clay, she thought, the sort of satiny clay that dried to fine powder. A puff of wind and it would be gone, and she remembered the way the bodies of the silver-slain soldiers had dispersed when the light fell upon their flesh.

Gloriana only patted her cheek, her expression unreadable in the shadows. "It was no help to you, child, don't you remember? The wolves don't hunt by sight—they hunt by scent. That cloak is effective against mortals, perhaps. But the wolves can smell you, I'm sure, even in here." She drew another deep breath and let it out in a long sigh. "Don't fret. My time was over long ago. And there's no other way. I, too, am a link that binds the Caul. When I am gone, another link, at least, shall be undone and only Timias will remain."

"But you don't know—" Delphinea began, her voice breaking. "How can you really be sure? Has anyone else ever come here—maybe they're only meant to go after you."

There was a long pause in which Gloriana let her remember last night. Then she said, "Try it, if you don't believe me."

Without another word, Delphinea jumped to her feet and threw her long skirts over her arm. She strode to the door and threw it open. A low warning growl sounded the moment her foot stepped over the threshold. On the opposite side of the clearing, the wolves were clustered in a pack, lying over each other like a pile of big rocks. But as she took another step over the threshold, they immediately re-arranged themselves into sitting sentries. She put her foot on the second step, and the biggest wolf threw back his head and howled. The others stared at her with hard, unshakable eyes and began to drool. Whatever Petri was or had become, he had not deserved such a terrible death. She slammed the door shut with a shaking hand, and Gloriana beckoned her close once more. "Come, child. Let's sit together, and I shall tell you stories of happier times than these."

"Where's that stink coming from, Hudibras?" Lord Philomemnon of the Southern Archipelago pressed his face against the small grille in the door of his Tower prison, and spoke through clenched teeth, even as beside him, Lord Berillian of the Western Reach, the first of Alemandine's Council to be imprisoned, passed him a linen square dampened with lavender water. "It's intolerable. What's Timias doing about it?"

"Nothing," Hudibras moaned. He leaned against the door frame, then startled back as the magical ward set around the door to keep the two councilors from escaping sparked a warning. He looked over his shoulder, out the door which led to the stairwell, as if he feared that guards with drawn swords would charge up the steps at any moment. He placed the back of one hand against his white forehead, as if the weight of his own head was suddenly too heavy to bear, and Philomemnon found himself suddenly riveted not so much by the way the double cuffs of foamy lace fell from the sleeves of his turquoise doublet in precisely perfect folds.

He forced himself to concentrate as Hudibras continued, "Timias—Timias isn't—Timias isn't doing *anything*. No one's even *seen* Timias since he went in to speak to Alemandine. And as for the smell—well, we all know it's terrible. We all know—we all smell it." He shook his head and closed his eyes against a sudden tide of tears that spilled down his cheeks like raindrops, and Philomemnon found himself captivated by the sheen of sunlight on Hudibras's burnished curls. "Everyone tells me that we're doing all we can, but all I see anyone do is dance and pretend they can't smell it. And I think it's that smell making my dear Alemandine sick."

"The Queen's still abed?" Berillian pushed Philomemnon aside. "Then what's that music we hear? And what about Vinaver? She was supposed to be back here before Samhain—"

"Oh, she'll be here soon enough—Timias sent a whole regiment after her—her and Delphinea both. And as for what's going on, don't you think I'd tell you if I could?" Hudibras sank to the floor, below the level of the grille. Philomemnon had to press his cheek to the door to see Hudibras reach into his scabbard and withdraw not the dagger one might expect, but instead, a large peacock-feather fan. He snapped it open and waved the brilliant blue-green feathers back and forth before his reddened face. "Round about the circle goes—dark to light and back it flows. Can't you feel it spinning?" He gave a little sob, extracted a large white linen square from somewhere deep inside his turquoise-studded doublet and blew his nose loudly. "The more things stay the same, the less they are the way they were before. Timias has set a ward upon the Queen's entire suite and now no one can get anywhere near the Queen. No one even knows how long ago. The clocks run backward, then forward, the hourglasses run down, then up. No one's even sure what day it is." His voice dissolved in a series of shuddering sobs.

"Backward? Where's your brother?" asked Philomemnon. "Hudibras, get off the floor and look at me. Where's Gorlias? And Rimbaud and Evardine? What about Commander Morais? Why hasn't someone set the Palace Guard to do something?"

It seemed to take an inordinate amount of effort for Hudibras to drag himself to his feet. "Morais has correctly pointed out that we have not been attacked. And as for everyone else—they're all—all of them—well, that is, most of them—" Hudibras drew a deep shuddering sigh, raised his eyes and pressed his lips together even as his eyes flooded again with tears. "They're dancing."

"Dancing?" Philomemnon looked at Berillian, who shrugged. "What do you mean? Are you telling me that the Revel yet continues?"

Hudibras shrugged, looked over his shoulder and turned back with a helpless little moan. "On and on. Around and around." Great tears rolled down his cheeks and stained the intricate embroidery on the collar of his shirt. "It hasn't stopped for days."

But Philomemnon could only stare at the fan. "Why do you carry a fan in place of a dagger?" Suddenly it troubled him that he was acutely aware of the subtle change in hue as Hudibras's tears darkened the color of the delicate candle-wicking. *A touch more blue to bring the turquoise out.* A shiver went down his spine as he realized how susceptible they all were. *Has the entire Court gone mad?*

Philomemnon wasn't aware he had spoken aloud until Hudibras answered, "Quite possibly. I'm beginning to think so. So I've come to get you out." Hudibras dragged himself up, mopped his face, then thrust the linen back into his doublet. He furled his fan and replaced it in the sheath. He took a deep breath, closed his eyes, shook his head as if to clear it, then came so close that all they could see was his smile through the grille. "You see, don't you, my dear friends? My dear cousins? We *are* cousins, did you know that? I had the genealogies drawn for Alemandine, but she didn't seem to care. Alemandine never actually seems to care about anything, have you noticed? I think she lives for Vinaver's possets. So it's up to us to do something, don't you see?"

"What exactly do you think we can do?" Berillian's fat chestnut-colored curls suddenly clogged Philomemnon's nose as he stuck his face in front of the grille. As Philomemnon pushed the mass of silky hair out of his face, Berillian swept around and looked at him. "And how, stuck in here?"

"We're going to go through that mirror—" Hudibras pointed to the opposite wall with his fan. "Someone has to find out where this stink is coming from—" He broke off and sniffed. "And make it stop. That's what's making Alemandine so sick. That's why she can't leave her bed. That's what's making everyone so miserable and so strange. It's this wretched smell and no one will *do* anything about it. But if we go through the mirrors—"

Philomemnon leaned against the door frame and felt a warning tingle from the door-ward. "How do you expect us to get out? Can't you feel the ward on this door? The guard who set it knew what he was doing. Both of us have been over it a dozen times, and we can't get it to budge."

"I came prepared." Hudibras reached inside his doublet and withdrew a slim beech wand topped with a sky-blue topaz.

Philomemnon frowned. "Hudibras, when was the last time you worked any magic beyond changing the color of your doublet?"

"It will be fine," he hissed, mopping away his tears, and stuffed his kerchief back inside his doublet. "I've been building this spell for days—well, I think it's been days. Seemed like it, anyway. See how the light is coming in just behind me?" He gestured over his gorgeously padded and jeweled shoulder. Rainbows danced over his face, reflected from the intricate knot-work of tiny gems on his padded shoulders. He placed one palm flat on the door and aimed the wand just below the grille, so that light refracted and focused through the tip.

In that very same moment, Philomemnon saw what Hudibras had failed to consider. The gems on the shoulders of his doublet—tiny crystals of aquamarine and diamond and pale blue topaz—also concentrated the sunlight, charging the tip with more energy than Hudibras realized. Philomemnon grabbed Berillian's shirt and pulled him back, even as a fireball of light exploded and the entire door splintered into javelin-sized shards that smoked and spat black ash. It singed the edges of his hair, and the rank aroma in the air was replaced by the odor of burning flesh and fabric. He waved the white smoke away and staggered toward the door, to see Hudibras sprawled out on the floor, a long spear of charred wood pinning him through the right side of his neck. "Great Hag," Philomemnon whispered. "Hudibras—" Behind him, Berillian gave a low moan, and Philomemnon turned in horror to see that Berillian's right hand was a burned and bloody mess. He'd used it to shield his face when the door had exploded.

With gritted teeth, Berillian lurched forward. "Hudibras, you fool," he managed through clenched teeth. "Look what you've done."

"Go." Hudibras's voice was a mangled gurgle through the fountain of pale pink blood that pulsed from the wound and spilled down his neck. For a long ghastly moment, Philomemnon was transfixed as it stained the pale blue embroidery a sickly violet. "Go." Hudibras writhed and scrabbled at his hip, and from his scabbard withdrew his peacock fan. He pressed it into Philomemnon's hand as more blood fountained up and soaked his chin in a gush. "Go."

As if from far away, Philomemnon heard doors slam and distant shouts. "What do you think I—" But even as he spoke, the fan stretched and reformed into a golden dagger, the hilt set with turquoise and onyx in such a way as to resemble a peacock's feathers. "Ah." He met Hudibras's pain-wracked eyes. From the bottom of the stairs, they could hear the heavy tramp of the guards' booted feet.

Berillian stumbled forward, and with his uninjured hand, picked up a long piece of wood. He spun it experimentally, and a fork of lightning crackled off the tip, singeing a black mark in the arched ceiling. His face was pocked with drops of sweat the size of hailstones.

"What are you doing?" Philomemnon gripped his uninjured arm. "We've got to—"

"You go—"

"But—"

"I can't get through the mirror like this and we've not the time to heal it. I was never much good at mirror magic. I can hold them off, give you a chance. And besides—" He gestured at the floor where Hudibras writhed and quivered like a felled stag.

He's going to kill him. The unthinkable thought paralyzed Philomemnon for a split second longer, and Berillian gave him a shove. "Go!"

He ran down the corridor just as the first guards emerged from the stairway arch, and jumped feetfirst through the gilt-edged frame, launching himself into that gray and shadowy dimension that existed behind every mirror in Faerie. As he fell, he caught a glimpse of Berillian's reflection as he drove his makeshift spear into Hudibras's heart, and behind them, the flash of the guards' weapons.

He landed with a hard thump on the floor below. Faint and far away he heard an agonized shriek and the splintering of glass. In the sudden silence, Philomemnon knew that Berillian, too, was quite possibly dead. It was only a matter of a few moments that they'd be after him, but he was forced to pause and consider which way to go.

Light filtered in at odd angles, reflected beams that changed as the sun moved across the sky, altering the dimensions of the space so that it expanded and shrank with the amount of light. The air inside the mirrors was stagnant with the stench. It was like immersing oneself in a pool of rotting water, and he wondered how he knew that. Nothing in Faerie ever rotted. At least, it never had before.

He forced himself to think of the task at hand. Within the mirrors, left was right, and right was left. As long as he remembered that, he had some chance of navigating through the mirrors' murky maze. But where to go? Not to his own chambers—that was surely the first place the guards would look.

First to the Queen, he thought. First to find out why Timias had set a ward about her entire suite of rooms. Poor Hudibras might have been infected with whatever madness now gripped most of the Court, but in his last coherent moments he'd been able to piece together some kind of plan. Philomemnon hoped he could stay sane long enough to accomplish at least as much.

For he could feel a wild chaotic energy slipping like tentacles around the edges of the mirror, sinuous as the rays of light that streamed around the squares of glass, seeking any channel, any outlet, heedless of focus or intent. Here, behind the mirrors, he was somewhat inured against it, as if the glass itself blocked most of it. But the concentrated stench was so putrid he could feel his gorge rising in his throat. *A fine choice, indeed—stay here and drown in stink, or go mad.* Resolutely, he worked his way through the twisted angles, up and over walls bent at odd angles, in what he hoped was the direction of the Queen's chambers, listening intently for any sounds of possible pursuit.

Without warning a lady's face appeared in one of the mirrors, and he startled back, dismayed yet transfixed. Delicately, deliberately, using two pale pink fingertips, she was systematically removing every eyebrow, every eyelash, until her face resembled a bloated moon, punctuated only by the valleys of her eye sockets, the high thin bridge of her nose, the pink slash of her mouth. Nausea churned his stomach as she bent her neck and removed her hair, peeling it away in one continuous sweep, leaving the bare white dome of her head. A faint melody, bright and lilting, permeated the miasma and he realized he was somewhere near the Great Hall.

She leaned forward and smiled at her reflection. As he watched in horror, she began to stroke her face with light, almost feathery touches, and as she stroked, black feathers, bluish and glossy, began to cover her face. But when she pulled her nose forward into a raven's beak, it broke the spell and he turned and fled, stumbling through the shadows, heedless of whether or not anyone might hear.

He slowed as the music swelled to a cacophonous crescendo and peered over his shoulder, for the music masked any other noise. On gentle feet, he eased past the huge mirrors that lined each side of the Hall, mirrors that not only sent floods of light into the dimension behind the mirrors, but also allowed any so inclined to see readily inside.

The tendrils of energy were thicker here, coiling like invisible snakes, and he felt himself drawn inextricably to a mirror, and before he realized what he was doing, he pressed his face to the surface of the glass itself and stared, riveted by the fantastic spectacle parading before him. The music's wrong was his first thought, and then he realized that the masked and costumed dancers weren't wearing masks or costumes at all. All of them had altered themselves into the semblance of animals of every cast—stags and hounds and birds of every description. Here, a lady spotted like a cow smiled up at a lord whose peacock feathers fanned out above his head, and there a lion danced with a lamb. The mottled light cast the faces of those who still resembled sidhe in parchment's brittle yellow.

The kaleidoscopic chaos swirled by, a discordant mix of

hue and scent, sound and texture that flashed and blared and spun, its impact perceptible even behind the glass. We'll all be taken up by it, he thought. The odor of jasmine, followed by lemon, blasted through the glass, and the effect was even more nauseating, if possible, than the foul aroma itself. He clapped a hand over his mouth and backed away, even as a voice from somewhere very close cried, "There he is."

The scent of lilies and clove exploded under his nose, wrenching him out of his reverie, and he looked over his shoulder to see green doublets and drawn swords. They'd found him.

Led by little more than instinct, he took off, followed closely by the thump of running feet and the clatter of weapons close behind. Maybe Hudibras was right. Maybe it was the foul stench that was affecting them so. He veered close to the Queen's quarters and was startled by the blast of energy from the ward around her suite. It sent him sprawling, tumbling down the shadowy reflection of a staircase. He lay, stunned. Timias must have set the ward from *behind* the mirror, which meant that he had left, leaving the Queen alone. Where could he have gone? Why would he prevent anyone from reaching Alemandine, in her condition, unless—perhaps he'd taken her somewhere? He slowly got to his feet, and as he rose, sniffing, he realized that the lower down he went, the stronger the smell. He ducked out of the nearest mirror and found himself in a small cloakroom off one of the entrances to the kitchens.

The angry face of one of his pursuers popped out of the mirror behind him and he took off once more through the deserted kitchens, following the stench down and down and down, until at last he stumbled down a narrow winding stair that led from the wine cellars into the gremlins' quarters in the very lowest reaches of the vast palace.

He paused to catch his breath, realizing he'd managed to lose his pursuers, at least for the moment, and looked around, taking stock of his surroundings. How bizarre, he thought. It appeared to be a narrow network of small grottoes hewn out of the bedrock beneath the palace. Their beds appeared to be no more than piles of earth surrounded by more rocks. What an amazingly strange way to sleep, he thought. He had never once before given any thought at all to how the gremlins lived. And, where, come to think of it, were they now?

He dodged behind a jagged outcropping as he heard footsteps overhead. At once a torch flared to life behind him. The wet miasma of stench seemed to cling to the rocks like a layer of oily grease. He heard the voices of the guards above him, arguing that they'd no need to go down there, they'd only need set a patrol around the entrances to the gremlins' quarters.

A shower of rocks near his shoulder made him look up. Another cascade of fine pebbles and showery sand nearly blinded him. Now what? he wondered. Could it be that the very foundations of the Palace were collapsing?

Another rock tumbled down, almost hitting his head, and this time the stench was unmistakable. He picked up the rock and noticed it was wet and covered with frothy slime. This is where that stink is coming from, he thought.

He could still hear the guards arguing above him. A blast of air, hot and fetid, hit his cheek, and he realized that it was coming from a small crevice just above his head. The stink was nearly unbearable here, and he could hear something that sounded like a combination of both gnawing and growling. Just a handspan above his face, he saw a rock move. Was something behind the wall? He kicked a few rocks from the nearest bed, piled them up and climbed on top, leaning into the wall to maintain his balance, trying to find an angle at which he could see.

He did not see the claw that swiped out his eye. He fell backward, his palm flat against the jellied smear within the socket, numb with shock, more overcome by the realization of what was causing the stench than pain. As he stumbled up the steps, heedless of capture, the only coherent thought that pounded through his head was *Goblins. That stench is goblins.* Let the guards kill him. They would all be dead soon, anyway. The goblins had found a way into the very center of Faerie, the place they all thought was safe.

He pulled himself up, feeling faint and weak, and as the guards surrounded him, he held up his one hand in surrender, while he kept the other pressed flat against his face. It didn't matter what they did to him. Was it his imagination or was the growling audible from where they stood? He sagged to the floor, overcome at last by the cloud of hot pain now blanketing his head. "Go...look...down there," he panted, fighting off the blackness that threatened to overwhelm him. Someone else had to see for themselves. "Go...look...be careful...they've got...claws—"

"Who has claws?" asked a voice on his left.

"Go look down there at what?" asked another.

"It's a trick, Sergeant, don't trust him—he's a councilor," interjected a third.

"You fool, can't you see he's bleeding?" There was the metallic sound of metal sliding over metal as a sword was sheathed, and then slim fingers gently lifted his chin, and Philomemnon met wary eyes as his chin was lifted. He felt the warmth of the torchlight on his face and horrified gasps from the guards now crowding close. "What did this to you, my lord?"

"Just go...look." Blackness enveloped him, soothing as a blanket, and his head fell back against the shoulder of the nearest guard. As if from very far away, he heard a shout and then the sound of booted feet pounding up the steps. He registered a few words, but enough to tell him the sergeant had seen for himself.

"Bring him...the Commander must... Now."

A pad of linen was thrust into Philomemnon's ruined eye socket, a linen strip hastily bound around his head. His head lolled against a guard's velvet chest as he was lifted, and he heard the man ask, "You mean to say the goblins are coming?"

"Oh no," Philomemnon managed. "They're already here."

What will happen if Faerie dies? Nessa's question echoed in Artimour's mind, triggering flashes of images from last night—the scent of her skin, the taste of her mouth, the texture of her hair—all making it more difficult than Artimour had ever imagined to leave her behind. The border was not as easily crossed as he expected, for it was as if a fine web of invisible filaments now stretched tenuously across it, not as solid as whatever spell of binding had blocked Nessa's return, but real enough to hinder his. There'd been some sort of corn magic worked last night, he remembered. Perhaps it was a hopeful sign that the mortals had a grasp of their own magic.

Or maybe it was that Faerie was already fading. That chilling thought spurred him on, and just as he was resigned to swim across the border, the first rays of sunlight, bursting above the trees, sliced like a dagger through the fragile magic, and allowed him to slip unheeded into Faerie. He emerged into an eerie stillness on the ancient road beside the River Afon, not far from where he'd been stabbed, that led directly to the ivory and crystal turrets of Alemandine's palace. The position of the sun told him in which direction to head, the slant of the light told him it was much later than dawn, maybe even late morning. White mist swirled over the ground between the moss-covered trees, drifting silent as the sprits of the dead on Samhain off the surface of the water. The hair rose on the back of his neck as he stared at the altered trees. Like their counterparts in Shadow, most now stood bare but for a few withering leaves that dangled from crooked branches like shreds of long-shed finery. Even the pines were tinged yellow and brown at the tips, as if they, too, were about to drop their needles.

This *is* Faerie, he reassured himself. He took a deep, experimental breath. The air itself was different from the danker atmosphere of Shadow—lighter, airier, more ethereal. *Not as real.* Out of nowhere, the thought intruded. *No,* he told himself. That way lies madness. Faerie is as real as the trunks of these elder-trees. And he would not think about what might happen if Faerie were to die.

He reached out, touched the nearest tree, ran his hand up and down its rough, ridged bark, felt the deep grooves channeled into the light brown bark. The branches drooped, heavy with fat bunches of black berries. He heard an odd sound, a swish, followed by a soft crunch, and turned to see a stag and three does, grazing. The sound was their hooves moving through the ankle-deep leaves.

The stag raised his head and looked at Artimour. Their eyes met, then the stag nudged the does. With a flick of white tails, the little herd turned and disappeared into the forest, and Artimour saw that their backs were covered in oozing sores. As he watched them leave, he noticed a huge oak tree, its trunk swollen and bloated, its bark stained with rivulets of some yellowish slime that foamed white as it touched the ground. A foul smell rose from the tree, a sickly-sweet odor that clogged his nose and clung to the back of his throat. He peered into the hollow of the tree, and saw, to his surprise, a dark bundle surrounded by a noxious bubbling liquid oozing out of the heartwood itself. Gingerly, he withdrew the bundle and flung it on the ground. He poked at it with a twig and gasped when he saw the bright silver edge. Surely it was the very dagger Finuviel had used to stab him, left within the tree. But why? Artimour wondered. Finuviel had stabbed him, then left the dagger here. If he'd intended to return for it...why hadn't he? Artimour rose to his feet, pondering, gazing back upstream, remembering the obvious marks of the host he'd seen along the river. He had originally thought the host had crossed the river for some inexplicable reason. Now he had a clearer understanding of the nature of Finuviel's bargain with Cadwyr. Finuviel had lent the host to Duke Cadwyr's cause. But where were they now? Still fighting with Cadwyr? How many battles was one silver dagger worth? And how long had Finuviel been planning to leave a silver dagger, no matter how well wrapped, inside a Faerie tree? What had he been thinking?

The silver had begun to rot the tree from the inside out and he was glad he'd decided to leave Nessa's sword in Shadow, even as the thought of Nessa triggered a memory of the smoky scent and salty taste of her skin above the steady pulse beating in the hollow of her throat. Had Finuviel understood what would happen to the tree? *Finuviel,* he thought. *Finuviel, what have you done? And why haven't you come to take your dagger?* This was the dagger Nessa made, he thought. He couldn't leave it here. It had already done enough damage. Perhaps he was fated to have a weapon of Nessa's by his side. He buckled the sheath to his belt and started off down the road with grim determination. Something was terribly wrong in Faerie. If he didn't discover what it was soon, and how to make it stop, all of his worst fears— and Nessa's—would be realized.

But he had not gone far when around a wide curve, an ornate coach and four came bearing down on him, driven at an amazing speed, even for the sidhe, who could cover great distances quickly. As Artimour jumped aside to get out of the way of the careening horses, he saw that the driver was barely in control, and he was braced against the block, in a manner most unseemly. His hat was all askew, his green velvet jacket half undone as if he'd jumped behind the reins in a hurry, and his white linen stock whipped around his face like a tail, his lace collar frothing beneath his chin.

There was something else odd, for the bridles were all entwined with green vines, vines that grew up and over and around the coach. As Artimour shaded his eyes to get a better look, the coachman caught sight of him. He struggled to bring the horses under control. "What are you doing here, mortal?" he cried as he fought the horses to a shuddering stop. Artimour stepped out from the shelter of the trees and looked up at the coachman. He recognized the intricate insignia on his sleeves as belonging to one of the Thirteen Noble Houses of the Court. "Coachman?"

But the coachman's face contorted in a rage, which in itself was odd, and he leaped from his perch, dragging Artimour down to the ground with hands wrapped around his neck. "What do you think you're doing here, mortal, standing in the way like that—"

"Don't you know me, Coachman?" asked Artimour, incredulous, even as he struggled to keep the coachman from strangling him.

At that moment, the coach doors opened and four be-winged ladies spilled out, dressed for what looked like some elaborate masquerade. One, in pink, sported pigs' ears; another, in white and black, a cow's snout; while a third's black-feathered wings arced like a raven's over her glossy feathered head. "Look, it's Artimour," one cried.

"Prince Artimour!" said another.

"Is it really you, Artimour?" said the bird-lady.

"It is Artimour," repeated one of the others.

"Yes, it's Artimour!" His name was taken up by a chorus that rose from both sides of the coach. Two more ladies, dressed in identical outfits of gray and salmon pink, wore scales that gleamed with opal iridescence on their wings and over the bridge of their noses.

"Don't you recognize Prince Artimour, Rodrigal?" The bird-lady stepped away from her companions and smiled up at him with all the predatory interest of a hawk.

"Amadahlia?" Her name rose effortlessly to his lips, thanks to an afternoon's dalliance, many, many seasons ago.

Her pale cheeks flushed the barest pink, and her dark lashes dipped low over her cheeks, but as she raised her eyes to his, he saw fear not flirtation.

Before he could ask what was wrong, the lady with the cow's mask poked her in the back. "We've not the time to dally, Amadahlia, get back in the coach."

Amadahlia turned on her with a squawk that sounded alarmingly birdlike and Artimour saw she was wearing tight black silk that extended all the way over the backs of her hands, leaving only her fingers exposed. "Where are you all going?" he asked. "Is this some sort of picnic or parade? Why are you all dressed like this—"

"It's what's been happening to us," Amadahlia choked. "It started as a—as a game, as a pastime but now—" she held up her arm "—I can't take it off."

He looked at her arm, at the other ladies crowding close, and realized with a pang of horror that these were not at all elaborate costumes but some strange metamorphosis that affected each of them differently. "We're going to Vinaver— she was supposed to be back with herbs for the Queen's possets, but she's left and Alemandine won't let anyone in to her chambers and Timias has put a spell of binding on the whole suite and the Palace is—"

"And the goblins are attacking—" put in one of the fish women.

The chatter of their voices rose to a dizzying pitch, and Artimour looked at the coachman, who was watching him with eyes narrowed with suspicion. Automatically, he felt in his belt for the silver dagger. "What goblins?"

"The ones at the Palace. What I've been trying to tell you, if my sisters would only stop chattering like magpies."

Amadahlia turned her huge eyes up to Artimour, sidled closer and laid her hand on his arm. He looked down and saw that the nails were shrinking, dwindling, into hard little bony lengths. Like claws. Another pang of nausea rose in his gorge, and he swallowed hard.

"Tell me again," he managed, fingering the silver dagger, cursing Finuviel silently. "Tell me where you are going. One at a time."

"We're going to the Forest House to fetch Vinaver. Because the Queen—" Amadahlia's eyes filled with tears and she broke off.

"Because the Queen," squealed the pink-gowned lady with the pig's ears. "The Queen has taken to her bed and now Timias has cast a spell around her and no one can get in."

"And the goblins—?" began Artimour, trying to comprehend everything all at once, even as the sheer implausibility struck him like a physical blow in the chest.

It was the driver who answered, leaning down to get a better look at Artimour's face. "They tunneled in through the gremlins' quarters, treacherous little scags that they are. We'd been smelling something since Samhain, but no one remembered what a goblin smelled like. They've already overrun nearly a quarter of the Palace, but the sunrise stopped them and sent them back below the ground." His eyes were cold and drained of color, so that instead of some customary shade of green, they appeared gray and empty. "There's only one Councilor left, and he's doing what he can."

"We must have the Queen's magic," said Amadahlia.

"And a full company of the Palace Guard was sent to arrest her, but they've not come back," continued the pig-eared lady. "And so we thought we'd better do something ourselves before it all changed—and the goblins were able to overcome the Queen—"

"Everything is different now," said Amadahlia, looking up at Artimour.

"It's all started to change," said Cow-snout.

"Like us," put in the ladies on the other side of the coach, their scales gleaming pink and gray in the sunlight.

Like me. Artimour felt a sweat break out on his forehead. He rubbed his hand across his chin and felt the growth of beard.

"And you—you do look very—very mortal," said Amadahlia.

"I fell into Shadow." Artimour bit his lip and looked around. There was no point in sharing his story with these frantic ladies, for it seemed that the entire reality of Faerie was beginning to fray. He remembered the expression in Nessa's eyes when they'd talked of Faerie dying and he knew he had to ask the question. "You haven't—you haven't, by any chance, met a mortal? On your way from the Palace?"

"Another mortal?" Rodrigal practically spat the words while the ladies all wrinkled their noses and looked at each other, clearly titillated at the prospect.

I'm not a mortal, Artimour wanted to shout, but he refrained. "A mortal blacksmith—a big man, tall, dark, with a beard?"

Rodrigal snorted, regarding Artimour with a dubious eye. "We've no time to dally with mortals. My prince."

"Not to dally with," Artimour shook his head, glancing around the forest for more signs of breakdown. But only the leaves drifting from the silent trees bore silent witness. "I'm talking about a mortal blacksmith? Named Dougal?" But at their blank and confused faces, he only waved a dismissive hand. "Never mind then."

"Take one of our horses, Artimour." Amadahlia plucked at his sleeve. "Alone you can ride faster than this thing can. Ride on ahead, and tell the Captain of the Third Company that they are needed posthaste to protect the Palace. Tell Vinaver we're coming and she must prepare—"

"She must help," echoed the pale pink lady.

"Yes, do it, Rodrigal," urged one of the fish twins. "Tell the guard we shall bring Vinaver back with us—there's no one to answer to at the moment, until she can get to the Queen, and before we go back, she has to tell us how to take these wings off—I can't bear them anymore."

"Wings? That's not the only thing she has to tell us how to stop. She has to tell us how to stop the rest of it!" said Cow-snout.

It all seems to come back to Vinaver and Finuviel, he thought. *I hope they can undo whatever it is they've wrought.*

The coachman unhitched one of the four horses and handed the reins to Artimour. There was more he wanted to ask, but he was too troubled both by what they told him and by what he saw to linger any longer, and so he only touched his heels to the horse's sides and galloped off down the road, leaving the golden coach trundling along, gradually falling farther and farther behind the curtain of drifting leaves.

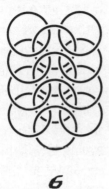

6

"How long to get to Gar?" Nessa asked as she and Uwen rode away from the shadows of Killcarrick's walls. Faint tendrils of dawn light threaded through the early-morning fog, and she asked more to keep her mind from wandering to Artimour and the fate of her parents in the OtherWorld than any real wish to know. The sword she'd made for Artimour hung against her thigh. If Uwen thought it odd that she should have chosen to arm herself, he'd said nothing. In this strange new world, it only made sense to carry a silver-edged weapon. Her body felt tender and sore, and her spirits were as dismal as the day. She supposed she understood why Artimour didn't want to take the sword with him. But what if he needed it? she wondered as she fingered the simple wooden hilt. She didn't like to think about what Artimour might find waiting for him in the OtherWorld. What would happen to him if Finuviel had already made himself

King? The thought of her parents trapped there as well made her wish she could find an excuse to go back to the OtherWorld herself.

She mustn't think like that, she told herself. Her father would expect her to stay put, for if Faerie had been a dangerous place before, it must be even more so now. But the ride didn't look to promise the distractions of the forge, and she had to force herself to focus on the leaf-littered road, eyeing Uwen. In the russet light now spilling over the hills, she saw that there were traces of blue in the creases of his neck, and his hair was damp, as if he'd come from a bath. His eyes were hollow in their sockets, his offset jaw clenched, his mouth drawn down and grim.

"If we don't stop, assuming we can get across the bridge at the Daraghduin, we could be at Gar by this time tomorrow. But it'll depend on what we find ahead, lass," he replied. "I wish I understood more about this bargain Cadwyr made with this sidhe. It seems lopsided somehow." There was a heaviness, a weightiness to his words that was never there before, and it perplexed her and worried her more in some ways than any of the other changes in him.

"What do you mean?" she asked, her attention momentarily diverted from the puffiness between her legs that the rocking motion of the horse was only exacerbating.

"Well, you think about it. An army for a dagger. Does it seem like an equal exchange to you?" For a long moment, Uwen held her eyes.

Nessa thought furiously. A dagger, a silver dagger, in exchange for a host of—how many had Artimour said? Five hundred knights?

Uwen was shaking his head. "Surely the sidhe have means

to kill each other without needing silver. Why they'd even need to make this bargain is a puzzle we might never understand. But look at it from Cadwyr's point of view. Part of the bargain—obviously—was that Cadwyr had to hand over the dagger *before* any battle could be fought. Wouldn't you force a sidhe to wait until after he'd done whatever it was he'd promised to do, before you handed over your part of the deal?"

She was silent for a moment, thinking it over. What did Dougal do when a customer placed an order for which the final payment would be sizable? Frequently, he kept something of the customer's in surety of payment—and such surety could vary, from a gold brooch or copper torque, or even, once or twice, a cow. "When my father wasn't sure if a customer could be trusted for final payment," she said slowly, "he'd hold something of theirs, something of near or equal value. Something they'd want to have back enough to guarantee they'd come back to pay." She paused, then looked at Uwen as something clicked into place. "Cadwyr made Finuviel gave him the Silver Caul."

"That's what I think, too. Which makes what Cadwyr did even worse, for why didn't he give it back, come Samhain, given all that was to happen? And what's more, now the question becomes, how long does Cadwyr mean to keep it, assuming he still has it? And if he had it, why didn't he warn us about what would happen on Samhain?"

"Are you saying you think Cadwyr doesn't intend to give it back?" Nessa asked incredulously.

"Think about it, Nessa." Uwen stared straight ahead, and for a long moment the silence was only broken by the steady rhythm of the horses' hooves. "It's one thing to use an army of the sidhe against a foreign threat. But to turn the goblins against your own kin, against your own coun-trymen—he did nothing to warn the rest of us—it's almost as if Cadwyr meant to turn the goblins on us. And not only did he turn the goblins on us, first he took away the ones who might've saved more of us if we'd had time and notice to prepare. So not only were we unknowing as newborn calves, we'd about the same ability to defend ourselves. Why? Why do such a thing? Unless it somehow benefited him? Or another ally?"

Nessa turned to Uwen, so horrified she could scarcely draw the breath to form the words. "Are you suggesting that Cadwyr has joined with the goblins against the sidhe?"

Uwen shrugged. "Think about it. Anything's possible."

Nessa's birch staff banged against her knee in its awkward binding on the horse's side. She put her hand on the staff to steady it and, as always, was oddly comforted by the touch of its cool smooth wood. It was always smooth, wherever she happened to place her hand, but it always seemed to oblige with a peel of birch bark, too, when needed. There was something about the staff that made her feel it was still alive, still connected in some way to the tree from which it had fallen. *The Mother-Tree.* The word fluttered through her mind like a breeze-blown leaf. "If Cadwyr has allied with the goblins against the sidhe, then he's turned against Finuviel."

"I'm not saying that's a fact, lass." Uwen's pale eyes were fixed on the road ahead, his expression like stone. "I'm just saying that's a possibility."

"But if he has—"

"It's a possibility, but not likely. I can't imagine anyone forming an alliance with the goblins. But I wouldn't put it past Cadwyr to use the goblins against the sidhe—soften them up in the same way they did us."

"Which means—" Nessa wrinkled her brow and tried to contemplate what all this could possibly mean for Artimour and her parents. "Which means Cadwyr means to rule the sidhe?"

For the first time that morning, Uwen turned to look at her directly. "That's another possibility, isn't it?"

They lapsed into silence while Nessa contemplated possibility after possibility, each one too horrific to really contemplate. Was Cadwyr building some super force of warriors, armed and armored in silver, capable of destroying both goblins and sidhe? Poor Griffin had been dragged away kicking and screaming according to Molly. She fingered the hilt of the sword and wished she'd insisted Artimour take it. He was assuming his enemies were either Finuviel or the goblins. He was not counting on running into mortals armed with silver. She knew all too well the stories told of the upland raids on cattle and homesteads, how long-festering slights could erupt from relatively routine cattle raiding into wholesale slaughter and rape. Now worried even more about the fate of her parents, especially her mother, who surely was as young and beautiful as the day she'd gone into the OtherWorld, Nessa was as pensive as Uwen.

All morning they rode, passing bedraggled groups of stunned refugees, most of whom were single survivors of once-larger groups. Uwen sent them back to Killcarrick, where the Sheriff, Nessa thought, would surely groan at the further strain upon his larders. She was about to ask Uwen if it would be wiser to allow the refugees to accompany them to Gar, when flashes of metal and muted shouts made Uwen motion to her to draw her reins in and step off through the trees. He gently swung out of his saddle, and slowly they crept through the wood flanking the road, until they came to the rear of a wagon train that consisted of perhaps ten wagons covered in canvases lashed down with thick ropes, and maybe a hundred riders, all fully armed as if for battle. Nessa didn't recognize the pattern of their plaid, but the shaggy, short-legged ponies they rode spoke of the barren hill country to the east. The hill country of Allovale, she remembered, and wondered if these were Cadwyr's kin.

"So that's what Mungo was talking about," Uwen spoke quietly, and she realized he was talking to himself.

"Who's Mungo?" she murmured back.

"The oldest chief among the Duchess's kin from up Garannon way. He was telling us about the wagon trains coming out of Allovale—all loaded with silver—all coming by different routes, trying to fool would-be raiders, I suppose. I guess these came down the opposite shore of the lake—not the most direct way south, but if you're trying to avoid robbers, I suppose it makes sense. We'll hang back here, watch and see where they're going. If we're stuck at night on the road, it might not be a bad idea to make our presence known."

Another look at Uwen's grim expression made her determined to understand the abrupt change that had come over him. But he motioned her to silence as he swung up into the saddle and gestured for her to do the same. For what seemed like a full turn of the glass or more, they stayed off the road, maintaining a delicate distance between detection and observation.

And so it was that too late Nessa noticed a low-lying branch trembling as they approached, and she gasped as a long blade slid out behind the tree and a second sword emerged from the underbrush in front of Uwen, effectively halting them both. A rumpled knight, his clothes streaked with mud and blood, his chin dark with grizzled beard and his braids in wild disarray around his face, stepped out from behind the tree and confronted Uwen with a drawn broadsword. For a moment, they both froze. Then Uwen broke into the first genuine grin she'd seen since Samhain and said, "Mother goddess, Tully. Put that blade down before either you do yourself a mischief or I'm forced to do one to you."

When they stopped for the night, Griffin found it as convenient to curl up in a corner of Cadwyr's tent as he had to ride in a wagon directly behind Cadwyr all that day. Orange flames leaped high in the bronze brazier, washing Cadwyr's clean-shaven cheeks with the copper-colored glow of a Lacquilean idol. He smiled at Griffin, crouching beside the copper-bound barrel, his hands cupped around the golden flagon. "Come here, boy, come closer. It must be cold over there."

Whenever Cadwyr looked at him, he grew warm all over. Griffin crept forward as his throat constricted, the flagon held in one hand. Cadwyr nodded, waving him closer.

"Here. Have a cushion."

Griffin caught the flying red silk square before it knocked into the flagon, and Cadwyr laughed. He was sprawled, as seemed to be his custom of an evening, across his broad hide folding chair. The chair itself was ornately carved and was placed on a thick carpet. More cushions, in colors of an intensity that defied any reality Griffin knew, surrounded the brazier, all embroidered in intricate patterns of bright indigo and red and green.

Cadwyr wore a white shirt of some fluid fabric that draped across his chest in graceful folds, and black trews that molded seamlessly into boots of leather so finely tooled that they, too, moved as supply as silk. Around Cadwyr's neck, on the same cord as his heavy silver amulet, and the ducal amulet of his rank, he wore a bag made of some pale tan leather. An unpleasant scent emanated from it, a smell Griffin was sure only his brew-honed senses could detect, but one which any mortal would now recognize all too well. For the bag stank clearly, though faintly, of goblin. Griffin wondered where Cadwyr could have gotten such a thing, and what he kept within it, that he needed to have it so close. And where in all of the known world was such finery as Cadwyr's found? He settled on his cushion, as far away from Cadwyr as he dared.

The colors, the scents, the textures, the brightness of the burning brazier assaulted him, so that his head spun and the world tilted a few times before it settled. The tent reeked of charcoal and wool and some heavy musky aroma, and Griffin looked down at the clear, apple-scented fluid in the flagon. Something about the furnishings of the tent tugged at his awareness like an angry tooth, and he gazed around the interior of the tent with new eyes. Cadwyr did not look like a simple country noble about to become elevated to head of one of the great houses of Brynhyvar. He looked the way Griffin had always imagined the Kings of Humbria or the Emperors of Lacquilea to look. Or a lord of the sidhe. A lord of the sidhe. He thought of Nessa, and he wondered if she had managed to return to this world, or if she'd fallen prey to some lord of the sidhe, a lord of the sidhe who smiled the way Cadwyr was smiling now. It unsettled him so much he spilled a drop or two, and the precious brew sloshed over the rim and he had to force himself not to lick the amber drops as they rolled down the flagon's curve.

"Sit, boy." The Duke might have been talking to a favored hound, but Griffin knew better than not to obey. "Tomorrow we'll be at Gar. Ever been there?"

He leaned against the square wooden crate he'd noticed that Cadwyr kept close always. "No, my lord, my master preferred to go alone, and the few times he did take anyone, he took his daughter instead. But he said it was to be my turn next year."

Cadwyr gave a short, delighted laugh. "You've never seen it? They say it's the grandest by far in all of Brynhyvar, save Ardagh itself. It's nothing at all like Allovale." Cadwyr leaned forward, and his mouth was wet with the wine Griffin smelled on his breath. In fact, he could smell everything about Cadwyr, from the damp sweat-stained wool of his tunic, to the grass that clung to the soles of his boots, to the stink from that bag dangling just above his heart. Griffin sniffed, even as Cadwyr continued, "Have you ever been to Allovale?"

The question took him aback, and he found himself searching Cadwyr's blue eyes. "N-no," he managed with a dry tongue. "I come from up Pentland way."

"Ah. Well. It's not much of a place, really. Mostly mountains covered in moors that grow some of the biggest rocks in Brynhyvar. There's no farmland worth tilling, no pastureland to speak of. There's a coast, but no harbor big enough for a ship of any consequence. So there's not much there but for a few peasants and wild pigs scratching a living out of the hills, if you get my meaning?" Dry-mouthed, Griffin nodded. Cadwyr's voice was husky, and his silken sleeves slithered over the armrest as he raised his goblet to his mouth. He smacked his lips and went on. "But there's one thing it does have. It's got silver, in veins thicker than the widest trees, and deep pockets, all through the mountains. They go down deeper than anyone's ever tried to mine. In the days before Bran Brownbeard, Allovale was rich and rivaled Ardagh for its grandeur." Cadwyr wrapped his hand around the little leather bag. "Because the silver was needed, then, you see. But since the Caul..." He paused, then shook his head. "Well, as you can imagine, silver's not been needed on such a scale in centuries. The miners all mostly moved or found other trades—oh, there's still one mine open, of course, though nothing like the way it was. But the silver's still there. Waiting, all these centuries. Just waiting for someone to come along who understands the true power of silver, the true power it gives us, over both goblin and sidhe." He paused and gazed over Griffin's shoulder. "It's all going to be different soon—very soon, as you'll see. You may even live long enough to see it, lad, if you keep drinking the brew."

"See what?" It was like magic, this spell that Cadwyr wove, Griffin thought, entranced by the captivating rise and fall of his mead-rough voice, the flush of color in his cheeks. Or was this another effect of the brew?

"The rise of the House of Allovale, boy. We were once the grandest name in all of Brynhyvar. We were called the

Silver Kings, and we lived higher than the King of Humbria himself in our palaces that were grander by far than either Ardagh or Gar. We were no dirt-digging farmers or cattle-raiding horse thieves like the rest of them that call themselves nobility." Cadwyr leaned forward and the hide bag swung out, and Griffin got a clear whiff of something that was as undeniably familiar as it was surprising. "But things are about to change."

"Why does that bag smell like goblin?"

Cadwyr leaned back, the small bag cradled protectively in his huge hand. "Ah, boy. That's what the brew does, you know. It enhances certain...sensitivities." He caressed the bag as if it were a lover's hand. Then he pinned Griffin with a look hotter than a metal brand. "Want to know a secret, boy?" He beckoned, and his breath was like a furnace blast. "Come here."

A spear of heat went straight down his spine to his groin and Griffin felt his body stiffen in response to—to what? To Cadwyr? He had no feelings but hatred for Cadwyr. He dragged Nessa's face out of his memory. But in some weird way, it seemed that Nessa's face superimposed itself over Cadwyr's, so that his eyes took on something of her dark depths, his brow broadened and lifted. Griffin gasped and blinked and gulped back a quick swallow.

Cadwyr shifted, knees spread wide, elbows on his thighs. "Have another drink, yes, that's right, a good one—I like to watch you drink, boy, did you know that?" His eyes lingered on Griffin's mouth, then his throat. "So come here, and let me tell you the closest secret in all of Brynhyvar. It's a se-cret some would die for. It's a secret some already have. Can you keep a secret like that, boy?" He caught Griffin's wet hair in one fist and swept it off his brow, twisting Griffin's head up and back, so that Cadwyr's own face filled Griffin's entire vision. "I reward my friends, boy. Have you noticed?"

The bag swung closer to his face, and Griffin smelled the rank, OtherWorldly stench of the goblins, and as it swung near, he had a chance to look at the leather. It was pale, almost white, and delicate, like kidskin. It dangled, turning, this way and that, and he caught a glimpse of the other side, and the faintest outline of a blue five-pointed pentacle.

Nausea boiled in his gut, and he doubted even the brew could quell it. For he knew what sort of hide the bag was made of, and it wasn't kid, or calf or pig or anything even of the OtherWorld. For the pentacle could only be a tattoo, the color indelibly marked into the skin, so that even whatever tanning process the goblins utilized couldn't erase it. Of course it stank of goblin. He could well imagine those monsters creating such a thing with the remains of their prey. But why would Cadwyr want such a horrible thing?

Griffin looked away, even as Cadwyr twined his hand in Griffin's hair and dragged Griffin's face back up to his. "The brew makes you mine, doesn't it?" His lips were stretched back across his teeth, exposing his white canines, and his eyes blazed azure blue in his reddened face. He gripped the bag with his other fist. "I'll tell you this much, boy. There's a whole world in this bag. You believe that? Well, do you?"

But Griffin could only dart his eyes from the fist that enclosed the bag, noting Cadwyr's thick, square fingers, the wiry blond hair on the back of his hand. This close the wine on his breath was as intoxicating as if Griffin had downed a flagon of it himself. Cadwyr's lips were thin, but wet, his chin stubbled with a rough gold haze. *He's going to kiss me,* thought Griffin. His head fell back, and his eyes closed, even as some more rational corner of his brain screamed at him to see what was in the bag.

But the pressure of Cadwyr's mouth on his never materialized. Instead, there was the sound of running footsteps, rough speech, shouts of greeting, or warning. Cadwyr whipped up and around as the leather flaps were flung aside and a guard entered. He stood just inside the tent, glanced back over his shoulder and advanced cautiously. "What is it?" asked Cadwyr. "What's wrong?" He let go of Griffin and coiled back into his chair like a great snake.

Griffin scuttled backward, next to the wooden crate.

The guard glanced in Griffin's direction, swallowed hard and advanced a few steps, clearly hesitating to speak in front of Griffin. "My lord—"

Cadwyr frowned. "Spit it out before you piss yourself. What's wrong?"

"There're two—" Again the guard looked at Griffin and Cadwyr snorted. "May I speak in front of—?"

"Pay him no mind. Two what? What're you talking about?"

"Two of the—two of *them,* my lord, if you take my meaning. Two of the sidhe. Warriors. Here. They say they're looking for someone."

"Is that so?" muttered Cadwyr. The odd look that crossed his face may have been a trick of the flames. "Well, show them in. Let's hear what they have to say."

With a quick nod and another bow, Dermott was gone. Cadwyr stretched out on his chair again. He caught Griffin's eye and grinned. "Looks like we're in for some fun tonight, boy." His gaze fell on the crate beside Griffin. "Do

you know you're leaning up against Donnor's head, boy?
Aye, and the coffer that holds the rest of him? Well, the
ashes of the rest of him. Can't be hauling corpses from place
to place with goblins on the hunt, can we?"

Griffin jumped away from the crate as if stung, splashing
the contents of the flagon down the opening of his linen
shirt. It ran down his neck and bare chest in a slow tickle like
a woman's finger down the back of his hand, a sensuous
downstroke of sensation that made Griffin gasp aloud as the
sidhe entered.

His first impression of them both was that they were tall
and slim and beautiful, and they shone. There was simply no
other way to describe the way light seemed to radiate from
their very flesh, making them appear at once translucent and
yet wholly solid. His mouth dropped open, and it was all he
could do not to fall forward, staring. At that moment, there
was nothing else he could even imagine wanting to do.

Despite his initial impression, he realized that they were
not identical, although they were clothed alike in moss-
green doublets of what appeared to be silk velvet. Pearl-
gray cloaks poured off their shoulders, the color of lake
water in winter. Their hose was dark, and disappeared
smoothly and seamlessly into their thigh-high boots.
They were armed with bow and broadsword and they
moved with the sinuous grace of wind moving over
wheat as they bowed briefly before Cadwyr. The flames
flared higher and yellower, as if in response, and in the
brighter light, he saw that one had hair the color of the
shiniest of acorns in autumn, and the other's was bound
into a braid that shone like honey in the sun. And then
one spoke, and Griffin found himself leaning forward,

lost in the melody now pouring from the sidhe's throat. And then he realized it wasn't music at all—it was merely the creature's speech. *By the goddess, if Nessa met one of these things, she must be lost, indeed,* he thought, recognizing in the small rational part of his mind he still possessed that he was only caught up in the seductive enchantment of the sidhe.

"Greetings, my lord." The one with the nut-brown hair rested his hand upon the hilt of his sword. "We come seeking another of our own, and our intention to find him has led us, much to our surprise, here, into Shadow. And thus we implore you to tell us if you or any of your people have yet seen or heard tell of this companion of ours whom we seek."

Griffin crept forward, more entranced than ever. The scent that wafted from them was a delicious combination of something grassy and green, yet sharp all at once. He sniffed, audibly, and the second one turned and pinned him with a gaze the color of the inlays on Cadwyr's torque.

"And who is it that you seek?" asked Cadwyr.

"His name is Artimour. Prince Artimour. Our captain and our friend."

"And how long has he been missing?" asked Cadwyr, and there was something in his tone that made Griffin think he knew who Artimour was. *But how is that possible?* he wondered, and he watched as the sidhe who'd noticed him tapped the other on the forearm, and gestured to Griffin with a quick nod.

But all the other answered was, "He left our garrison just before Samhain, but he has not returned and events in Faerie have been proceeding—" He broke off. "We have reason to be concerned."

"And what makes you think he's here?" Cadwyr sat up and leaned forward, knotting his fingers across his chest.

They hesitated and glanced at each other, and Griffin was struck by the sheer beauty of the delicate arching angles of their faces. How could anything be so perfect and yet live? Griffin licked his lips. For the first time in a long time there was something he wanted more than the brew. He wanted them to keep talking. Finally the first replied, "We set our intent to find him, and our footsteps led us here. Can you tell us anything of him?"

"Did it now?" Cadwyr stretched out his legs, crossed his black boots at the ankles and pursed his lips, raising his steepled fingertips to touch his mouth reflexively. "Did it now, indeed?" He leaned forward, shaking his head slowly. "Nothing—nothing at all concerning this Prince—what did you call him? Artimour?—has come to me, but we shall ask about the camp. Perhaps someone has seen something." He gestured to the cushions. "Sit, if you will. Ale? Mead? Wine?"

Again they glanced at each other. "Your hospitality does you credit, Lord Duke," answered the second, a trifle slowly. "But perhaps you could tell me how it is that a mortal boy comes to reek of may-apple wine?"

The other took a single step forward and gestured in the direction of the bag Cadwyr wore around his neck. "And you, Lord Duke, that bag around your neck, it stinks of goblin make."

"Well," said Cadwyr with a little smile and a graceful shrug. "From time to time, I've come across an oddity here and there." He shrugged again and glanced at Griffin, and Griffin saw the edge of steel in his eyes. "Griffin, be a good lad and call for the guard, will you?"

There was something in the way the shadows moved across Cadwyr's face that made Griffin wary as he edged over to the tent flaps. He beckoned the guard standing a few feet away, noticing immediately that Cadwyr's tent was now surrounded by guards, whose breastplates flashed silver in the orange torchlight. He turned back to Cadwyr as the guard nodded and raised his thumb, as if in some prearranged signal. He looked over his shoulder at Cadwyr, who was watching him and stroking his chin.

"May-apple wine is hardly an oddity, my lord," said the second sidhe.

"Forgive me that I cannot be of further service," replied Cadwyr. He gestured to the guard. "Conn here will take you through the camp. Feel free to ask who you will." Cadwyr looked at Griffin, then beckoned. "Come here, boy. We don't want you in the way."

Confused, Griffin scurried to crouch upon the cushion to which Cadwyr pointed. And to his horror, as the tent flaps fell upon the sidhe, he saw the flash of a silver blade, and two short high-pitched shrieks sliced high and wailing through the night. They ended in a long gurgle. Griffin looked at the tent flap, eyes wide, nostrils quivering with fear. Was it possible the two sidhe were dead? He looked up at Cadwyr, who was smiling at the entrance, as if he could see through the skins. He glanced down at Griffin. "I can't take any chances," he said. He beckoned with his forefinger and gently pushed Griffin's head down on his knee. There was more noise now, low, indistinguishable voices, grunts, a few curses sharply silenced. He stroked Griffin's rough hair, then twisted it around his hand and brought Griffin's face up to his. "You see this bag, boy? You know what it's made of, don't you, lad? You're a smart lad, aren't you? You know."

Terrified, Griffin could only nod. Cadwyr had slaughtered the sidhe. They were dead, he knew it, he could feel it, somehow, their deaths burning in the marrow of his bones, making him ache for the brew.

"But you don't know what's in it, do you?" Cadwyr moistened his lips with the tip of his tongue, reached down with his other hand and brought up his goblet from the floor. He waved it gently under Griffin's nose from side to side. The scent of the brew tickled the end of his nose like a feather, and involuntarily he leaned toward it. But Cadwyr held him hard. "Look at me, boy. I'm going to show you a secret. I'm going to give you a secret." He let go his hold on Griffin's hair just enough to let him sag a bit, just enough for him to reach the lip of the goblet, even as Cadwyr pulled it out of the way. "You want it, don't you?"

Griffin glanced at Cadwyr, then at the cup. The need for the brew was boiling in him now, he could feel it coiling and twisting in the pit of his belly. The smell alone was inciting him, so that he could only nod and swallow hard, eyes fastened on the gleaming edge of the goblet.

"Well, then, boy, I've a bargain to offer you." Cadwyr lifted the goblet and touched it briefly to his mouth, enough to leave a residue that gleamed on his lips. Griffin licked his. Cadwyr smiled and set the goblet down and Griffin could not control a disappointed gasp. The need was on him now, and he looked down at himself and realized he was fully erect. Cadwyr tightened his grip on Griffin's hair and brought him higher, so that he was forced to half crouch beside the chair, his groin against Cadwyr's knee. "I'll make sure you have all you need of the brew, forever. For however you long wish to drink it, it's yours, as much as you wish." He wrapped his other hand around the bag and lifted his knee up and down against Griffin, who closed his eyes and groaned. A fire was raging through him, and soon, there would be nothing left of him at all but this hungry, angry, all-consuming need. "And all I ask, boy," he said as he let go of Griffin and he fell, half sprawling over Cadwyr's lap. Cadwyr twisted the cord off his head and ran his hand down Griffin's back, around the curve of his buttocks, feeling the muscles with the same hard and casual hand he might a favorite horse. "All I ask is this."

Suddenly he pushed Griffin off him, and he sprawled backward. He was dizzy and his head was spinning, his tongue sticky and dry. If he could only have a drink, a single drink from the goblet next to Cadwyr, he'd be able to think again, he knew. Involuntarily, he scuttled closer, and Cadwyr reached down and hauled him once more to his knees. He dragged the black leather cord down and around Griffin's neck, allowing it to twine with the cord from which Nessa's amulet hung. The unmistakable reek of goblin filled Griffin's nostrils and he gagged, twisting his face away. Cadwyr pushed it down beneath his shirt, and Griffin fancied he could feel it burn against his wet skin. "Just give it back to me when I ask you for it, all right? You promise?"

He raised the goblet to Griffin's lips, running the lip of it gently over Griffin's, so that he parted his mouth and, to his shame, tried to swipe a taste with this tongue. Cadwyr laughed delightedly. "You promise?"

Griffin nodded and Cadwyr raised the goblet to his own mouth, tipping it back and draining it in one mighty swallow that left Griffin sagging between his thighs. "Oh, yes," he whispered, thinking he'd be more than happy to surrender the disgusting thing at any time, and Cadwyr dragged him up once more.

"A kiss to seal the bargain," he said, and he plunged his brew-drenched tongue into Griffin's mouth.

"I'm not sure he'll live." Cecily spoke softly to Uwen, but Nessa heard every word as clearly as if she'd spoken in Nessa's ear. "The leg wound's the bad one—it goes all the way to the bone. Even if he lives, he may lose the use of it." She pulled her filthy plaid around her thin shoulders and gently brushed her dirt-smudged fingers over Kian's face.

She loves him, thought Nessa, *and she is terribly afraid he will die.* The Duchess looked young and tired and fragile, her dark blond hair loosely braided and held with a strip of linen torn from her hem, her shift ragged and bound at the waist with a strip of leather that looked as if it had been cut from a horse's bridle. She looked nothing at all like the woman Nessa remembered from the trip to Gar she and Dougal had taken a few years ago. Then Cecily had been dressed in a sumptuous gown embroidered at cuffs and hem and throat with gold, finery that, to Nessa's eyes, surely rivaled that of the Faerie Queen herself. She'd been surrounded by her ladies and her pages, her belly vast with a long-looked-for heir. But it was her hands that Nessa remembered most, white as new-made cream, the nails pink and smooth and round, her fingers soft as goose down as she'd gently touched Nessa's cheek. The child had died either at birth, or shortly after, Nessa remembered, and there had never been another. She remembered the Duke, too. He'd been older than Dougal, a bald, paunchy old man who'd forgot her existence the moment Dougal unwrapped their wares.

She could certainly understand why Cecily might prefer the tall knight to the old Duke. And looking at Kian, she understood Cecily's fear as well. It was not simply his terrible stillness as he lay beneath the dirty, bloodstained plaid. It was in the way his mouth was a dry, drawn slash, slack at the corners; in the way his eyes were sunk in their sockets so that his lids looked like wrinkled parchment; in the wet gleam on his forehead that Cecily dabbed away with a piece of linen torn from her sleeve. On the other side of the fire, the two knights snored, propped up against each other, and in the nearby clearing the ragtag band of refugees slept in and under their wagons, arranged around a crackling fire.

Beside Nessa, the birch staff seemed to quiver. Startled, she looked down. The staff lay beside her, quiescent as usual. She glanced up but Uwen was listening to the Duchess's soft voice, smoking his pipe and staring into the fire with that faraway expression.

"It's not fair," Cecily was saying, her face white and pinched. "It's just not fair."

The birch staff gave another palpable throb, and Nessa jumped. Uwen looked at her over his pipe, a question in his eyes, and she shrugged and smiled. She wished Granny Molly were there. She wished she knew what to do. She could feel a kind of incipient energy building in the staff, but here, alone, in the dark wood, without Molly's guiding presence, she hesitated to do or say anything. After all, hadn't she snapped at Uwen not long ago, over a fire much like this that she'd no knowledge of healing? "Kian won't die," Nessa blurted. "Once we get to Killcarrick, Granny Molly will know what to do."

"Your Grace," said Uwen as he drew on his long clay pipe. "When we reach Killcarrick, there'll be other matters to attend to. You understand what I mean. You've got to prepare yourself. The clans have begun to arrive. They'll be looking for a strong hand and a high heart."

For a long moment, Cecily stared at Uwen.

She's afraid, thought Nessa. From somewhere in the tree-tops, an owl hooted and she jumped. *Well, who isn't?* She touched the silvered sword which lay beside her and wondered what had happened to Artimour. The night was quiet all around them, but there'd been no sign at all of the goblins. *Maybe they're full.* She pushed the gory thought away in time to hear Cecily say, "That was the second wagon train we passed heading toward Gar out of the Allovale uplands. What else is he moving but silver?"

"That's exactly what he's moving," Uwen agreed. "Mungo's lads helped themselves to a bit of it already."

Silver, thought Nessa, silver and smiths. She thought of poor Griffin, who'd survived the harrowing attack on their own village only to be drafted into the service of the Duke of Allovale. Cadwyr still had the Caul. He was still moving silver. And he still had the smiths. "Do you think Cadwyr means to rule the sidhe?" Nessa blurted, surprised by her own boldness.

But Cecily only raised her head and looked at Nessa. "Nothing Cadwyr's planned would surprise me." She pushed her hair back off her face. "This is what I think. I think he murdered Donnor on the battlefield." She broke off and looked at Uwen. "I think he used this bargain with the sidhe to take Ardagh. And now he's amassing a great force, of men and silver. The men I understand—even the merce-naries—in light of the Humbrian threat. But the silver—"

"What Humbrian threat?" asked Nessa.

"The King of Humbria won't want to let Brynhyvar go without a fight, Nessa," answered Uwen. "You see, once we get the goblins and the sidhe and the country itself sorted out, we've still to face the King across the sea. We can't lose sight of what started this mess, for the lords and the chiefs surely won't. That's the problem now—consolidating them behind Cecily, convincing them to support her on the throne. Cadwyr's made his position plain by raising his colors over Ardagh."

"And so now," Cecily said with a sigh, looking down at Kian. "Now—"

But Uwen leaned forward. "There're plenty who don't like Cadwyr."

"But that's not enough to keep them from supporting him if they believe he will be able to hold back the Humbrians. And if he's set to conquer TirNa'lugh—"

"He'll destroy Faerie, if he does," blurted Nessa. Both Uwen and Cecily turned to look at her.

"It won't matter to him if he does," said Uwen.

"My parents are there," Nessa whispered. She pressed her lips together, remembering the shadowy faces, the sad eyes of the shades she'd seen on Samhain, the soft chorus that echoed even now like the whisper of a breeze through the branches overhead. *Help Essa. Help Essa come home.* If it all just disappeared, both Dougal and Essa would be lost to the Wild Hunt. Forever. Suddenly she felt more alone in the dark night than she'd ever felt in her life. Beside her, the birch staff throbbed palpably and Nessa glanced down, half expecting to see it pulsating. But the staff looked no different, and when she touched it, it felt the same as ever, cool and

round and as smooth-fitting in her hand as the touch of Artimour's glove, and as still. *It's my imagination,* she told herself. Limbs of trees don't beat like hearts. She glanced across
the fire, but neither Uwen nor Cecily had noticed.

Uwen's eyes flickered down to Kian's face and then back
at Cecily. "I know you're worried about the Chief." His
voice was soft, and in the glow of the fire, Nessa saw that
his expression was soft. *Why, he loves her,* thought Nessa,
and wondered if either of them knew it. "There're skilled
grannies at Killcarrick. You'll see."

Nessa thought of Molly and was a little comforted.

"I wish there were some way to prove he murdered Donnor," said Cecily. She stared into the fire with hard eyes and
a grim mouth, her chin resting on her knees. "Cadwyr came
to me the night before they left. He brought me a rose—it
was the most perfect thing I ever saw. Now I've a better idea
where he got it from."

"From TirNa'lugh?" asked Nessa.

"Alone?" asked Uwen.

Cecily nodded. "He waited til my maid was gone on some
errand, and slipped in. Cadwyr told me he sent Donnor to
my parents to ask for my hand on his own behalf. But when
Donnor arrived, he decided to ask for me for himself."

"Maybe Duke Donnor assumed he'd leave you to Cadwyr, along with everything else," put in Nessa, and this
time, Uwen raised an eyebrow and removed his pipe from
his mouth.

But before he could speak, Cecily laughed, even though
her face was set and angry. "That's exactly what I think,"
said Cecily. "Or at least that's how Cadwyr sees it."

"You got away just in time," said Nessa.

"Aye," said Cecily, and for the first time, Nessa heard the northern burr in her speech. "Poor Granny Lyss." She shifted on her haunches and looked at Uwen. "Kian told the Arch-Druid that there might be another claimant to Donnor's title," Cecily said. "He didn't say who—but I hope to the Great Horned One himself he shows himself soon. That's one thing Cadwyr is definitely not expecting."

"It is, isn't it?" said Uwen. He placed his pipe down and fumbled for a moment with something around his neck. He held up a gold medallion on a gold chain, the sort given to every child of noble blood at birth, which recorded by rune and jewel and sigil the complicated net of kinship that stretched across Brynhyvar like a caul. For a split second, Nessa saw a flash of the old Uwen, the merry Uwen who'd always been ready with the unexpected joke. "Then I suppose now's as good a time as any to tell the both of you that it would be me."

7

Griffin tried not to gawk as the narrow forest road broke through the trees and opened into the broad avenue that led across a dun-brown meadow up to the gray granite rock pile that was Castle Gar. Positioned against the high mound of Gar Tor, it reminded Griffin of a predator poised to pounce. Black pennants flew from its towers, long tails that whipped in the bitter wind like the hungry tongues of angry snakes. *Or goblins.* The thought made him shiver and reach for Gareth's flask at his hip. He uncorked it, and chugged a long swig and replaced it in one practiced motion. The black shrouds draped across the tops of the walls looked as if a flock of giant ravens hugged the gray stones to their breasts. Above the shrouds, he could see a dark line that seemed to undulate, and he realized it was the press of those crowding at the walls, watching their approach. For a split second, Griffin wondered if their arrival would be welcomed or repelled.

But then the intermittent notes of a lone pipe floated across the broad valley and a shiver ran down his spine as he recognized the ancient Lament of the House of Gar. *They know,* he realized. *They know the Duke is dead.* He nearly reached for the flask again, but a thin thread of warmth still pushed through his veins. It steadied him enough that he was able to grip the reins and focus straight ahead on the plaid-draped full-size coffin in which Donnor's remains were now encased.

Cadwyr held up his hand, and as a series of barked orders filtered back through the ranks, turned to his second and said, "I thought I gave the order that no word of Gar's death was to reach the Duchess."

The other man, big and burly as Cadwyr, but dark like Dougal, shrugged. "What will it matter?"

The two men looked at each other and laughed, and another chill went down Griffin's back, forcing him to take another quick swallow. Since he'd watched Cadwyr so casually slaughter the sidhe, he had tried, as much as possible, to keep his distance, even while the question as to what Cadwyr kept in that bag he wore around his neck occupied Griffin's thoughts more and more. But did he want to get close enough to find out?

The ragged lines arranged themselves in tighter formation, and the drummers took up a steady march. Lulled by the up-and-down rhythm of the horse's slow jog over the relatively flat meadow road, and the soft tattoo of the muffled drums, Griffin fell into a sort of a drowse, his head lolling over his chest. Automatically, his fingers fumbled for the flask at his side. As he tipped his head back, one of the guards who rode in Cadwyr's company caught his eye. "You sure drink a lot of that stuff, lad."

Griffin nodded as he self-consciously replaced the flask. "It's—uh—special medicine the granny made for me— cure my goblin bite."

"Oh." The man's raised brow was enough to tell him he didn't believe that. "Goblin bite? I heard you were found with not a mark on you."

"Oh, no," replied Griffin, thinking as furiously as he could. "My head—" He pointed to his scalp and bent to show the man the thick scab of crusted blood still tangled in his hair. "Fang got me just as it collapsed."

"Ah." But just as Griffin relaxed back into his saddle, the soldier continued, "But you do sure drink a lot. For a lad and all." He licked his lips, and Griffin understood. He wanted some.

"Oh, no," said Griffin. "You don't want to try this stuff, not at all—" And then he broke off, for they had reached the outer ramparts. The black shrouds hung from scaffolding erected to begin the repair of the heavy damage the goblins had inflicted on the outer walls. Things must be bleak in Brynhyvar if a fortress as big as Gar had suffered such damage. The ground surrounding the castle was heaped with rubble, and chunks of huge stones lay strewn in random piles.

Ahead, the black iron portcullis shrieked on its chains as it was raised. A silence, oppressive as the damaged walls, rose all around them, broken only by the lament, the hollow ring of the horses' hooves, the creak and bounce of the wagon wheels and the heavy tramp of booted feet, despite what seemed like thousands who crowded into the wards, clung to perches on walls and roofs, and watched with sullen eyes. Griffin reached for his flask as they marched through the narrow entrance, following Cadwyr, who guided the procession through the outer wards, until at last, they entered the innermost courtyard.

On the dais, a group of white-robed druids stood in a cluster. They drew together as Cadwyr approached, clustering behind a taut-mouthed leader who gripped his staff with a white-knuckled hand. Cadwyr rode right up to the dais, forcing the druids to step back.

"Where's Cecily?" Cadwyr asked by way of greeting. "Bedridden with grief?"

But while a shallow ripple of laughter filtered back through the ranks of Cadwyr's men, the druids only gathered closer, and the one Cadwyr addressed visibly quailed. "She—she's not here, my lord Duke."

A hush fell over the company. Cadwyr dismounted, tossing the reins carelessly in the direction of a groom who ran forward just in time to catch them, and stalked up the steps. He paused on the third step, so that his eyes were equal to the druid's. "What do you mean, not here?"

"He means she left." The boy who blurted out an answer looked not much older than Griffin, and his grayish robes were trimmed in a bard's dark blue. The druid shot the boy a murderous look, and at once, he was dragged back, thrust behind a group who shuffled him away.

"She left, did she?" Cadwyr stroked his chin and advanced up the steps until he stood towering over the druid. "So where, then, did she go?"

"North," the druid whispered.

Griffin looked up to see the outline of a single piper on Gar Tor, standing like a huge crow among the black standing stones. A blast of rain-flecked wind gusted through his hair and plastered it against his wet cheeks. The faces around him were wet, too, old and young, shriveled and smooth alike, streaked with tears, or rigid with suppressed emotion. An image of Jemmy's head, eyes living and aware, bouncing into the mud, mouth still working in a silent scream, flashed through his mind, and he uncorked the flask and took a quick slug, all the time aware of the guard's eyes on him. But only a hard hot swallow would keep the rising tide of memory and emotion from choking him. A blast of sleet stung his cheeks, anchoring him firmly in the present.

Cadwyr's jaw tightened, and his back went rigid. One hand tightened on the hilt of the dagger in his belt, the other balled into a fist. "Come with me," was all he said as he pushed past the druid. The others parted like a river flowing around a rock as he advanced. Griffin stumbled after Cadwyr, intent on following at a safe distance. He'd no idea where Cadwyr would lodge in such an enormous place, and he had no intention of letting the brew out of his sight. The need for another quick slug was making his head ache, and the hard sleet stung his ears. He would be glad to get out of this weather, out of this tense and charged atmosphere. But the casket was lifted off the cart and carried into the hall, and the crowds surged forward, cutting off his access to Cadwyr and the druids who scampered in his wake like frightened rabbits behind the hound. The funeral drums picked up the beat and the piper high above lifted a trill of notes in a long and complicated skirl. The entire crowd pressed forward, carrying Griffin along with it, following Donnor's casket into the hall.

As if some beast was let unleashed, the whole company burst into loud wails and long moaning keens. Griffin staggered on his feet, the smells alone making his head spin. He had to get out of the human flood before it overwhelmed him. He felt desperately for the flask at his hip. Just holding it enabled him to push his way through, overcome by a panic he did not understand. The scene dissolved into a madhouse as he stumbled out the door into the ante-chamber that led directly outside, head spinning, mouth dry as cotton. He pressed his hot face against a cold stone wall, listening to the muted shrieks and cries and the wild howl-ing of the pipes as Donnor's people gave vent to their grief. The antechamber was cool and dim, lit only by a few tapers, but beyond the doors, he could hear the wake getting louder. If he didn't find his way somewhere else, it was only a matter of time before some drunkard found him out here and seized him back inside.

He wandered down the corridor, and peering down a darkened branch, noticed a staircase, lit by big torches in heavy iron brackets, in the gloom. He tightened his hand around Cadwyr's bag, careful to hold it through the fabric of his tunic. He didn't like the greasy feel of it touching his skin. The brew, he thought. He sniffed, then sniffed again. There it was, like the first hint of spring on a winter's wind. He sniffed a third time, then started up the steps, confident of the direction.

Out of the corner of his eye, he thought he saw a flicker of a movement. He unbuckled the flask, swallowed quickly and replaced it before he started off. At the top of the steps, he heard Cadwyr's voice rising above the general lament. He crept closer, easing all the way past the door, following the scent of the brew. A door across the hall stood slightly ajar, and he pushed it open, sniffing. A small antechamber opened into a bigger bedroom. Cadwyr's bedroom. He swallowed hard. In a small dressing room off to one side, a barrel of the brew stood, its copper fittings gleaming. He licked his lips, uncorked his flask and took a good, hard swallow, then instantly chided himself. It was dangerous to take too much at any one time, he could sense that. But the immediate bolt of energy that shot through his veins made him smile.

It also brought the stink of the bag beneath his shirt more acutely to his nose. He sniffed again, and wrinkled his nostrils. The bag had to go. He tiptoed to the doorway of the bedroom and pressed his ear to the door, listening to Cadwyr continuing to grill the druids. He met the eyes of another druid peering out into the hall, a young one, of about the same age, and darted back into the room, easing the door shut.

This time a noise made him turn and pause, and he thought he saw a cat, or perhaps a small dog, scamper beneath the bed. "What the—" he began. He raised a hand to his head and rubbed his temples. He should've known better than to have such a hard slug of brew. But he listened a moment, making sure that he heard nothing, saw nothing, and he stepped closer to the window and shook the contents of the bag into his hand. For a long moment, he could only stare at what at first appeared to be a puddle of shimmering starlight. And then the reality of what he held hit him, the identity of what the thing could be, must be, hit him, and he gripped it hard within his fist, casting a desperate glance over his shoulder. He had the Silver Caul. The Silver Caul of Bran Brownbeard—what else could it be?

But he wasn't going to keep it in the disgusting bag made

of human flesh. Clutching the Caul, he opened one of Cadwyr's chests, pawing through shirts and underlinens, until at last he seized upon a plain linen square. Another noise behind him made him nearly drop the Caul and he half turned, to see something that looked like a big cat leaping out of the shadows at him. As Griffin instinctively dodged out of its way, it grabbed right for the bag, leaped upon it and darted away, leaving him gasping, sitting in a heap as the door slammed open, and Cadwyr, followed by at least half a dozen druids, strode into the room.

He hauled Griffin to his feet and shook him. "What was that thing?"

Griffin shook his head, too terrified to speak.

Cadwyr dropped Griffin so that he splattered onto the floor with a loud thud. "Where's the bag, boy?"

The tone in Cadwyr's voice warned Griffin not to look up. But he had no choice, for he was picked up and slammed backward, so that his head knocked against the stone wall and his teeth rattled in his skull. As the druids rushed forward to hold Cadwyr back, Griffin puddled into a miserable heap and dared to raise his eyes as Cadwyr bellowed like a bull, "Where is it? What did you do with it, ya lackwit?"

Griffin pointed one shaking finger. "It—the thing—it took it—and disappeared."

"A thing?" Cadwyr shook off the druids who clung to his shoulders like a stallion a troublesome moth. "A thing? What manner of thing was it?"

"Small." Griffin held up his hand at about knee height. "With a tail. Big eyes. Claws. And teeth."

"A cat. A cat took it? You're saying a cat took it?" Cadwyr lunged at Griffin and he slipped away, out of his grasp, and hid behind the nearest druid, quivering, wishing he dared reach for the flask.

"Not a cat," Griffin moaned. "Of course it wasn't a cat—I thought it was a cat, too, but it wasn't—"

"A trixie?" put in the same young druid as before. "Think of it, Master Kestrel? Doesn't that sound like a trixie to you?"

"There's no such things as trixies!" snarled the druid holding on to Cadwyr's left.

With another shake, Cadwyr flung them all aside and picked up Griffin by the tunic. "A trixie? You're saying a trixie was here? And took the bag? Which way did he go?"

Terrified, Griffin could only nod and point. Cadwyr spoke over his shoulder. "Bring me that sidhe. I want that sidhe. Hag knows he should be well cooked by now and of a mood to cooperate. Maybe he can tell me what a trixie wants with the Caul. And if he can't—well—"

He flung Griffin to the floor, and stepped over him, but one of the knights paused in front of Griffin's prone body as he moved to do Cadwyr's bidding. "What about this one?"

"Drop him in the dungeon."

Cadwyr stalked away with a nasty chuckle, and Griffin was dragged after, still half-numb with shock. He was glad to be rid of the bag, for he'd hated the feeling of it around his neck, the smooth, greasy feel of it, the slimy stink of it, and he thought he might vomit, or possibly even faint. He struggled against the nausea that threatened to overwhelm him and called after Cadwyr, in a voice hoarse with longing, "But, my lord Duke—" he gasped and held out his hand. "My lord Duke, it only got the bag. I've—I've got the—the—the thing itself here—safe—" And then he did faint, and the last thing he remembered was Cadwyr turning on his heel and lifting him into an embrace with a triumphant laugh.

"What are you talking about, Artimour? How could goblins have invaded the Palace? The border's not been breached—there's been no word to even suggest—" The commander of the Third Company of the Palace Guard did not even attempt to conceal the contempt and suspicion with which he gazed at Artimour and his mortal garb. His name—Gillieas—bubbled up from the bottom of Artimour's memory, a recollection that rubbed raw even now. *Let me at the mortal—I hear his form with rapier-and-dagger is best described as knife-and-fork.* They'd disliked each other from the moment they'd met, but it had been some time since they'd crossed paths.

"Shouldn't we be arresting him, too, Captain?" Gillieas's lieutenant spoke from his right side, a sergeant now stared suspiciously from his left. "This isn't border country—and look at him. Maybe he's had something to do with—" He broke off and arched his eyebrow significantly. "You know."

"Something to do with what?" asked Artimour. "Have you not heard a word I've said? There's a carriage full of the Queen's ladies come to fetch Vinaver—you've no time to stand and question me. You're all needed back at the Palace—post, posthaste."

But Gillieas only strode a few paces and turned back, stroking his chin.

Artimour pointed over his shoulder. "If you don't believe me, ask Lady Amadahlia and the rest of them. I'm sure you'll pass them on the road. Now, if you don't mind, I'd like to see my sister before I go. The coach's not far behind—you'll meet them on the road."

Gillieas asked, "And where exactly do you intend to go?"

"Back to my border garrison," answered Artimour, spreading his hands. He cocked his head, confused by Gillieas's blatant hostility. "I'll bring back the border guard—surely you agree they're needed—" He broke off as the lieutenant whispered something to the sergeant. "What is it? Is it my clothes? Yes, I'm dressed like a mortal, but I've not the time to explain to you—there'll be time later, when the goblins—"

The gates opened behind him, and he turned to see a load of armor and weapons and bridles being led in, and neatly stacked by the soldiers of the guard. He gazed around the vaulted space that was the courtyard of the Forest House, and noticed, for the first time, a large amount of weapons and armor and bridles that were all sorted into neat piles of equipment and goods. "What is all this? Are you preparing for some sort of siege?"

"What an interesting question you ask, my lord, under the circumstances." Gillieas folded his arms across his chest.

"Under what circumstances? What are you talking about? This is not the time for talk and explanations, Gillieas. Faerie is dying. Don't you understand?"

"But how is it you've come to be here, Artimour?" asked Gillieas. "How is it again you know the Palace is attacked?"

"I met a carriage full of ladies on the road. And they told me the Palace was attacked by goblins. They asked me to ride on ahead, to summon you and then to go on, to the border. And the host."

"The host, you say. The host that rode out before Samhain?"

"What other is there?"

"There's the one we found slain, my lord Prince. The five hundred we found within the wood, all dead."

Artimour heard the words, but for a moment, they made no sense. He shook his head as if to clear it, and looked around the faces now drawing close, cold and beautiful and terrible in their unyielding expressions of distrust. He remembered the only evidence he'd seen of the passing of the host—all the hoofprints leading into the river that he'd come upon just before he'd met Finuviel. He glanced around the courtyard once more and this time saw the indigo banner wrapped around its golden pole, propped against a tree. "You're telling me the host is dead? All of them?"

"But for thirteen. The thirteen Finuviel ordered to stay here and guard his mother."

"And what about Finuviel?"

"What about Finuviel?" asked Gillieas. "When was the last time *you* saw him?"

The circle of soldiers was drawing closer. *He's accusing me,* Artimour thought, and he squared his shoulders. "The last time I saw Finuviel, he tried to kill me with this dagger," Artimour replied. He ripped the silver dagger from its sheath and waved it beneath their noses, taking a grim satisfaction in the way they all dodged back with hisses and stifled cries. He pulled aside his tunic, stripping off the bandage to reveal the angry purplish line slanting above his heart. "See? Finuviel stabbed me with this dagger, then pushed me in the river and left me there to bleed to death or drown. I happened to wash up in Shadow, which is how I came to be wearing these mortal clothes. The mortals who found me there saved me." He thrust the dagger back into its sheath. "You've wasted enough time."

Gillieas shrugged. "Perhaps, perhaps not. But if Finuviel used the dagger to stab you, how do you happen to have it?"

"I found it in a tree." As Artimour stepped forward, his arms were seized and dragged behind him. "What in the name of the Hag are you doing, Gillieas? Want me to show you the tree, Gillieas? It'll be easy to find—you can smell it rotting from the inside out." Artimour struggled, but the two guards held him hard.

"He even stinks like a mortal," said one.

"What do you think you're doing, Gillieas?"

"I want answers and I want them now. Bring him upstairs. I don't care how sick with mourning Vinaver claims to be. We'll sort this out now."

"Sort what out?" Artimour struggled as they lifted him off his feet and half dragged, half carried him up the stairs and into the house proper.

"Your sister, as you call her, seems to think Finuviel's out there—among the host. At least that's why she's got us out there searching."

"Searching for what?"

"Searching for Finuviel, of course. Aren't you interested to hear how they died?" Gillieas swung around as the guards brought Artimour to a halt.

"Well?" he asked.

"They were killed with mortal weapons made of silver. Edged in silver, at any rate. There's no doubt at all."

"Weapons like this one," put in the lieutenant.

"Finuviel used that to try to kill me," Artimour nearly shouted. "I'm not the one you should be arresting—he's the one to arrest—he's the one who's in league with the mortals—where do you think he got this dagger from?"

"Odd, then, that you should have it."

"I told you how I came to have it."

"And you expect me to believe that? As well as some idiotic story about goblins invading the Palace? About ladies who are turning into pigs, riding in a golden coach?"

Shouts from the gates interrupted Gillieas and he paused and frowned as the gates swung hastily open and the very same carriage as Artimour had met on the road spilled into the courtyard, the white horses wild and foaming. Guards reached for their bridles and the three animals pranced and whinnied and tossed their heads as they slowly quieted.

Gillieas pushed Artimour out of the way and tore the door open. The coachman was nowhere to be seen. "What the Hag—" he began as a raven flew out of the coach, shrieking displeasure. She circled once, twice, then settled on the nearest branch and cawed three times. Then a pig and a cow ambled out, looking confused, blinking in the bright light.

"Amadahlia," Artimour whispered, between the guards. "Amadahlia?" The raven shrieked again as nausea stirred in Artimour's gut. "You've got to get back to the Palace. There's no time, don't you see? Get Vinaver and make her explain. Something terrible's happening—"

"Something terrible has already happened," whispered the soft voice from above. They all turned, and Artimour saw Vinaver clinging to the railing of the central staircase. "Something terrible is happening now. You must go back, Captain, and if you want me to come, I will."

"Lady Vinaver?" Gillieas turned, squinting up into the

halo of light surrounding Vinaver. Behind her, dark shapes loomed and Artimour peered up, trying to see who it was that held Vinaver up on both sides.

"Vinaver?" Artimour asked. "Who's that with you? Is that Finuviel there?"

"Oh, no," she answered. "Would that it were Finuviel and we should not be in the state we're in now." She gripped the railing with both hands and began to descend, her back hunched and misshapen, and he saw that her wings were gone. Her eyes were huge and green in her pale, pain-pinched face. But as she stepped out of the pool of light and set foot on the bottom step, he saw the faces of the two behind her, and he gasped.

The one was an unfamiliar lady, reed-thin and gowned in russet. But it was the big mortal who crept down the stairs behind Vinaver who made Artimour's jaw drop. He moved slowly, painfully, as if every movement was agony. His white hairy face was incongruous above the vivid green tufted silk of the robe he wore belted with a scarlet sash. The rich clothes were a painful contrast to his unhealthy air. But there was no doubt at all who he was, for there was simply no mistaking the shadowed depths of his black eyes, the determined set of his gray-lipped mouth and the proud lift of his furrowed brow. "Horned Herne," said Artimour. "You're Dougal. The blacksmith of Killcairn."

It was the scent of may-apple wine that lured Delphinea into the great pile of rock and stone that was the Castle of Gar, at once surprising and distracting her. The barest trace of it tickled her nostrils, startling her out of her concentration as she darted into the black wells of early-morning shadow puddled at the base of the enormous stone walls. She sniffed, then eased past the drowsy watch leaning on their weapons in the gray, predawn light. Her first sight of the huge castle had made her think that perhaps she had made a mistake in thinking she had any chance at all of finding Finuviel, but the scent of the wine of the sidhe was unmistakable.

The mortals—men and women and even children—lay sprawled in snoring heaps beneath a motley of blankets and shawls and cloaks of every garish color and combination imaginable. They slept like the hounds lolling among them, apparently all where they'd fallen the night before. Every story ever told about the way the mortals lived appeared to be true, for the Castle seemed crammed to the rafters, both with mortals and the amazing amount of equipment they apparently needed to eke out their lives. The doors of the Great Hall stood open, and within she could see barrels piled on barrels, and the remains of great carcasses of deer and ox hanging off iron spits in the huge hearths, and the stink of grease and sweat and damp peat-scented wool mingled in the heavy air.

But even so, Delphinea sensed something of their lure, for as she stole from shadow to shadow, she saw, amazingly, tiny lights that danced and sparked in the dimness, wherever flesh was exposed, in showery patterns of fiery color. She pinched herself to remain focused on the scent. *Remember what they do to us.* Vinaver's warning, repeated by Gloriana, echoed silently. *Don't look at them,* she told herself. *Concentrate on the scent.* Silently, she made her through corridors so deep in shadow, she was able to tiptoe past three yawning kitchenmaids without so much as a flicker of notice. It helped that every available space was piled high with baskets and barrels and bundles of all sorts. The walls were stacked with weapons, and from the rafters hung implements and tools of every size and shape.

The smell of death and rot was thick in the air, and she drew the cloak close about her face. She took another sniff, for trying to detect the delicate may-apple scent was like finding a fine silk skein laced through mud. But the fragrance was there, faint but unmistakable, beckoning her above. She skirted pockets of graying light, staring up and around at the crude stone walls, the iron brackets where cold torches hung, some still smoking. Wood burned in the kitchens, and the smell of cooked oats wafted on the foul air. The Castle was beginning to wake. She hurried on, nearly colliding with a sleepy scullion who lurched out of a dark doorway, muttering to himself. She dodged back, flattening against a wall, and he glanced over his shoulder, then went on, muttering and shaking his head.

She took another experimental sniff. The seductive fragrance was stronger now, leading her to the wide stone staircase, beckoning her above. She gathered her skirts, took another look right and left, and darted up the stairs to the floor just above. But the scent led her up another level, until she turned a corner and saw that the stairwell opened up into a short corridor with two doorways set on either side of it.

A lone torch flickered sullenly in an iron bracket. She paused a moment, listening carefully. Below her, she could hear the great Castle beginning to stir to life, and a pale ray of sunshine gleamed suddenly on the floor at her feet. The scent of cooking meat blended with the may-apple smell.

She tiptoed down the corridor, placed her ear against the closest door. She heard nothing, and pushed it open slowly. It opened with a soft creak, and she peered inside, to see a long table of crude planks surrounded by benches, but the room was empty otherwise. She let the door close with a soft click and flitted across the hall. This time she heard the unmistakable sound of mortal snoring and she tiptoed to the next door. The aroma was strongest here, and her next inhalation was practically as intoxicating as a draft. There was quite a lot of it behind this door, she thought as she gently lifted the latch.

The barrel stood just opposite the door, beneath the room's lone window, set high above in the gray stone wall, which was unrelieved by tapestry or hanging of any kind. Delphinea pushed the door open slowly, and saw that it was a dressing room, for several large chests stood beside the barrel and lined the nearest wall. As she peered around the door, she saw a low mattress, covered in blankets, on which a figure crouched, head hung low between splayed knees. He wore a filthy white shirt and baggy black breeches. Between his thighs, a flagon, gold and crusted in gems, glittered in the dull light, and she gasped softly, daring to hope that she'd found Finuviel. Then the figure raised his head, and she saw it was not the face from her dreams at all. Tanned flesh hung like sagging leather from the bony ridges around his eyes, his dark brown hair hung lank against a skull that seemed far too large for his body. Black eyes burned in their hollow sockets and Delphinea felt her heart leap into her throat as he looked straight at her and said, "Who in the name of the Great Horned One are you?"

Delphinea froze. She held her cloak tight to her throat,

hardly believing that this strange-looking mortal had the ability to see through the sidhe-spell. "Who are *you* that you can see me?" Delphinea whispered back. She peered cautiously around the door. There was no one else in the room and she saw he wore a long length of chain around his waist, the other end of which was bolted into the wall behind his bed. "And why are you chained?"

"I ran afoul of the Duke. He means to teach me a lesson, that's all." He uncorked his flask and the scent of the may-apple wine burst into the air. He swallowed quickly and recorded it with a gesture so practiced Delphinea peered at him more closely. "But the question still is, who are you and what are you doing here?"

There're many more questions than that, thought Delphinea, but she forbore to ask them. There was something strange about this near-grown mortal she didn't think she wanted to understand. "I'm here to find Finuviel, the Prince of the sidhe. Do you know where he is?"

At that the boy looked slyly sideways. "I know where he'll be." He held out the flask. "Want some?"

Delphinea slipped into the room. She did want some, but it seemed less than wise to share it with this strange boy. "My name is Delphinea. If you can tell me where Finuviel—"

"I already told you—I don't know where he *is*. I told you I know where he'll *be*." Again, he took a quick swallow, and the aroma hit her like a punch between the eyes. "Soon. Very soon." He held out the flask. "Are you sure you don't want some?"

"You shouldn't drink so much of it," she murmured, amazed that he drank it at all, for even the sidhe were cautioned against drinking too much too often. Brewed only between Beltane and Mid-Summer, its distilled essence was the pure energy of raw fire. And it must account, she thought, for why he could see her and why he didn't quite glimmer like the other mortals. But she couldn't think about the wine. "Where *will* he be then?" she asked.

The boy held out the flask and his chain clinked. "Are you sure you don't want some? You look as if you'd like it."

"N-no, no, thank you, I wouldn't. I only came to find Finuviel."

"Well, you've only to wait. But I wouldn't wait here." He glanced at the door that led into the chamber where the mortal still snored, and took another sip. She followed his eyes.

"Who's in there?"

"The Duke, of course. I don't think it's wise to let him see you."

"Why not?"

But his reasons, whatever they were, went unspoken, for the door opened suddenly, and a big mortal loomed in the threshold, bare chested, hair still sleep tousled. Potent as fire, as the may-apple wine, twinkling showers of gold and red and orange light sparked off his body in a dazzling display that made her dizzy. *Remember what they do to us.* Between the heady aroma of the may-apple wine and the dazzle of the lights, she had to fight not to forget who she was and why she was there.

"Well, well, Griffin. Who have we here?" The mortal's voice rasped like sand-washed silk and the light patterns shifted and spun, dizzying in their intensity.

"She's come to find Finuviel," said the boy as he took another swallow.

His name's Griffin, thought Delphinea, struggling to maintain some sort of grasp of time and place.

"Has she, now?" The big mortal smiled, bowed. He reached out, touched her cheek, and Delphinea drew back. "Well, then, she's come to the right place. Come now, little sidhe, I won't hurt you. No one will hurt you."

From his bed the boy cackled and Delphinea glanced at him and then back at the big mortal who was looming over her like a living tower of flame. "Are you the Duke of Gar?" she managed.

He smiled at that. "Tell her, Griffin. Tell her who I am."

"Well, you will be the Duke of Gar, Your Grace." Was it fear that made the boy's voice quiver as he answered? She glanced at Griffin, but he was chugging back another swallow.

He shouldn't drink so much, she thought. Briefly it occurred to her that he was encouraged to drink it for some reason beyond her comprehension, and then a swirl of bright gold tinged with green exploded in her face as the mortal picked up her hand and brought it to his lips.

"He's a very promising boy." The mortal flung his hair off his face and smiled at Delphinea. "My name is Cadwyr, and I am most humbled to make your acquaintance, lady of the sidhe. Your Prince will be here soon—tomorrow at the latest. I'm sure it will gladden him to see you."

The boy took another quick swallow and nodded, with another clink of his chain.

Suddenly the room seemed very small and very hot and the fragrance of the may-apple wine was stifling in the thick, heavy atmosphere. The lights arcing off Cadwyr were making her head spin and she blinked, pressing her nails into the palms of her hands in a vain effort to keep her wits. There

was something so strange, so odd about the whole thing—
the dismal gray dressing room, the chained boy, and the
Duke himself, who was smiling at her with long white teeth
and red lips. Red lips, she thought, and it occurred to her she
had never noticed how red the lips of mortals were. His eyes
were blue, she realized with a start. *Blue like mine,* and she
realized she'd never seen a living person—mortal or sidhe—
with eyes the color of hers. She leaned forward, involuntarily, spellbound by the green and gold and even orange
swirling around the dark center.

"I've come to take Finuviel back to Faerie," Delphinea
blurted. Her mind felt thick and slow and stupid but she
could feel her heart racing in her chest.

"Of course you have," Cadwyr said as he drew one finger down her cheek. "And so you shall. We'll all go back to
Faerie. Very soon."

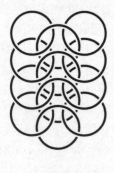

8

"**D**o you think he'll live?" Nessa peered over Granny Molly's shoulder, watching as the wicce-woman rang out the comfrey-leaf compresses and applied them gently to the angry red flesh of the wound. Kian lay facedown, his breathing shallow, his flesh hot.

Molly didn't answer immediately. She expertly rebandaged the wound, then wiped her hands on a linen towel. She tucked the blankets up over Kian's shoulders and motioned Nessa to follow her out of the makeshift shelter that had been set up for Cecily on the roof of the keep. It was the only place within the walls where there'd been space to set up something that would allow for a modicum of privacy, for the Sheriff had reclaimed his bedroom the moment Artimour had vacated, and refused to surrender it to anyone else.

Now the hall was in an uproar. Even from this height, they could hear the bellowing that accompanied the recognition of Uwen's claim to Donnor's title, of Cecily's claim to the throne of Brynhyvar. Molly listened a moment, leaning on the battlements, letting the breeze whip little tendrils of her iron-gray curls around her flushed cheeks. "We'll boil up some cabbage leaf and see if we can get him to drink it," she said, more to herself than to Nessa. "There's scarcely any supplies here, and too late in the year to think of gathering any. But the sloes the Duchess brought—those will help, I think."

"But will he live?"

Molly leaned against the stones, gazing out over the dark landscape. Below, in the courtyard, the warriors of lesser rank crowded closely, alternating shouting and shushing each other, as they jockeyed for a closer position within the ranks. "Don't you want to be down there, to see what's going on? Great doings are afoot—they're making a new Queen—"

"You're not answering me."

Molly put her arm around Nessa and drew her close, turning her so that they both faced the battlement. "There're a few things you should know if you're going to spend time with sick people, Nessa. And one's that hearing comes to us first, and leaves us last." Molly met Nessa's eyes squarely. "Sir Kian's a warrior. Do you think he expected to live to be an old man?"

Nessa dropped her eyes and took a step backward. "Are you saying he'll die?" she asked in a hushed whisper, lest her voice carry on the fickle breeze.

"We all die, sooner or later, Nessa. But of Kian, I'm saying at this point it could go either way." Molly glanced at the makeshift bed of piled straw and blankets and sighed. "I'm thinking something's gone bad, deep in the leg. Even the birch bark doesn't seem to help much. We'll see what the comfrey can do. He's young and strong—it just depends how hard a bite the Marrihugh took."

Nessa shifted on her feet. She had hesitated to mention it before, but there seemed to be nothing to lose at this point. Molly had never thought her mad before. She gestured to her birch staff, which she'd left leaning against one of the wooden supports of the canvas roof. "Last night, in the woods, when we were sitting by the fire, and I was listening to Her Grace and Uwen talk, I thought I felt—" She broke off, trying to think of the best way to describe the sensation. "I thought I felt my staff move. By itself. I wasn't touching it. It was just lying next to me. And I felt it—move."

"In what way? Was it an animal?" Molly folded her arms over her breasts and looked more closely at Nessa.

"Molly, there've been few animals in the woods since before Samhain. Uwen remarked on it before, when he brought me and Granny Wren down from Killcairn. No, I felt it twice more after that. It gave a little jump. Like it wanted me to pick it up." *That's exactly what it wanted me to do,* she thought. *Only I was too afraid to do it.*

"And did you?"

Nessa shook her head. Her palms were itching now, in fact, to go over and pick it up, but she resisted. "I—I didn't know what to think. You weren't there. I couldn't imagine what I was supposed to do after that. I was afraid I'd look foolish—I told Uwen before I knew nothing about healing and I was afraid he—he'd think I was mad if I picked up that staff and started waving it around."

"Ah, Uwen." Molly smiled. "You might've been surprised by Uwen's reaction. But the next time you feel such an urge, you might want to keep in mind that such directions tend to come one after the other, in their turn."

"You mean, if I'd picked it up, it would've come to me what to do next?" Nessa glanced at the staff. The skin of her palms felt warm.

"That would seem to make sense now, wouldn't it? The tree wouldn't waste her energy telling you all of it if she can't get you to pay attention to the first thing she wants you to do, would she now?"

Nessa thought for a moment, then glanced again at the staff. "No. I suppose not."

"Why don't you go try picking up that birch staff now?" Molly nodded. "And maybe Sir Kian has more of a chance than I thought he had."

"What does that mean?" Cecily's voice startled them both, and Nessa turned to see that the Duchess was standing in the doorway that led down the steps. As both she and Molly bobbed quick curtsies, she came forward. "How is he? Is he better?"

Both Molly's face and voice were smooth. "I can't say yet, my lady. When the Marrihugh puts her mark on a man, it's a hard thing to shake it off."

"I won't accept that." Cecily raised her chin and crossed her arms over her breasts. "There must be something we can try."

"Well, Your Grace, perhaps there is," Molly replied with a troubled look. "You have your staff, Nessa?"

"And what is it exactly you mean to do, Granny?" Cecily looked at both of them with a raised brow.

"Well, I'm not quite sure what to call it, Your Grace. Maybe a bit of tree magic, I suppose?"

"I thought only druids worked tree magic," Cecily said.

"Things are changing," blurted Nessa, and when both Cecily and Molly looked at her, she didn't know what to say next.

"The lass's right about that, Your Grace. Things are changing. But magic is magic—it all comes from the same place, don't you think?" said Molly. "There're corn grannies who use the trees in their rituals, you know."

Cecily looked dubious and Nessa felt a pang of doubt. She glanced at Molly, holding out the staff. "Maybe—maybe you should do this."

But Molly only smiled and shook her head. "Child, don't you understand? I don't know what to do. You do." She glanced at Cecily. "Would you like us to leave?"

"No," said Nessa suddenly. The staff jumped to life between her palms, and she felt a sudden throb so intense she was amazed neither of the other women had seen it. "No, both of you. Both of you, stay. Three—and one." She shook her head, for the significance of the numbers escaped her entirely. But it seemed very important that there were four of them—and that three of them were women and one was a man. The staff beat like a living heart in her hands.

"What do you want us to do?" asked Cecily. She drew a little closer and Nessa sank to her knees beside Kian. Out of the corner of her eye, she saw Molly casting salt in all four directions.

Uncertainly, Nessa held the staff over Kian and closed her eyes. It was throbbing now, pulsing so strongly she could feel it expanding and contracting against her palms. She felt Cecily and Molly kneel on either side of her, and she nodded, beginning to sway back and forth to the beat pulsating through the staff. Beside her, Molly whispered, "All right, girl?"

"I can feel it," she whispered back. "It's in the wood. It's beating. Like a heart. Do you think I'm mad?"

"No, no, Nessa." Molly wrapped one strong arm around her. "No, don't think that. Just do what seems right. Let the tree guide you. All right? Can you do that?"

"I can try," Nessa answered, even as inside she quailed. She could feel Kian beneath the staff, feel his life draining out of him in a slow steady stream. She could feel Cecily beside her, desperation oozing out of her from every pore. *I don't know what to do,* she wanted to say. *It's not like smithing,* she thought. Her father had been right there beside her, guiding her through every step of each process until she felt assured. But this—

You're not alone, Nessa. It was a voice like Molly's, but not Molly's, rich and strong like Molly's, but stronger, even, than Molly's, somehow. *Trust the tree. Trust yourself.* The energy was building now, beneath the bark, and her hands quivered of their own volition, as a current of energy swept up and down and through her, and she felt as if she'd been seized in the grip of something huge.

"Go with it, child," murmured Molly. "Let it come."

The pulse was stronger now, so strong that she was scarcely aware of Molly's steadying arm around her. Her feet seemed to grow roots, roots that stretched down through all the layers of rock and wood to the earth below, connecting to some vast source flowing like a mighty river through the land itself. The floor beneath her was pulsing now, too, rising and falling in perfect time. She remembered the feeling the day she'd been healed herself by the birch tree. She spread her knees so that her thighs were wide and splayed apart, and her spine bent backward, as a surge of energy flowed from her thighs into the base of her spine to the top of her head, then down her arms all the way to the tips of her fingers. It leaped from her fingers into the living wood. She was the spark, she realized. She, herself, somehow, was the very thing that ignited the power in the land. She felt it rising up now, through her own bones, into her muscles so that she began to tremble and shake from head to toe. Sounds now were bubbling up out of her mouth as if from a suddenly uncovered spring. They were nonsense, burbles and bubbles that made her teeth and her tongue vibrate against her lips and the roof of her mouth, so that she began to mutter and groan, even as she began to move up and down, as if she rode a great, bare-backed beast.

"That's right, child," whispered Molly against her hair. "Let it come. Let it come. Breathe now, and let it come."

Breathing. A most remarkable idea, Nessa thought, and she drew a deep gulping breath like a drowning man.

She heard Cecily whisper, "What's happening to her?" But Molly's quick mutter of a reply was drowned by the noises she heard pouring out of her own mouth.

As if the air fed the fire within, the sounds suddenly resolved themselves into words, words that boiled up and spilled over her lips of their own volition. Her heart beat in time to the steady rhythm of the pulsing tree and she understood, on some very elementary level, that the part of herself she knew as herself had somehow retreated, allowing this other part to emerge, another part she had somehow always dimly sensed, buried deep within, all along. She took another breath, and heard herself begin to chant:

"By Alder, Ash and Aspen Tree,
By Birch and Beech and Rowan Three,
Hazel, Holly, Elder, Vine,
Yew and Apple, Oak to bind.
Name I now each sacred tree,
And all thirteen I call to me
To bind to me the power that runs
From root to trunk to leaf to sun;
Up and down the trunk it goes,
Dark to light and back it flows,
All healed now Sir Kian be,
All healed now I say he'll be,
All healed by power of sacred trees."

In the background, she could hear Cecily and Molly chanting, "All we say three times shall be, as we will so let it be." She felt their arms around her, and as she repeated the last three lines, she concentrated on the energy she felt building into what felt like an enormous mass under her hands.

"All we say three times shall be," echoed Cecily's voice in her ear, her breath hot as the blast of the forge, and Nessa felt a punch, a burst so strong, the staff bucked up and down in her hands.

Scarcely believing what she did, Nessa lowered the staff down on Kian's chest, and felt the power roll out of it in a slow, pulsing wave across and into his body, moving with sure and slow deliberateness across his chest, down his arms, up his neck, down his spine and through his legs. As if from far away, she heard distant fluids hiss and gush, steam and burn as the healing force seared into the marrow of his bones, spurring the sinews and vessels to knit themselves whole. Against the backdrop of her eyelids, she watched the tissues form and spread and grow, branching out like a canopy of new leaves against the glowing face of the sun. The images faded, and she felt great drops of sweat running down her face, and a sudden gust of breeze made her shiver violently in Molly's protective embrace. Molly gently removed the birch staff from her quivering hands and placed it delicately on the floor beside Kian. She took the shawl that Cecily handed her, wrapped it around Nessa, gestured for the wine, then raised the cup to Nessa's lips. "There you are, girl, there you are. That was—" She broke off, and Nessa saw that there were tears on her cheeks, and her eyes were watery. She pressed a quick kiss on Nessa's cheek.

Nessa managed a smile and a glance at Kian, but before she could speak, Cecily gasped and picked up Kian's hand. "Kian?"

Kian's eyes were open, his eyes alert without a feverish gleam, his face a healthy pink without fever's wet flush. "Cecily?" he said.

"I'm here." She caught up his hand and kissed it. "Oh, Great Mother, thank you." She looked at Nessa wonderingly. "And thank you—I've never seen anything like that—"

"I don't think anyone has, my lady," said Molly as she drew Nessa away. "I don't think anyone has in quite some time."

What does that mean? Nessa wondered as a dreamy calm descended upon her. From the corner of her eye, she saw Cecily pick up Kian's hand, kiss it, and begin to weep. Her head felt almost too heavy for her neck to hold, and her limbs felt slushy and soft, as if her bones had turned to oatmeal. *Oatmeal.* An image of a bowl piled with steaming oats drenched in honey topped with melting butter rose before her eyes, and she realized she was ravenously hungry. "I'm hungry, Molly," she murmured against Molly's shoulder. The older woman was guiding her down the winding stairs, letting her lean on her broad bosom, so that Nessa felt nearly cradled.

"I know, child," whispered Molly.

"I feel so strange, Molly," she said. The shadows were moving, shifting, forming and reforming into images and patterns she could not begin to comprehend.

"We'll get you fixed right up," said Molly. "Just put one foot in front of the other for now. One foot in front of the other."

Somehow, they reached the kitchens, and Nessa found herself bundled into several sets of capable arms, who wrapped her in blankets and fed her oatmeal sweet with honey and apples and rich with cream and butter, until she fell into a deep and sudden sleep.

"Is he even alive in there?" Voices, rough as the gravel on which Finuviel lay, penetrated the red fog of his agony. Every jarring pound of their booted feet throbbed through the earth, wracking his spine. He curled his blistered fingers in the coarse wool blanket and gasped as cold air free of silver's taint blasted into his prison. He tried to open his eyes but he found that the lids were sealed against his cheek by a dried crust of the fluid that seeped from his silver-scorched skin. But the air was cold and tasted sweet, and he opened his mouth as he was lifted, then dragged up and out of the mine.

As soon as he reached the surface, he felt it in the same moment the sunlight stung his face—a questioning awareness and the face of a young sidhe he knew he'd never seen before exploded from out of the half-remembered fragments of his tormented dreams. Her eyes were blue, he saw. *Blue is the color of surcease.*

"He's not so pretty anymore," said a voice, and this time there were chuckles of assent.

Finuviel sensed movement beside him, and he tensed. He felt the splintered boards on which the straw was piled. A wagon, he thought. They were taking him somewhere. He heard a creak and a jounce, and realized someone else had gotten into the wagon beside him.

"Ah." The quick intake of breath contained both pity and disgust, and Finuviel wondered what exactly the silver had done to him. It felt as if it had eaten away at his exposed skin, leaving the sinews and the tendons all exposed.

"What'd ya think, Bard? Will he make it back to Gar?" One of his unseen guards spared him the trouble of trying to talk immediately.

There was a long sigh and then a pause. "Fetch more water." Finuviel felt the air on his chest as the shreds of his clothing were shifted aside with what felt like one very tentative finger. "Bring my bag. If we pass a village with a corn granny, we'll have to stop and ask her what she thinks. I've a few simples in there—may have some affect upon him— 'tis a monstrous thing that Cadwyr's done."

Finuviel bit back a moan as his hand was picked up, accompanied by that same soft hiss of dismay.

Immediately, the mortal laid Finuviel's hand down gently. "Lord sidhe?" The voice was gentle, soft, as if he feared Finuviel's hearing might've been affected as well. Finuviel felt hot mortal breath in his ear, then a cool shadow fell across his face and he turned his head in its direction. "You can hear me?"

Finuviel nodded. Pain seared down his throat as he tried to move his tongue.

"I'm here to try and help you, my lord. I'll do what I can—I'm a bard, trained in healing. My name's Lavram. Let me know if—if anything I do is too painful for you, my lord, for to tell you the Hag's truth, I'm not quite certain how to—how to help."

Agony lanced down Finuviel's arm as he beckoned the mortal closer, until he could smell the mortal's rancid breath. "Silver's poison—must draw out the poison."

"Draw out the poison? I have some drawing salve. Will that work?"

He had no idea what drawing salve might be or what it might contain, and so he nodded, exhausted by the effort, swallowing the spongy wetness welling up in his throat that he realized was not only blood but a bit of the tissue lining his mouth as well. For the first time, he realized how terribly the silver must've affected him, and he reached up, intent on touching his cheeks, when the mortal pulled his hand back and he realized he had no feeling at all in his fingertips.

"No, no, my lord. We don't want to touch that cheek. Not yet, anyway. Let's get it all clean, shall we?" The mortal's voice was determinedly cheerful.

His arms were lowered gently once again, and placed deliberately by his sides. Finuviel felt the mortal moving, heard the clink of hard-bottomed containers and the sudden splash of water, then smelled a grassy peppermint. There was the slosh of linen dipped and wrung out. A few droplets landed on his face before the entire compress was placed gently on his cheek. It cooled but could not entirely stop the fire Finuviel felt burning in his skin. But at least it eased the worst of the pain, so that he plucked at the mortal's garment and said, "Bard?"

"Don't talk, my lord. Just let me bathe you with this—it feels all right? Try to rest."

"Where're we going?"

"To Gar, my lord. Duke Cadwyr has called for you."

There was a rush of breeze. He smelled horses, wet grass and rushing water. The rough boards beneath him jolted forward and the liquid spilled over his hand. "Help me," he choked out.

There was a long silence and Finuviel wondered if the mortal had heard him. Then another wet linen compress was applied to his other cheek and the mortal whispered, "My lord, I cannot."

"I'm dying, can't you see that? Do you really think there's anything you can do to help me, mortal?" Finuviel tried to struggle upright, but a wave of searing fire and dizziness overwhelmed him, and the bard easily pushed him flat once more.

"Please rest, my lord."

"Listen to me, Bard. If I don't return to Faerie, I'll die, and so will all my kind. I know what Cadwyr means to do— Is that what you want, Bard? Please—"

"I cannot, my lord." The hot breath blasted directly into his ear. "There're a hundred riders to guard you—the Duke's not taking any chances. I could no more let you go than I could sprout wings and fly."

Finuviel felt the wet cloth daubed on his eyelids, softening and loosening the thick crust that sealed them shut.

Water ran down into his eyes. He managed to open one eye, and blinked against the sudden flash of sunlight. He lifted his arm and saw that his hand was something out of a goblin horror, for the skin hung off it in shreds, nails blackened and charred into claws.

"N-no, my lord, easy, easy." The mortal was fussing over him, pouring something into a goblet that suddenly sang to him of Faerie. Finuviel turned his head, seeking the source of that extraordinary and unexpected scent, and the bard touched the lip of a mortal cup to his mouth. "The Duke sent this brew—he said it might ease you."

May-apple wine burned on his ruined lips, swirled on his charred tongue, washed down the raw tissues of his throat, burning like liquid fire all the way to his gut, sending a ripple of strength through his entire body. He drew a deep breath and smelled water—fresh water, running water. The sky above him flashed blue through the broad canopy of dark evergreens above their heads. *Blue is the color of surcease.* He saw again the face of the woman with eyes the color of that sky. He heard the shriek of a gull, and realized they were taking a road along some large body of water— a river, perhaps, or a lake. For the first time since leaving the mine, Finuviel began to believe he might survive on more than hope alone. He smiled up at the mortal, willingly bending his head to take another sip. With enough may-apple wine, and water close by, he might not need the mortal's help to escape. *I'm coming,* he thought, to whatever, or whoever, might be at the other end of this strange new sense of connection. Faerie, itself, he thought. Surely it's Faerie itself. *I'm coming,* he thought again, and the may-apple wine rushed to his head and all his thoughts dissolved into a shower of rainbow sparks.

"Kian?" Cecily whispered, scarcely daring to believe what she'd witnessed. She touched his forehead once more. In the gloom, his face was pale but felt warm and dry to the touch. But not too warm, thank the goddess. She had no doubt that the goddess deserved to be thanked. But which goddess? A chill went down her spine as she remembered the still echo that had reverberated through her mind the day after they'd escaped. She felt first his forehead and then his cheek with the back of her hand, and his eyes fluttered open more. He turned his head on the pillow and looked at her.

"Cecily," he said again.

She picked up his hand and brought it to her lips. "How do you feel?"

He smiled, shifted beneath the blankets, stretched and flexed his arms and hands. She struggled to blink away the tears that flooded her eyes, even as his answer sent a cold finger of fear down her spine. "As if I'll live to die another day."

Oh, no, don't say that, she thought. She pushed the whisper of a laugh out of her mind, and shook the impending sense of doom away. She forced herself to smile back. "We're at Killcarrick," she whispered.

He smiled again, and nodded, just a little. "I know."

Of course he did, she thought. "Uwen's the Duke of Gar."

He nodded, mouth quirked up in a little smile. "I know that, too. The grannies who were just here could talk of nothing else."

Their eyes met and he was hers again, solid and strong. Desire and gratitude and love rolled through her, forcing words to spill from her lips she'd no intention of speaking yet. "Well, then, Sir Kian of Garn, who knows so much and hears so well, perhaps you also know I bear your child."

She was never sure which of them looked more surprised, and his answer was lost in the harsh shrieks of the flock of crows that swept low over the tower and circled off, screeching their obvious displeasure.

It was very late by the time Nessa made her way back to the forge, having no real idea how long she'd slept cocooned before the kitchen fire. It occurred to her that the Sheriff must have some regard for her, for no one had moved into the blacksmith's quarters, and there seemed to be a tacit understanding that they were hers til Engus came back. If he came back. But she was still so tired she did not see Uwen crouching beside the fire until he stood up, startling her as she set her birch staff beside the forge and reached for an iron to poke a flame out of the red embers. "Sorry to frighten you, lass. I heard what happened—everyone's heard it now. How's the Chief?"

"Well," said Nessa slowly, "I—I'm not quite sure—"

"No? That's not what I heard—though I wasn't sure I heard it right. Didn't you tell me you knew nothing about healing?"

"I still don't know anything about it," she said.

"The word's spreading quick he's healed by some new magic that got worked by you. They're saying you're a Beltane child."

"Me?" Nessa flushed and looked down at her hands. "My birthday's about a month away from Beltane—I couldn't claim to be a Beltane child if I wanted to." She nodded at the staff. "It was the tree—this staff. I was just—I was just the one it used—the one it *wanted* to use. Does that make sense?"

Uwen nodded slowly, then he smiled. "I'm only teasing you, lass. And yes, it does make sense, quite a lot of it. But I still think you're wrong. I think you know quite a bit more about healing than you think you do."

"What happened today, in the councils?" Nessa set her birch staff in a corner of the forge and poked the red embers in the forge to life. She was equally sure Uwen—and all the rest—were wrong. She had a connection to the tree of some sort—it wasn't any healing ability of her own. Certainly she'd never healed so much as a torn toenail before. It was ridiculous to think she herself had anything to do with it. *But Molly couldn't feel the staff move.* She shoved that disturbing thought away and concentrated on building up the fire.

The nights were getting cold. Soon she'd be forced to rummage through Engus's chests for something warmer to wear, unless a market were held. But it didn't seem like anyone had much time or thought for a market. Briefly, she wondered if the weather turned as cold in Faerie, if Faerie would survive long enough for her father to escape, and what Artimour might have found waiting there. She was tempted to go and find out for herself. After all, this time she had a silvered sword.

But Uwen sighed and paced to the door. He leaned on the threshold and peered out into the courtyard, which even at this hour still bustled with activity. "I'll say one thing, since Cecily's got here, this whole keep's looking much better organized. But as far as the chiefs go, it's not so much Cecily they like, as Cadwyr, at the moment, they distrust. The scouts have gone out—there're plans afoot to block the routes he's using to bring the silver down to Gar—he won't like that, and it'll force him to show his hand. And everyone likes the idea of helping themselves to Cadwyr's silver."

"What about the Duchess? Will they elect her Queen?"

"There're plenty who are at this moment inclined to support her against Cadwyr. But whether or not she's elected—well, that will depend on who wins the fight. Understand?"

Nessa took a deep breath. "And what about you?"

"A couple of the druids examined my medallion and pronounced it genuine. But again, there're more sitting on the fence to see which way the apples fall."

"And what will you do?"

"Wait til the scouts come back—see what they can tell us. But what about you, Nessa?"

"Me?" His question startled her, and took her unaware.

"There's been talk among a whole group from up your way that they intend to leave soon. I wasn't sure if you planned to go with them or not."

"I—I didn't even know there was talk of leaving." Did it matter? she wondered. Artimour would come here to look for her.

"Well, that's good then."

"It is?"

"I wanted to make sure you weren't leaving before I came to ask you for a favor, lass."

"Of me? What do you need?"

"Not me. Cecily. She came away with scarcely a shift on her back. She needs a sword, and armor—something to make her look as strong as I know she is—as strong as Kian knows she is."

Who could doubt that Cecily was strong? Nessa wondered. She nodded at the courtyard, where ever since Cecily's arrival, the chaos had magically resolved into order. Even the smell was diminishing, replaced by the scent of soap from the great billows of steam issued from the laundry cauldrons now steaming in the courtyard, stirred by a veritable company of stable hands and scullions. But she understood why Uwen asked. "A sword will take some time, though. It's no simple thing, you know. I'll have a hilt from something here—I don't think—"

"You do what you can, lass." He touched her cheek as he turned on his heel. "You're needed here, Nessa. Don't ever doubt that."

Had he guessed she'd thought of going into the Other-World again? she wondered as she watched him make his way across the courtyard. She lifted a sword from the pile of discarded weapons, assessing its hilt. The Duchess was small—she'd need a smaller hilt, thought Nessa as she began to ponder how to do what Uwen asked. *A sword's not like any other weapon, you know, Nessie.* Instantly she was six years old, perched on a table, watching her father pound a length of iron into steel, his skin and black hair shining with sweat so that he shone the way she imagined a sidhe must. *And why's that, Papa?* her own childish treble echoed across the years. *You can hunt with a bow, or a spear, or build a house with an ax, cut your meat with a knife. But a sword alone is made to kill men, and so you must be careful of the intent you put in it. A sword that looks for blood too eagerly can be as deadly to its owner as one that's drawn too reluctantly.* She'd been far too young to understand what Dougal had meant, but she remembered how she'd clasped her fingers and watched him turn all his fierce attention to the metal on his anvil, and she remembered the shivery feeling that swept over her as the walls themselves shuddered with the force of his blows.

But it made more sense now, and as she lifted the lantern from over the anvil and blew out the stub of the candle, she wondered what sort of intention Dougal would have put in a sword for Cecily. But the only image that came to her mind, just as she was falling asleep, still planning the construction, was of her birch staff, curiously with three leaves sprouting from one end.

9

"Still-wife? Still-wife, are you here?" Jammor bit his lip and peered inside the dim stillroom, glancing over his shoulder. Below, in the outer wards, the mercenaries from Lacquilea drilled their complicated drills, their camp spread out across the meadow all the way to the treeline, and he could smell the unfamiliar scents rising from their cooking fires, their foreign accents harsh and loud upon the wind. He eased inside the room. Bunches of drying herbs hung from the low beams, and the shelves were full of neatly arranged jars and flasks and implements. "Still-wife?" A figure looked up from her place at a table, pulling her black shawl off her head. "Mag?"

"Who's that?" She was pounding some green mixture with a pestle, working with two of the other grannies. One was sorting through a pile of stems and stalks and leaves, and the other was carefully straining some sort of tincture through a cheesecloth sieve.

"It's me, Jammor. Jammor of the Rill."

"What do you want?" Mag kept her eyes fixed on her work.

"I came to ask—to ask—how the granny was."

"She's dead. You can tell your master that, boy." Mag worked the pestle hard, as if she could grind the herb into the very mortar itself. Then she turned away with a heavy sigh, tugging her shawl back up over her head.

"Wait—no, wait, Mag—that's not at all why I came—"

The older woman turned back. "Then why did you come? To find out for your master what the Duchess might have planned? To work your way into our number again?"

Jammor twisted his hands in the fabric of his gray robe. "Kestrel didn't send me. I came because there's something very strange going on with Cadwyr. And I had a dream last night—a dream about trees."

"What about trees?" Mag put her pestle down.

"I dreamed the trees were dead. Not just around the castle. All over Brynhyvar."

Mag rolled her eyes. "Go ask your master what that means. We grannies have no tree lore, right, Corka?"

The granny with the sieve looked and made a small noise of disgust, then turned back to her work with what could have been a curse.

"Still-wife, I want to help you—I don't know what the dream means but I do know Cadwyr's mad."

At that they all looked up. "What makes you say he's mad?"

"Have you seen that boy he keeps?" Jammor peered over his shoulder. "The one who's always got his flagon to his mouth?"

"I got a good look at him when they first came in," Corka said. "There's something wrong with him. Very wrong."

"It's that stuff Cadwyr has him drinking. There's barrels of it in the stables now. Cadwyr's only been here a day and already he called for another barrel of it. How can any one person drink so much? It looks as if it's burning the boy up from the inside out, but Cadwyr keeps feeding it to him. Why?" Jammor advanced a few more paces. "And all these mercenaries and all the silver—I think Cadwyr means to conquer all TirNa'lugh—Mag, I'm not joking."

The third granny rose to her feet and shut the door. "You should learn to keep your voice low, young bard."

But Mag beckoned to him, as she said to the others, "Her Grace said Cadwyr was in league with the sidhe long before Samhain. But now you think he's turned on them?"

Jammor leaned forward, deliberately lowering his voice, until the grannies cocked their heads and gathered close. "There's another one now. A lady. I don't know where he found her, but he's got her upstairs. And another still—one he had inside a silver mine—the King, they say, of all the sidhe."

Corka exchanged looks with the others. "That answers why he's turning the silver into weapons. I told you it wasn't to pay those Lacquilean vultures."

"What about this lady, boy?" Mag crossed her arms over her breasts and cocked her head.

"She's a lady of the sidhe—I glimpsed her and that was enough. He's got her in the Duchess's rooms—with a moon-mazed uplander girl to tend her."

"Interesting," said Corka, nodding at Mag. She reached for a basket.

"Someone has to get word of this to Her Grace," said the third granny at his elbow. "If this is true, Cadwyr must be stopped before he has the might of TirNa'lugh behind him—if that happens, no one shall stand against him."

"That's right, boy." Mag nodded. "You've got to get word of this to Her Grace."

"Me?" Jammor looked from one granny to the other. "I—I don't know—what about Kestrel?"

"What about him? If he knows you've come to us, what's your life worth to him? Or to the Duke? They'll give you a horse at the stables. Just tell them—"

"Tell them you've been summoned for a funeral."

Jammor looked from one granny to the other. "That won't work—ah, you're teasing." He took a deep breath and let it out in a long sigh. "All right. I suppose you're right. I'll think of something and I'll go."

The wind was cold as it whined through the battlements, and Cecily pulled her shawl tighter over her shoulders, even as she tried to shake off the sense of disbelief that they could even be having this debate. "Kian, I don't think you're ready to ride. Please listen to me. You were nearly dead—you lost more blood than I thought a man could hold. It took a marvel to cure you—the blacksmith girl worked magic of a kind even the grannies say they never saw. Tree magic, of some sort—the druids right now are speaking to her." Cecily crossed her arms over her breasts and shook her head. "Please, won't you at least talk to the granny—"

"I can't listen to some cud-chewing country granny, Cecily—"

"Cud-chewing granny? Since when do you call them

that? You were willing to listen on Samhain. You were willing to listen when it came to the goblins. Why won't you listen now?" She tossed her head and her hair tumbled out of her loose kerchief, and she thrust it off her face, bundling it back into a loose knot. "I know why you won't listen. You want to ride out, don't you? You don't want to wait and take on Cadwyr until you're healed. But you're not ready. How can you possibly be ready?"

"Look at this, Cecily." Kian turned his shoulder to her and showed her the back of his arm. "This is nothing more than a scratch. And this—" He patted his leg. "Whatever kind of magic Nessa worked, it was extremely effective. Look— it's clean—it's healed." He turned his leg. "And you cannot bolt me to your side. Maybe it wasn't just Nessa's magic." He walked naked to stand beside her, and tilted her chin up to his. "Maybe the leg wasn't as bad as you thought. You know some wounds look worse than they really are."

"I saw how much blood you lost." She turned her face away and bit her lip. "I don't mean to keep you bolted to my side. I just don't want to see you ride out before you're really ready."

"Cecily, it's just a scouting trip. I want to see for myself the way the land lies east of the lake. I know the upland country, but those passes out of Allovale aren't near as familiar. We'll be gone just a night or two. Surely you can spare me that long?"

"It's not about sparing you. It's about losing you." She stared down into the courtyard, where the repairs had largely been completed. She had immediately assigned the mothers and children and those too old to fight to the most protected area of the keep, thus ensuring an instant relief of most of the mayhem. Now a sergeant bawled a drill as Kian reached out and drew her close. Involuntarily she leaned into him, letting her head fall into the hollow of his chest. "Can't you send Uwen?"

He shook his head. "You know I can't send Uwen. With Donnor's death, the Company doesn't exist anymore and Uwen's got a claim to the duchy of Gar. I've no call to order him to go anywhere. You know that."

"I know that you're the dearest thing in life to me, Kian of Garn. I nearly lost you and we haven't even begun."

"Ah, Cecily." He tilted her head and dropped light kisses on her cheeks, on her eyes, and then finally, he gathered her mouth with his. They leaned into each other, and she let herself sink into the warm solidity of his arms and chest and thighs. Then he turned her face gently around and pointed out across the land. The land lay brown and sere beneath the crisp sky, the evergreens dark spikes on the thickly forested hills that reflected in the breeze-blown lake. "You can't think like that, Cecily. This land, all this before us and beyond, and all those people down there and out across the hills, that's what must be the dearest thing in life to you, Cecily. I can be replaced. I'm just a warrior, and there are a thousand knights within these walls, or just outside, who would gladly give up an arm to stay home and sit by your side, or warm your bed any night you asked it of them. It's the land you must love, Cecily, for the land goes on forever. We—the warriors and the druids and the rest of us—we come and we go in and out of the Summerlands." He paused, then said, "I'll tell you the truth. I know you're right. I was nearly at the Summerlands—I could hear the feast, smell the oxen and the stags roasting on huge spits, I even smelled the mead flowing like water through the air. If I've been called back, Cecily, surely it's for more than a couple of days." He wrapped his arms around her and his hand crept low, gently cradling the low swell of her belly, nestling her close. He pulled the kerchief off her head and let her hair tumble around her shoulders.

"I don't want you to die," she said in a fierce whisper between clenched teeth.

"Well, I don't want to die either." He spun her around to face him. "I want to see you crowned. I want to see my son born. I want to see him grow to be a man. But I also know it's not that we die, but how that matters."

It's not that we die, but how. The ancient tenet of her House echoed through her mind, and she crossed her arms over her breasts, as she would shield herself and the child within. But it was the ancient creed of her warrior race, and Kian was, before anything else, a warrior. *That's why they all love him,* she thought. *He's just and brave and loyal; he's everything a warrior should be. Even in the acceptance of his death.* With a deep sigh, she let him turn her in his arms and lead her to their bed, let him ease her down on the coarse straw-pricked homespun sheets, let him lift her tunic and her kirtle over her head. "I promise I'll come back to you, Cecily," he murmured as he moved up over her body. He touched one rosy-brown nipple gently with the tip of his tongue, licking delicately until she cried out involuntarily, and he raised his head and smiled. "How could you think me eager to ride away from this?"

But you are, she wanted to say. Instead, she reached for him, and he covered her mouth with his, one big hand splayed over her slightly rounding belly. "I shall come back to you, Cecily, I swear. I shall come back to you, and to our son."

"Could be a daughter, you know," she murmured as she ran her flat palms over the lightly furred planes of his chest.

"Could be both," he murmured back, and then he made the world dissolve into a soft warm haze of long-denied desire.

"Blacksmith?"

Nessa looked up from her work to see a crowd of white-robed druids clustered in the doorway of the forge, with Molly and a couple of the corn grannies, Morag and Bethy, hovering close around the edges. "Aye?" She put her hammer down and stepped around the forge, wiping her hands on a wet rag. "Master Druid? Molly?"

"Master Druid here has heard about your healing of Sir Kian, Nessa. He wanted to ask you about it."

"My name's Collum, maiden. My fellow druids and I— we're from up Pentland way, and we have some questions about the healing it's been said you performed over Sir Kian of Garn."

"What sort of questions?" asked Nessa.

"It's being said you invoked some sort of tree magic. We hoped that you could help us."

Nessa glanced at her staff, which still stood, just as she'd placed it last night, in a corner of the smithy. No leaves had sprouted on it overnight. Nessa looked from the druids to Molly. "I don't really remember what I did. Or what I said."

"I told you, I doubted the girl would remember," Molly put in, chin raised, arms crossed over her breasts. "The words come through her, not of her."

But the druid ignored Molly and fixed his intent stare on Nessa. "Would you come with us?"

Nessa glanced again at Molly. "Where do you want me to go?"

"We need to know the thirteen trees. Do you remember what they were?"

"The thirteen?" She blinked. "Alder, ash, aspen. Birch and beech and rowan." But the rest were a blank, and there was a low groan from the druids as she shook her head and spread her hands helplessly. "I—I didn't think it was something I had to remember, I'm sorry."

"We know oak and holly, Master Collum," said one of the other druids.

But the first druid only waved him away impatiently. "It's what we don't know that matters, Master Bard." He turned back to Nessa. "At the full of the moon, maiden, we plan to do a working, a ritual, to connect us back to the Sacred Thirteen. But—"

"But you're not certain what they are?"

"It didn't matter before," whispered one of the other druids.

Nessa looked up, met Molly's eyes. "I'll try to remember," she said.

"That's why we want you to come with us." The druid gestured to his fellows. "We think the best way for you to repeat yourself is to heal someone else. Don't you think?"

Nessa opened her mouth to protest, but before Nessa got a word out, Molly said, "I don't see how that necessarily follows, Master Druid."

But the druid leaned forward, eyes desperate beneath his furrowed brow. "Please, maiden. My brothers and I—the druidic verses are obscure. The people looked to us for help on Samhain, and we had little to offer—"

"If you'd come and try for us, maiden," said another. His speech was thick with a northern burr, and he wore an unfamiliar plaid over his blue-trimmed robes. There was such distress in their faces, such anxiety in their stances, that Nessa wiped her hands once more on her rag and reached around her neck.

"All right," she said. "I'll come."

The druids bowed and turned, striding away from the forge, as if they expected her and the grannies to follow. Nessa threw her apron over the anvil and tossed aside the vambraces, then scampered after them, even as Molly called, "Don't forget this!"

"Molly, what if I can't remember what I said?" Nessa asked as she gripped the staff.

Molly made a little sound that might've been a sigh. "Do your best, child. Go with it. Remember?"

Nessa clutched the staff, trying to recall the phrases that had seemed to flow so easily. *Birch and beech and rowan three, elder, apple, holly vine*—was that it? "Molly," Nessa asked as they followed the druids out of the keep and into the wood, "Why is this happening to me?"

The grannies glanced at each other. "If you weren't so sure of your birthday, Nessa, I'd say you were a Beltane child," Molly answered slowly. "But since you are—" she shrugged. "Who's to say? I don't understand it. The druids have starcraft, perhaps Master Collum can tell you."

"What makes you so sure, Nessa, of the day you were born?" asked Morag, struggling to keep up. She huffed and puffed, her plump cheeks red with her effort.

"It's the day my father told me I was born," Nessa replied slowly. "And he was there, so he should know—"

"Unless he deliberately told you another day," put in Bethy.

"Hush now, Bethy," said Molly. "Don't be putting it in the girl's head her father would lie to her—you've no call to do that. But maybe he was mistaken, Nessa? Could that be it?"

But Nessa only shook her head and finally the grannies exchanged glances and shrugged. "Well, then, there's none to know for sure," said Morag. "Where in the name of the Great Mother do these druids mean to drag us?"

They had left the beaten track now, and were on a new path, which wound through the Killcarrick woods, into the low hills just beyond the keep. The wood was quiet but for the loud crunch of the leaves beneath their boots and the swish of the grannies' skirts.

The wood opened up into a clearing, and Nessa saw they were at the bottom of a little hill, a little tor, the top of which was visible from Killcarrick's tower. "What's up there?" she asked, for the druids were clustered at the base, waiting.

"We've rekindled the sacred fire, and we've begun to clear the sacred space. But there're more than thirteen trees in these groves now—more or less and all different ones—" began Collum.

"They've been let to run wild, you see," put in another druid.

"Will you come?"

They started up the hillside and Nessa followed. It gave her a cold and empty feeling as she followed them up the hill, their ragged hems dragging in the thick underbrush. Whatever had been here once wasn't here anymore, she thought as they reached the summit. She gazed around, and saw what looked like the ancient remains of a great bonfire. "What is this place?" she asked.

"It's the old Killcarrick Tor, isn't it, druid?" Molly replied as she stepped into the low ring of stones. Nessa noticed them. They were no higher than anyone's knee, covered in moss and leaning at crooked angles. They were stained and blackened too, in places, as if they'd been too close to too many fires.

"Aye," replied one of the druids.

"Why was it abandoned?" asked Morag.

A shiver went through Nessa as she looked around. It was cold up here, cold and empty, despite the thick wood all around. The trees were bare up here, their leaves long blown away.

"They couldn't get the fires lit up here, isn't that so?" said Molly. "They moved it to the tor they use now perhaps twenty years ago. Isn't that right?"

"Something about the way the wind blows off the lake, Granny," added another druid.

Nessa had been to the rituals on Killcarrick Tor more times than she could count, and she had never heard about this place. She looked around the barren overgrown tor and gripped her staff. The wood was cold, unyielding. A pang went through her. "What is it you want me to do here, Master Druid?"

"Please come." He beckoned to her, and she followed through a copse of young trees that had grown up in the very center of the ring of crooked stones.

She gasped. An old man lay on a wooden pallet, his arm torn off at the shoulder, a thick bloodstained bandage awkwardly bound around it. He looked up at her and smiled. "Beltane-born?"

"No," cried Nessa.

He looked around at the other druids, his long white hair

spilling over his chest, his face gray with exhausted pain. "I thought you went to fetch the Beltane-born?"

"She says she's not," said Collum. "Please, my lord, won't you at least let her try?"

"Come here, girl." The old druid raised his head and beckoned with his one hand. "What's your name and where're you from? And why are you all covered in soot?"

"I'm Nessa from the village of Killcairn. I'm a blacksmith."

The old druid looked up at Collum. "What nonsense is this that's got into your head? Do I look like a horse that's lost a shoe?"

Alarmed, Nessa backed away. "Perhaps—perhaps you better find another—"

"Come back here, girl," Collum said. "Please," he finished as Molly stepped forward, ever vigilant, with a firm "Now, see here, Master Druid—"

Collum looked down at the old man on the pallet. A fine sheen of sweat covered his forehead and Nessa saw his lips were thin and blue. He's dying, she thought. "What happened to your arm, Master Druid?"

"A goblin took it on Samhain."

Nessa backed away, uncertain, even as Collum caught her arm. "Please—please won't you try?"

"I—I'm not sure this is something I can heal," Nessa answered. The whole grove, the whole place, it was sick and sad and quiet and cold—as if whatever had once lived here was gone. Gone or sleeping. Waiting for something to wake it. She wondered how the fires had been lit that blackened the old stones.

"She knows her limits," grunted the old druid. "At least she's that wise."

"What is it you expected the girl to do?" asked Molly, stepping forward.

"The bleeding won't stop, wise-woman," said the druid on the ground. "I can feel the life leaking out of me a drop at a time." He glanced from Nessa to Molly and the other corn grannies. "Maybe you've something to ease my passing, sisters?"

The women glanced at each other, and Nessa stepped forward. A pang of sympathy ran through her for the old man before her, and she glanced around the group. "I'll try. I'm not sure I can do much good. But I'll try." She looked down at the old man.

He met her eyes then and her heart sank, for she doubted very much she would be able to help him. The staff felt cold and lifeless in her hand. *But why?* she wondered. Why save Sir Kian, and not this wise old man? Wasn't his knowledge needed? Surely as one of the ArchDruids, he'd spent his whole lifetime learning their lore.

As she fell to her knees beside him, he looked at her and smiled. "It's not your fault, girl."

A cool breeze rustled through the branches overhead. Somewhere a bird trilled and was immediately still. Nessa felt what she thought was a definite throb in the staff. But there was nothing else. The land, she thought. She had no sense of the land beneath her feet. *Maybe we're too far from the Mother-Tree.* But she hesitated to give up, even as the druid sighed on the ground and she felt Molly's hand on her shoulder, just there, strong and comforting. She took a deep breath, held the staff out over the old druid, willing herself to feel that sense of connection, of communion with the land. But there's nothing there, she thought again. It's like the house is empty and still. Like there's no one home. But there're trees all around here, she thought. The standing stones are blasted with fire. Could something have happened here to shut it all off?

At last she had to acknowledge it was futile. She sank back and shook her head, opening her eyes to see the old druid watching her. "It's not your fault, girl," he said again.

"I don't understand," Nessa said, looking up at Molly. "It's just not—it's just not there." It was an emptiness she felt, a hollow feeling, as if, quite strongly beneath her feet, something wasn't there.

"We told you, Collum, you were casting good seed after bad—to think a blacksmith girl, of all things—"

"Doubtless the knight was not so hurt—"

The mutters stung Nessa like stones. She backed away, clutching the staff, feeling it like a stick in her hand. It felt as lifeless as a stick and she was tempted, for a moment, to throw it away, into the brambles and vines. Behind her, she heard Molly shout "Nessa!" But she kept on running, out of the brambles, into the forest, blindly running until at last she paused, and looked around. Something swung down, low, out of the branches, like a large cat, and she swung her staff and hit it to the ground. It fell, hissing, and Nessa crouched, paused, the staff held like a weapon. The thing that sprawled before her hissed and grunted, and she drew back, staring at it in the gloomy forest light. It looked like a large-eared, miniature version of the goblins, she thought, only very very dirty, smeared with dirt, in fact, and covered with leaves, so that it looked as if it had deliberately tried to camouflage itself. Which probably, she thought, it had. It got to its feet, hissed and showed its teeth, then ran away, deeper into the woods. What in the name of Herne was that? she wondered, squinting after it. But there was no time to follow it, for she heard Molly and the other grannies calling for her, and she knew she could not make them think she'd been lost within the wood. "I'm here," she called, staring in the direction the thing had gone. A small goblin? she wondered. Did goblins even have young?

"Nessa?" Molly broke through the underbrush, closely followed by Morag and Bethy. "Nessa, are you all right?"

"Don't let them make you feel bad, Nessa," cut in Bethy.

"Her Grace knows what you did for Sir Kian, Nessa," said Morag.

"Nessa?" The grannies halted a few paces away.

"I thought I saw something, Molly," said Nessa. "Something that looked like a little goblin. Only it was brown and covered in leaves."

The three women gasped. "A trixie?"

"Did you hear that, she saw a trixie!"

But Molly held up her hand. "Enough, sisters! The girl's head is full enough as it is—she doesn't need more speculation from you forcing it to spill. Leave her be. You know just now was hard."

Nessa turned to face them. "I know what I saw. I knocked it down, in fact—look, see that mark in the leaves? That's where it fell."

"What did it do?"

"It hissed at me and ran off when I threatened it again with my staff."

"And it was brown?"

"Aye, and covered with leaves." She dusted off her tunic. "I'm sorry I ran off just now."

"They're scared old men, Nessie," began Morag.

"That's not it," Nessa said. "It wasn't what they said. It wasn't just that."

"What was it, child?" asked Molly as they headed toward the keep.

"It was the strangest thing, Molly. When we stood on the tor—the land didn't feel the same as it felt in the keep. Do you think it had something to do with—with this staff? Closer to the keep we're closer to its tree?"

Molly glanced at the other two grannies. "Well, child. It could make sense."

"But it doesn't explain why I was able to help Sir Kian and not the old druid."

The grannies looked at each other, and finally Molly patted her back. "There're many things we can't explain, Nessie. Maybe it's best to let it lie a bit."

"Think on it," Morag said.

"Sleep on it," added Bethy.

But it troubled her, all the way back to the forge, through the rest of the afternoon and into the evening, until finally, as the shadows were falling, she tore off her apron and went to find the druid. She found Collum inside the keep bent over a bowl of stew. As she hesitated, debating whether or not to disturb his supper, he looked up and saw her. He dabbed at his mouth with a napkin and waved her over. "I meant to come and find you, blacksmith," he said, before she could speak. "I wanted to apologize for what happened today. In our zeal to understand, we did not consider you at all. My brothers and I—I must apologize for our behavior."

"Thank you," Nessa said, wondering what had brought about this change of heart.

"The Duchess—" Collum said, wiping his lips again. "She made it clear—the nature of Sir Kian's wound, the spell you worked—we don't understand how or why it worked, but it's clear you made something happen." He motioned her to sit down, and thrust a wooden bowl at her, then waved for the serving bowl at the other end of the table. "That's what I wanted to talk to you about. It's clear you worked some sort of magic. I—I want to ask your help in understanding what sort of magic it was."

Nessa put the spoon to her lips and took a bite of soup. "But, Master Druid, don't you—don't you have magic? Of your own sort?"

But the druid shook his head, and spoke so softly beneath the din of the crowd, that Nessa had to lean down to hear him. "Don't you understand, maiden? Our magic—druid magic, tree magic, whatever you wish to call it—isn't much more than ceremony at this point."

"But I thought—I thought some of you northern druids were able to call up the dead on Samhain—you saved your people—"

"Aye, that was old Lugh who did that. He didn't know it would work." Collum put the spoon down and sought her eyes. His eyebrows were thick and sprinkled through with gray, and arcane tattoos wound up and down his arms. "We don't have time for rivalry. The Duchess has spoke true—corn magic, tree magic—what we need to find is the real magic. The magic that keeps the goblins out of Brynhyvar. It must've worked once."

"When?"

Collum broke off and glanced up at the high table on the dais that the Sheriff had set up on the Duchess's arrival. The

Duchess herself was eating, flanked by Sir Kian, the lords and chiefs and as many of those who'd brought their ladies crowding close at the board. "A thousand years ago, I suppose. Before the days of Bran Brownbeard. You know the lore, don't you, maiden?"

She only nodded and turned back to her soup. Papa, she thought. Mother. And Artimour. She realized the druid had asked her a question.

"—perhaps it's not the healing, maiden. Perhaps it's something else. What do you think?"

"I—I'm sorry. What did you ask me?"

"Perhaps there's more to it than simple healing, maiden. Could you maybe think about what was different today out on the tor, and here, within the keep? You don't have to answer me now. Just think about it."

"I can tell you one thing," Nessa said slowly. "Before, with Sir Kian, I felt this connection with something—something in the land—something that felt like water, and air and fire, but all at once, and inside the land. It was like I suddenly stepped into the middle of this great river and I could feel the water wash all around me." She broke off, thinking that her words were barely adequate to describe the intimate connection. But he nodded for her to continue and so she said, "Today, on the tor, I felt nothing. It was like the land itself wasn't there, or wasn't aware." She broke off once more, struggling to find the words. "The staff is part of it— but I don't understand how."

The druid leaned back and regarded her with troubled eyes. He looked from Nessa to Cecily, then back again. "I must consult the lore. I know it's in there. It's just a question of understanding it."

"The grannies say their magic is the magic that cannot be taught, only remembered. If tree magic and corn magic are the same, maybe yours can't really be taught either?"

"Then I fear we may be truly lost, maiden. Mid-Winter approaches. Did you see those things that came on Samhain? I fear they'll come back at Mid-Winter. It is the longest night of the year, after all. But the land cannot be dead. Only sleeping."

"Maybe there's something in your lore to wake the land," Nessa said.

She meant to be funny, but the druid's mouth dropped open and he stared at her, his face flushing, then whitening then flushing again, and for a split second, Nessa feared he might be in the grip of some sort of fit. He glanced up the dais, then back at Nessa. "Maiden..." He reached out and touched her cheek with a trembling hand. "Maiden, you don't know what it is you've just said." He flung his plaid over his arm and, leaping to his feet, pressed a quick kiss on the top of her head. "A blessing on your house, child. A blessing on your house!" And then he bolted from the room, running like a young lad through the crowd, an eager smile dancing on his face, leaving Nessa to eat her soup in silent shock.

The sound of trickling water roused Finuviel from his drowse, even as an abrupt jounce of the wagon caused a splinter to stab through the blanket into Finuviel's back. He gasped as Lavram's thick fingers gently pulled the compresses off his face. He felt another rush of cold, sweet air. He tried to open his eyes, but another thick crust of blood and pus had formed over his eyelids. He lay, cursing Cadwyr silently, as Lavram gently dislodged it once more with a piece of linen that felt as if it had been woven out of sand. Finuviel's eyes finally flickered open and he focused. Even the stars were silver in the flat black sky. The face that peered down at him was rough with whiskers, lined and furrowed, but the eyes were kind. Brown eyes. Mortal eyes. "Lavram?" he managed.

"Please try not to talk, my lord." Lavram gently removed the rest of Finuviel's bandages, daubing at his cheeks with something that smelled like grass and stunk like dung. "If your throat's but half as raw as your face, you must save it, my lord. Duke Cadwyr has questions."

Finuviel shut his eyes. *Shaft Cadwyr*, he wanted to say. But it wasn't worth what the effort would cause. Every part of him stung and burned as if a thousand needles burrowed into his flesh, but his face felt as if the skin had been peeled away, leaving only raw sinew and bone. The rough edge of the clay cup touched his lips and he felt the trickle of something liquid on his tongue, heavy and solid seeming, dense as everything in Shadow. "Give me—" He tried to turn his head away. "Give me more may-apple wine." If it burned, at least it burned with the fire of Faerie.

"There's only a little of that, my lord, I want to try and eke it—"

"Give it to me." Finuviel's hand snaked out, strong with desperation, and he twined his fist in the bard's robe and dragged him down so that he was nearly nose to nose with the mortal. That was when he realized his own nose was a cratered pit. He clamped his lips against the sudden wave of nausea and said through clenched teeth, "Give it to me now."

"All—all right, my lord."

"Here, here, what's this?" A hand leaned over the edge of the wagon and shook Finuviel's hand off, and another whiskered face leaned over.

"Nothing, Sergeant. We're fine." Lavram shook himself, picked up Finuviel's hand. When the guard had ridden off, he looked down at Finuviel. "Now do you believe me? They're crawling all over us. I can't help you get away. They'll bring Cadwyr my head on a pike."

"Not if you come with me," Finuviel whispered. They were heading through mountains, he thought, the torch-lit carts trundling through dark hills to reach Cadwyr quickly if they must needs travel at night. He stared up as an orange tail of fire whipped high above him. The stars flickered, shuddered, grew and shrunk. He forced himself to breathe, to press his ruined hands into the hard surface of the wagon, fighting the oblivion that threatened to overwhelm him.

With a shocked hiss, the bard drew back, shaking his head. "N-no, my lord, I—I can't—the Duke would—"

"I can reward you, mortal, beyond your dreams." But the words were lost in the flood of blood that bubbled up and spooled down his chin.

But the mortal was already turning away with a look of pained sympathy. "Rest, my lord. Just rest."

With a gurgle that would have been a cry of frustration, Finuviel fell back, shutting his eyes once more. The black blank before his eyes filled immediately with blue. *Blue*, he thought. *Blue is the color of surcease.* Something cold and wet touched his face, something soft was laid gently upon it. His hands were picked up one by one, bandages unwrapped and replaced. The wagon swayed in rhythm to the soft clop of the horses, and the voices in the wind moaned around the mountains he could not see but felt rising all around him, peaks silent, still and snowcapped. A vision of white snow and blue sky filled his mind, and as if from very far away he thought he heard a woman's voice calling his name. *Finuviel.*

I'm coming, he wanted to cry, but his head was being lifted, and a crude beaker put to his mouth. Liquid, sweet and bitter, spilled down his chin, down his neck and into his mouth, seeping down the back of his throat, coating the ruined tissue with something that felt like thick sludge. He choked, swallowed and turned his head, wondering if it were possible that something more tangible than fog lay beyond his visions.

10

"What more evidence do we need that Cadwyr plans to make himself king?" Mungo said as he leaned belligerently on the table. "Maybe ten thousand is an exaggeration, but what if it isn't? You don't think he invited them for his uncle's funeral, do you?"

"It's not as simple as you want to make it sound," spat Tuirnach. "All this talk of sidhe and bargains—without hearing from anyone who was there, how are we to know what happened at Ardagh?"

"But isn't that odd enough, Tuirnach?" Cecily said from her place she'd appropriated at the center of the table. The chiefs and the lords were restless—a general belligerence was breaking out between rival septs and it was becoming obvious to her that she'd better form these battle-primed louts into some sort of cohesive force before they all killed each other.

"Maybe he's brought in the those mercenaries 'gainst Humbria, Mungo," put in a third chief.

"You don't even know how many there are," argued Tuirnach.

"Enough that someone at least thought there were ten thousand. If ten thousand's too many, how many will we believe in? Five thousand? Two?" asked Uwen.

"He moved them up from the south following his rout of Ardagh," said Cecily. "And why would he want to feed them over the winter? We need not fear Humbria til spring."

"Maybe he's planning on using them against the goblins. After all, we've all suffered huge losses. If this is Cadwyr's idea of help—"

"Aye, and all the smiths he took," put in the Sheriff of Kill-cairn. "He took them to share their wares with us, no doubt?" He sat back with a snort.

"It's rather the kind of help you'd get from the fox if you asked him to come in and tend the henhouse, isn't it?" asked Cecily tartly. "When has Lacquilea ever looked at us without an appetite?"

"I say it comes down to this." A big woman, all fuzzy red braids and a freckled face like a horse, strode up the center of the hall and shoved the men aside. Her leather armor was stained, her plaid was frayed and she smelled rather strongly of fish. Cecily recognized her as a distant cousin of Uwen's from the Outermost Isles. "He put his colors up over Ardagh. He's welcomed a foreign army to our land. Do we want Cadwyr for our king, or don't we? That's the only issue I say we have to settle. After that, the rest will fall in place."

"Ah, Durlagh, your tongue cuts as quick as your sword," Uwen murmured as he raised his glass to her.

Cecily flung the end of her plaid over her shoulder and tried not to quail. "You're right, my lady," she replied. "That's exactly what it comes down to." Kian and his scouts were not even a dot on the horizon, she thought, and already it was before them. She'd hoped the vote would come while he was there, standing tall and strong and silent beside her, an obvious link to Donnor, a reassurance that the one who would lead them all into battle was recognized by all as more than equal to the task. She let her gaze range down the table, meeting each pair of eyes in turn.

"Well, Cecily, there's no doubt here who's got the better claim—" began Mungo.

"Now, just wait—what's been settled here?" interrupted Tuirnach. "Cadwyr's Donnor's heir—should we not consider the wishes of a man whose bones have scarce had time to warm in the Summerlands? Donnor wanted that Cadwyr should inherit—"

"Donnor is dead." Cecily saw every face react. "Donnor is dead and the world's a different place. What Donnor wanted was for his blood to continue through the House of Gar. But even if we assume Cadwyr is Donnor's only heir, my claim and my blood are still better."

"If you married Cadwyr—"

"No." She stood up. "Absolutely not. I am a free woman of Brynhyvar and a widow and I will not marry Cadwyr. Do I make myself plain to all of you?" As the nods and shrugs went round the table, Cecily continued, "You see, Tuirnach, Durlagh's right. Are you content to allow Cadwyr's colors to remain over Ardagh? And if you are, can you remember that this is the man who loosed the goblins on us at Samhain?"

"That's a very weighty charge," said Tuirnach. "You better be very sure of yourself, lady, before you come saying such things before an assembly like this." Cecily read the indecision on the old man's wrinkled face. He had been absolutely loyal to Donnor, and his preference was to transfer that loyalty, unquestioned, to Donnor's designated heir. "To say he loosed the goblins on us is tantamount to claiming wholesale murder."

Careful, Cecily, careful, she thought. She raised her chin. "There's a witness to the bargain Cadwyr made the sidhe."

"What witness?" asked Tuirnach. "I never heard there was a witness—oh, some moon-mazed lass, eh? Cecily, please—this is not—"

"Maybe you better talk to the witness, Tuirnach," Uwen said. "She may be many things, but I wouldn't ever called her mazed. She's the blacksmith girl that's been doing most of the work here herself—helped keep us alive on Samhain. We can fetch her now if you like."

But before Tuirnach could answer, a contingent of druids, arms tucked into the deep sleeves of their robes, marched into the hall. For a moment, Cecily remembered the druids of Gar and she was forced to keep a smile on her face. She hadn't liked the way this group had challenged her about Nessa. It reminded her too acutely of the way Kestrel and his brethren dismissed the corn grannies of Gar. Poor grannies, she thought as a pang went through her, and not for the first time, she thought of Granny Lyss, and Mag and the others, and of her promise to come back.

"A word, if you will, Your Grace? My lords?"

Cecily rose to her feet as the others turned or shifted in their chairs. "Yes, Master Druid?"

"My brothers and I—we've been conferring, Your Grace, among ourselves, with the late ArchDruid. It's become clear to us that in order to awaken the latent magic in the land, the magic that the old druids refer to, that a new monarch must be accepted by the land itself."

"Accepted by the land? What's that supposed to mean?"

"In the years since the Silver Caul of Bran Brownbeard was forged to protect us from the goblins, the magic that used to hold them fell into disuse, for there was no longer any real need to tap into it. The land, itself, in some way, has fallen asleep. I realize that explanation is somewhat lacking and I understand that you all are looking at me and calling me a typically obtuse druid. But I assure you, my lords, my ladies, chiefs and dames, that is the clearest answer we have for you."

"So we've reached close to the same conclusion," said Mungo. "We crown Cecily here, we take her up the hillside, she lies with the land—" here he broke off and winked "—and we take out Cadwyr in the morning?"

The druid pursed his lips as a snicker and a chuckle went round the room. "I'm afraid it's not that simple. The crowning—the awakening—must be performed on Ardagh Tor. The Tor of Ardagh is the central point in all of Brynhyvar. It stretches out equally in all directions for at least two hundred and fifty leagues. The name itself, Ar-dagh, in the old language means *the* place, the one, central place where it is all joined together and flowing out from, all at once. If the land accepts the new monarch, and answers yes, then the bonfires shall be lit, all across the land."

"I don't understand," said Mungo. "You can see a signal fire from the other tors—why not crown her now, and let the fire run out from Killcarrick Tor—"

"Mungo." Uwen nudged him. "When was the last time you got a woman pregnant spilling your seed in her mouth?"

"Might've happened this morning." The grizzled warrior winked.

"Well, if it does, you warn all the women, Uncle."

"I see Sir Uwen understands me." Collum shook his head. "Forgive me, our ArchDruid died in the night. I'm not in a mood to be amusing. You've come to us for answers, and I'm giving you the best answer that we have right now. There're two levels of magic, so to speak, at least in our understanding of what we've discerned so far. There are some here, even now, among my brethren who disagree with me on this and other points. But they have agreed that it is the easiest and the simplest way to explain it, if not the truest and the deepest. The first level is the level of the corn magic—were that to fail, the people would starve. But there's another level, one rooted in the land, and the ruler. And that's the magic that's fallen asleep, that's the magic we've not needed all these years. Caul or no Caul, its obvious whatever kept the goblins away doesn't seem to be working anymore." A shadow darkened his face and he paused, then said, "If it's all right with you, Sheriff, we'd like to put the ArchDruid's pyre up on the old tor."

"Why the old tor?" asked the Sheriff, leaning forward.

"He insisted to the end that the old tor was the real tor."

"What's wrong with the new one?" The Sheriff sounded almost insulted.

"He didn't say there was anything wrong with it, my lord Sheriff, and he meant no insult. Just that it wasn't the correct tor to use. But since the magic hadn't correctly been invoked in so long, it hadn't much mattered."

"But I thought..." Cecily paused. "They had to move the tors, I mean they had to find another place to hold the ceremonies—the fires wouldn't stay lit because of the winds off the lake?"

Collum nodded. His eyes pinned Cecily and the rest of them, but his expression was very far away, and he gazed out into some point beyond Cecily's shoulder. "That seems to be true, my lady. That's what everyone's told me. What no one has told me is how the old stones still up there—the ones nearly worn away to nothing—if there's no way to keep a fire burning up there, what then burnt those old stones so black?"

"Look there, by the Hag, Chief, I think that's them." Tuavhal pointed across the meadow as the unmistakable glint of metal flashed through the trees. "Look, there—isn't that exactly what Mungo described? Those carts covered with canvas and lashed down with rope—look, I see one now—in that gap between those trees."

Kian held up his hand and the riders slowed. "And they're coming right for us. Let's pull back—into those highlands there. That'll give us a good look at them."

"Are you sure that's them, Tully?" asked another. "I only count three carts so far."

"Well, I guess we'll see," he replied. "That's definitely Cadwyr's plaid on those riders. And those ponies—Allovale's the only place in Brynhyvar that grows such stunt-legged runts."

They dismounted and guided their horses onto the ridge above the road, flattening down into the underbrush, crawling up to the ridge, where the concealing brambles stuck into their garments and scattered in their hair. Kian spat dried leaves out of his mouth as he crawled on his belly, easing as close as he dared to the edge. In less time than he'd thought, they heard the approaching hoofbeats.

"They're coming on fast," muttered Tuavhal, and his companions nudged him quiet.

Kian nodded. They were indeed coming on fast, especially for a wagon train weighted down by clumsy loads of silver. But while the number of riders appeared about the same as Mungo and the others described, somewhere between sixty and seventy, there were in fact, only three carts.

"Why so many, Chief, to guard so few?" whispered Tully against his ear.

Kian shrugged and another answered, "Maybe the bastard's finally out of silver." Soft chuckles followed that remark and Kian raised his head, quelling them with a look. There was something odd about it, he thought, the speed with which they were trundling along, the number of armed warriors to guard what seemed like a relatively small amount of silver.

"There're three more wagons coming, Chief." The knight to his right, Darrag, nudged his shoulder. "Look there. But they're not covered in canvas."

"Supply wagons," whispered Tully. "For a troop this big you'd need—"

"Hush," said Kian between clenched teeth. He looked down, for the first was passing right beneath him, and it was, as Tully suggested, a supply wagon filled with barrels and rolls and string-tied bundles. Then the second rolled beneath them, and Kian caught a glimpse of something so monstrous, he wasn't sure he'd seen it, raw and pink and wet-looking as bloodless meat, something so revolting he wasn't sure what it was at first, and then he realized it had to be a face, a face that a gray-robed bard leaned over, placing linen compresses gently onto the cheeks. The eyes opened, and focused, and for a moment, Kian saw them blaze such a vivid green in the morning sunlight that he was suddenly certain the manner of creature in the wagon below. "That's a sidhe," he whispered.

"What'd you say, Chief?" asked Darrag, but Kian shook his head and held up his hand, peering over the ridge.

The wagon trundled on, and the bard leaned over the still form, reaching for a bandaged hand.

That's a wounded sidhe, thought Kian. Hurt in some way, maybe on Samhain, maybe in the fight against Hoell—maybe the very one Nessa had seen with Cadwyr? Whoever it was, it seemed that there would be a lot to be learned about Cadwyr's plans if they were to somehow get their hands on the sidhe. He craned his neck, thinking furiously, risking exposure to the point where Tully tapped him on the shoulder and he drew back, eyes still fastened on the dust cloud now dissipating. A cook's wagon took up the rear, followed by another calvacade of warriors on horseback. When the dust cloud disappeared, Kian slowly rose, dusting off his trews, adjusting his plaid, so deep in thought he didn't realize Darrag repeated his question, until Tully jostled his arm.

"Begging your pardon, Chief. But what did you say that was?"

And motioning them all close, Kian explained as much as he possibly could.

"So what do we do about it?" asked Tully. "Take him? That'd ruin Cadwyr's day, don't you think?"

Kian drew a quick breath. He'd known immediately that once he'd mentioned the word *sidhe,* they'd be of one mind. But was that wise? He glanced up at the sun. It was getting on to noon—they could trail the troop til nightfall and plan a midnight raid.

As if he'd heard the echo of Kian's thoughts, a knight behind Tully said, "We could trail them til they make camp, and take him in the night, before anyone was awake enough to know we'd been there."

"I should point out," said Kian, "there's at least ten of them to every one of us."

"Ah, Chief." Darrag nudged his ribs. "That hardly makes us even."

Kian heard his own voice echoing through his mind as an image of Cecily's concerned face rose to taunt him. *A scouting expedition. We'll only be gone a night or two. Surely you can spare me that long?* Capturing Cadwyr's sidhe wasn't part of the plan. But who would've expected him to pass right beneath their very noses? "All right," said Kian. He took a deep breath and the wind ruffled the branches over their heads, dipping low to tangle in his hair. He pushed the tree out of his way. "Darrag, Hugh and Eagen, get the horses. We won't ride yet. Let's wait here, just a bit."

As the three knights turned to do Kian's bidding, Garth, the youngest of the riders who'd only won his belt at Samhain, and whose pink face belied a razor's touch, asked, "What for, Sir Kian?"

Kian turned and pointed down the road, where a couple of riders, garbed in Cadwyr's plaid, trotted after the rest. "To see if there're any more like them following. No matter how even the odds, we don't need them knowing we're coming after them."

"I meant what I said, mortal. I can reward you beyond anything you've dreamed." Finuviel grasped Lavram's wrist as he leaned over to peel away once more the stiffened compresses. They smelled like muddy honey mixed with grass. Finuviel doubted they had any real benefit, and the bard's attempts to heal him only frustrated him that the stubborn mortal wouldn't listen. The light had long since faded over the western hills, and the river finally presented them with a barrier the wagoners refused to cross until the morning. He could smell burning wood and cooking meat. It would be so easy to slip into Faerie if Lavram would only help him over the side.

"My lord, I can't." Lavram's face flushed a dark red as he wrung out the compresses in fresh solution. He glanced over his shoulder. "The guards are already nervous. Cadwyr will have their heads on pikes. And they're watching me— we've all been warned, you know."

"Warned about what?" asked Finuviel, beneath the bawled orders for the watch.

Lavram started, spilling the basin, and the water splashed a dark stain on his robe that he ignored as he leaned forward. "Warned about you, my lord." He glanced away, as if embarrassed. "Warned about the enchantment of the sidhe. That's why none of the others will come near you. But they're all watching. Believe me." He glanced up, smiled and nodded, then looked over his shoulder, and his lips quirked up again. "You see? There're guards not just posted around the camp—they're around this wagon as well."

Warned about me. The enchantment of the sidhe was as nothing, he thought. He was dying, he could feel the silver eating its way into his flesh, boring into his sinews, all the way to his bones. He was poisoned and it was spreading through his flesh even as they spoke. He had to warn his people, and then somehow prepare to face the biggest and most ferocious goblin army in centuries. Or it was finished. Even without the Caul. "Don't you understand?" Finuviel croaked. He twined one hand in Lavram's robe and dragged the man down to his ear. His lips cracked, and pale fluid, whether blood or pus or some combination, seeped into his mouth and down his chin. "If I die, Faerie dies. If Faerie dies, this world dies. Don't you understand that, you foolish, foolish mortal?" Something sparked in the mortal's eyes, fear and something else. "Cadwyr's *betrayed* me. Broke his word, imprisoned me and took the Silver Caul. Does that mean nothing to you, mortal? Has it not occurred to any of you that the man who'd betray one ally will just as easily betray another? And the goblin raids on Samhain? Those were his fault, mortal. If I'd had my way, the goblins would never have been free to rampage as they did." Liquid welled up in Finuviel's throat and he swallowed hard, staring into the bard's eyes with every measure of will he yet possessed. "Don't you understand? He betrayed all of you on Samhain. Cadwyr had the means to stop the goblins. But he didn't."

"Wh-what are you talking about, my lord?" Lavram shrank down, ostensibly busying himself with his vials and unguents and compresses.

Finuviel lay back. "Give me a drink of that may-apple

wine, Bard, and I'll tell you a story, a story such that when you carry it back to your fellow bards, your name will be added to the annals of your mortal history."

"What story?" The lip of the cup the bard held beneath his chin trembled, and a bit of the may-apple wine oozed down Finuviel's chin.

It seared a path into the marrow of his bones and as the fluid trickled down his throat, he felt another burst of strength flow into his veins. He had to keep the mortal feeding it to him. "I make you a bargain, Bard," he whispered, holding the mortal's eyes with his. "Keep that wine flowing down my throat and I will spin you a tale such as has never been heard in your world or mine."

Lavram's eyes lit up and he held the cup up to Finuviel's mouth once more. "I'm not supposed to let you talk, my lord. They say that's the way you win our hearts—with your songs, with your words—"

"Would you like the story, or not, Bard?"

"All right." Lavram shrank down, glancing around. The guards were moving all around them, lining up around the cooking fire, claiming rations from the wagon for the night. He filled the cup once more from the skin and nodded. "All right, my lord, just whisper."

It was nearly midnight when Griffin heard Cadwyr stride into his bedchamber. He stirred on his mattress, the chain around his waist chafing at his flesh. He took another sip of brew and curled up uneasily, watching the door. It bothered him to think of the sidhe-lady here, beneath Cadwyr's roof. There was no telling what he might do to her. The door between the two rooms swung open abruptly and there he was, standing in the door, a big black shape against the dim glow of a lone candle. "Hello, boy."

"You're not going to hurt her, are you?" Griffin asked. The words were out of his lips before he could call them back, and he clutched his flask.

"Hurt a creature as lovely as that?" Cadwyr shook his head. "What sort of monster do you take me for, boy? Of course not." In three long strides, he was across the room, twisting his hand in Griffin's hair, searching for the lacy silken kerchief now knotted on a chain around his neck. "Now, you, boy—if you lose this—"

The roots of his hair began to burn. Griffin wet his lips and itched for a drink. "I swear, I swear I won't lose it—"

"You like the drink, don't you?" Cadwyr let him go with a laugh. "So does she. In fact, she asked about you, Griffin— who you are, where you come from. She seems quite taken with the fact you're a smith."

"M-me?" He scrambled backward, bumping his head against the stone, even as he fumbled for his flask.

"Aye, boy. You. So we'll get you prettied up tomorrow. I'm expecting a most important visitor, after all."

"Wh-who's that?" whispered Griffin. Although he was quite certain he already know.

"Why the King of the sidhe, of course. The King of Tir-Na'lugh." With a soft chuckle, Cadwyr walked across the room, his boots making no sound at all. At the door he turned. "Good night, Griffin. Sleep well. We'll make you all pretty tomorrow. The Queen of Faerie herself requests your presence."

Griffin settled back against his mattress, the flask secure against his hip. A cold breeze blew through the opened window above his head, and he leaped up in order to shut it. But his fingers faltered on the latch when he noticed the unmistakable blood-red ring around the moon.

"...and so, that's why he put me in the silver mine, but still, he keeps the Caul." Finuviel paused, motioned once more for a sip of wine and fell back on his pillow, exhausted.

The mortal was silent as he lowered the cup. Then he said, "Did your people kill the Old Lion of Gar? Duke Donnor?"

"He did not fall at the hands of my people, Bard, and I have no knowledge of how otherwise it might have happened. But part of my bargain with Cadwyr was that not one of his side shall fall by our hand. And not one other did. Not one."

"What about the Caul? Won't you all need that back?"

Finuviel nodded. "Of course. But I would rather fight Cadwyr with my own army at my back, and not his."

There was another brief silence, and then Lavram whispered quickly, "All right. I'll help you. On one condition."

"What do you want?"

"I want you to take me with you."

"To Faerie?" Finuviel whispered. "Are you sure you want such a thing, mortal? Faerie is not entirely safe right now."

"I've no choice, really," Lavram said with a bitter little laugh. "Once you're found missing, my life's not worth the pike Cadwyr will stick my head on. Do you understand? I believe you that Cadwyr's a monster. But don't leave me here to get eaten in your place."

"It's not simple a thing, mortal. Don't you understand? There's danger for you in Faerie. Once you cross over, you most likely won't be able to come back."

Lavram swallowed hard and his eyes swam with unshed tears. "I was nearly there, once." He glanced over his shoulder. "One Beltane. I went up on the tor, Gar Tor, and there I saw a woman dancing in the center of the ring." He pressed his lips together and stared out into the night. "I watched her, and as she danced, I could see the sky behind her was blue, even though it was the middle of the night. I wanted to join her—I would've joined her, but three of my brothers came up and saved me."

"As long as you understand, mortal, your brothers will not come to save you this time. Once you taste the food and drink of Faerie, you'll become forever changed. You may not be able to return to this world, no matter how much you might come to wish it."

"I've thought about this," he said. "I've thought about it for a long time. What is it you want me to do, my lord?"

Finuviel struggled to raise himself high enough to see over the side of the wagon. The guards were drowsing, the night was still and the gurgle of the river soothing as it lapped against the rocky shore. "Help me. Help me get to the river."

"The river? And then where?"

"Into it." Finuviel smiled in the face of Lavram's startled look. "Water, you see, is the surest conduit from Faerie into Shadow and back."

The measured footfalls of a guard pacing the perimeter of the camp made Lavram duck. "It takes them about twenty minutes to walk all the way around. If we wait til his next circuit and follow him, we can get to the river as he passes it."

He barely nodded but his lips moved twice. "All right, my lord. All right." The camp continued to settle down. In the wagon, Finuviel listened to the bard's steady breathing and stared up at the sky. He could hear the gurgle of the water somewhere on his right, and he could feel the infinitesimal particles of silver gnawing through his flesh. If he didn't reach Faerie soon, he would die, and he itched to rise up and leap into the water, flitting away like a salmon into the shadowy water, down and through and across and into the world that was his. Then a guard hawked and spat and another muttered a curse, and he peered out, over the edge. Most of the men snored in a ring, indistinguishable lumps of plaid and saddle blankets. He thought about his mother, about the single-minded determination that had led her to manipulate and scheme across two worlds, and wondered if she even yet still lived. He held his hands up to his face, and in the shadowy torchlight and the nearly full moon, he unwrapped the bandages.

The skin was mostly gone, his hands pale sinews laced around the white bones, the charred and blackened fingertips. The sidhe could heal themselves, but what sidhe had ever endured something like this? Would he ever be able to return himself to the way he'd been before? A monster's hands, a monster's face...he touched his cheek and winced. He could not lift a sword with them. He closed his lashless lids, murmuring another curse, and as he fell back on the blanket, his hands touched the rough splintered wood. A latent warmth seemed to rise from somewhere in the center, a warmth that soothed his tortured hand. *They say the trees of Faerie and the trees of Shadow are one and the same.* His mother's voice echoed through his mind. *Mother, I think we somehow got it all wrong.* The question was, was it too late to save it all?

A volley of arrows burst across the night sky. Finuviel flattened himself, staring up in disbelief as the camp roused itself. Shouted orders blasted through the quiet, accompanied by crashes and the screams of startled horses. Finuviel peered over the edge of the wagon and stared in shocked disbelief. A small band of mortals was riding straight for him, swords drawn. He dropped down, even as Lavram raised his head experimentally, then immediately bent low. An arrow whistled over their heads. "Lie low, my lord, they're after the sil—"

"Oh no we're not," cut in a tall warrior with long blond braids who bounded up to Finuviel's side. "We're here for you."

"Who are you?" Finuviel demanded.

"Enemies of Cadwyr," the mortal replied. "That good enough for now?" The knight extended his arm, and with Lavram's help, Finuviel just barely rolled onto the back of the horse. From very far away, he thought he heard the cold ring of a Faerie horn. *The warhorns of Faerie,* he thought in a daze of smoke and pain and flashing silver blades. The knight swung his sword in a vicious arc as a guard approached, and he lashed the horse, spurring him on as Finuviel clung with all his strength to the knight's waist. The horns sounded again, pure and unmistakable, but the camp was fully roused now, the guards rushing at them from all directions. Beside him, he saw Lavram take an arrow directly in the chest, and he cried out as the horse reared and screamed, hooves flailing as a battle-ax connected with its leg. He and the knight came crashing down, and he rolled under one of the wagons, in time to see the blond knight fall, his neck sprouting a fountaining arc of bright red mortal blood.

* * *

Cecily sat up, gasping. Air blasted through a gap in the shelter, where one of the ropes had come undone. Sweat ran down her neck, streamed down her back, and her whole belly wrenched and clenched so that she leaned forward and gasped, clutching at her midsection. Was she losing this child, too?

She waited a moment, but the pain didn't return, and she felt no telltale trickle or warm gush of fluid from between her legs. The night was still. Somewhere far below, she heard the changing of the watch called and she heard the snap of the banners off the walls. From very far away, wolves howled. Winter was here, she thought. Soon it would snow, and the chiefs would go back to their mountains and their strongholds and hunker down until the spring. There wasn't much time left to move against Cadwyr. Whatever they would do had to be done quickly.

She reached for a shawl and thrust her feet into slippers, then went to stand on the battlements, overlooking the keep. She heard a sound like a distant roar, and realized it was the wind moving through the distant trees. Sharp as a blade, the air cut through her woolen gown, her thick slippers and shawl. She shivered, hesitating a moment longer just to make sure the pain had only been part of a dream. As she turned to go back to bed, she glanced up at the sky and gasped to see a blood-red ring around the moon.

11

The news that a druid had come in from Gar brought Cecily flying down the stairs to the hall, where the druids and several of the chiefs had already gathered around a figure wrapped in an unfamiliar plaid. For a moment, she wondered if Kestrel had sent a spy, and then she recognized the young bard who'd volunteered at first to join the corn grannies in their rite. "You're Jammor, aren't you?" she said as the boy rose to his feet, bowing awkwardly over his bowl of porridge.

"Your Grace." He uncovered his head. "The grannies of Gar have sent me to tell you Cadwyr's got an army of twenty thousand men camped around Gar—and more silver arriving every—"

"Twenty thousand men?" interrupted Uwen, who'd come into the hall without Cecily realizing it. He leaned over the boy's chair. "Where in the name of Great Herne did he find twenty thousand men?"

"He's hired twenty companies of Lacquilean—"

"Companies or cohorts, boy?" asked Uwen.

"I—I'm not sure—what's the difference?"

"Ten companies make up a cohort, and ten cohorts is a legion. A legion is an army. If he's got two legions of Lacquileans—he's got more than ten thousand, I warrant."

"But I thought that Kian said the scout exaggerated?" Cecily said, sinking onto the bench beside the boy.

"Maybe Kian was only hoping the scout was exaggerating?" For a long moment, their eyes met and Uwen let out a long sigh.

"But that's not all," Jammor continued. "There's something going on with Cadwyr—even Kestrel says he's not the same. There's a lady of the sidhe at the Castle now, and Cadwyr's set her up in your old chambers, my lady. He told Kestrel that she was the Queen of the sidhe, and he's got a boy, a very strange boy he keeps chained to the wall, who drinks barrels and barrels of this strange brew that only a few of the guards are allowed to touch."

"But," Uwen asked, "the sidhe Nessa saw with Cadwyr was angling to be King—"

"That's the one he's imprisoned in the silver mine—the one he's sent for—"

"Slow up, boy," said one of the other chiefs. "What do you mean imprisoned? Even the woman?"

"Aye, that's what I've been trying to tell you," Jammor said. A pot of mead was put in front of him and he took a long quaff. "He's not put her in the dungeon, but he's keeping her under wraps. Her door is guarded day and night, and

Mag and a few of the grannies went to see her and no one was allowed in. Cadwyr's found some half-mazed island girl to see to her. And that's why I've come. Because Cadwyr's not thinking just of ruling Brynhyvar. Cadwyr intends to conquer the OtherWorld as well."

"I suppose that answers the question as to how he means to pay so many mercenaries," said Mungo. As Jammor talked, the hall had gradually grown more crowded. "And here I was thinking that's why he wanted all that silver."

"This silver they're making into weapons," said Jammor.

"Who is?" put in the Sheriff. "Is that where all our smiths ended up? At Gar?"

A stricken look crossed the young bard's face. "Not exactly, my lord Sheriff." He hesitated. "It's my understanding that the entire party of the smiths were wiped out on Samhain. There's a rumor going around that Cadwyr's boy—the one he keeps chained to a wall in his rooms—was one of them, but I've seen him and he no more looks capable of blacksmith work than I do."

"What's wrong with this boy, Jammor?" asked Cecily. She had a sad, sick feeling in her heart and in her gut, for this was what she had suspected all along. If only Donnor had listened to her.

"I—I don't rightly know what's wrong with him. The still-wife can't get in to see him, either. But he's skinny as a stick of wood and his head's as big as a squash and his skin just hangs off him like an old bag of leather. I've seen him two or three times, skulking around behind Cadwyr. Cadwyr keeps him chained in his dressing room most of the time. I'm not sure why."

"And you say that Cadwyr's been keeping another sidhe in a silver mine?"

"Aye, my lord. Rumor is that he's the one that's supposed to be the King."

"Great Mother," swore Cecily, biting back a curse as crude as any Kian might use. "So he intends to conquer the OtherWorld then turn upon the rest of us?"

"Or turn upon the rest of us then conquer TirNa'lugh," replied Mungo.

"Let him wear himself out fighting the sidhe," put in a faceless voice from deep within the crowd.

Cecily gathered her plaid around her shoulders and scanned the throng, searching for the one who'd spoken, but others now were chiming in. She drew herself up to her full height and stepped onto the dais. "We can't let that happen," Cecily said. "Don't you all see? He's not going to wear himself out—he's got twenty thousand men armed with silver. He's going to chew through the sidhe and the goblins, and then, when his mercenaries are fat and well rewarded, then he'll turn on us."

"What makes you so sure he's turned on the very creatures that you say handed him Ardagh?" asked Tuirnach.

It was Jammor who answered him, rising from his chair beside the fire, projecting his bard's voice across the crowd, so that there could be no doubt who answered. "Did you not hear me say he put the King in a silver mine? His personal guard is armed with weapons made of silver through and through. But that's not all, my lords, my ladies." Jammor took a wide step and came to stand beside Cecily on the dais, his woad-blue robes dusty and travel-stained. "There's this look that Cadwyr wears—a hunger that nothing quite satisfies. It's a look I've only seen on the faces of mad dogs."

"Are you telling us Cadwyr should be put down like one?"

"I'm telling you I don't think we have a choice," Cecily replied. "If Cadwyr conquers the OtherWorld with his silver and his mercenaries, he'll be able to use the sidhe and maybe the goblins, too, against any who would stand against him. And we don't have Cadwyr's silver mines."

"We could try taking one or two, to even things up a bit, lass," suggested Mungo.

"It may come to that, Uncle," said Cecily. "But it would be better if we can stop Cadwyr before he gets any bigger."

"So now you believe we should attack as soon as possible?" Tuirnach folded his arms over his chest.

But Cecily's answer was forestalled by the entrance of one of the watch, who came with the unprecedented announcement that a company of the sidhe themselves, riding milk-white horses under white flags of truce, and leading what appeared to be half a dozen mortal horses, were approaching the gates of Killcarrick.

At once the speculative hubbub rose, like the buzzing of a huge hive, and Cecily had to raise her voice to be heard above it. "Let them come," she said, and they settled back to wait.

Uwen took the place on her left, and gasped when the dark-haired leader clad in a moss-green doublet, flanked by half a dozen companions, strode unblinking into the hall. He walks as if he's been here before, Cecily thought, suddenly acutely aware of how primitive and crude the hall and all its inhabitants must appear as she was swept into the shining beauty of the sidhe. "That's Artimour," Uwen murmured. "The one that was found along the banks here."

"He—he looks almost mortal," replied Cecily with a frown, and then she stopped and gasped, for she recognized the shield that they bore.

"He's half-mortal," said Uwen, and then he, too, broke off, and the two of them rose to their feet at once.

The crowd parted like a muddy river for a shining silver fish. Artimour paused a few paces from the dais and bowed. "Sir Uwen. My ladies, and my lords. My name's Artimour. I am the Captain of this last company of the Guard of Her Majesty, Alemandine the Illustrious of Faerie. We come to you in peace, but the news we bring you will not be welcome." A shaft of afternoon sun streaked across his face, highlighting the deep furrow between his brows, casting circles beneath his shadowed eyes. The clothes of the sidhe molded seamlessly to his body, but the light was so stark he looked as mortal as any other warrior in the room. The light glinted off the edges of the shields his companions carried, stinging her eyes like knives.

Don't cry and don't faint. Cecily raised her chin. "It is the custom of our country that guests are fed and watered and welcomed with a story before anything is asked of them."

"We would refuse your mortal food and drink, my lady, and we'd rather give you a story than have one."

"Tell us your story, then," whispered Cecily in a high, soft voice, and she braced herself, for she knew, as surely as she recognized the shield and the shards of the sword, that they brought her word of his death.

Nessa heard the news in the forge, when one of the scullions who'd been helping her stuck his head inside the window and shouted, "The sidhe are back and Kian's dead."

Kian's dead? she wanted to call, but he was gone, swallowed up into the press of the crowd now pushing toward the hall. From everywhere, more and more came hurrying. She glimpsed the gleaming white horses, the moss-green doublets and pearl-gray cloaks, and she heard a name whispered through the crowd, passed around like a platter. "Artimour," someone said.

She gripped the arm of the nearest woman, and recognized Bethy the corn granny. "What's happening, Bethy?" she asked, for the woman's eyes were streaked with tears.

"Sir Kian's dead," she replied. "Sir Kian's dead and that— that sidhe who was here has come back."

Artimour! Her heart sang the name, even as the news of Kian's death fell heavy as a lump of lead on her ears. "How can he be dead?" Nessa asked. "He was only just healed—"

"They're talking about it now, in there—the lords and the chiefs. Stay here, Nessa, news will filter out—"

"I'm going to see if I can get a bit closer," Nessa said. She patted Bethy's arm and eased her way past two big men, then found her way blocked once more. The people were muttering, speculating, and she heard more wild rumors of the sort that had run rampant after Samhain. A disturbance in the crowd pushed Nessa against a stone wall, and she saw a weeping groom leading a familiar horse in the direction of the stables. That's Kian's, she thought as she remembered her first sight of Kian's great warhorse as it churned the dirt in the smithy yard back in Killcairn to muck with its great hooves. With his shining hair, Kian had looked like a hero out of one of Granny Wren's stories. *Who wants to be a hero?* Griffin's voice echoed in her mind. It was after one of the storytelling sessions Dougal had insisted they attend. *The heroes always die.* All around her, men were weeping, great drops running down weathered faces, shoulders heaving with silent sobs.

She looked up. The sun was shining like a gold coin in the sky, and the light turned even the dullest browns and duns and grays into a shifting canvas of colors that held hints of richest indigo and green and red, and even the blue of the sky wasn't hard and blank and cold like it usually was in winter, but bright and soft, as if it was remembering summer. Now it seemed a mockery. *What did I save him for?* she wondered. *Why was he healed? To go forth and fight and fall? And fail?*

Her face crumpled as a wave of loss and grief swept over her. It had been a long time since she'd thought of Griffin. A long time, indeed. And he loved her, Molly said. She fingered his amulet and hesitated in the courtyard, wanting to press forward and learn more, yet at the same time, wanting to go back to the sure refuge of the forge. Now she understood better than she ever had why her father so often buried himself in his work. The intense focus blunted the pain of everything else.

"Are you coming, lassie?" A warrior from one of the northern clans pushed behind her, easing her deeper into the crowd, and just as they reached the open doors of the keep, through which Nessa could glimpse the shimmering cluster of the sidhe, someone jostled her arm, and she turned to see a blue-robed bard holding out a bundle.

"Are you Nessa?" he asked. She stared at him uncomprehending and he repeated the question. "Are you?" he asked a third time. The crowd was pushing them against the door, and with a stifled curse, he gripped her forearm and dragged her back out into the courtyard. "Are you Nessa the blacksmith or not?"

"Aye," she managed at last. "Who're you?"

"My name's Jammor of the Rill, Maid Nessa. Sir Uwen of the Isles bid me bring this to you. He said you would know what to do with it." He held out a rectangular bundle wrapped awkwardly in something that fell like thick black silk.

She looked up, and saw that the bard was about her age, with grayish eyes that reminded her of Artimour's, the same color as the tiny-leaved thyme in winter that grew on the banks of Killcarrick Lake, and suddenly she wanted to go home, wanted her father and the forge, the smell of the charcoal. Kian was dead, she could hear the chiefs bellowing like frightened cattle trapped in a burning barn. She had never felt so lost nor so alone standing in that courtyard, surrounded on all sides by people who pressed and whispered and wept. She had been so brave for so long—she had faced goblins and Herne and the druid. A wave of loneliness and fear and grief and homesickness crashed over her, and her eyes flooded with tears and she had to press her lips together not to sob audibly. She raised her hand to her mouth.

"Maid Nessa?" Jammor was looking at her, puzzled. "Are you all right?" She tried to nod, but couldn't, for her throat was suddenly too full of tears. He made a little noise, and gripped her arm, leading her back through the worst of the throng to the fringes. He hesitated only a moment, then found their way to the forge. Just inside the threshold he paused. "You heard about Sir Kian?"

She nodded and the tears spilled over and she wiped them

on her sleeve. "I'm sorry," she finally managed to say. "It's just..." She paused, wondering how much to say to this kind-faced stranger. "It's just I had a hand in healing him."

"That's what Collum was saying just now. That's why I offered to bring this to you when Sir Uwen looked for someone. I wanted to meet you." He held out the silk-wrapped bundle. "Be careful—it's wrapped in leather but it's in pieces."

"What is this?" she asked as she reached for the bundle, but even as her fingers made contact, she knew exactly what it was. A vision exploded in her mind, an upraised arm, glowing steel, a new-forged blade. A spark seemed to flare at the base of her spine, running up and down her back, down to the earth. And once more, she felt that same amazing sense of connection to the land, the earth, that had been missing up on the sleeping tor. And she knew exactly what to do.

She didn't really hear Jammor tell her that these were the shards of Kian's sword. She cradled the bundle to her breast as if it were a newborn infant, and said, "When Master Collum has a moment, please ask him to come to the forge. The first moment he has."

Don't faint and don't weep. But Cecily could not help her eyes filling up with tears as she listened to the song of Kian's death, for in the manner of the sidhe's telling, it was a song, a song that spoke of grief and loss and everything she had ever been afraid of losing.

"Are you all right?" Uwen's hoarse whisper penetrated the blanket of numbness that was descending on her like a cloak. Donnor's death had not hit her half so hard and, in retrospect, not at half so hard a time.

"This is bad," Tuirnach was muttering. "This is very bad. We've scarcely the men to meet Cadwyr on our own terms, and now you, lord sidhe, have come to ask for help? Do we look as if we're in any state to lend you any kind of help at all? Why, it seems to me that it's your kind that's responsible for this mess if it's one of your kind that made a bargain with Cadwyr in the first place."

"It was meant to benefit us all," replied Artimour. "It was Cadwyr who turned against my kin. We but come to ask for weapons and armor to withstand silver. Ordinary mortal weapons only so that we have a chance against Cadwyr's silver."

A few cries of "Give it to them!" rose from the crowd, but boos and hisses rose as well, and Tuirnach looked at Cecily pointedly. *They're expecting me to fall apart,* she thought. *They're all expecting me to shrivel up and die now that Kian's gone. Donnor died because he wouldn't listen to me. And now Kian's dead for the same reason.* Tuirnach was speaking. "What good ever came of anything our kind has ever had with yours?"

It was meant as a challenge, and Cecily leaned forward, ready to argue that here was an opportunity to truly take Cadwyr by surprise, for surely he would not at all expect them to have allied with each other.

But Artimour's reply surprised her and took her breath away by the savagery of his response. "You're right, my lord. You're right." He flung back his cloak and paced a few steps back and forth. "You're absolutely right. There's never been any good to be gained by any interaction between my kind and yours. I admit that, for I have seen that firsthand, and I would not willingly entangle myself with any mortal, for whatever reason. But if you will be so generous as to help us in our hour of need, we will help you in yours. For whatever might divide us, we have a common enemy."

Cecily rose shaking, to her feet. She looked straight at Tuirnach. "You know what I think worse than losing Kian?" She hesitated a moment, then continued, "Allowing Cadwyr to be King. You don't want to ride with us, Tuirnach, keep your sons and your horses and your warriors safe at home. You do that if you wish. But I for one will call up all my kin and all my warriors, because I will never, so long as I have breath in my body, bend my knee to Cadwyr." She threw back her head and the words poured out of her throat, words that she knew she could never have said for Donnor, a lament that came up from the depth of her soul.

> "Dead, are you, Kian, brave battle-brother,
> Cold as the ice that now flows through my veins,
> Hard as the rock that now beats in my chest.
> Bitter your loss as the edge of the blade
> That severed you from us."

The warriors were beating their shields now, in time to the rhythm of her speech, and more than a few had begun to hum the plaintive melody of the House of Mochmorna's Lament.

> "Let your soul now be tempered
> In the fires of the Summerlands.
> As ours will be tempered in the heat of the war—
> For I vow to you, Kian, as I stand here in company,
> Of all the brave brothers who saw when you fell,

I'll send you the coward who sent dogs after warriors,
     I'll send you the viper that came in the night,
I'll send you the one who now holds your head high."

Only a few of the chiefs stood gape-faced, but even Tuirnach was beating the table with both fists. Cecily took a deep breath and met Artimour's eyes squarely. "So I say, yes, lord sidhe, we will help your people rescue their King and their Queen. We will give you weapons to withstand silver and we will welcome your aid."

"There are ten thousand Lacquileans and ten thousand others he's gathered to him, lassie," snarled Tuirnach. "We're two thousand at best, even with perhaps two hundred or so of sidhe. He's sitting behind that great pile of rock called Gar and we'll have to attack it. What do you call those odds?"

There was a long pause and Cecily stared back at him, her mouth tense and tight and drawn, but she would not be cowed. The wooden floor beneath her feet quivered in a long slow throb and she startled, looked down, as if she half expected to see a wave pass beneath her feet. Then she looked back at Tuirnach and smiled. "I call them even." She leaned forward, pressing her advantage in the face of his silent shock. "After all, my lord, it's not that we die, but how."

"Not that we die, but how!" The battle cry was taken up by the warriors, who whooped and cried and raised their swords to beat upon the tables with the hilts.

In the forge, Nessa heard the chanting and the singing, the cheers and the cries, and she knew that something had happened, some decision had been reached. She was tempted once more to brave the crowd in the courtyard and try to reach the hall, but the courtyard seemed more crowded than ever now, noisy and smoky, and here, in the darkened forge, was relative peace. And besides, the young bard had promised to send the druid.

And so she was expecting to see Collum when the footsteps hesitated on the threshold and she looked up, to see Artimour standing in the door. "Artimour!" she cried as wild joy leaped within her. She threw aside the thick black wrappings and ran to meet him, but he only pressed a gentle kiss on her forehead and drew back, when she would've reached for his mouth with hers.

"What's wrong?" she said at once. She touched his chest and he withdrew visibly. "Artimour? What is it?"

"I need to talk to you, Nessa. Can we sit? And talk?"

"A-all right," she replied. "What about—" She gestured to the bedroom behind the hearth. "What about back there?"

He looked less than happy but nodded. "All right."

But once she'd sunk down onto the rough wool cover, he did not join her on the bed. Instead, he stood at the end of the bedstead, his hands on the rail. "What's wrong?" she asked again. "What happened when you went back? What did you find?"

He shook his head. "What we did was wrong, Nessa. I should never have touched you. It was wrong."

"Wrong?" She stood up, hands on her hips. "How can you say that was wrong? It was the rightest thing I've ever done. I've never imagined that anything could be like that." She waited for him to respond, but when he didn't, she sank back down on the bed, her eyes suddenly flooded with tears. He had been the one bright spot in this whole terrible lonely day, and now, somehow, he was so frighteningly different, it bewildered her. "It was the rightest thing of all."

"Listen to me, Nessa. This has nothing to do with how I feel about you. When I went back—"

"What? Tell me. What is it?"

"I found out a lot of things when I went back, Nessa. I found what's really going on—I found out that my sister Vinaver and nephew Finuviel are the ones behind it all. And I found your father and your mother."

"You did?" Her head snapped up and she had to control the impulse to wrap her arms around his neck. "Really? He's alive? He's all right? They're both of them all right?"

"They're alive. They're alive, Nessa, but they're not all right. Not in the sense you are. They can't come back—they'll die if they do. They've had too much Faerie drink and food to live here anymore. They've become what we call changelings. What Vinaver did to them was wrong—oh, yes, it was no accident that led her to choose your father—"

"For what? It was my mother that was lost there, first—"

"No, Nessa. That story you believe is just a story. That's not what really happened at all. My sister needed a blacksmith, a mortal blacksmith to help her with the Caul's un-Making. So, one Beltane, when the veil between the worlds was thinnest, she slipped across the border and found your father with your mother within their Beltane bower. And somehow she wove her enchantments and spirited Dougal out of there, but she didn't count on your mother coming to find him. What she did to the two of them, and to you, was terrible. She used you all like you were nothings.

"Don't you see, Nessa? The Caul has anchored our

worlds so tightly together, it's like they're strangling each other. That's why I've come. I'm here to find Finuviel and the Caul and take them back to Faerie so that this terrible union can be undone at last. That's why I was wrong to touch you, to take you. Even if you wanted me. That was wrong, too."

He dropped down beside her and picked up her hand. "I saw the terrible things that happen when my kind mixes with yours. Your world's not mine, and mine's not yours, and those old chiefs in there who said we're better off apart are right. I saw in your father's eyes when he spoke of you—the kind of man he is, the kind of man he wants for you, the kind of man you should have. Not someone like me that's neither swan nor salmon, bee nor bear, who may be dead with the unMaking of this cursed object."

"How dare you say you know what my father wants for me?" She flung off his hand. "You spend an hour or two with him out of his whole life, and you dare to tell me you think you know what he wants for me? I'll tell you what I think he wants for me. He spent one moment with my mother on a Beltane hill and that's lasted him nearly twenty years." Even as the words left her lips, she paused, realizing on some other level the import of what she'd said and her own words intermingled with those of Molly and the druids and the other grannies. *One moment with my mother on a Beltane hill... Are you sure you're not Beltane-made?... Were you a Beltane child we'd have no question...*

But the tangle of overlapping voices meant nothing at the moment, for Artimour only shrugged, with a look of sadness and regret. "Then we had our moment, maiden." He left her staring after him in silent disbelief.

* * *

In the tunnels below the palace of the Faerie Queen, bone crunched and flesh splattered as Xerruw strode through the knee-deep corpses of the goblings who'd died in the first wave of the assault, the gremlin Khouri scampering over them in his effort to keep up. Many of their older brethren had already chewed away much of the fallen. It had not been quite the surprise he'd hoped it would be, for the sidhe had been able to mobilize in surprisingly fast fashion, once they'd realized the imminent threat. But it was a start.

"My lord." His new second in command, Kubai—an altogether more obsequious fellow than Iruk—bowed. "We have discovered two more ways up into the main part of the Palace. The earth beneath the stables is soft and easy to dig, and in the throne room, there is a soft shaft around the marble core."

Xerruw paused, sniffed and licked his chops. "Excellent." He looked up and sniffed once more.

"My lord? There's something wrong?"

Kubai showed the proper attitude. Xerruw liked that. "Nothing amiss. Just a strong smell of mortal—ah. Look there, Khouri. Who is this and what is here?"

At once, Khouri leaped forward, hissing and spitting in what he assumed must be its own tongue, and Xerruw snarled at the guards and snapped his tail. The other gremlin slid out of the guards' grip, but it stumbled and could hardly stand. Xerruw drew back, eyeing the newcomer suspiciously. It looked sick, unhealthy, gray, rather than golden-brown like the other. He sniffed. The smell of man-meat was strong on it, and from the dirt that clung to its feet, the leaves clinging to its head, he realized it must have come from Shadow. "I thought your kind was all in the Palace and couldn't leave."

"We can if we're willing to die," Khouri said. The second gremlin's eyes were closed and it appeared to have stopped breathing. One guard stepped forward and sniffed, then licked its maw. Khouri looked up at it and snarled as menacingly as if he dwarfed the guard.

Xerruw grunted. "Enough. It's not man-meat, though it surely smells of Shadow. Can it talk?"

"Petri?" Khouri leaned down and shook the other's shoulder. "Well?"

The gremlin stared up at him with hollow eyes. "I have it." He held up the bag of pale human hide, and took a deep shuddering breath.

Khouri's small paw closed over the bag and he smiled as he patted Petri's head with the other, then licked the thin film of dirt off his finger. "Rest, brother, you've earned it." He sniffed the bag, then handed it up to Xerruw. "The battle, Great King, is half won. He has the Caul. The smallest of the small has triumphed once again." He licked his fingers, rubbed his hand over Petri's head, and this time, licked his whole palm, an expression of ecstasy on his face.

Suspicious, that anything should be so easy, Xerruw examined the bag, recognized it as being of goblin make, and sniffed it again.

"Soon, so soon, my brother," Khouri was murmuring as he alternately rubbed and sniffed. "Soon."

Xerruw peered inside, tipped it upside down, and shook it, then turned the bag inside out. He held out his open palm. It was empty. "Little brother," he said, his voice curiously soft. "There is yet work to do. There's nothing in the bag at all."

But even Xerruw was not prepared for the savagery with which Khouri ripped the other's throat open and, reaching within the body cavity, withdrew Petri's still-beating heart.

12

"With all due respect, my lord Duke, but my master, General Lussius, has bid me offer you the information that the legions are growing restless. Our soldiers are not accustomed to wasting such fine fighting weather. When do we march and when will you reveal your battle plan?" The Lacquilean translator spoke in such heavily accented Brynnish that Cadwyr only stared at him with a blank face. He opened his mouth to begin his speech once more, but Cadwyr cut him off.

"What? Oh." Cadwyr gestured to the window. "You want to know what we're waiting for? We're waiting for a prisoner, and then another two days, for the full of the moon."

The translator, a slender young man not much more than boy, frowned as if he was not quite certain he'd understood. "Please, you will repeat?"

Cadwyr pressed his lips together to control his impatience. The mercenaries of the Lacquilean Empire were indisputably the most professional army in the known world, and one of the main reasons the Humbrians had not tried to annex Brynhyvar long before this. The Lacquileans had jumped at the chance to get their hands into the Brynnish pot. But soon, he'd no doubt that he would have both King of Humbria and Emperor of Lacquilea bowing at his feet. So he leaned forward and replied again, this time very slowly, as he gestured once more to the window. "The moon—we must wait for it to be at its fullest, for its power to be at its apex."

The boy turned to the man who wore a polished steel breastplate over a short red tunic. His cloak was shot through with imperial purple—he was a member of one of the First Families. Ottavius Lussius folded his arms and listened to the rapid explanation. The side of his mouth quirked down, but that was his only reaction. He gestured at the hide map, and ran a finger along the border of the riverbank, then spread his hands and looked at Cadwyr, obviously asking a question.

The translator said, "General Lussius begs to be allowed to comprehend the intricacies of your strat—"

"Shut up, Phoebius." The general himself pushed his chair away from the table. His Brynnish was actually far less accented than the translator's. "You're a translator not a diplomat. You repeat what I say, you don't coat it in sugar. I've enough Brynnish for this. What game is this you're playing, my lord? You've yet to lay out an objective, save to issue us those ridiculous silver arms. Half those blades wouldn't cut butter. How do you expect my men to fight with them? And for what, exactly, are we waiting? The moon is full enough if you wish to march at night—we could be moving our troops into position all along the river, and be across before they ever suspect—"

"We have to wait for the moon, General." There was a petulant note in Cadwyr's voice that made Lussius look at him more closely. There was a fine gleam of sweat on his smooth-shaven cheeks, cheeks that were as closely shaven in the Lacquilean manner as his own. He had at first assumed it was an obsequious gesture on Cadwyr's part to ingratiate himself with his more civilized allies. But now he wasn't so certain. "When the moon is at its fullest, the boundary between the worlds will be the thinnest."

Lussius cocked his head, calculating the likelihood that what he'd thought he heard was what Cadwyr had actually said. "Are you telling me that you're basing the timing of this battle on the moon? But we're nowhere near the enemy—"

"We're closer than you think, General. This is a very... elusive...enemy." Cadwyr leaned forward and met Lussius's contempt with brazen assurance. "Now, one more thing, since you've inquired about our battle plan. Woolen plugs will be distributed to your troops. They must plug their ears—"

"You must be joking. Phoebius, did I really hear him say he expects me to send my soldiers into battle deaf? You're a madman, Cadwyr of Allovale, just like the rest of your countrymen."

But Cadwyr refused to be cowed. He only narrowed his eyes and raised his chin and smiled. "Why such undue haste to ride to battle, General Lussius? When you, of all your countrymen, have such a reputation for coolheaded decision-making. Perhaps there's something calling you back to the city? Or someone?"

Lussius did a double take, but Cadwyr only chuckled and patted his side. "I've got your commission papers right here, signed by the Vox himself. Your own father wants you kept up here and out of the way—for as long as I need you. No one's looking for you, General, to arrive back home anytime soon."

"No one's looking for me to allow my troops to commit mass suicide, either. What's your reason for the plugs? Are you going to tell me your enemies have horns such as will drive a man mad?"

"Yes," answered Cadwyr. "That's exactly what I'm telling you."

Lussius bit back the curse but not before "Superstitious tribesman," slipped out. He shook his head then pinned Cadwyr with a look that would've warned every man who knew him. "All right, my lord Duke. Assuming you know this enemy and I do not, how far will we march at the full of the moon?"

"I don't know."

"You don't know." Lussius's expression darkened another shade.

But Cadwyr would not be cowed. "The hostage—remember, my hostage? The one who should be arriving any day now? He'll be able to give me more information on what we'll find once we cross the border."

"I see. You expect him to so readily betray his people?"

But Cadwyr only had the chance to answer with a smile. There was a rapid knock on the door, which then opened to reveal an eager guard. "My lord Cadwyr, great news has come—not only does has the hostage been delivered without fail, but they have brought you the head of Sir Kian of Garn!"

Cadwyr leaped to his feet and howled like an animal. Lussius relaxed against the back of his chair, watching him closely. He was a second son and his survival instincts had been honed in the corridors of his own home before he was ten. An instinct to pay close attention to Cadwyr flared into life. But Cadwyr was practically dancing around the table, still howling, patting the boy's face, hugging the guard. He stopped short when he reached Lussius. "Oh, wipe that sour look off your face, Lussius. This news means you and I will feast in Ardagh 'ere the snow begins to fall."

"It's like this, the way I see it." Uwen leaned over the hide map pinned to the top of the long plank table and tapped his finger on the dark *X* that indicated Gar Castle. At the head of the table, Cecily sat, flanked by her foster brothers, Collum and Jammor next to Mungo on her right side, and Tuirnach beside Uwen. Artimour stood on Uwen's left, and Nessa huddled just behind his right, careful not to look at Artimour. "It's clear to me that Cadwyr will first attack the OtherWorld, and only then, once he has his position consolidated there, turn on us. But the fact is, we have to keep the fight here. We can't risk him winning in TirNa'lugh, for considering what Artimour has told us, he may, given his silver and his troops, have an excellent chance of winning. Right now, he thinks we're beaten."

There are some here who think we are, thought Nessa as she watched doubt flicker across more than one face, just as there were more than one who wondered what exactly she was doing pushing her way into the circle crowding round the table. But ever since the realization that there was a possibility—no, a likelihood—that she *was* indeed a

Beltane child had somehow embued her with more confidence in her abilities. There was a reason, now, at least, she had such gifts, that made her better able to claim them as her own. It even emboldened her to claim a place at the council table.

"But there are some things he doesn't know," Cecily said. She tapped the hide map. "He doesn't know we've made our own alliance with the sidhe. He doesn't know we know about his hostages. And he doesn't know we've an inkling of his plans, or any ability at all to respond to them."

"And how would you suggest we do that, my lady?" asked a chief in an unfamiliar plaid.

"If Cadwyr means to cross into Faerie," said Artimour, to Nessa's surprise, "he only has a limited window of opportunity. He has to wait for a portal large enough for so many mortals to cross over, to open up. And he can only cross in certain places. Water is the most reliable conduit, and a branch of the Darraghduin winds through the valley where the Castle sits. In looking at the map, from what Sir Uwen and the rest of you have told me, he's got two times he can move so many across—the dusk of the Full Moon, and at dawn. He'll have to march them down, here, across the meadow, and into Faerie, right here—where the riverbank opens up. The Full Moon is in two days. It's not likely he'll try to cross at dusk, but he may, depending on his alliances within Faerie."

"I beg your pardon, my lord sidhe," put in Mungo, "but are you telling me you suspect Cadwyr of involving himself in some sort of plot within your world?"

"We cannot assume that all the sidhe are Cadwyr's enemies, my lord," replied Artimour. "And as Sir Uwen pointed out, there's nothing to suppose he hasn't made some sort of alliance with the Goblin King himself. The fact that he not only has Finuviel apparently a prisoner, but the Queen herself, tells me that there has been more than one betrayal in Faerie." There was a black, bitter edge to his voice that made Nessa look at him despite her resolve. She could only see the back of his head, but she saw how rigid his shoulders were with suppressed tension.

"I suppose it must be done," said Mungo. "The druids say we have to crown the Queen at Ardagh—we have to go through Cadwyr to get to Ardagh. We might as well fight him sooner rather than later and while he's got his mind focused on other things and other places—"

"But what about these hostages of his? What about the Queen of Faerie?" asked Nessa. She poked her head around Uwen. "What about the Caul? I think you're underestimating Cadwyr. He'll outright kill them once the fighting starts. Someone has to try to get them out of there—help them find a way into Faerie. If he's distracted by the fighting, wouldn't it be possible for someone inside the Castle to free them?"

"Nessa," began Uwen, "we've scarcely the time to get this—"

"No, she's right," Cecily interrupted. "He will kill them. He's already shown he'll kill the sidhe without so much as a blink, and I know in my heart he murdered Donnor. Before the battle, someone has to get in there and get them out."

There was a long silence. Then Nessa said, "I'll do it." As a low rumble of disbelief and protest went around the table, she continued, "I've been to Gar. I know some parts like the back of my hand, and I've been in the Hall enough to know the general layout. I'm a blacksmith. They'll let me in. I can use a dagger and an ax, and I can swing a broadsword if I must. And I can say I'm looking for my foster brother, the apprentice smith from Killcairn. Shouldn't all the smiths be there?" She'd get Griffin to help her both free the hostages and cross into Faerie to free her parents.

"I thought the young bard from Gar said they were all killed on Samhain—" blurted Mungo, then bit his tongue and looked contrite. "Oh, lassie, if you did lose a fosterkin, I'm sorry for your loss."

A wave of numbness swept over her, blunting the first sharp edge of anguish, enabling her to raise her head and look straight at Cecily. "Well," she said, "I can still ask." She really was all alone in the world, she thought, and suddenly she was even more resolved than ever to find her parents and get them home. From the head of the table, the Duchess met her eyes, and in them, Nessa read a silent acknowledgment, and she felt a kinship with Cecily, as if she were a sister or a cousin, and a connection she had felt to few other women in her life. "Let me do this. Please."

"You shall not—" began Artimour, and Nessa rounded on him with a vengeance.

"Who're you to tell me what to do, my lord? You've made enough decisions for me, thank you very much. I'll leave this one to my lady."

Cecily leaned forward with steepled fingertips. "Why not, Lord Artimour? Why do you so object?"

He knows the real reason I want to do it, Nessa thought. She met his eyes, daring him to speak.

His answer took her by surprise. "Nessa may be both brave and strong, but she's yet a girl."

"Then who would you suggest accompany her, my lord?" asked Uwen.

"I'll go," he said.

He thinks he can keep me out of the OtherWorld that way, she thought. *Well, we'll see.*

"You, Lord Artimour?" asked Cecily.

"The command of my company can be left to one of the other captains. I can catch up to them as soon as I make sure the hostages return."

"All right then," said Cecily. "If that will suit you."

"Believe me, my lady, it suits my purposes very well, indeed."

There was some dark satisfaction in Artimour's voice that made Nessa glance over involuntarily once more. He was looking at her, his eyes hooded and angry, and she raised her chin and would not be cowed. *So he wanted to travel with her all the way to Gar, did he?* She favored him with a wink and turned on her heel and stalked away, leaving the rest to plan the logistics of moving down into the thickly forested hills surrounding Castle Gar.

She heard his footsteps behind her, but she kept going all the way to the forge, and when she would've slammed the door behind her, he stuck his boot in the doorway and prevented it from closing. "Why, Lord Artimour, to what do I owe the courtesy of a call?" she said, mimicking as best she could the stilted phrases of the stories.

"You know why I'm here. You think you're clever, don't you? I know what you're planning."

"Oh? And what's that?"

"You're planning on using this to get your parents out of Faerie."

"And you blame me for that? By your own admission Faerie is dying—"

"I don't expect Faerie to die. I seek to save it. But that's not why you can't get them out. It'll kill them to leave. You have to accept that. They're not coming back to you. Your father—"

"You don't know my father any more than you knew yours." Her words struck home and he staggered a little as if she'd physically slapped him. "And I know one thing for sure. He'd never want to linger there. He hated Faerie, and the last thing he'd want is to be kept there—"

"He's with your mother."

"Are you saying he wants to stay there with her?" When he didn't answer, she said, "Maybe you're right. But I want to hear them tell me that themselves."

"Why do you have to be so stubborn?"

"Why do you care?"

"Because it's too dangerous—"

"Too dangerous for who?"

"For you—for all mortals."

But the slip lingered. "I think I understand how dangerous Faerie is." She looked at his face, and knew he too had heard the slip and it mortified him on some level. And so she took the opportunity to ask a few questions of her own. "How is it you knew Finuviel was there?"

"When my horse returned without me, the border garrison sent out three search parties. One has never returned, one was driven back by the goblins on Samhain, and one returned to say they'd spotted Finuviel being removed from the mine."

"And how is it you've come to rescue him?"

"Rescue him? Take him back to Timias and have him answer for his betrayal of the Queen and all that's Faerie is what I intend to do with him. Believe me, Nessa, I wash my hands of both Vinaver and her son. They sicken me. Vinaver explained why Finuviel stabbed me, you see. She thinks I'll die anyway when the Caul is unMade."

"What? But that's terrible, is it true?"

He didn't answer for a moment. "I don't think I understand anymore what's true. To tell you the truth, I'm not sure I care. If it happens, and that's what must be, then so be it. I saw firsthand what silver does in Faerie. And it has to be stopped. At least I have the satisfaction of knowing that if I die, Vinaver is likely to die as well."

"I have to get ready," said Nessa, abruptly refusing to continue the discussion.

"For what?"

"I've druid work."

"Now you're a druid?"

"I'm a blacksmith. And that's what they've need of." She slapped leather vambraces over her forearms and crossed her arms across her chest. She understood a little better now why he kept his distance, but it didn't make it any easier to bear. Why not make the most of the time we have? she wanted to say. But she wouldn't beg.

"Then good night, Nessa. We ride at dawn."

"I'll see you at dawn," she said, and she looked pointedly at the door. He took the hint and she watched him leave. His head was bowed, his shoulders low, and she saw something new in the way he walked. He walks like an old man, she thought as a wave of sympathy went over her. An old, old man, much burdened by care. But shadows were lengthening across the courtyard, and there were things she had to do to prepare. She turned away and thought she saw Artimour dart back out of the corner of her eye. *Don't be moon-mazed, Nessa.*

"—preparations?" It was Molly, speaking from the doorway, a basket in her arms.

"Oh!" Nessa lost her grip on the window frame and the pane swung in, bumping her on the nose.

"What're you doing there, girl, half leaning out the window?" scolded Molly. "Come, if you're to leave at dawn, we need to get to this swordmaking at once. The druids say that fortunately, tonight is an auspicious night."

"Finally," said Nessa.

Molly chuckled. "Ah, child, one thing I've learned about Hag's days like these, it always seems the bleakest just when things begin to turn."

"Do you really think that's what's happening, Molly?"

"It's what I believe every night when the sun goes into the West." She patted Nessa's cheek. "Come, child. Let's get to work. The druids will be here before sundown."

An orange sun was setting behind the western hills when Uwen found her, but Cecily was not surprised to see him. He paused just on the edge of the stairs, and said, "Do I disturb you, Your Grace?"

How could you disturb me? she thought. *You're the closest one to Kian I know.* But the burden of the day hung on her like a lead shroud. Talking seemed so hard. She only shook her head.

"I know—I know you've scarce had a moment of your own since the word came in. But I wanted to tell you I know he'd be proud of you—how strong you've been. We all miss the Chief. And we know you miss him most of all."

Cecily drew a deep breath and bit down on her tongue to dull the uprush of grief and loss that threatened to drown her with its dizzying intensity. She clutched the stone battlements and stared out blindly over the darkly forested hills, the shimmering surface of the black lake. "I don't understand one thing, Uwen."

"What's that?" His voice was very soft, very kind, and she turned.

"Why did Nessa save him? Just to prove to us that she could?"

"Ah, Cecily, from what you told me and from what the granny said, 'twasn't anything Nessa could really control. She couldn't heal the old druid, now."

"Then why Kian? Why did the goddess let her save him, if she only wanted him back?" The tears spilled down her cheeks then, and her face crumpled. He reached out and drew her close, and she stiffened, then relaxed against him, sobbing, until she realized her tears were soaking through his shirt all the way to his skin. "I'm sorry," she said at last as she raised her head and wiped at her eyes. "I just..."

But Uwen only wiped away his own tears and said, "We all miss the Chief, Cecily. And you need to cry. Only you've been right not to. There'll be a time to mourn him. But we all know now isn't it." He took a deep breath. It was the first time he'd used her name but it didn't seem to matter.

She wiped her face again on her linen square. "I wanted to ask you if you knew what happened to Kian's sword? I know it was in pieces, but you see, I bear his child, Uwen, and I'd like to be able to show his son his sword."

"Ah." Uwen touched her cheek gently. "Well. That's why I came up here, you see. Nessa, and the druids, they have some great doing for that sword, and they sent me to ask you if you would care to come."

At some point, Nessa became aware that the grannies and the druids had begun to sing, a kind of bridal chant, soft and wooing, similar to the songs sung to invite the brides of Brynhyvar to come and meet their grooms. It *was* a bridal chant, she realized, a soft and wooing call to—to whom? she wondered as she picked up her hammer and her attention was drawn to the metal before her. She dug her feet down into the flagstone floor, and once more, she felt that undeniable surge of some connection into something like a great river, and she knew that it was the roots of the great birch tree on the hill, that somehow, by extending all the way into the ground beneath Killcarrick, that enabled her to link into this enormous flow. She remembered how it had felt the first time she had connected to the tree, and she took a deep breath of the hot, dense air. Perspiration trickled down her neck. The druids and the wicce-women had stopped moving now, and were gathered around Cecily and Uwen, who stood opposite the anvil. She met Uwen's eyes.

"Looks good, lass," he said.

She held the rough-hewn blade of glowing metal up and immediately had a sense that she'd already seen this and remembered her vision. Holding it by the tang, she plunged it into the waiting vat of water. It hissed and smoked, and in the light, the water looked red. Twelve times she hammered out the metal, and twelve times she immersed it in the water. *It needs thirteen,* she thought. She felt the words begin to bubble, boiling up like bits of shimmering color in the darkness of her mind. The hammer sang and sparks flew and the forge reeked of human sweat and salt and the acrid smell of metal. To the rhythm of her hammer, she felt words begin to flow, and she looked up to see the druids, and the grannies, the Duchess and Uwen, all moving in time to an unheard beat. Or was it? she thought. *Birch and Beech and Rowan tree—no, that's not right. The A's came first—Alder, Ash and Aspen Tree; Birch and Beech and Rowan three—yes, that's it.* The hammer's ring echoed in the night, white smoke belched up the chimney. *Round about the circle goes dark to light and back it flows—by the Sacred Thirteen trees, by the power I bind to me—through this metal let it run—from root to trunk to leaf to sun.*

The fire sparked and flared, the forge reddened and the light grew brighter. Sweat ran down her arms, her sides, and she felt her belly quicken, the same sort of throb as Artimour roused. She was in the center now, and looking around, she saw that between the druids and the grannies and the Duchess and Uwen there were twelve. She herself in the middle was the thirteenth. *That's where the magic is,* Nessa realized. *In the middle of things—in the place that holds it all together. The power that binds, the force that loosens. Right here, where I am standing.* Words leaped once more to her lips, and as she slammed the hammer down with all of Dougal's focus, she heard herself say with sure certainty:

"By Alder, Ash and Aspen Tree,
By Birch and Beech and Rowan Three..."

The druids gasped when they heard the words begin to flow, and Collum called, "Listen well, my brethren!"

Nessa took a deep breath and the words rushed out of her mouth, charged with the strength of air and fire and water and earth, for the words were shaped by her very being, which was all of those elements combined, endowing the metal with such force of purpose that she almost felt as if the sword, in some way, became aware:

"Hazel, Holly, Elder, Vine,
Yew and Apple, Oak to bind.
Name I now each sacred tree,
And all thirteen I call to me
Call to me the power that runs
From root to trunk to leaf to sun;
Up and down the trunk it goes,
Dark to light and back it flows,
By the Thirteen Sacred trees,
By the power I bind to me,
Through this metal let it run.
From root to trunk to leaf to sun:
A sword of healing let this become
No true wrong let it not right
And only foul the flesh it bites.
Great God and Goddess of the land
Great God and Goddess guide my hand
All we say three times shall be—
As we will, so let it be."

Up through the ground, the power flowed, connecting in her belly with hot air she drew into her lungs, rushing through her limbs, up and down her spine, until the back of her neck tingled and the sensation rolled down her arms in a steady pulse. The very discipline of the craft allowed her to control the force of the magic, so that the tools became extensions of herself, enabling her to shape the hot and burning metal as if it were cool and malleable as clay.

The sword took shape before their eyes, the power wreathing the edges in flames of glowing blue. *All we say three times shall be,* thought Nessa, *All we say three times shall be.* She felt a massive, growing tingle at the base of her neck, as if a burst of energy was growing, charging, blooming, and with a last, focused thought, straight as an arrow or the edge of the blade, she let the final thought roll through her mind, down her arms, forcing the churning energy into shape, so that the metal glowed and shimmered and in the combination of the fire and the moonlight, the spark and the steam, the sword itself took form. "As we will, so let it be."

She raised the sword by the tang and held it up, let it shimmer like a silver arrow in the moonlight, then plunged it into the waiting vat of water. It hissed and steamed and she raised it high, so that the water droplets ran like pearls down its gleaming sides. She was trembling, her arms were shaking and great drops of sweat were rolling down her sides, down her back. She nearly dropped the sword, and Uwen rushed forward to catch her as the blade fell into a shaft of moonlight.

When Nessa opened her eyes, she thought she was alone in the little bedroom behind the smithy. Then a flicker on the periphery of her vision caught her eye and she turned to see Artimour sitting on a stool beside the bed and she sat up so quickly the room spun. "What are you doing here?"

"I saw what you did tonight. I'm not sure why I'm here, really. But I think it's to apologize."

She rose up on one elbow and pushed the sooty tumble of her hair out of her eyes. "For what?"

"For doubting you. I still don't think it's wise of you to go into Faerie. But I saw—I saw what you did tonight. It's not for me to tell you whether to go or stay. I was wrong to tell you otherwise." He got to his feet. "Now I see you're all right, I'll leave you to rest. We leave—"

She caught his hand and when he went to pull it away, she said, "Stay with me tonight."

He hesitated, then shook his head. "It's better this way, Nessa. Just better."

Better for who? she wanted to scream. But she was too tired to argue and too proud to beg for information. She fell asleep the moment her face touched the pillow.

She was surprised to meet Uwen in the stables at dawn. "I didn't know you were coming with us."

"Ssh." He pressed a finger against his lips. "Neither does anyone else. But it seems to me you're going to need someone else who knows Gar to get you around. Because I think it's pretty clear there're only two places Cadwyr would hold either the Caul or the sidhe. One's in his bedchamber, and the other's the dungeons. I know where Cadwyr's chambers used to be, at any rate, and I know what lies beneath the Castle as well. So you'll get us in, Nessa. I'll help you find them, and Artimour will get them over the border."

"Then what about you, Uwen? What will you do to get out of Gar?"

"Well," he said as he checked the buckles of her saddle and the pack across the horse's back, "let's just say this gives me the chance to pay a private call on Cadwyr."

13

The end was coming fast. From the highest turret of the Palace, Vinaver watched a red sun rise at last over the eastern hills. She could not see the light penetrate the lower floors where the battle had raged since dusk, nor hear the goblins' clawed feet scamper back to the safety of the darkness, but she could smell the reek of goblin entrails and she could imagine the purple rivers of goblin blood that fouled the marble halls. The door opened without ceremony, and Morais, the beleaguered-looking Commander of the Palace Guard, stepped into the room, his face drawn and pale. Even the shaft of rosy light that fell across his brow did nothing to lighten his expression, but turned his moss-green doublet dark gray.

"What word, Commander?" Philomemnon turned away from the window, his ruined eye covered by a black silk patch. He would never be the same again, thought Vinaver, but then again, which of them would?

The floor shuddered as the entire palace shook, and Morais looked wearier than Vinaver had ever imagined a sidhe could look. How ironic, she thought, that she should see the end come here, high in this airy tower of crystal and ivory. How many times in her quest to find the Hag had she pleaded with whatever force guided her path to let the fresh clean air of Faerie be her last breath. It appeared she was about to get her wish.

Morais answered, "The initial spells of binding we set were done too quickly to have much effect, and so were broken through almost immediately. The ones on the floors above held almost the entire night—"

"But did not even hold til dawn?"

Morais spread his hands. "My lord, our magic is sorely lacking without the Queen. That's what I've come to tell you, my lord, my lady. We must break into the Queen's chambers, for we have no choice. My concern is that they will discover the Sacred Grove within the center of the Palace. It appears they're tunneling beneath the stables as well—they could well find their way into the throne room. But it's the Sacred Grove that concerns me the most. So far, the spells around the Queen's rooms are intact. But we need her. We cannot hold another night without her."

"But how do you intend to get in if the spells of binding hold?"

"To tell you the truth, I'm not sure. I'm open to all your ideas. But my concern is that as thorough a spell of binding Timias may have set, I'm quite sure there's no such ward on the floors. He wouldn't have expected anything to come from below."

"Can we not use fire to blast—"

"No," interrupted Morais. "Fire of a force sufficiently necessary to rout the goblins would weaken the foundations of the Palace. If that's what we must ultimately do, so be it, but I would not wish to direct a force that great without the Queen's magic to fortify and sustain it. And we cannot do that anyway, as long as Timias and the Queen herself are barricaded in the very heart of the Palace."

The sunrise was turning the sky the color of mortal blood. *The holly bears the berry as red as mortal blood.* The old line ran through Vinaver's mind as she turned away from the window. Another day in Faerie was dawning, glorious as always, the sunlight spilling over the emerald-green hills as if nothing was wrong. The wounds in her back were still open and seeping, but she was growing used to the pain, felt it becoming a part of herself, hardening a familiar path in her sinews and her muscles and her skin, shriveling her from the center out. We're all dying, she thought. "So what you're saying, Commander, is that it's only a matter of time?"

There was a long silence and then Morais nodded. "I am afraid, my lady, that is exactly what I am saying. There are simply too many of them. And far too few of us."

"All right, Morais. We'll think of some way into the Queen's chambers. You get some rest," Philomemnon said. After Morais had bowed himself away, they were quiet for a long time. As the sunlight strengthened, Philomemnon said, "What if we made another Caul? We have silver, we have a smith—you even have the tools—"

"What good would another Caul do us at this point, Philo?" Vinaver sighed. "There's only one thing to do but wait and hope that Artimour arrives in time."

"Vinaver, I hope you haven't made another mistake."

"What do you mean, another mistake?"

"I don't mean to criticize you, Vinaver, I know you've done nothing but what you've believed to be best. But maybe—maybe you've not been quite accurate in your assessments of those you've chosen to help you. The gremlin betrayed you. The mortal betrayed you. And now—now it all rests on someone your son stabbed."

"Artimour understands…"

"Vinaver, my dear." Philomemnon looked at her sadly and shook his head. "I think you may have made yet another terrible mistake."

Uwen reined his horse at the top of the ridge, close to where the tree line ended and the broad meadow sloped down to the river. "Great Mother. Would you look at that?" he asked.

Nessa came up behind him and gasped. She had been to Gar, had been prepared for the imposing sight of the great Castle rising up out of the rolling meadow, but the sheer size of the camp spread out across the valley took her breath away. The plain was a solid encampment of soldiers, mostly Lacquilean, their red and gold and purple banners snapping brazenly in the wind. There were so many of them, too, she thought as she followed Artimour and Uwen out of the reassuring cover of the trees. The Lacquileans were dark, she saw, but olive-skinned, their faces clean-shaven. They were camped in groups of ten or twelve, it seemed, and all the men were busy, mending gear, polishing armor, sharpening swords. Here and there, around the fringes, she saw plaid battle banners stuck up on stakes that looked especially crude beside the mercenaries' eagle-topped flagpoles.

They eyed the little party, sized them up as Brynnish and turned their attention away. She heard a few call after them in their language that sounded like gobbled gibberish, but those were quickly hushed. They were disciplined deliverers of death, she thought, chilled by the sterile precision of the camp and the almost preternatural neatness about the soldiers themselves. Death's not really that clean, she thought as she rode past them through what had once been the gatehouse of Gar. She looked up at the ruins, realizing that what looked like piled faggots were all that remained of the gates. The huge iron portcullis that led to the entrance of the second ward was intact, however, and a temporary gatehouse had been set up.

As they approached, Nessa flung back her hood to reveal her face, and Artimour allowed his to fall back. Uwen pulled a linen bandage over the lower half of his face. The guards at the makeshift gate wore Cadwyr's plaid, and showed no sign of recognizing Uwen. But they exchanged a skeptical look when Nessa said she was a blacksmith. "Oh, really?" the one demanded.

"Oh, really," she replied. "Is Master Lear here? Master Lear the smith?" She named Donnor's Master Smith, a cantankerous man who nonetheless seemed to have respected Dougal enough to allow him the use of his forge on occasion.

"Lear's dead, maidy," another replied, leaning on his spear.

"I heard the Duke needed smiths. I heard that most of those he rounded up were slain on Samhain." She raised her chin. "Is that so?"

The two guards leaned on their spears and the first nodded at Artimour and Uwen. "And who're these? More smiths?"

"These're men are from Killcairn," Nessa replied, struggling to keep her voice steady. "We decided to come south since Killcarrick was so crowded—" here Uwen coughed "—and Killcairn destroyed." She looked over her shoulder. They hadn't thought such improvisation would be necessary. Cadwyr, it seemed, was more cautious than they'd expected.

"All right. You can go in. But we'll be looking for you in the forge, maidy." The first winked and waved them through.

The second gestured with his spear. "I've got a spear with a point that needs some trimming."

Artimour turned and looked at him, and this time it was Nessa who placed a hand on his arm, leading him into the second ward of the great keep. Uwen gestured them to keep walking. "This way," he said. "We'll go round to the stables first. See who's about."

But as they drew near to the Hall, Artimour sniffed and turned his head, looking puzzled. "That's a most unexpected odor—"

"What is it?" asked Nessa, taking a big sniff. "What do you smell?"

"It's very faint." Artimour closed his eyes and sniffed again, and this time shook his head. "I must've been mistaken."

"By what?" asked Nessa.

"I could've sworn I smelled may-apple wine. It's a particularly potent brew, and even the sidhe don't drink it regularly..." His voice trailed off as he looked around the crowded ward.

Uwen held his shoulders crookedly now, exaggerating his limp, as he shepherded them across the uneven cobbles, navigating with unerring instinct toward the stables. For if

there were ten thousand men without the walls, there must
be nearly that number within, thought Nessa, wide-eyed at
the number of soldiers and stacks of equipment. All silver,
she saw. No wonder the young druid was so certain of Cadwyr's plans. He might as well advertise them the length of
Brynhyvar. Well, she thought, missing Artimour's reply,
what did he care? Soon, she realized, that was exactly what
he intended. "What was that you smelled again?"

Both men hushed her until, as they rounded a corner and
found themselves in a less crowded area of the Castle, Artimour paused and cocked his head, sniffing again. "There
it is again."

"I don't smell anything." Nessa took a deep breath and
all she could smell was horse manure. They were obviously
near the stables.

"It's coming from that direction—" Artimour pointed.

"Those are the kitchens over there," said Uwen. "Let's
turn the horses over to a groom, and then we'll take a walk
toward the kitchens. No one'll think it odd if we go get a bite
to eat."

"Uwen, everyone seems too busy to notice us much," said
Nessa. "What do you think?"

"I think we got here just in time." Uwen adjusted his bandage across his face and pulled his cloak low over his eyes
and said nothing more until they'd left the horses with a
surly stable boy, then silently pointed them in the direction
of the kitchens.

But they never got quite that far, for Artimour pulled
them toward a flight of stone steps that led down into a black
well where an unlit torch hung in a rusty grate. "Down
there," he said. "Definitely down there."

Try as she might, Nessa couldn't smell it. Uwen grabbed the torch and lit it with a flint scraped over the stone. "These are the old wine cellars," he said as he held the torch up. "They opened them up right after Donnor threw the gauntlet down." The walls were crusted with lichen, the floor crunched beneath their feet, dry with dust and the bones of mice. Several times Nessa sniffed surreptitiously, and the last time she was rewarded with something more than dust and cobwebs. But even as she opened her mouth to ask if whatever it was smelled like roses, Artimour made one last turn and stopped in front of an alcove where a dozen or more wooden barrels stood piled, their copper bindings gleaming orange in the flickering torchlight. The three stood staring.

"So is this where the smell's coming from?" Uwen asked after a long silence.

Nessa sniffed again, and this time she was sure of it. "It smells like roses."

"I knew I smelled it," Artimour said with a look of grim satisfaction. "The question is, what's it doing here, and why is there so much?"

"What is this stuff, anyway?" asked Uwen. He tapped on the closest barrel, but the sound was muted, dull.

"It's may-apple wine—it's like drinking pure fire. Even the sidhe can't take too much. So why is it here at all?"

"Perhaps the Queen, or Finuviel—" began Nessa, breaking off at the sound of echoing footsteps. The three of them dodged into a room a few measures away and Uwen extinguished the torch, leaving them huddling in nearly total darkness, scarcely daring to breathe.

"...so what's the lad going to do when they run out of this stuff?" The first voice wasn't so much loud as it reverberated, so that it seemed as if it was right on top of them. Instinctively, Nessa flattened back against the wall and found she pressed against Artimour's lean body. Desire speared through her and she stiffened, forcing herself to concentrate instead on the three distinctive voices coming ever closer.

"At the rate he's drinking it, it'll all be gone by next week."

"Well, he won't be here next week, not him nor Cadwyr neither," said the third voice. "And neither will we—didn't you hear the orders just come down? We're on the march day after tomorrow—going back to get more where this stuff came from."

"So it's true what they say about this stuff? It's the wine of TirNa'lugh?"

Crouched between the men, Nessa shifted carefully on her feet and her leather boot creaked against the cobbled floor.

"Did you hear that?" The guards paused and listened and immediately Nessa froze.

"Oh, it's just a rat."

"Maybe it's a trixie—you know, I heard a trixie was seen in this very castle. Now that can't be a good sign."

"There're no such things as trixies." Light flared as torches were placed in iron brackets.

"You're a fool, Robb, you're the one who said there were no such things as goblins. What do you know about anything?"

"I know if we don't get this barrel moved there'll be no extra ration of mead for us tonight. Would you like to shut up and grab one?"

On the other side of what now seemed like a low pile of stone, the three guards wrestled a barrel onto its side. Then one retrieved a torch, as the other two rolled the heavy barrel back down the cobbled passageway. "What about the torch?" asked one.

"Ah, leave it. It will burn out soon," said another. "And no, not that way—they said take it over this way."

"That way? That's where the—"

"We just follow orders, remember, Robb? We don't ask a lot of questions."

Still bickering beneath the rumbling barrel, the guards' voices faded down another branching corridor.

They waited until the rumble of the barrel had faded completely before they stepped out of their hiding place. "Might be interested to know where it's going," said Uwen.

"All right," said Nessa. "Where to now?"

But Uwen's suggestion was lost in the inhuman shrieks that echoed down the vaulted corridors, sounds of such agony and despair, they looked at each other in alarm. "Well," he said. "Whatever's making that noise certainly sounds inhuman."

"You think that's where they were taking the barrel?" asked Nessa.

"It's coming from roughly the same direction. But it's hard to tell down here—sounds carry and echo. Nothing is necessarily what it seems."

The screaming came again, a high-pitched wail that raised the hair on Nessa's neck. Nothing, not even the naked women who'd come after the goblins on Samhain had sounded so hollow and so—so empty. So empty and so lost. "Should we go find out what's making that noise?" she asked.

"Well," said Uwen, "it seems to me there's a chance Cadwyr's brought Finuviel from the silver mine and put him down here and he's the one making that horrible noise. So we may as well go and check it out now, while we're down here. We can always explore the top part of the Castle later tonight, when things start to settle down." He lifted the torch and beckoned, but as the eerie wailing began again, Nessa wondered if she really wanted to see whatever it was that was capable of making noises like that.

"No! No! No!" Griffin fought the guards with all his might, kicking and twisting and writhing. He clamped down on a hairy slab of a hand, and was rewarded with a cuff and a curse. "You little scat-head, you'll pay for that. Just watch."

Beneath Griffin's renewed shrieks, one of his other captors asked, "What in the name of the Hag are we moving him for, anyway?"

"Cadwyr wants him safe and out of the way and until he's wanted."

"Wanted for what?" The guards laughed and gripped him hard despite his struggles. Deeper and deeper they carried him, down farther and farther into the dark bowels of Gar, until at last they came to what was clearly a long-unused dungeon cell.

"No, don't put me in there," he shrieked, to absolutely no avail, because they heaved him onto the moldering pile of hay with no more care than if he were a carcass. His head knocked against the stone wall, and stars exploded across his eyes. As he groaned, and felt for his flask, he was aware that a barrel of brew was being rolled into the cell. He squinted up as a heavy hand jerked his chin up and he met the angry eyes of a guard, who waved a bloody hand in his face.

"Now here's where I pay you back for that bite, dog-boy.

Cadwyr said to put the barrel in the cell with you. But he didn't say to open it. So since you like to chew so much, have fun biting it open."

The door slammed shut in Griffin's face. "No! No! No!" He twined his fingers in the iron grate and pulled frantically, then took a quick sip from his flask. He screamed once more, just in frustration, then dropped to his knees in front of the barrel and began to feel along the copper bindings very carefully with fingertips and tongue.

In the dank cell across the corridor, Delphinea huddled beside Finuviel's pallet and listened to Griffin's agony. In the dark, Griffin began to sob, deep, screaming wails that seemed to come from someplace so far deep within, she felt as if the sound was being dragged up from the depths of the earth itself. It was a cry that gave voice to her own fear, her own terrible sense of having failed. *Just give me one sign, Great Mother, one sign that all's not lost. Just one.* Every time she looked at Finuviel, glanced at the terrible results of the silver mine, or remembered the touch of Cadwyr's hands on her skin, she felt an overwhelming sense of despair. But she dragged herself to her knees and pressed her face against the iron grate. "Griffin? Griffin, is that you?"

There was a long silence, and she began to think he did not intend to answer her. "Lady? Is that *you?*"

"What happened, Griffin?"

"I don't know," he sniffed. "Cadwyr came up like a madman, and told them to bring me down here. But I didn't do anything—" His voice rose in a petulant whine followed by loud thuds, and she realized he was knocking or kicking against the barrel in frustration. "I didn't do anything at all!"

"Griffin, stop that!" A draft blew against one cheek and light flickered in the corner of her eye. She pushed her cheek so deeply into the iron grate she could feel the scabs of rust, but saw nothing. "I think someone's coming. Can you see who it is?"

"Hello?" The unfamiliar voice echoed softly in the darkness. "Hello? Is anyone down that way?"

"Yes! Yes!" shouted Griffin, pulling at the grate as if he would pull it off. The thumping began again, and Delphinea realized that he was throwing himself against the door. "Please, please, I'm here, I'm here—they left the barrel, I can't get it open. They wouldn't open it and I've no way—"

The bobbing light came closer, and Delphinea saw three long shadows silhouetted on the floor. A mortal man asked, "Who's there?" as another voice, equally unfamiliar, but with the unmistakable lilt of a sidhe, said, "They put that wine in—"

"It's me—it's me, Griffin—" Griffin interrupted the sidhe, and Delphinea could see his eyes gleam green, his teeth flash white. "Help me. I have to have the brew."

Delphinea heard a soft gasp, and a sound that might have been a sob. The third figure took a step or two forward, and Delphinea saw that it was a mortal woman—tall and broad and armed as heavily as a man with an ax across her back and a short sword at her hip. But her voice as she approached the cell door warily was feminine and soft, and in it, Delphinea heard both disbelief and fear. "Griffin? Great Mother, oh, Griffin, is that you?"

Nessa squinted into the square opening, scarcely daring to believe that the pale lank-haired figure that clutched at the iron grate with skeletal fingers could really be Griffin, for he more closely resembled a Samhain shade than the strongly muscled lad she'd bid good-bye to scant weeks ago. "Griffin?" she whispered again, unwilling to believe the evidence of her own eyes.

"Nessa?" Her name ended in a plaintive sigh that held an undeniably familiar cadence. And unbelievably, when he pressed his face to the grate, she saw that it was indeed a Griffin who'd shrunk down to a bony scarecrow, with a grin like a death's head, and eyes that burned with hungry light. "Do you have a knife? Or the keys?" he asked. His voice sounded strange, too, as if his mouth was tinder dry. He licked his lips and took a sip from a flask.

Nessa wrinkled her nose and got a stronger whiff of the wine. "Are you drinking that wine, Griffin?"

"Good gentles." The voice was delicate as a song, and Nessa jumped and turned to see the pale luminous face of a sidhe peering up from another cell across the hall. But her eyes were a deep and startling blue.

Artimour turned to her at once. "Who are you? And who's that—" He gasped and turned to Uwen. "Shine the light there, please? Great Herne, who is that?"

"That's Finuviel," said the soft voice. "And my name is Delphinea."

Nessa turned back to Griffin as Artimour and Uwen peered into the opposite cell. She had to understand what was wrong with Griffin. "Griffin, what's happened to you?"

"Nothing," he answered, his eyes gleaming in the torch-light. "I just need—I need a drink of my—my medicine there. The stuff in the barrel. I take it and it makes me feel better."

"That's not medicine. Who told you it was medicine? And what's wrong with you? You look like you're sick."

"No, I'm fine, I had a horrible experience on Samhain, that's all. I was the only one to live, you know. All the rest got—taken."

"Then why are you down here? What have you done?"

"I haven't done anything," he howled. "They put me down here for no reason! I was minding my own business and doing exactly what he told me and then all of a sudden—"

"Hold on, boy." Uwen came up behind Nessa. "Hush that. We'll get you out—I know where the keys are. At least I used to. The sidhe over there are in a bad way—both of them."

But Artimour had turned away from the door, his face pale, his lips pressed tight together. "We have to move quickly. He—he's nearly dead."

"Who *are* they? Is that really the Queen of Faerie?" asked Nessa, torn between her curiosity about the sidhe, especially the woman, and Griffin's plight.

"I'm not sure who *she* is, I can't say—she's not Alemandine. But the other is Finuviel. And what Cadwyr did to him...I'll say this, Finuviel may have stabbed me, but what's he going through a dog shouldn't suffer." He turned away and shook his head, and Nessa dared to peek inside the cell. On the floor, beside the door, a small, dark-haired woman crouched beside a low pallet. A figure lay still beneath a rough wool blanket. The woman raised her eyes to Nessa, and she gasped, for if she'd thought the men of the sidhe fair to behold, they were not half so fair as this woman, who was surely not much more than a girl, for she appeared, in fact, to be younger than Nessa herself. Then the figure on the pallet moved, and the flickering torch fell upon his face, and Nessa started back in horror.

"That's Finuviel?" she whispered to Artimour.

Griffin rattled his grate. "Won't one of you give me a knife? All I need is a knife."

"Steady there, boy." Uwen's voice was soft and soothing, the same tone Dougal might use to an injured animal. "We'll have you all out of there in a trice—"

"I don't care about getting out," Griffin hissed. "I want to open the barrel."

"I don't think you should be drinking that stuff, Griffin." Nessa snapped her head around.

"Even we don't drink it with such abandon." The sidhe-girl's voice was as lovely as her face, a gentle sound that reminded Nessa of a spring breeze through cherry blossoms, and made her realize in an instant why Artimour rejected her. If all the women of the sidhe were half so lovely as this creature, it was no wonder he preferred them. "He calls it brew."

"Brew?" Nessa repeated. "Griffin, it's not some brew, it's Faerie wine—"

"I don't care what it is," he howled suddenly. "I want you to open the barrel."

Artimour said, "How quickly can we be out of here?"

Uwen smacked Griffin's hand on the grate. "Enough, boy. We'll get it open as quick as we can, but your noise is going to draw attention. Unwelcome attention at this point, so shut your mouth." He took a deep breath and turned back to Artimour. "I'd say—a turn of the glass, maybe less. Depends if they've moved the keys, who's got them, and who's guarding them. Boy, how soon do the guards come by?"

"How do you expect me to know?" Griffin spat. "I've only just been put in here—Hag knows why."

Uwen shut his eyes and whispered something. Then he looked at Griffin and said, "I'm trying to help you, lad. The least you can do is cooperate."

"I said I didn't know." Again his tone was petulant as a sulky child's, and Nessa sighed. This was a new Griffin, a different Griffin, a Griffin she wasn't sure she liked.

"All right, I'll be back." Uwen patted Nessa's cheek, slapped Artimour's shoulder and peered inside Griffin's cell. "You stay quiet, or I'll cut your throat myself."

The hard edge in Uwen's voice frightened Nessa, as well as the realization that he was indeed capable of such an action if it came down to such a choice.

As Uwen's footsteps faded down the dark corridor, Griffin rattled his grate. "Nessa, give me your dagger."

"Griffin, I don't think it's a good idea for you to drink that. Why don't you—"

Artimour spoke softly in her ear. "He can't help himself."

Griffin tried to force his hand through the grate, flaking off his skin nearly to the bone, and Nessa stifled a shriek. "Enough, Griffin! All right. Here." She tried to hand him her dagger but the crosspiece wouldn't fit.

"Twist it," he hissed. "Twist it."

"Griffin, it just won't fit," Nessa replied. "Can't you just wait—"

"Try mine," said Artimour.

But that, too, failed to fit, and Griffin howled again, jerking against the grate as if he would rip the door off by the hinges, and to her amazement, Nessa saw the hinges start to give. "Griffin, calm down. Once we're out of here—"

He pressed his face to the grate. "Nessa, I can't leave. The Duke'll kill me—"

"He's already killed you, lad," said Artimour. "You just don't know it yet."

"What kind of thing is that to say?" Nessa rounded on him. "Griffin's just sick, he'll be fine once we get him where—"

"I can't go anywhere, Nessa. I have to stay right here. Didn't you hear the lady? He wants to keep me safe. 'Twas those guards that wouldn't open the brew for me—'cause I bit their hands. But—"

"Griffin..." Nessa swallowed hard and covered his claw-like fingers with her own. The flesh felt hot and dry as leather set out in the sun, and the bones felt like sticks bound together with stringy twine. "Griffin, listen to me. Cadwyr's about to go to war. You can't stay here, it isn't safe. You have to come with us—"

"Nooo," he howled, banging against the door like one demented. "You don't understand."

"Then tell me and I will." There was something terrifying about this strange new Griffin.

Griffin's face crumpled. "I have to stay with him. I made a bargain with him. And if I don't stay with him, I'll die."

"Griffin, no, don't think that. It's not so bad—" She twined her fingers in his. "Granny Molly—you remember Granny Molly, right? She knows lots, and the druids—"

"Nooo!" he cried and he flung himself over the barrel, sniffing and licking every joint, every casing.

"Nessa..." Artimour touched her shoulder. "He can't help himself. Cadwyr got him on that stuff for some reason, and now—" He broke off and glared over his shoulder. "I only wonder where the hell he got it from, and who could've been so stupid as to give a mortal as many barrels of mayapple wine as he's got stored in the wine cellars." Nessa glanced at the opposite cell and saw Delphinea's startling blue eyes peering through the grate.

"But why does Cadwyr want to keep him safe? Griffin, stop making that terrible noise and answer me. What sort of bargain did you make with Cadwyr?"

"He's the one who has the Caul," Delphinea answered beneath Griffin's piercing howls of frustration. "Cadwyr made him wear it for some reason. First he kept him chained in his rooms. But Cadwyr put him down here with us. I don't think he wants everyone to know we're here."

It was Nessa's turn to press her face to the grate. "Griffin, be still!" His howling choked off, and he looked up from crouching crablike beside the barrel. "Is it true you have the Caul?"

He glanced right and left and nodded.

"Give it to me!"

"I can't!" screamed Griffin.

Nessa turned to look at him, her fist pressed to her mouth. The creature that threw itself against the walls wasn't Griffin. Behind her, Artimour spoke in her ear. "Now, do you see what I meant when I said nothing good ever comes when our two worlds meet?" But before she could respond, he said, "If he keeps that up, he'll draw the guards. See if you can get him to talk."

Nessa gulped, then peered through the grate. Griffin had quieted. In the rushlight, he was crouched again beside the barrel, a flask held to his lips. His head was tilted as far back as it was possible, and he tapped the bottom with desperate fingers. She could see his throat move and his mouth work. "Griffin? Griffin, talk to me."

He lowered the flask and his lips looked plump and oily. "I'm sorry, Nessa." He licked his lips, and his tongue darted out and took another swipe around the flask's rim. "I'm sorry. I have to drink this stuff. When I don't have it, I feel bad."

"Griffin, what happened to you?" She leaned into the grate until she felt the rusted edges press into her cheeks, and whispered, "Where did they take you? Who made you drink this stuff and why?"

He took another swallow and replaced the flask in a one-handed motion so swift and practiced her heart twisted. "They gave us the brew to make us work. We worked night and day, me and all the others, in Ardagh Vale."

"What did you do?"

"We made things out of silver—axes and swords and knives and mail and shields—or we coated ordinary things with silver, and the last day we made a lot of chains. I remember all those damn links. Then they took us back to Gar, but we never got there, because Samhain came, and the goblins came back." His face darkened and he turned aside.

"But you survived."

"Because of the brew." He patted the flask. "No, that's not exactly true. I survived because of a boy who gave it to me to drink. They wouldn't give it to us on the journey, see? Without it, we were easy to guard, all loggy and thick and slow. The captain, to his credit, gave us some as dusk fell on Samhain, but it wasn't soon enough, you see. We were mostly half-asleep still. This was Gareth's flask. He dropped it when they took him."

His voice faltered and his eyes dropped, and Nessa twined

her fingers in the grate, feeling helpless to comfort him. "Griffin, tell me about this bargain with Cadwyr. We need the Caul, Griffin. You know we need the Caul. Things can't be made better if we don't take it back to Faerie. You don't want the goblins to come again, do you?"

"But I promised him—" Griffin began. "I—I already nearly lost it once. He'll kill me for sure—"

"He's already half killed you!" The whining note in Griffin's voice made her angry. "Can't you see that? He's using you like a human—like a human treasure chest. He's feeding you stuff that's making you sick—have you seen yourself in a mirror at all? Have you looked at the way your clothes hang on you?"

"I just haven't been very hungry. That's all. The stink makes me sick."

"You know that's not true." She broke off and turned her head away lest he see the tears threatening to spill down her cheeks. A sick feeling was growing in the pit of her gut, a feeling that had nothing to do with the nauseating odor rising all around them. It was as if the very earth and rocks around them were sick, she thought. "Griffin? What exactly did you promise Cadwyr? And what did he promise you?"

"I promised I'd give him the Caul back if he ever asked for it. And he promised to give me all the brew I ever wanted. Nessa," he said as the whine crept into his voice. "Whatever you think of me, I really do need this brew. Please, I'll tell you everything, just help me get the barrel open. Please."

"Give me your dagger." Nessa held out her hand to Artimour. She removed her own dagger from her scabbard and knelt down on one knee, the toe of her boot on the blade of the dagger. Using Artimour's dagger, she worked apart the hilt, separating it from the metal blade. When it lay in pieces at her feet, she handed the blade and the hilt through the grate. "Be careful. It's not held together by anything."

As Griffin uttered a little cry of pure joy, and a scent like funeral flowers mushroomed from his cell, the tramp of booted feet made Artimour and Nessa freeze. Immediately, he beckoned to her, leading her farther down the passage. But as she gripped her staff, she realized the end of it was glowing. "Wh-what?" she began, scarcely daring to believe her eyes.

"It's a lych-light," said Artimour. "That staff of yours, there's magic in it. It's responding to Finuviel and Delphinea. Some say the trees of Faerie and the trees of Shadow are the same."

The booted feet approached. "But—but what do we do about it?"

"Cover it with your cloak." He shrugged. "Hurry, they're at the end of the corridor."

She thrust it under her cloak and flattened herself against the wall. "So it's not responding to *you?*"

His eyes gleamed almost sidhe-like as he swiftly turned to face her and she knew she'd struck a nerve. You could use a shave, she wanted to say, but just then, Uwen entered the passage, flanked by five knights. He looked first into Griffin's cell, and then into Delphinea's. "Nessa? Artimour?"

She uncovered the lych-lit staff and stepped forward, Artimour at her elbow. "Who—where'd you find—"

"These are the knights of Donnor's Company—all who are left, at any rate. Cadwyr's found no excuse to kill them yet, so he was planning on keeping them for ransom. Fortunately, Cadwyr's never been a knight of Donnor's Company, so he doesn't know all the ways in and out of our billets. They've already been planning a few surprises of their own." He made introductions so quickly Nessa knew she'd never remember their names, then said to the knights, "The one on the floor in there is the one I'm worried about. He's not able to walk from what I can see—"

"Give him some of the wine," said Delphinea.

"Will it help him enough that he needn't be carried?"

"He said it helped him before on the journey here."

He can talk? thought Nessa. It seemed unbelievable that intelligible sounds could issue from that ruined throat, but as Delphinea's mournful words faded, Nessa understood what she had to do. She looked into Griffin's cell, where he slurped the brew from the opened tap, like some obscene nursling. "Griffin?" As much as she pitied him, it appalled her to see him like this. "Griffin! Stop that. Listen to me."

He pulled away, licking his lips and the back of his hand. He looked almost sleepy with satiation. "What is it?" Even his voice was syrupy and slow.

"The sidhe needs some of the wine, Griffin."

"This is my brew." He rose to his feet and he looked bigger somehow, stronger. "It's *my* brew, Nessa."

"Griffin." Nessa could barely control the urge to slap him. "We'll get you more. We know where there're barrels of it. Please." On the other side, behind her, the knights were digging into the rotting wood frame with crowbars around the ancient hinges. She looked at Uwen questioningly.

"I couldn't waste time with keys. We brought tools."

In a few moments, the men had hacked the ancient hinges out of the rotting wood. "How'd you know it would be so easy?" she asked as they pushed the thick wooden door aside.

"Donnor never used these dungeons. We used them for fun—sent the fosterlings down here on Samhain and such."

"Remember the races?" put in one of the knights as they bent their backs to the hinges on Griffin's cell. In even less time, the rotting wood gave way and the door was lifted off with a creak.

But Griffin still crouched around his barrel. "Please, Griffin?" Nessa held out her hand. "I understand it's your brew. Won't you please share? Papa would expect you to share. Griffin—remember how he always said a guest was to be given the best of what we had, no matter how high or low? And these two sidhe, they clearly haven't been treated all that well. This is a chance to make that right."

He didn't answer, but he unbuckled the flask and filled, then corked it carefully, and held it out with a shaking hand. "They can have the brew but not the flask. They can't have the flask. It—it helps me sleep."

Oh, Griffin. Grief went through her like a spear. He was so very, very different, how could he ever be himself again? She pressed her lips together to keep from sighing audibly and handed over the flask. Across the passage, Uwen and the other knights were conferring with Artimour over Finuviel's pallet. As Griffin crouched once more beneath the tap as if it were a teat, Nessa stepped through the doorway and touched his shoulder. "Griffin?"

He took a quick gulp, then turned to her, and his eyes flashed green. He's drinking so much of that stuff, it's changing him, she thought. But his face was crumpling as he looked at her, and he fumbled at his neck and withdrew the amulet she recognized as hers. "Look, Nessa, I have your amulet. I think that's what kept me safe, it brought me luck. Did you see I left mine for you?"

It touched her at first, and then the expression in his eyes frightened her. But she fumbled beneath her tunic and finally pulled out his amulet from under her shift. "I've got it right here."

"I would've waited for you—"

From somewhere far away, a door slammed, and Uwen stuck his head into the cell. "Come on, we've got to go."

Nessa jumped to her feet. "We have to leave, Griffin." A sulky look passed over his face, and she reached down and shook his arm. "Come on."

He raised his face and she saw his cheeks were wet with tears. "Nessa," he whispered. "I haven't thought of anyone but you." He wrapped his hand around hers in an iron grip and pulled her down beside him.

"Griffin, we can't stay here. You have to come." She could hear the men discussing escape routes, the sidhe's muted groans and Delphinea's lilting murmurs of encouragement.

"When I—when I left you that amulet, I wanted you to know how I felt about you."

A chill went through her as she looked at his skeletal face. Uwen tapped her shoulder. "Come, Nessa."

But Griffin had her hand twined in his fist, and for a terrible moment, she thought he didn't intend to let her go. In the corridor, she heard Artimour say, "I hear someone coming."

The lad loves you. The incongruous memory ran through her mind. "Oh, Griffin—" Nessa broke off, feeling helpless. "Come with me, Griffin, and we'll go back to Killcairn. Come on, don't you want to go back?" It was the only thing she could think of to say. And after all, they were going back to Killcairn—eventually.

"I'll come with you, Nessa, on one condition." His voice sounded like the leathery scuttle of a beetle over old parchment, and it made the hair on the back of her neck stand straight up. "Marry me. Promise you'll marry me and I'll come with you."

"Griffin?" She startled back and his grip held her firm.

"Nessa," said Uwen right behind her. "We have to go. Now."

"All right, Griffin, I'll marry you as soon as we go back to Killcairn." The words tumbled out of her mouth, and Uwen squeezed her shoulder. That she should have said something so—so unthinkingly, so uncaring of their meaning and their import, startled her even more than the way Griffin took one last long swallow of wine, then rose to his feet in a swift fluid motion, dragging her upright with him.

"Let's go." His teeth flashed white.

She caught Artimour's eye and read his thoughts as clearly as if he had spoken. *See what happens when our two worlds meet?* Was this what her parents had become? A chill ran down her spine as she realized that a fate like this was what he sought to protect her from.

"I need the flask," Griffin hissed as they hastened down the dank, dark corridor, two of the knights supporting Finuviel.

"As soon as we get out of here," Nessa answered. "Let go of my wrist, Griffin, you're starting to hurt me."

But he only tugged at it harder, so that she spun around in front of him and nearly fell. She could hear the tramp of booted feet behind them, followed by a shouted outburst. "Great Herne, Griffin, not now!"

"Pick them up," ordered Uwen, and one of the knights slung Finuviel over his shoulder like a side of ham, and another swept Delphinea into his arms. As the knights began to run down the corridor, he turned to Griffin. "Boy, you either run or I kill you myself."

Griffin let go of Nessa's wrist and advanced on Uwen, his eyes shining an inhuman shade of green, his words a high, weird hiss. "I want my brew." He might've lunged on Uwen, but an arrow thudded into his back. His eyes flew open and blood belched from his mouth.

"Run, Nessa," said Uwen as he drew his sword.

"We need the Caul," she cried. She patted his tunic, his breeches, examined his belt for pouches, as Uwen stood over her practically dancing with desperation.

"Try his neck," he said as another arrow whistled over them.

"There they are!"

As the dozen or so guards rounded the end of the corridor, Nessa's fingers closed around the lace-edged pouch. She ripped the bundle away, and as they ran with frantic haste, she thought she heard Griffin whisper, "Nessa."

14

"**G**ive me the Caul." Somewhere in the confusion, in the darkness and the damp sweat that filled her nose, Delphinea clearly heard Artimour ask the girl for the Caul. It distracted her momentarily from the terror and the confusion, but there was no time to see if Nessa handed it over or not, for the big knight who held her only gripped her tighter and ran on. Fear scented the heavy air, rising like a miasma from the knights' sweat, filling her throat, making her palms sweat. They had the Caul. They had Finuviel. *Let it not be too late,* she whispered to whoever might be listening in the same rhythm as the pounding feet.

Somehow, they navigated the twisting passageways, until at last, they spilled out into a cold clear night. The big knight set her on her feet, and she realized they were underneath a low arch, in a narrow passageway within a wall. The wet wind licked at her face, and she saw Finuviel moan and fall to his knees. She bent over him as the two knights beside him helped him upright. He was gasping, and the air was gurgling in his throat, while pale bubbles of blood pearled around his mouth. He opened his eyes and stared at her, so full of pain and misery that her heart clenched, and her hand hovered in the air, helpless to heal. "Help me," he mouthed.

Just a sign, Great Mother, thought Delphinea. *Just one simple sign that it's not too late, that we have any chance at all of succeeding.* "Who has the flask?" she whispered. Someone put it in her hand and she held it to Finuviel's lips, supporting his head, and she saw that the last strands of long black hair, limp as sodden feather, hung over her arm.

Uwen was speaking in a hoarse whisper, "If our luck holds we'll be able to get through the piles of rubble, but we'll have to stay close together."

"Where are we heading?" asked Artimour.

"I supposed we'd head down to the riverbank—didn't you say that would be the largest portal, the easiest place to slip through?"

"No," said Delphinea suddenly. She touched Uwen's arm, and he startled. "We don't need the riverbank, Captain." She had no idea if such was his proper form of address, but the others used it to defer to him. "The border's close here. I can feel it."

"I can walk." Finuviel's voice was a harsh gurgle.

"Then let's go," said Artimour.

"I'm coming," said Nessa.

"You can't come, Nessa," he said at once, and Delphinea was surprised by how angry he sounded. "Faerie is dying—we've no time for—"

"And what do you expect me to do here?" Nessa hissed.

"Hide in the forge? Have them do to me what was done to the other blacksmiths?"

Delphinea's head jerked up. Nessa's phrase was echoing in her ears, ringing like a chime, even as Artimour continued to insist. "No," she said, interrupting the flow of his reasons why not. "Maiden, Nessa—that's your name?" When Nessa nodded, she said, "And you—*you* are a blacksmith?"

"Aye, lady," replied Nessa, sounding confused.

It's the sign. Delphinea choked back the tears that sprang to her eyes and raised her chin. "Lord Artimour," she said with all the dignity she could muster. "With all due respect, Nessa must come. We need her—"

"Vinaver has her mortal smith, my lady," Artimour interrupted. "Nessa's not—"

"But she's a woman," said Delphinea. "It needs a mortal woman to unMake the Caul—"

"How do you know that?" In the gloom, Artimour's expression was dark with suspicion.

"Gloriana told me." Delphinea confronted Artimour.

"Enough," said Uwen. "She can explain it all to you when you're safe across the border, but whoever's going had better go quickly, before Cadwyr's guards figure out the shortcut."

At the base of the tor, Delphinea paused. "It's here," she whispered. "We've but to walk around it against the sun—"

One moment, they were walking on the path which led around the base of Gar Tor, and the next, they were stepping out of the trees and onto a grassy lawn, to see the white turrets rising, the crystal panes flashing like rubies in the rising sun. "The Palace still stands," she cried over her shoulder. But almost immediately, the illusion that all was as it should be was shattered, as the unmistakable reek of goblin hit her nose, and she realized that the white mist rising from the base of the Palace was not mist at all, but smoke.

Finuviel dropped to his knees in the soft green grass, breathing hard, his terrible face turned up to the sky. "Wine," he breathed.

Delphinea offered him the flask again, and with Nessa and Artimour on either side, they made their way across the deserted green lawn. But to Delphinea's alarm, the closer they got to the Palace, the more Finuviel's strength failed. "Look," Nessa whispered, pointing even as she staggered under Finuviel's weight. "The hedges are all brown."

Faerie is dying, thought Delphinea. *But it can't be too late.* The gates were open, and only a lone guard stood watch. When he saw them coming, he dropped his spear and ran down the avenue, shouting for his fellows. He didn't even seem to notice the presence of a mortal. "Lord Artimour," he said, and she saw that there were tears on his face. "You've come back just in time." And then Finuviel turned his head, and let the hood fall back, and the sidhe gasped. "Who—who—" He broke off, then said, "My lord Finuviel, is it truly you?"

Finuviel turned away with a sigh, and Delphinea stepped forward. "Where's Vinaver?"

"The Court's all taken refuge in the highest tower, my lady. We'll take you there now. It should be safe—the first ray of sun sent them all back below the surface." He paused and looked pointedly out the gates. "But to tell the truth, my lord, we looked to you to bring reinforcements—the border guard—"

"They'll be here 'ere nightfall," answered Artimour.

"That's good, my lord, for I doubt we can last another full night. The goblin hordes are huge, and voracious—we've never seen or heard tell of the like..." The sidhe's voice continued on, rising and falling, describing a situation so dire, Delphinea felt sicker every step she took.

Someone pulled open the great bronze doors that led into the innermost ward, and then the full horror hit her, for it was here that goblin carcasses lay strewn, and here and there lay what looked like empty suits of clothing. Purple goblin blood spattered the halls, smeared the silken hangings, ran in rivulets down the mosaics. A silent, exhausted-looking guard pointed up at the base of great curving staircase, a white confection that swirled so high Nessa thought surely its tip touched the fluffy white clouds she saw floating peacefully in the perfectly blue sky. The sky was the same color as Delphinea's eyes, which she turned on Nessa as the men eased Finuviel, stumbling, up the steps.

Delphinea turned to Nessa, and beckoned. "Come," she said. "I realize now who you must be. There's someone here you will be happy to meet." The sheer joy that broke over Nessa's face poured through Delphinea, refreshing and pure as Mid-Winter snow. Despite the pain she felt creeping into her joints, into her fingers, she smiled back as she turned to continue up the steps. Each step somehow got harder, and harder, the higher they climbed, and as they climbed, the end of Nessa's birch staff begin to glow.

"Why—why does it do that?" she whispered.

Delphinea stole a glance up at Nessa. "The trees of Faerie and the trees of Shadow are one, some say. Look—" She fumbled at her waist, in what looked like a black bag covered in feathers. "This does it, too." As she withdrew a slender piece of wood, Nessa saw that it was obviously a piece of holly, for from it, in a manner that reminded her of her dream, three small leaves grew from a twig near the tip, and clustered at the base were four small berries, glowing a soft bright red.

They had reached a landing. A tall woman, dressed in a long russet gown, carrying a basket, was walking down the steps. She dropped the basket when she saw the little party heading up the steps. "Delphinea! Artimour!" she cried. "Call my lady," she called back over her shoulder, even as she scrambled down to meet them. "Delphinea, child, we thought for sure you'd been—oh!" She broke off and covered her mouth with her hand as Finuviel raised his raw, cratered face.

"Good morning, Lady Leonine," he managed. A drop of opalescent blood spooled down his chin. "Perhaps you would do my mother the courtesy to tell her...that her son...begs an audien—"

He toppled forward then, into a big dark figure that suddenly loomed out of a doorway, followed by a red-haired woman in a white gown, slender as a reed, whose pearl-like face glowed with the unmistakable translucency that marked a mortal taken into Faerie. Delphinea felt a sudden jolt of an emotion so piercingly sweet it brought tears to her eyes, as Nessa cried, "Papa!" and then, in the soft wondering voice of a very small child, "Mama?"

But Griffin wasn't dead, much as he wished at the moment he was. Cadwyr had strung him up, his scrawny wrists bound in leather, and now he struggled to stand on his toes, as his arms were dragged out of their sockets by the weight of his body. A low brazier stood to one side, a variety of implements glowing red, and Griffin had already screamed himself hoarse.

"Tell me." At some point Cadwyr's voice had ceased to be a voice, and was instead a monstrous insidious creature that wormed through Griffin's burning skull, slipping and sliding with razor-sharp spines. Cadwyr's breath seared against his ear. "Tell me."

As if from far away, he heard a heavily accented voice say, "You're going to kill him." Griffin peered around and saw a Lacquilean of some high rank standing in the doorway, arms folded, looking distinctly uncomfortable. "He should be dead already. It was his screaming that alerted the guard. Must you continue to torture him?"

Cadwyr bit back an oath. He stalked away from Griffin, and Griffin blessed the god in the form of the Lacquilean, as the stranger continued, "Isn't it obvious what's happened, my lord? Someone got into the castle, didn't they, boy?" When Griffin nodded, he said, "If it upsets you this much to lose the hostages, you should've taken the precaution of killing them."

"Well, General, your troops are ready to march at a moment's notice, aren't they? Fine. We'll leave at dusk. Give the order, Sergeant. We march at dusk." He turned on his heel and strode from the room, spitting orders as he went.

Ottavius Lussius stood a moment longer. As the last guard went to rush past him, after Cadwyr, he stopped the man with a single nod. "Cut him down."

The guard did so at once, then bolted from the room, and Lussius let him go. Dispassionately, as both his rank and his profession demanded, Lussius walked over to the body. His face was as shriveled as a date, but his voice had sounded so young, so high. Well, that happened sometimes under torture. This one looked like an old man, though Lussius was certain Cadwyr'd referred to him as "the boy." Lussius squatted down, examining the agonized features. It wasn't just that he looked old, Lussius decided. He looked...different. Something about the way the boy slumped over made Lussius look at his back. He pushed him down gently and frowned. An arrow had penetrated just to the left of his spine, between his shoulder blades. The head was still in the wound, and an inch of the shaft still protruded, brown blood clotted thickly all around it. This boy should be dead. Unbelievably, he stirred beneath Lussius's hand, raising a tortured face. "I'll be right back," said Lussius, wondering why he should so concern himself over the fate of this boy. But there was something odd about this whole affair, and this boy was part of the mystery. He'd take him to his own quarters, and see what he could learn there.

The mortals—Dougal, Nessa and Nessa's mother, Essa—were all huddled in one of the wide window seats of the tower room, whispering and kissing and hugging amongst themselves, and every now and then, Delphinea turned her head, as if just a glimpse of their happiness was enough to keep her from despairing altogether.

"It doesn't seem to be working," Vinaver whispered. She had withdrawn with Leonine and Delphinea. Finuviel lay on a low couch, and it was obvious that the silver continued to work its way through his body. His strength was beginning to ebb, and even his mind, it seemed, was drifting off, for he muttered as they worked over him. Delphinea herself could feel a weakness that continued to seep insidiously into the marrow of her bones. For nearly a full turn of the glass, she'd been patient, watching Vinaver and her lady daub the contents of a small crystal vial on him, to very little affect.

"I don't think anything can work," Delphinea said. "We have to destroy the Caul."

She looked up at Artimour, who lingered beside the door, his attention divided between what was going on in the room and the conference between Morais and two of his captains in the hall. Several times, she heard him ask, "But there's no way you know into the Caul Chamber?" His insistence seemed somehow odd, and she was reminded that he was the one who held the Caul. She leaned forward and said, "My lady, maybe you have it backward."

"What are you talking about?" Vinaver demanded.

Delphinea summoned up all her courage and said, "You believe that Finuviel must be healed in order to unMake the Caul. But what if it's really that the Caul must be destroyed, for Finuviel to be healed?" She leaned forward, pressing on, even in the face of Vinaver's gathering rage. "My lady, think. You've been wrong about a lot of things—you don't remember what the Hag showed you, not exactly. You don't hear the trees clearly—you told me so yourself. Surely you can see, we have to try something. Before the sun goes down and the goblins come back, and it's not safe down there. I don't think he'll last another night, any more than we will."

Behind her, she heard Artimour say, "And what do you suggest, my lady? I'd gladly go to the Caul Chamber, but the commander here tells me every way is warded."

She turned. "I've heard what you say. I'm sure I can find

a way in—Timias's wards would not have included mirrors within the Queen's suite itself. Once inside the mirrors, we can go directly to a mirror already within the Queen's rooms, like the one opposite the Caul Chamber. So let Nessa and me and—"

"And me," said Artimour.

"We do need a third," said Delphinea warily, trying to remember what it was that Gloriana had said.

"You need the true King," hissed Vinaver, "not that—"

"Abomination?" finished Artimour. "Never mind, sister."

"Whoever's going had better hurry," said Philomemnon. He pointed to the western windows, where the sun was hanging just above the green ridge of the hills.

In the window seat, Nessa embraced her parents, and when she would've handed Dougal her sword, he stopped her. "You're not to worry about us, girl. I've got a silver dagger-blade—it's half-made and not yet sharp, but it's the reason I'm alive."

As the mortals embraced each other once more, Vinaver caught Delphinea's hand. "I hope you know what you're doing, girl."

"We have to hope Gloriana did," Delphinea replied. She felt at her waist for the raven bag, and Leonine handed Nessa a leather-wrapped bundle, half as long as a man's arm and twice as thick. "There's a hammer in there, and tongs—mortal tools, to work the silver."

"All right," said Nessa as she fit them into the pack she wore across her back. As she straightened, she looked at Delphinea, and a horrified look crossed her face.

"What is it?" asked Delphinea.

Nessa bit her lip. "My lady—" she began, then nodded

at the tall attendant who was removing a heavy velvet curtain from an enormous mirror with an ornately carved and painted frame, and Delphinea was standing right before it, as though it were a doorway and she meant to step right through. "Your face."

"What about my face?" asked Delphinea.

Nessa nodded at the mirror. "Look."

Delphinea turned to her reflection and stifled a little cry as her hand flew automatically to her face. Without even being aware, a pinkish patch was spreading across her cheeks, around her eyes, like a mask. She looked over her shoulder. "I don't think we've much time. Hurry."

"But how are we getting there?" asked Nessa.

"Like this," said Delphinea. And seizing Nessa and Artimour by the wrists, she ducked into the mirror and pulled them both through.

"Looks like there's a change in plans," mused Uwen as the sudden confusion brought troops running from what seemed like every corner of the castle. It was an easy thing to slip in among them, blending in with those running in response to the sudden alarm bells.

The moon was already up over the walls and hung fat and bloated in the still-blue sky. It had a reddish cast, the kind of moon the wicce-women called a blood moon, a hunter's moon. But who would be the hunter and who the hunted tonight? He beckoned to his foster brother, Ygerne, and said, "Go back to the stables—make sure we've horses saddled and ready in the Company's practice yard."

"What's going on, do you think?" Sir Urchart asked.

"Looks to me Cadwyr's discovered his hostages have

gone missing, and that the Caul is gone. So I'd reckon, for the way they're all arming for battle—" Uwen paused as the knights flattened themselves into an alcove to let a squad of cavalry on the way to the stables dash past "—that he's decided to march ahead of schedule—at dusk, rather than dawn—and hope to chase them down."

"What's that going to mean for the Duchess?" the fourth knight, Tomough, said.

Uwen shrugged as he beckoned them to continue on their way. "I'm sure they'll notice when all those men outside start kicking up the dust. And if we have our way— well..." He paused. They had reached the junction where the corridor branched off in two directions, one that led to the hall, and the other to the kitchens, beyond which lay the practice yard of Donnor's First Company. "Come on, lads. Let's see how brave Cadwyr is in a truly fair fight."

The boy's voice haunted Lussius, whispering through his mind even as he gave the orders for the attack, and the boy's eyes rose up even before his closed eyelids as his squire dressed him and armed him for battle. Now he sat uneasily on his horse and watched the ordered chaos of the regiments assembling. He felt increasingly uneasy as the red sun sank lower behind the hills, and a red moon rose above the trees. A line from an ancient treatise on military strategy ran through his head. *The art of war is the art of deception.* But whatever it was he sensed that Cadwyr had done went beyond the pall of ordinary strategy.

The veteran of a hundred battles, Lussius understood the tricks of making an enemy believe one marched south when one really marched east, of tricking the enemy that one was weak when one was truly strong. But that boy... He gazed around at the thick forest that covered the surrounding hills. They provided excellent cover—for anyone or anything that might have a mind to attack ordered rows of advancing troops. He signaled to the centuries and said, "Watch your flanks." He pointed to the hills rising up on either side of the broad meadow. "Any attack has to come from there."

"You see something up there, General?" asked one of the younger ones, turning to at the eastern hills. A cloud of dust, raised by the first line of Cadwyr's cavalry, partially obscured the view.

"No," said Lussius, reluctant to confess his uneasiness. Superstition was the last thing he wanted encouraged in the ranks. He opened his mouth to give the final orders, when his body servant, an older man who'd been with him since he was a boy, rushed up.

"My lord, my lord, the boy! The boy's gone."

He frowned down, for the centuries were exchanging curious glances. "What do you mean, gone?"

"He told me he was going to the privy and he's not come back. So I went to search for him, and he—he's just vanished."

"Don't worry, Leptus, he can't have gone far. He's in very bad condition. He probably took cover in some tent or other when the alarms started. He'll show up as soon as the camp quiets down." He frowned then, waving the old man away more impatiently than he meant, and barked, "To your places, gentlemen. Watch your flanks."

Another squadron of cavalry whooped down the road, raising dust, forcing a row of legionaries to break ranks. Lussius frowned. He admired Cadwyr's daring, Cadwyr's ambition, and Cadwyr's willingness to play the might of

Lacquilea against the appetites of Humbria. But there was something about that boy... He shouldn't have been able to crawl, let alone get himself to a privy. It was too late, now, however. He dismissed the feeling, and with a snap of his fingers at his standard bearers and his personal guards, he rode to take his own place amid the ranks.

From their encampment on the ridge, Cecily peered down. It was one thing to speak of ten thousand men, and another to actually see them, spread out in their hundreds in neatly ordered camps, the last of the afternoon light glittering on weapons and armor. Behind the camp, the great castle crouched against the landscape like a wounded cat with its back against the tor. Cadwyr's banner flew brazenly against the sky, replacing the mourning black that she had left flying. The walls were in no better state of repair, either.

"You didn't mention how bad the walls were, Cecily," said Mungo beside her. "That's not quite the fortress it was. And look there—didn't the sidhe-lord say he'd go at dawn tomorrow? Looks to me he's going at dusk. Tonight." As they watched, movement began to stir through the ranks; the cooking fires began to spume white smoke as they were doused, and the camps sprang from quiet order to disciplined chaos before their eyes.

"They're fools to go at dusk," muttered Artimour's designated lieutenant, a tall, thin, pale sidhe named Eberiel.

A fat moon had already risen, and hung low and bloated in the sky. Cecily pointed to it. "Perhaps that's the reason. He sees no need to wait."

"Either that, or the maidy and the sidhe-lord were successful and he's after them," put in Mungo.

The sidhe gathered his reins. "I shall alert my fellows, my lady. Remember to remind your men to use the woolen plugs to stop their ears. The warhorns of the sidhe will strike a man dead from fear alone."

"Time to ride, lassie," said Mungo, his eyes blazing, his worn leather breastplate gleaming with fresh oil.

She cast one last look around, the sword Nessa had made her heavy on her hip, and saw torches flare to life on the walls. Pipes screamed and skirled, and a black puff of smoke drew her eye to a line of pikes set above the gates. For a moment, she wasn't sure what she was seeing, and then she realized she was looking at heads. One of them could be Kian's, she thought, for Cadwyr had it, he'd display it with glee. Nausea roiled in her gut and she swallowed hard, for now was not the time or place to show any sort of weakness. "Let's ride," she said. "It's not that we die, but how, right?"

"That's what Sir Kian always said," murmured someone behind her. She whipped her head around. In the mix of battle-ready men and horses, the speaker was impossible to discern, but she felt strangely comforted, confident and calm as they galloped back to the camp.

"Keep the lamps burning," said Cadwyr as his body squire settled his shirt of silver mail over his leather tunic and woolen hose. He held out his arms as the squire strapped on the silver vambraces, then sat as the man bent to attach the full greaves that covered his legs from ankles to knees. Cadwyr reached for his swordbelt. "Fetch my dagger from the other belt."

The man nodded, bowed, then left the room. Cadwyr

paced to the window and peered out, where the first ranks of his cavalry were already marching through the improvised gates. On the walls above the gates, he saw the heads of Kian and the other knights of Donnor's Company, a warning to all who considered challenging him. He took a deep breath and the smell of incipient battle was on the wind—that heady mix of leather and horses and men and steel. A taste of that Faerie stuff was called for. And where was that squire? The hour was getting late.

He strode to the door of his dressing room and pulled it open. A figure was huddled on Griffin's mattress, and he frowned. He toed it with his boot, and he saw it was his body squire, still alive, but out cold. His hand went automatically to his side. His sword wasn't there. On the other side of his bedroom, he heard a latch click softly. In one stride, he was across the narrow room. He opened the corridor door, and stepped out to see Uwen, Donnor's Second Knight, standing in the middle of the corridor, holding his sword. "You mean to kill an unarmed man, Sir Uwen?"

"Oh, no, Cadwyr." He tossed Cadwyr his sword, and Cadwyr caught it by the hilt and unsheathed it in one fast motion. "I'm going to kill you in a fair fight. Maybe the first fair fight you've fought in a while."

"Six to one is fair?" Cadwyr gestured to the other knights crowding the end of the corridor.

"They'll not interfere. They're just here to make sure your lads don't try to interfere." Uwen swung his sword up and the two blades rang together.

"I'm going to kill you, you crook-face cripple."

"Not if I kill you first."

In the narrow confines of the corridor, the two men cir-

cled, wary. Cadwyr lunged with fierce intensity, picking a
moment when Uwen's step was cramped by the wall.

Uwen blocked the blow and riposted, swinging the blade
in a wide arc. Cadwyr parried and lunged again. With a
curse, Uwen dodged the blow and slammed a bench into
Cadwyr's knees, even as the point of Cadwyr's sword slid
down his forearm, raising a bright red line. He pressed his
advantage, feinting one way, then another, dodging Uwen's
next blow that shattered the bench to bits. "Surrender now
and swear your oath to me and I'll reward you greatly,
Uwen of the Isles."

"With what, Cadwyr? The wine of the sidhe? Will you
turn us all into monsters like that poor boy below?" Uwen
threw a dagger as another crushing blow from Cadwyr sent
his sword spinning out of reach. He grabbed his broadsword
and blocked Cadwyr's thrust just in time.

"So that's how he got out." Cadwyr spoke through
clenched teeth as he evaded the dagger. Faintly, as if from
very far away, he heard what sounded like the echo of a distant horn. His attention was distracted just long enough for
Uwen to slide his blade around and under, dealing a glancing blow to his thigh. Cadwyr faltered, stumbled, then recovered, even as blood began to arc in a steady pulse.

"Surrender now and I'll make sure you don't have to pay
the blood-fine with your head."

"What blood-fine?" Behind Uwen, Cadwyr could see his
own men fighting with Uwen's knights, so that the corridor
emptied out, and the two of them were alone. Steadily, he
pushed Uwen toward the railing, and the steps, in the same
direction as his knights.

"The one you owe every man, woman and child who lost

someone on Samhain, monster." Uwen spat the word, feinted left then right, then attacked, whipping Cadwyr around so that he fell down to his knees. He stumbled, but recovered, and backed up, easing down the steps. Uwen advanced warily, and Cadwyr waited, breathing hard, until just at the moment Uwen raised his arm to strike, Cadwyr darted up like a snake, rushing forward, his face contorted, gold braids flying around his red face like the rays of the sun. Uwen stumbled back, and Cadwyr dealt him a quick blow to the right arm and then to the left. They smashed together, hilts grinding together, and blue sparks leaped off the metal. "You give my regards to Donnor tonight."

"You give him mine for me," spat Cadwyr. He thrust Uwen back with one mighty heave, and another stroke swept the sword from Uwen's hand. Blood arced from the palm, and Uwen drew the long dagger he wore strapped to his right boot.

He crouched, and Cadwyr raised his arm once more.

And in that moment, another blade swiped across Cadwyr's throat, and Griffin's face peered over Cadwyr's shoulder as he toppled and he fell. "You give him *mine, from me.*"

"Boy," breathed Uwen, scarcely daring to believe his luck. "Boy—we saw you take the arrow—"

But Griffin only licked his lips and patted his flask. "It's the brew, you see, Sir Uwen. It's keeping me alive." He took a step forward, and Cadwyr's arm came up and thrust his blade through Griffin's chest.

"Change—ling trai—tor," grunted Cadwyr as he died.

The blade hissed and steamed and Griffin screamed, then turned his face to the wall. Inexplicably, his expression brightened. "I hear the horns. I hear them blowing—

the sidhe have come—the sidhe have come—" And in a gurgle of dark blood, he died.

It was chaos on the field before Gar—a mayhem of troops tangled with tents and horses and equipment. From her position upon the ridge, Cecily watched the battle rage with the other chiefs, her ears plugged against the horns of the sidhe. The wool muted the worst of the screams and the clanging metal, but the sights were still terrible.

"Look there—" said Mungo, tugging on her arm. On the walls of Gar, the standards bearing Cadwyr's colors were being pulled down, and from the walls, the pipes began to scream a retreat. And as they watched, a tiny figure on the walls raised a stake with a pale round object on it, and as the moonlight fell full upon it, Cecily knew exactly who it was by the color of that golden hair.

"He's dead," she cried. "They did it—Uwen did it—" And as they watched, the tide of battle turned, and Cadwyr's men, as well as the mercenaries, began to run from a chilling sound that rose from the river itself, a sound that came in a cold line of pure white light, as the sidhe came singing and blowing their unearthly horns.

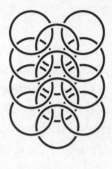

15

It was the shadowy world behind the mirrors, where the light was perpetually silver, and sound was flat, that made Nessa realize how different Faerie really was. She stumbled wide-eyed after Delphinea, trying to control her urge to clutch the sidhe-girl's hand in a bone-breaking grip. She felt at her side for the sword she had originally made for Artimour, and was comforted to know it was still there. And it comforted her to know her father and her mother were above, though she was beginning to think it likely the three of them would be trapped in Herne's Wild Hunt forever. It was the sore on Delphinea's cheek that had made her realize how dire the situation truly was.

But Delphinea was charging on ahead, slipping through corners, weaving down stairs, seemingly effortlessly. It was only when they reached what appeared to be the lowest level that she paused, bit her lip and whispered, as if to herself, "Left is right, and right is left." She looked one way and then the other. "Or is it the other way 'round?"

There was something eerie and unnatural about this place within a place, and Nessa wrapped her arms around herself and told herself there was really no reason to shiver. "Don't you know where we're going?"

"I know *where*," Delphinea replied with a puckered frown. "It's—it's just *how* to get there." She shook her head as if to clear it. "It's just—it's not as clear to me as it was..." She raised her face and looked back over her shoulder in the direction from which they'd come, and Nessa saw that the sore looked as if it was spreading. *Maybe it's only a trick of the light,* she thought.

"Things are reversed within the mirror," Delphinea was saying. "So, yes, that has to be the way to go. What else could it be? Left is right, and right is left. All right. Come."

"But where exactly are you taking us?" Nessa insisted. The mirror-world was a labyrinthine maze of sudden wells of deep shadows and dizzying jolts and shifts of perception.

"To the Caul Chamber, of course. As I said to Vinaver, I doubt Timias remembered to ward every mirror *within* the Queen's suite. I think we can get inside the Caul Chamber from the mirror that's opposite the doors. We'll hope Timias forgot to extend his ward so far. And we'll hope that we're in time."

As they rushed past the mirrors, Nessa glimpsed golden chandeliers and multicolored blurs that seemed to sparkle and move. But Artimour would not let her stop, and at last they paused before a huge light gray rectangle. Delphinea nodded. "It's this one, I'm sure of it." She took a deep breath and confidently stepped through.

Artimour looked at Nessa. "After you, my lady."

Nessa closed her eyes and stepped through, then gasped, for Delphinea was pushing her back through the glass. "I was wrong," she said, "and we'd better hurry."

"Why?" asked Artimour as he tried to stick his head through.

"No!" cried Nessa, for she, too, had glimpsed what Delphinea saw. A huge goblin leaped full body at the glass, and as Artimour stumbled back, it smashed into the mirror, shattering the glass and sending the three of them flying back. From the other side of the mirror, they could hear muted roars. "They're here," Nessa whispered.

"This way," said Delphinea.

"Are you sure?" asked Artimour.

"I can't be sure of anything anymore," she said, but she led them back through the maze, apparently retracing their steps to a certain junction. She bit her lip, as the corridor branched off in three more directions.

"Which way?" asked Artimour. They could hear screams now, and wild howls, and smoke was beginning to drift from between a few of the frames.

Nessa choked, and Delphinea said, "Down here."

At last they stood before another broad gray expanse, but the light was different in front of it, and Delphinea placed one hand experimentally against the glass. Amazingly, unlike the other glass, it resisted. "What's wrong?" Nessa asked. "Why's this one different? Are you sure this is the right one?"

"I'm sure. It's the Caul," Delphinea whispered. "That's why there's dust across the glass." She looked at Nessa with a rueful little smile. "There's no such thing as dust in Faerie."

Before Nessa could respond, Delphinea pushed through the sticky surface, then turned back and held out her hand to Nessa. "Come, it's hard, but I'll help you."

It was difficult, like trying to push one's way through a thick spiderweb, but at last they managed, and finally the three of them stood before a set of huge bronze doors covered in thick scabrous flakes that oozed a fine film of foul-smelling condensation. "Oh, Great Mother," whispered Nessa, for she had never seen such deep deterioration in metal before. "It was in there?"

Delphinea nodded. "Now we just have to get those doors open." She glanced at Artimour nervously, thought Nessa, and wondered why. "We have to touch the doors—you and I, Artimour—each of us lay a palm on the door—"

"I wouldn't touch that," interrupted Nessa. "That metal looks burned. Maybe the lock will just give if we push it."

Artimour kicked first one door, then the other, but the golden latch, pitted and fouled as it was, held firm. From behind the doors, a terrible cacophony arose.

"What's that?" whispered Nessa.

"The gremlins," replied Delphinea. "This is where Timias put them—after Samhain." She glanced at Artimour. "You have the Caul?"

"I have the Caul. Let me try this." Artimour swung his sword, but the blade only bit into the rotting metal and stuck there, shivering, and he wrenched it out, frowning.

"Try mine," said Nessa as she unsheathed her sword. One swipe of the silver-coated edge was all that was needed to slice through the golden latch. She looked at Artimour, wiped the edge on her tunic and resheathed it. But there was no more time than to throw him more than one triumphant glance, for the doors were swinging open, and together, the three stepped over the threshold into a scene that was more surreal than anything Nessa had yet encountered.

The room seemed vast, but that was partially because the ceiling soared high above their heads. In the center, a marble column stood, and beneath it, an old, old man sat, clutching a staff in one hand. On top of the marble column, a pale green globe shimmered in the light that filtered down from the arching windows set in the vaulted walls that stretched far above their heads.

Clustered around the edges of the room, what looked like hundreds of small goblins huddled in small groups, and here and there small bodies lay charred. The old man rose to his full height when he saw the doors swing open, and as he pointed the staff, a ball of greenish light gathered at the ends, and both Artimour and Delphinea cried, "No, Timias!"

At once, Timias lowered the staff and smiled. "Children. How wonderful to see you."

"Where's the Queen, Timias?" Artimour asked.

Timias gave a great sigh and spread his arms wide. "The Queen is dead, I'm afraid. And without the Caul—"

"I have the Caul," said Artimour.

"We've come to unMake it, Timias," said Delphinea. She held up something that looked as if it were covered in black feathers and her slender holly wand.

But he only leaned upon his staff. "Are you sure that's wise?"

Delphinea looked taken aback and he glanced at Artimour, then at Nessa, and Nessa saw Timias's eyes flash red. Not green, like any other sidhe's, and suddenly, she was very, very afraid, and her fingers surreptitiously tightened on the hilt of her sword. He smiled directly at her, pointed the staff, and suddenly the hilt disintegrated in her fingers and the blade clattered to the floor, where the silver edge hissed. But neither Artimour nor Delphinea appeared to have noticed.

"You have the Caul, Artimour?" Timias smiled.

He nodded, and drew the small bundle of lace-edged linen from around his neck.

"You know," said Timias, leaning forward. "If you just replace the Caul all this—" with a sweep of his staff "—all this just goes back to just the way it was. Well, perhaps not exactly the way it was. But very nearly."

"Don't listen to him, Artimour," said Delphinea. "I told you what he did—how our mother died—"

"Is it true?" Artimour asked.

Nessa felt something like a heavy web twist around her ankles. She looked down, but saw nothing. Artimour hung riveted on Timias's every word and Delphinea's lips moved, but no sound came out. "You could be King, Artimour," said Timias.

"Me?" he asked, his face blank.

"Why not? Were you not born of Gloriana? You are every bit as much her child as Alemandine, as Vinaver. And Alemandine is dead."

"Artimour," whispered Nessa. "Don't listen to him. Remember what you said yourself. He's just trying to get you to give him the Caul." All around them, the gremlins were beginning to slither and hiss, their huge eyes reflecting green and violet and red. Timias reacted at once, sending a bolt of light from the end of the staff into first one corner of the room, and then the other. The gremlins screamed and shrieked and then withdrew, hands, tails and ears flickering, and Nessa realized they were speaking to each other. "Delphinea," she whispered as Timias turned back to Artimour. "Do you understand how to talk to the gremlins?"

"Enough from you, mortal." Timias leveled the staff at her, and a bolt of light drove her back nearly to the door, knocking her flat. "Give me the Caul, boy. We'll put it back where it belongs, I'll give you the staff, and you'll be King. Be King, or be unMade."

Be King, or be unMade. Timias's words echoed over and over in Artimour's mind. Vinaver had said as much to him. After all, wasn't that the reason Finuviel had felt it perfectly justified to stab him? But it had never occurred to him he might be King—King of all the sidhe. What a turnaround that would be. He could imagine the look on Gillieas's face, on Morais's, on Vinaver's, on Finuviel's for that matter—if he were to simply put the Caul back on the moonstone globe and return it to its place. The threat from the mortals would cease to exist—surely, even the goblins themselves would be dragged back to the Wastelands, once he claimed the oak staff for his own. All around him the floors, the walls shuddered.

"Hurry," said Timias. "Give it to me. The goblins are nearly here. Can't you feel it? Give it to me, and you will have the power to defeat the Goblin King himself. You and only you, Artimour. Artimour, son of Gloriana, King of all the sidhe."

King of all the sidhe. The choice was obvious—be King, or be unMade. He took a single step forward, and Nessa's voice stopped him.

"Artimour." Her voice was weak, and when he looked at her, he saw red mortal blood running down her face. "Artimour, don't listen to him. He's lying. He's just trying to get you to do what he wants. Look all around you. Look at Delphinea. Look at the doors. You said yourself the Caul is poison and it must be unMade—"

Another bolt of light from Timias's staff ripped through Nessa, this time choking off her words and sending her sprawling limply on the floor. "I said *enough,* mortal. Destroy her, my prince. We've no need of *her.*"

Artimour walked to stand above her and paused. Her face was smooth, the blood bright scarlet in the light, her curly hair black as a raven's wing against the white marble floor. It reminded him of how she'd looked asleep, and a wave of tenderness swept over him. He looked up and saw that the gremlins were gesturing frantically among themselves. *Be King, or be unMade.* Delphinea's great blue eyes were full of anguish as her mouth worked silently.

He's lying, Delphinea signaled feebly, and at once all the gremlins repeated the gesture. *He will be the one unMade.*

And then Nessa opened her eyes. "He's lying," she said. Their eyes met. Artimour reached for the silver dagger and threw it in one fast motion at Timias. It landed with a searing hiss directly into his belly and the old man jerked, his eyes huge and wide. He leveled the staff at Artimour and, as one huge bolt of light exploded out of its tip, Nessa pushed him down, so that he collapsed beside her on the marble floor.

With Timias's death, whatever spell he'd woven around Delphinea dispersed. She frantically bent over Artimour and Nessa, even as the gremlins exploded from the perimeters of the room, their shrill shrieks creating a blaring echo that surely would draw every goblin in hearing. She strode to the marble column and pried off the moonstone. Inside, a collection of crystals sparkled dully. "Come," Delphinea cried to the gremlins. "Come take what's yours and go." *Never trust a trixie.* "Go and none of your tricks!" she cried.

"We don't have any tricks," said one of the gremlins as he edged closer to the columns.

"How do we know you'll unMake the Caul?" shrieked another.

"We're still bound here til you do," hissed a third.

Delphinea picked up the oak staff and held it out. It felt like a dead stick to her, without so much as the tremor of life she'd felt the few times she'd brushed near Nessa's staff. But pointing it seemed to have the desired effect. "Take your crystals. I swear we'll unMake the Caul. You go back to Shadow and stay there. Is that a bargain?"

They muttered and hissed and gestured among themselves, and finally the first nodded. "We agree. We will keep to our part if you will keep to yours."

"Go on, then." Delphinea ran over to Nessa and Artimour, both of whom were beginning to stir. "Are you all right? Nessa? Artimour?"

They nodded, both staggering a little as they got to their feet and Nessa wiped away the blood on the side of her face with her sleeve. "Now where?"

"The rock where the Caul was forged is below the column," said Artimour. "My mother showed me once." He gave them both a sad smile and beckoned. As Nessa passed him, he held out the linen bundle. "Take it now. Don't you see?" he asked in response to her unspoken question. "As long as it exists, the temptation to do as Timias wanted me to do is still there."

"Let's hurry," said Delphinea as the floor began to shake.

"What about Nessa?" asked Cecily. She seemed to have grown taller in the last few days, as if she'd stepped into a new, fuller version of herself. The aftermath of the battle continued all around them, and it seemed, thought Uwen, almost unreal that they were back once more to the place where they had started. Not all of them, of course. He had felt Kian's absence keenly, though he had felt his presence, too, especially in the fight with Cadwyr.

Now Cadwyr's corpse lay with all the others, awaiting its turn on the funeral pyres the druids were now, at last, burning. The sidhe had returned to fight their own battle, and the dawn light was beginning to burn through the early-morning mist that lay like a shroud over the remains of the Lacquilean tent city. For the sight and sound of the sidhe had utterly defeated them. The earth still shook from the thunder of their feet running back to Lacquilea.

But Cecily was continuing, like some soft-voiced raven, less shrill but just as insistent. "What about Nessa? Her father? He deserves better than to die in the midst of some battle that's not even his."

Uwen sighed. He was tired, and he was wounded. He thought of the barrels of the brew down in the cellars, and he wondered what a drop or two would do for him. It had helped the sidhe lord temporarily, that was for sure. But then he remembered poor Griffin, and he reached for the sword belt he'd slung over his chair. "All right, I'll go. I'll go and bring the child home." He dropped the belt over his head and pressed a quick kiss on her cheek. It was streaked with dirt and tasted salty. "You're such a mother hen, Cecily."

"That's what Kian always said," she answered.

"Well, it's true." He picked up her hand and hoped that the kiss he pressed upon her cold palm burned for a long time.

"We can't stay up here any longer," said Dougal as the tower shuddered so violently that crystal windowpanes began to shatter. With all the strength he could muster, he ripped a length of silk away from the window and held it over his frail wife's head. "We must go lower. Where's the safest place within the Palace?"

"The throne room," offered Leonine from her place beside Finuviel's couch. "The marble arch over the throne—it's carved out of solid marble—nothing around it will collapse."

"But the goblins—" began Vinaver as the tower shook.

Essa looked up at Dougal. "Nessa?" she whispered.

He shepherded her away from the window, trying to think of something that might comfort her.

But before anything occurred to him, the door opened, and Philomemnon looked within. "Come. We must move lower. The towers are no longer safe—the goblins have overrun the stables and the guard has fallen back to the one tower."

"He can't be moved," said Vinaver.

"I'll carry him if I must," said Dougal. "Come, Essa." Another tremor rocked the tower, and this time the window above Finuviel exploded in a shower of twinkling crystal, and shards of slivered crystal rained down.

"Now, Vinaver," cried Philomenon. "Now."

"It could kill Finuviel," cried Vinaver.

"Mother." Finuviel struggled to sit up. "It will kill us all to stay."

"Nessa?" asked Essa. "What about her?"

All Dougal could think to say was, "She's lower than we are."

The lower they climbed, the louder the screams and shouts, the stronger the stench of goblin and the smell of smoke. "What're they doing?" asked Dougal as he wiped sweat off his brow.

"All they can do, Master Smith. Fight the goblins with fire. Light is the last defense of the sidhe," replied Finuviel, waving Dougal away when he bent to help him. "I think I can walk. The reek of goblin makes me strong." He hauled himself upright, and immediately his knees buckled.

"More determined than strong, I think," said Dougal.

A squadron of guards ran up. "Come, my lady," the sergeant said, without pausing to bow or acknowledge the rest of the group in any way. "Come with us and we'll take you—"

"To the throne room," said Finuviel. "We'll be safe there."

"Sir, there's evidence that the goblins have begun to tunnel—"

"But it's the safest place in the Palace," cried Vinaver. "And it's nearer the Caul Chamber than—"

"All right, my lady, if you insist."

"Sir, the main force of the attack is all coming from the stables," interjected one of the other guards.

They heard the faint sound of horns. "The border guard," cried one of the guards. "They're coming."

"Let's hope they've come in time," said Dougal.

Far too slowly for the liking of the sidhe soldiers, they made their way through the darkened halls, until they came at last to the silent throne room. The guards paused, and Vinaver staggered forward. "The doors," she said. "Well?" Gingerly, the sergeant pushed, and the door fell open with a creak. "Interesting," Vinaver whispered. She cleared her throat. "Sergeant, I suggest you alert Morais that his worst fears have been realized. Timias must be dead, for the ward has failed. If the goblins do tunnel up through the middle of the Sacred Grove, my sister's life is—"

"May well be over now," Dougal said. The floor trembled, and somewhere very close, there was the sound of splintering glass and the rumble of collapsing walls. He reached out and steadied himself against the wall. "We'd better take what shelter we can, and hope that border guard of yours can draw them off long enough. Let's get inside."

The sergeant and another guard pushed open the huge doors and a rush of cold air hit them like a wall. Cold prickled at the back of Dougal's neck as he gazed around the empty room, supporting Finuviel with one arm, and Essa with the other. She met his eyes, and he knew what she was thinking. Somewhere in this Palace, their daughter worked some strange magic. Dougal took a deep breath and stepped over the threshold, staring up.

The vaulted ceiling was nearly invisible, for hardly any light at all filtered down through the black squares of the arching windows that ended in a rose window of pale pink glass. Heavy silken draperies, in Alemandine's favorite palest green, puddled on the floor. There were cracks in the marble walls, he saw, and running through the marble floors jagged gaps broke it into a dangerous puzzle. The walls were mostly in shadow, but he could see what looked like cracks running up and down them at uneven intervals, creating the illusion that the wall behind the throne was rounding out. And it *was* rounding out, he realized, even as the others began to fan out across the room, holding up their torches, and even as he put his arm around Essa, to draw her behind himself, he saw the wall behind the throne shift and shudder, and with the same sound as a rumble of rocks down a hillside, a huge goblin stepped out before them, flicking his black forked tongue, his leathery tail snapping around his legs.

He heard Vinaver take a swift breath, saw Philomemnon turn white and faint. But Finuviel pulled himself upright and muttered, to the sergeant, "Hand me your sword."

"You can't be serious," said Dougal. "You can scarcely stand, my lord—"

"I'm the one he wants," replied Finuviel. "I'm the one he's here to kill."

"Well, let's not make it any easier for him than it has to be, all right?" From within his belt, Dougal pulled out the rough silver blade.

"Soldiers, spread out," ordered the sergeant. He slapped a sword into Finuviel's hand and grabbed a spear from one of the others.

The sound of the horns was louder now, but the cries and screams were getting louder now too, and the reek of goblin blood was strong in the air. But there was another stink too, and it emanated off the goblin like a fetid miasma so thick one could feel it like a shield around him. It was the reek of human flesh.

"Little king, I am Xerruw, King of the Goblins, and now

King of all worlds," said the huge goblin. "I have a special
place in my hall for your head. It will bring my people great
pleasure to watch it rot." He leaped at Finuviel then, and his
long tail snapped out like a whip.

In the rock-hewn grotto beneath the Caul Chamber, a thin
fountain bubbled up from an underground spring, but other
than a flat rock beside the spring, with a shallow depression
in which lay a small pile of ash, there didn't seem to be much
else to work with. Delphinea held up the raven bag. "We
have to wash this in the fountain."

"What's that?" asked Nessa.

"It's one of the Hag's cauldrons made from one of the
Marrihugh's ravens. When we wash it in this water—" Delphinea began to rinse it in the small fountain "—it's supposed to turn into—" And sure enough, as she twisted and
turned and splashed the thick water on the bag, it began to
harden and to round. The water didn't seem like ordinary
water, somehow, thought Nessa as she watched. It was vis-
cous and gooey, and it wasn't so much rinsing the feathers
as coating them, turning them into something round and
black and very glossy. Finally Delphinea held up a perfect little cauldron. "Well?"

"We need fire to melt it down," said Nessa. "Anyone have
a flint? And some coal?"

"We don't need either," said Delphinea. "Gloriana said the
fire must be kindled from the oak staff—" She nodded at
the staff in Artimour's hand. "Maybe point it? The way
Timias did?"

Artimour shook his head. "You know I can't do this." He
handed it to Delphinea. "You try."

Nessa was shifting from foot to foot, watching as Delphinea took the staff. She placed the cauldron in the middle of the pile of ash, then unknotted the small linen square. A shadow passed over her face, and Delphinea knew she was remembering the sad, sick boy who had tried to bargain for her hand. Nessa withdrew the hammer and tongs from the pack, and placed them on the rock. She stepped back and handed Artimour her staff. "I guess we're ready."

"I don't know if I'm the one to try this," said Delphinea. The holly berries were glowing a soft red, as warm a red as the burning feeling that was spreading across her cheek by slow degrees.

"Just try," said Nessa. "Just try."

But the wood was dead. Finally Delphinea said, "It doesn't work."

Nessa ran her fingers through her hair. The Caul was glimmering in the bottom of the cauldron, innocent and deadly. She sniffed. "I smell smoke."

"They're getting closer," Delphinea said. "I—I think if we don't destroy the Caul, the Goblin King will kill Finuviel. And then—and then—"

Think, Nessa, think. Nessa bit her lip. The trees of Shadow and the trees of Faerie are linked. Maybe—maybe they weren't so far from help after all. They were underground, where the roots were. She took her staff from Artimour and placed it deliberately in front of her, held it with both hands and leaned the middle of her forehead against it. *Give me your wisdom,* she thought. *Great Mother-Tree, hear my prayer and grant my plea. You healed me once, and Kian made two. Now three times healed, the land of the sidhe.* A jolt slammed through her feet, taking her breath away, sliding up through her hands, into the middle of her forehead. As if against a dark backdrop, she saw the answer, as clearly as if it happened before her. "Delphinea," she said. "Your holly wand. Ignite the oak. Awaken the land. The Queen—the Queen awakens to land—Artimour—hold the staff—"

It all seemed to happen at once, somehow, for Delphinea moved and Artimour took up the staff and in the instant that the holly berries touched the tip of the oak staff, the oak and the holly flared into a hot fire that surrounded the tiny cauldron. At once, the silver began to bubble, and as the Caul began to melt into shimmery rivulets, Nessa took a deep breath, and once again felt the words begin to bubble up and through her:

"By Alder, Ash and Aspen Tree,
By Birch and Beech and Rowan Three,
Hazel, Holly, Elder, Vine,
Yew and Apple, Oak to bind,
Bring me now a flame to burn
That dark to light may now return,
Let round about the circle go,
That light to dark and back may flow."

She wasn't chanting, alone, she realized, for Delphinea was reciting the same words, her voice as chiming and melodic as a bell, Artimour's fair tenor a poignant counterpoint. The sound blended and echoed and amplified off the rocks, ringing as loud as a hammer, and as Nessa repeated the final phrase a third time, she used the tongs to pick up the pliant metal. "Now what?" she whispered. "Now what?"

And suddenly the image exploded in her mind, and she knew exactly what to do. In a few short strikes, she shaped the softened metal into a flattened circle that surrounded a five-pointed star. When the amulet had taken shape, she picked it up with the tongs and held it in the bubbling fountain.

As the silver began to steam and hiss and harden, the entire room tilted, the floor cracked apart with a tremendous shriek and half the roof collapsed, so that the entrance was now a huge gaping hole in the Caul Chamber's floor. Delphinea cried out, and Nessa felt an enormous wave of exhaustion roll over her, similar to what happened when she'd healed Kian, and when she'd made the sword. She swayed, and the amulet rolled out of her grasp, to lie beneath the collapsed portion of the roof.

"We can't stay here, Nessa," said Artimour. "Come, Delphinea, we have to leave it—it isn't safe to go over there."

The world was spinning now, and she was swaying on her feet. Artimour caught her as she fell, swinging her up against his chest. She heard him say, "Take the staffs and the wand," and then, with another ominous rumble, the world went black.

Finuviel could feel the moment the Caul was undone. The constant burning was immediately extinguished, a subtle constriction in his sinews eased. A sense of healing washed over him, and he felt his hands strengthen to the point where he could grip his sword. As Xerruw flung the last of the guards away, he turned to Finuviel with a broad grin. "Feel better, little king?" He licked his lips. "Me, too."

With a snap of his tail, he had Finuviel on the ground, backing away, as Xerruw advanced.

Dougal staggered forward, silver blade raised, and with a mighty cry, he buried it into the Goblin King's back.

"Not fair!" Xerruw screamed, and threw both Dougal and the dagger across the room in one mighty heave. Dougal sprawled beneath the bottom of a huge gilt-framed mirror.

Finuviel scrambled to his feet, holding his sword, as Delphinea and Artimour, carrying Nessa, stepped out of the mirror. At once, Artimour handed Nessa to Dougal and drew his sword. As Xerruw lunged at Finuviel, Artimour stuck his own blade into the Goblin King, and he responded with a hiss and a whip of his tail that sent Artimour sprawling, even as Nessa sat up and looked around. She jumped to her feet, over Dougal's protests, and drew the sword at her hip.

Finuviel saw her attack, opened his mouth, but Artimour was there first, slicing away at the Goblin King's tail before it could whip her legs out from under her and crush her with a claw. The sword clattered out of her hand, spinning out of her reach, and landed by Finuviel's foot. He dropped his own dagger and picked it up. As the silvered edge caught the light, Xerruw hissed and backed away. Artimour scrambled backward, pulling Nessa out of immediate danger. A snowflake drifted down, and they all looked up. A portion of the roof had collapsed, and snow was beginning to fall.

"Oh, Great Herne," muttered Artimour as he and Nessa dragged themselves to the alcove where Dougal and Delphinea huddled with Essa, Vinaver and Leonine.

"I hear pipes, Papa," said Nessa.

Finuviel and Xerruw were circling each other now, Xerruw snarling and snapping his tail, Finuviel leaping ever more nimbly to avoid it.

"Can't you help?" whispered Nessa.

"No one can help," said Artimour. "Only the King—the true King—can slay the Goblin King. Besides—" He pointed to a crevice in the base of the marble throne. As they all watched, horrified, it got bigger. "The goblins—there're more coming—"

Across the throne room, Finuviel launched himself at Xerruw, attacking with both swords. As in a skirl of pipes, Uwen and a dozen warriors rode into the ruined throne room. With a mighty scream, Xerruw toppled over, the hilt of Nessa's sword reverberating from his eye socket.

Finuviel stood upright, for just a moment longer, looked at Nessa, and smiled. Then he sank to his knees, breathing hard, as the snow began to fall harder.

"Get them out of here," cried Artimour. The ominous rumbles were continuing, and deep cracks snaked suddenly across the marble floor. He handed Nessa up to Uwen, as another knight reached for Dougal and a third took Essa.

"Come with us!" she shrieked.

"No, maiden." He shook his head. "Faerie is my world—I don't belong in yours."

"Let's go," cried Uwen as another wall collapsed, falling with a sound that felt like the wave of grief and weariness that overtook Nessa as he held her close against his chest with one arm and guided them back around to the other side of the tor, where the sun was just coming up and Uwen's own colors were flying over Castle Gar.

* * *

Snow fell, crystalline as diamond dust, wafting gently through the broken roofs of the fallen turrets from the soft gray sky. It blanketed the floors, softened the edges of jagged marble and splintered glass. It drifted over and around the sleeping sidhe, and in their sleep, they dreamed. In the Caul Chamber, the amulet gleamed silver in the shifting shadows. The great rock on which it had been forged trembled, shuddered, and unfolded itself into the craggy features and lumpen shape of the Hag.

Muttering softly to herself, she reached for her bag, hissing through her yellowed teeth as her claws wrapped themselves around her moonstone globe. She stuffed it into her bag, then sniffed, searching out the items that belonged to her. She took Timias's head next, and pushed it in beside the globe, cackling softly. "Dark to light and back it flows— thought you'd stop me, did you?" She picked up the amulet, sniffed it, licked it, then held it out so that the five-pointed star within the circle threw its reflection over the walls. "Not bad, not bad." *What will you pay for the knowledge of the Hag?* Maybe the girl hadn't paid quite enough, yet, but she would, she would. It was always easier to extract payment from mortals.

A sudden wave of weariness swept over her, so that her ancient bones felt heavy as boulders beneath her skin. Soon, she thought, soon, she too would rest. But for now, there was one more thing left to do. She slung her bag over her hunched back and made her way through the darkness to the ruined throne room, where most of the sidhe slept and the fallen corpse of the Goblin King rested on the base of the throne.

With a deep sigh and a mighty heave, she pulled the silver-edged sword out of his eye socket and extended her hand. The Goblin King opened his eyes, and Herne stepped up and out of his body, rivulets of dark red blood drying in the gaping wound where his antlers had been. "You always win," he said.

"*We* always win," she corrected. "But we very nearly didn't this time, no thanks to you." She shook her head. "You're quite impossible in the things you insist on hiding from me. I don't understand why you do it."

An angry light flared in her eyes, but Herne only chuckled. "I like to keep you guessing."

A retort leaped to her lips but she bit it back, for suddenly, she was too tired to speak. She leaned heavily on her staff and gazed around the chamber. "Shall we finish here?"

With Herne's strength, it was easy to position Finuviel and Delphinea on their thrones, the oak staff and the holly wand crossed together. "I don't know what you were thinking to leave him looking like this," Herne grumbled as the Hag gently whisked the snow off Finuviel's scarred and pitted face. "He'll never be what I made him. Hardly seems fair."

"The girl has a choice—she needn't take him for her Consort. And besides, look at this cheek. You think she'll wake up the beauty that she was? They all have choices, you know. Everyone does."

"But that's going to change it all before it ever begins. And I know your idea of choices—between bad and worse."

"When will you learn to trust me?" she asked.

Herne leaned across the thrones and chucked the Hag under the chin. His smile was like the first true ray of Spring. "I can hear the Spring coming."

"Well, that's one of us, then," she sighed. She took another breath and looked around. The shadows were thicker now, the snow higher. She was so tired. He was tired, too, though he'd rather die again than admit it.

"What about this one?" Herne stood over Artimour's body.

"What about him? He's one of yours—you decide."

"Oh, no, I've learned that much, you old hen. You'll not trap me like that. We'll let him decide."

"Well, then," said the Hag. "I'll show you I'm not half so cruel as you make me out to be." She reached into her bag and gently placed the amulet between Artimour's hands. As Herne blew a soft breath over Artimour's face, she chuckled softly. "Let's see how long it takes him to figure it out."

Herne looked up at the Hag but he didn't laugh. "Are you all right?" he asked again, and this time, his voice was as soft as a shallow wave upon the shore.

In some places, the snow was halfway up her thighs and it was getting hard to walk through it. It was time to go. "I'm a little tired, that's all."

"As well you should be." He had come to stand behind her, and she felt his strength, felt the charge of his restless vitality. "A thousand years is far too long. Are we finished here?"

"For the moment." She looked around at the silent ruins, at the sleeping sidhe, and nodded, satisfied.

"All right then." He gathered her up and lifted her in his arms as easily as if she were a child, and tucked her black cloak tenderly over her face to keep the snow off. He cradled her close, so that she could hear the strong, slow beat of his heart. It was like the throb of a great eternal drum, pounding out the pulse of life itself. With a deep sigh, she turned her face into the warm soft hair on his chest and closed her eyes. She drew a deep breath, letting herself slip away into sleep, and she, too, began to dream, of herself, as a child running through a sunlit meadow scented with thyme where a little boy, naked and brown, awaited her in the shadow of a spreading oak.

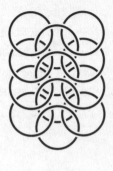

16

"**I**s that Nessa?" Bethy's voice split the evening twilight as she reached for the girl. Nessa clutched her new plaid close and surrendered to the woman's bear hug. The wind was cold around the base of Ardagh Tor at Mid-Winter, and the broad granny's hug was a dose of welcome warmth. "And how are your parents, poor lamb?"

It was a question Nessa didn't like to answer, but she knew the granny meant well, so she shrugged and tried to smile. "They're not bad—not as bad as might be expected. They're at Gar, you know, the Queen's own still-wife is looking after them. They both wanted me to come." She fingered her new gown of fine white wool, which was easily the most beautiful article of clothing she'd ever owned. Her mother had helped her pick it out, and it was special for that reason alone. She smoothed its silken folds and glanced excitedly through the crowd of corn grannies.

"Look, they're coming," cried someone from farther down the path.

"They're coming!" The cry was taken up, and the sound of the pipes and drums rose on the air and the crowd parted as the new-crowned Queen and her chosen escort made their way up the path strewn with pine and lit with high torches garlanded with holly. In the leaping firelight, she saw the holly berries shine a waxy red, and the old nursery line danced through her mind: *When the berry glows, the holly knows the Queen of Faerie comes.* What had happened to them all in Faerie? she wondered fleetingly. Were they all still sleeping under a blanket of snow? Frost crunched beneath her new boots and Molly gripped her hand.

"Come, child, look, here they are." Her cheeks were as rosy as a girl's.

Cecily did look beautiful, thought Nessa, her long blond hair flowing freely down her back, held by only the thinnest circlet of gold and silver and copper all twined together. Her gown was pure white wool, and Uwen, next to her, wore his plaid and nothing, as far as Nessa could tell, underneath.

"Be strong, now!" cried some faceless voice from the crowd, and a roar and a cheer went up, and Uwen raised his arm and gave a cheerful wave and a grin.

Nessa skipped up the hill after Molly, joining the ranks of the grannies who had taken up the song from the maidens leading Cecily up the hill.

It was amazing to think that this tor rising out of the vale was the very center of Brynhyvar, and it was here that Cecily would join with the land. It was all very mysterious, she thought, watching the white-gowned maidens carrying their beeswax tapers garlanded in gold. "She's like a bride," she breathed to Molly as Cecily paused at the very top, and the newly elected ArchDruid of Ardagh stepped forward. In one hand he held an oak staff, and in the other, a holly wand.

"She *is* a bride," answered Molly with a smile. "She's the bride of the land."

As she passed, Nessa could see the mound of Cecily's belly, just now beginning to swell with Kian's child. *How she must miss him,* she thought, and she thought of Artimour, and a pang went through her. Had any even survived? she wondered, and then her attention was drawn to the ArchDruid's stern face.

"Whyfore have you come?"

"I come at the call of the land," replied Cecily, her voice carrying on the cold wind.

Nessa felt her nipples harden into tight buds, and she leaned over to Molly with a shiver. "Does she really have to lie naked on the rock in this weather?" It seemed somehow more than indecent—almost cruel. But the druids and the grannies had all insisted that Mid-Winter night under a new moon was the most auspicious time to begin anything new. Molly only turned to her with a finger pressed tight to her lips.

"And will you accept the land's answer, for aye or nay, whatever it may be?"

Cecily raised her chin and squared her shoulders. "I do."

"How'll we know the land's answer, Molly?" whispered Nessa.

"Will you hush, girl," said Molly. "You want to make noise, come sing. And don't you worry—there'll be no doubt of the land's answer. Not if—" She broke off and exchanged some sort of significant look with the other grannies. "Not if the answer's yes, at any rate."

As the druid stepped aside to let Cecily pass, the music swelled around the base of the tor, and somehow, Nessa found herself part of a long line of women that wove in and around and through a long line of men. Up and down and around, they danced, weaving and out, and Nessa looked up at the dark, star-scattered sky, and felt a slow ripple move like a waking hound in the ground beneath her feet. "Molly—" she said, reaching forward to grab the older woman's shoulder. "Molly, I think I felt the beginning of the answer!"

Within the center ring of standing stones, the night was very dark. The flat rock in the very middle, the rock of the land, lay silent and black and cold. Cecily glanced over her shoulder as Uwen led her through the center ring. At the base of the tor, the people had begun to dance, and the wind carried their song, wooing and slow, past them both and out again to the night. The torches and the fires flared orange and blue, a marked contrast to the piled faggots of the huge bonfire arranged around the stones. If the land accepted her as its Queen, those faggots were supposed to spontaneously kindle, thus sending a beacon of flame to all those gathered around stones and tors and bonfires across Brynhyvar. If. A light dusting of snow was on the rock, and the wind cut through the thick soft wool of her gown like a blade. She shivered, pulling her plaid higher.

Uwen dusted off the snow on the low rock and turned to face her. She could barely hear the music and the voices down below, but she could smell the smoke of the fires drifting higher. His face was pale in the shadows, his red hair pulled back and arranged in neat braids around his face. "Cecily," he said softly.

She nearly quailed. This was the moment Kian had fore-
seen, and he wasn't here to share it with her. She had
thought, that by choosing Uwen, it would help ease the
pain of Kian's loss. But it didn't seem to be helping, because
all she saw when she looked at Uwen was how much he
wasn't the man she wanted him to be.

But his words made her head snap up and pay attention.
"I know I'm not the man you want me to be." *Had he read
her mind?* she wondered. She took a step forward, the better
to see him in the silver starlight. It was a new moon, the time,
the druids all agreed, when the ancient lore indicated the
most auspicious to begin again. He continued, "I am honored
and I am humbled that you did, however, choose me. I come
here not just to honor you and the land, but the Chief, as well,
for he was a warrior among warriors, and for all the causes
for which he might have died, this was the one he would've
chosen. So I honor his life, and I honor his death and I honor
the love you bear for him." And he shivered, as a harsh wind
whined around the stones, obliterating completely the music
floating up, intermittently louder now, from below.

The softness in his eyes made her reach for him, made her
draw his face to hers and press one gentle kiss on his lips.
"Thank you," she whispered, "Sir Uwen of the Isles, Duke
of Gar. Will you—please—take me to the land?"

He smiled then, and led her forward, letting his plaid drop
so that she lay upon it. She opened hers, and covered them
both, and they both gasped as cold flesh met cold flesh.
"I'm not sure what happens next," she whispered.

"Oh, Cecily," he sighed. "I am." He raised her chin and
gazed down at her. "You are most lovely and most fair, Cecily of Mochmorna and Queen of Brynhyvar." He bent his

head then, and kissed her, and he wasn't Kian, and he wasn't Donnor and he wasn't any of the boys she'd ever dallied with long ago among the heather and mountain thyme. But somehow, he was all of them, wooing and shy and knowing and bold all at once. And as their limbs twined together and the music drifted fitfully up the tor, and his flesh warmed against hers, she felt him change beneath her hands, felt his shoulders broaden in her embrace, his chest widen and his thighs swell. She heard a low deep chuckle, like the rumble of distant thunder and she opened her eyes and gasped.

He wasn't Uwen anymore, either. In the starlight, he was green. His hair was leafy, and his face seemed carved from wood. She knew exactly who he was, even without the huge antlers, for she'd seen him before. In the Hall, on Samhain, leading the Wild Hunt, and she scrambled back. "Great Herne," she breathed.

She drew back, holding one hand against her mouth, and he bent and picked up her other hand and brought it to his lips. "Don't be afraid, Cecily, daughter of the land," Herne breathed. "So comely and so fair." He smiled at her, and his eyes blazed bright green, and she wasn't afraid of him at all, any more than she'd been afraid of Uwen. "The land has but answered your call."

"You—you owe me a favor." She picked up her plaid and wrapped it around herself. The night air was cold, and it unnerved her that the god himself radiated a most pleasing warmth.

His face crinkled into a delighted grin. "There are some who would say that my very appearance here is a favor. But it's no favor—I am bound to come, to bring you the answer of the land. And so, for you—" He broke off and brought her hand to his lips again and kissed each finger gently in turn. It was Kian's gesture, and it twisted in her heart. "Ask of me what you will."

She swallowed hard. She had thought about this, over and over, since her first encounter with him, and she had known from the very beginning the first thing she wanted. But now there was another, another that seemed even more pressing, and she hesitated, not sure of which to ask. So she gambled and said, "I want two things."

He threw his head back and laughed. "One favor, two things. And doesn't the Great Mother make you all in her image? Go on."

She pulled her gown back together and squared her shoulders, and tried not to stare at the thickness of the phallus rising from the curly brown nest between Herne's thighs. "I want the souls you stole on Samhain released. They were warriors, all. They deserve to go to the Summerlands and feast, not dance to your tune forever."

He shook his head, and his shoulders heaved as if at some enormous joke. "So you'd have me give back the very thing that earned your favor? Go on. What's the other part?"

She leaned forward and turned her face, and listened for a moment to the slow beat of the drums, the high notes of the pipes and the voices of her people. "There is a blacksmith girl named Nessa, whose parents, Dougal and Essa, of a village called Killcairn, were sorely used by the sidhe. Without her help, without her skill, I would not be Queen—and Brynhyvar would not be here. If it's within your ken, Great Herne, I ask you to give them back their years. They're fading here, and Nessa told me they will be gone by Imbolc. She never knew her mother, and her father was tricked into giving her mother up. That's what I ask of you, Great Herne. Those two things. For my people."

"And is there nothing you would have for yourself, my lady?"

She glanced up at him then. His face was smooth, his eyes were hooded, and there was a sulky turn to his mouth that made her wary. "What do you mean?"

"You know what I mean. Is there nothing—or no one— for yourself you would have?" He leaned forward and his face was dark, his eyes glowing violet, flickering red.

And suddenly she understood. This was a test of some sort—a test of worthiness—and all at once, she knew exactly the nature of the test. Her heart began to pound and her breasts heaved and a wave of dizziness swept over her. Kian's face rose before her and his voice echoed in her mind. *Warriors come and warriors go, but the land goes on forever.* She stiffened her spine, bracing herself against the flood of memories that spilled from the deep well within like bitter water. "I know what you expect me to ask."

"Do you, now?" His eyes flared dark red.

"Yes," she said. She gripped her plaid more tightly as if that would shield her from the seduction of the possibility he represented. "You expect me to ask for Kian's life." Tears filled her eyes and she choked back the lump that had suddenly clogged her throat. "But I won't. Kian's death changed me. I don't know how, I don't exactly know why, but I know that it did. It was Kian's death that made me realize why I had to be Queen—it was Kian's death that showed me how cheap Cadwyr held us all. It was Kian's death that made me see that Cadwyr mustn't win. And if you give me back Kian, maybe that will change. And I can't risk that. I can't be Queen and risk that." She wiped the tears off her face and squared her shoulders. *I'd rather face the Goblin King,* she thought, *than this elusive being.* "I know Kian feasts in the Summerlands. I know I'll feast there with him some day. But I also know that for now, I must be Queen of Brynhyvar, and nothing—not even a change in the past—must threaten it."

Herne did not move, and as the moment lengthened, Cecily wondered if she had said the wrong thing, after all. But he bowed and said, "I see you are not only comely and fair, sweet daughter of the land, but you're growing wise as well. The Hag always knows, somehow. She always knows. And so I shall do what you ask and then one, for all things come in threes. I grant you a favor of my own, just for you, you wise, sweet Queen of Brynhyvar, that your years shall be long, and your land shall be fruitful." He extended his hand. "Come, let me give you the answer of the land."

Tentatively, she took it, placing her cold white fingers into his huge brown palm, and his fingers closed hers, drawing her closer, until she felt her head fall back into the hollow of his chest. He was still Herne, but he was Uwen, too, Uwen and Kian, and every man who'd ever kissed her or moved her or ever even glanced her way. And he knew her, too, it seemed, for he moved over her with the deep knowledge of her body and her pleasure in ways that only the most attentive of her lovers had ever known. He pressed her down and stretched above her, but she winced at the hard rock. In one smooth motion, he turned her, so that he was lying on the rock, and she was crouched above him. His hands cupped her breasts and she saw the brown hair that curled close on his forearms and the backs of his hands, and he raised his head, and brought her nipples, one after the other, to his mouth, so gently, so tenderly, as if he understood that they were swollen and sensitive with the coming child. Her body hummed and sung and thrummed and even though the wind was cold, he warmed her blood so that she threw off her gown and her plaid. The starlight poured down, bathing her in its silvery light, and she felt something hot and red leap up from the rock, so that red and silver, within and without, above and below, all blended and swirled somewhere deep within her. She placed the palms of her hand flat on the planes of his chest and looked into his eyes. They were Uwen's eyes, warm and real and loving, and she knew in that instant, that if he was the god, she was the goddess.

His phallus slipped easily between her naked thighs, her body opening as effortlessly as the earth around a seed. She felt rather than heard the drums now, pulsing in her veins, pounding in her heart, and she felt the rock itself, not cold and unyielding, but warm as sun-softened soil. The music swelled around them and as they began to move, she felt their bodies moving to the same steady rhythm as the beat that seemed to rise up from the land itself. The pleasure was mounting too, building in the base of her belly, the color of molten gold. She felt his phallus harden and swell, and her own body swelled in response, rich and ripe as a hot red fruit, and her womb shuddered, and pleasure flowed like molten gold flowed from the very center of herself. She arched her back and reached for the rock, steadying herself against it as she was gripped by another enormous wave that rose and crested and rolled down her spine and through her arms and legs and feet and hands, into the very rock, and beneath her, Uwen arched his back and cried and she felt a gush as his seed boiled up and spilled within her.

She gasped, collapsing on top of him, and felt another wave of pleasure rip through her, then down and out, into the rock and down, into the earth itself. The standing stones seemed to shudder as if a gigantic wave rolled beneath them, and as she watched, too astonished to really comprehend what she was seeing, the cold faggots and snow-covered wood around the standing stones crackled like lightning and roared into flame that leaped so high into the night, for a moment they were surrounded by a solid orange glow. From the crowd far below she heard a collective gasp and then a mighty cheer. Horns blasted and the pipes rang out a victory song, and she lay, gasping, cradled against his suddenly diminished chest. Gradually, she came back to herself. Uwen lay flat on his back, staring up at the stars, his pale face streaked with sweat and bits of leaves and twigs stuck in his hair. "Great Herne," he breathed, his chest still visibly pounding. "Great Herne, I think the land said yes."

Nessa stumbled forward as the initial wave rolled beneath her feet, catching onto Molly as she fell, and all around her, she saw that others felt it, too, for men and women both were losing their footing and toppling over, grabbing onto each other as another wave rolled down the mountain. She looked up instinctively and saw the wood crackle and then the great flames explode from the very heart of the faggots. "Molly," she cried. "Molly, look, the bonfire—there're no torches at all—"

The people began to cheer, the pipes skirled a victory

song and the horns sang out. All around her, the crowd was laughing and hugging, and as Molly grabbed her, pulling her into a fierce bear hug, Nessa pointed, out toward the horizon. Another wave rolled beneath their feet, and on the closest peaks she saw the signal fires igniting, each ring simultaneously, rolling out in all directions, so that at last it seemed they stood within the fiery ring. "Well, girl," said Molly as she put an arm around Nessa, and watched the bonfires springing to life all across the land, "you believe me now when I said you'd know?"

The blackbird's song made Delphinea open her eyes. She rose up on one elbow, and looked around and saw that she and Finuviel and perhaps two hundred others were in the middle of a great shallow dell. It was coming on to twilight, and a thin sickle moon was rising in the pink and violet sky. The grass on which they lay was very thick and very soft, and very, very green. *Spring grass,* she thought, the sort that sprang up at the base of the rocks. From far away, she heard a horse whinny, and she looked up. In the distance, on the rolling green hills, she saw milk-white horses gamboling, and a herd of white cows with red ears was slowly meandering through the gloaming. It was all so peaceful and so still. In her lap lay the holly wand, and in Finuviel's lay the oak staff. *You could do what Gloriana did, and take them both,* a small voice seemed to whisper. *Or you can accept Finuviel as your Consort. Just the way he is.*

She leaned over and examined his sleeping face. He was completely bald and his skin still bore the pitted scars from the silver poisoning. The other sidhe lying all around them sported long, silky locks of every color imaginable, even green and blue and pink and purple. And some, she saw, had stayed the way they'd fallen asleep—some had horns and beaks and pointed ears. They'd changed, she thought. They all looked different now. Her blue eyes were almost commonplace.

She could smell the apple blossoms wafting on the soft Spring breeze, feel the dew falling. She stretched out beside Finuviel and saw that in the vaulted arch of the indigo sky, the stars burned silver. The berries on the holly wand glowed a gentle red. It was Finuviel's face that had haunted her dreams, Finuviel's voice that had whispered to her for so long. She thought of the poor sick calves and foals. She had not loved them any less when the silver poisoning made them ugly. She knelt down beside him and saw how gracefully his scarred hands lay upon the oak staff. His form was as straight and fair as ever—it was only his face that was so marred. She took a deep breath, leaned forward, then pressed a single kiss upon the thin gash where his lips had been.

To Nessa's surprise, neither Dougal nor Essa remained at Gar, and when she questioned Mag, all the still-wife would tell her was that the two of them had insisted that they would both see Killcairn before they died, and so had left immediately after Mid-Winter. "But the snow, the weather," cried Nessa. "Still-wife, were you daft to let them go in their state?"

But Mag held firm, and the winter weather, which had held off in the weeks before Cecily's crowning, now descended full force, so that it was nearly a full month before Nessa could return to Killcairn. "You can always come and stay with me, Nessa," Molly said as she kissed the girl good-bye and pressed a basket filled with various tinctures and balms into her arms. "That's not so heavy for you to carry, is it?"

"No." Nessa smiled. "Not so heavy at all." She hesitated. The air was cold but the sun was warm today. The days were lengthening, the sun was growing stronger. Soon it would be Spring. "I'll think about it, Molly. I don't quite know how long they have left. Papa wasn't there very long, but he was sick. And Mother—well, twenty years wasn't as bad as it could've been. But they're both so weak, Molly, that's what's so hard. It's like watching them fade away right before my eyes. I take comfort that they're going to the Summerlands together. But it's—it's just so hard to watch." Her eyes filled with tears and she bit her lip. "Just when I got them both back."

"I'll look in on you day after tomorrow, all right?" Molly patted Nessa's cheek and pressed a quick kiss on the other. "You're not alone, Nessa. Don't be afraid to send for me, either, if you need anything at all. But go on now, before the sun starts to drop and it gets cold."

"You're such a mother hen, Molly."

But it felt good. She pressed another kiss on Molly's warm soft cheek, then waved good-bye at the end of the lane. As she started up the river road to Killcairn, she remembered the last time she'd walked from Killcrag to Killcairn. If possible, the day had been the very opposite of this, the air as heavy and gray then as now it was bright and clear. The world felt different, somehow. Younger, newer and cleaner. She smiled and gripped her staff and hummed to herself as she walked.

She passed flocks of geese herded by giggling girls, and a sulky boy driving a herd of sheep farther up the hill. A soft breeze blew off the lake, and in the sunlight, the water sparkled. *A Queen has been called to the Land and the Land has known her as its own!* The ArchDruid's triumphant cry reverberated silently.

The sun had turned the corner in the sky, as Dougal liked to say, by the time she reached Killcairn. She waved to the few of the villagers who had returned. So many had been lost, but a few new people had come—people whose old homes had been destroyed in the goblin rampage, kin of those who'd lived here. For Killcairn, the first to be raided, had been spared on Samhain and the rampage of the bigger hordes. So it looked just the way it always had, thought Nessa as she set her hand upon the gate of the smithy yard, and noticed then the white smoke billowing from the chimney. She heard a woman's voice singing, and the steady ring of the hammer. She thought she smelled a chicken roasting and bread baking. But that's not possible, she thought. Her father had been scarcely able to stand by the time she'd left to go to Ardagh. There was simply no way he'd be able to swing a hammer like that. Her mother had barely been able to raise her head off the pillow.

Nessa gathered up her skirts and ran directly into the forge, then gasped as she reached the threshold. Dougal stood behind the forge, a leather apron tied around his neck and waist, leather vambraces covering his arms. A linen rag was wrapped around his forehead, and his face was wet and streaked with soot. He paused when he saw her and smiled. "Finally, lass. We thought for sure you'd lost your way, then word reached us you were with the grannies."

"Papa?" Nessa said wonderingly. She edged into the forge, then gasped as her mother, wearing a plain gray homespun kirtle covered in a large apron spotted with grease, stepped in from the kitchen, wiping her hands, a broad smile of welcome on her face. "Mother?"

"Nessa, sweetheart. At last." Essa folded Nessa into a firm hug and Nessa drew back, scarcely daring to believe what she saw.

For the change was most apparent in her mother. Instead of that frightening translucency, her flesh had a reassuring solidity. Instead of the unearthly luminescence, her face was lined and reassuringly pink. Her hair was threaded with gray and the flesh sagged a bit beneath her eyes. She looked the way she should look, thought Nessa. As if she'd been here the last twenty years, instead of in the OtherWorld. "M-mother?" she tried again. "Is it really you? Wh-what's happened?"

"Ah, you poor girl, I see we've shocked you. But it's the most wonderful thing, isn't it? It happened right at Mid-Winter, when the bonfires lit the land. We lay down to sleep, your father and I, and when we woke up—well, this is how we found ourselves. I'm not quite as young as I was—" She laughed and patted her middle and glanced flirtatiously over her shoulder at Dougal, who actually winked. "But it's like we got those years back, somehow, Nessa. I don't quite know how else to describe it."

"I'm so happy," she began, "to see you like this." She put out her hand and touched her mother's face and it felt warm and fleshy in a way it had not been before. Her mother felt like Molly now—strong and soft and cushiony. She bit her lip as her eyes welled with tears, and as her mother reached

out to draw her close, a tall figure entered through the
kitchen door, wiping his hands on a linen rag. Artimour
wore an apron, similar to her father's, and his linen shirt
sleeves were rolled up to reveal his forearms, which looked
almost delicate beside Dougal's.

Nessa's head shot up from Essa's shoulder, and she staggered a little, her mouth dropping open as if she'd been
punched in the gut.

"Nessa?" Her mother wrapped an arm around her shoulders to steady her. "Nessa, are you all right?"

"Wh-what's *he* doing here?" she asked. "Artimour?
What in the name of the Hag are you doing here?" She fumbled beneath her tunic and withdrew the ring he'd given her,
the one she now wore on a leather cord. "Did you come
back for this?"

But before Artimour could answer, Dougal said, "Well, it's
like this, Nessa. You know we need an apprentice. You're a
strong girl, but you're still a girl, and Artimour here—well,
he applied for the job. Assuming, of course, you agree. I
won't bring anyone here you're not comfortable about,
Nessa. Your mother and I agree."

She dropped her pack and handed Essa the basket. "Can
I please talk to you?" she asked Artimour. Without waiting
for a reply, she turned on her heel, whipping the end of her
plaid over her shoulder. Her cheeks burned and the wind off
the lake suddenly had an icy edge. She strode down the
path to the beach because it was the only place she could
think of that she knew would be deserted.

"Nessa?"

He hadn't even bothered to grab a plaid, she saw, and
there was gooseflesh on his bare arms and the wind ruffled

his long dark hair. "You'll catch your death here running around like that in winter. Doesn't it get cold in Faerie?"

"Not like this." He crossed his arms across his chest and shivered. "Look, Nessa, if you want me to leave, I will. But when we all woke up, I looked around—and it was all beautiful again. The grass was turning green, the skies were blue, even the rain was beautiful as it fell. But I—I was holding the silver amulet—the one you made—" He fumbled beneath his shirt and to her utter amazement, he pulled it out. "I was holding it, and it didn't burn me. So I realized I had changed, just like the other sidhe, only it seemed that I...I was mortal."

"What happened then?"

"They told me I could stay. Finuviel offered a thousand apologies, all the land I desired, all the cattle I wished to claim. But all I could think about was what it would be like to be here with you."

"You told me I was a terrible mistake."

"Nessa, I'm sorry. You made me feel things I never knew I could feel. It was the hardest thing in the world to tell you I wanted nothing more to do with you. But when I saw what happened to your parents—when I saw what happened to Griffin—I didn't want anything like that to happen to you. And you're so determined, so stubborn. Once you make up your mind, there's no going back with you. I knew if you decided to follow me into Faerie, I'd never be able to prevent you. And so I hurt you. And I'm sorry. And if you let me stay and learn your craft, I swear I'll never hurt you again."

"And what does happen if you stay? Don't you realize how you made me feel about you? You made me feel things I didn't know I could feel either. I didn't just want you the way a mortal wants a sidhe—I cared about you, I made you the sword, I melted the amulet—"

He took a single step forward, and she saw that his lips were blue with cold. "I know you did, and I see that now, and I'm sorry. I can't undo what I did, and I'm very bad at this, clearly. I'm trying to tell you that I believe that what I feel for you is love—mortal love—and I would like to stay with you and—"

She stepped back, holding her hand over her mouth, fighting the tears that were threatening to spill down her cheeks. She flung back her head. Now he comes, she thought, ready to tell him to go back to Faerie and dance forever to Finuviel's tune.

Yes, now. The still small voice within echoed and she glanced up, her attention momentarily diverted by the dancing pattern of light leaping off the surface of the lake. *Now, when the world is new.* The scent of the tiny-leaved thyme crushed beneath her boots rose to her nostrils. *Do you really want him to go?* This was a choice, she understood in a flash of clarity. An important choice. A choice she didn't want to get wrong.

"I don't know how to say it, Nessa," he finished, looking miserable. "I don't know how to tell you that I love you and I'm sorry and I want to stay here, in this world, for as many years as you and the Hag allow."

"Tell me later," she said, knowing exactly what she wanted and feeling a delirious happiness sweep over her, so that she felt flushed and giddy and glad. The lakewater lapped against the shore and he began to shiver. She opened her plaid and spread her arms wide as the light leaped like silver salmon off the wind-whipped waves. "Show me now."

AFTERWARD

The timbers creaked as the waves pounded against the sides of the sleek, fast-moving Humbrian battle-boats. "A fair sky and a following wind." A grizzled old sailor winked at Hoell as he nimbly scampered up the lines.

The sailors were skipping up and down the rigging, and the oarsmen were rowing in fast time to the beat of the drum. Hoell wrapped an arm around a mast and leaned out as far as he dared, searching for some sign of his homeland through the shifting purple mists ahead. A flash of green, and he turned to face the dour expression of the Commander of the Humbrian Army. "I see it up ahead." He pointed.

The Commander, in his elaborate gold uniform, bent his thin lips into what might've passed as a smile, and said, "You're mistaken, Your Grace." Despite Hoell's rank, he refused to address him as if he were an equal to the King of Humbria. It grated on Merle, Hoell knew, but it didn't bother him. He would be happy to return to the green land of his birth, to swim the rocky shoals of the peat-black lake. It was the sea that made him nervous, the green, shifting waters that rose and fell like a rolling road beneath the shuddering deck. White flecks of flung foam dotted even the Commander's face. "We'll come about as soon as we make landfall and wait for dusk—"

At that, a tremor went through Hoell. "Wait for dusk? No, that's not a good idea at—"

"If you remember, Your Grace, you participated in these discussions."

An ancient fear swept over Hoell with all the force of one of the rolling waves. "But I told you then, I remember distinctly telling you—dusk is not—"

"My lord, the plan is made."

"But you don't understand," Hoell murmured. How to explain to this stiff-backed, wood-mouthed puppet that dusk was the most dangerous time of all, the time when the borders between the worlds blurred, when the goblins came hunting, when all who'd had sense were under a sturdy roof and behind four square walls? "Why not wait til dark, then? Midnight? The settlements will be all qui—"

"My lord, this is not a raid. If dusk will drive the Brynnish indoors, so much the better. We seek to establish a beachhead."

"Land-ho!" The cry went up from the lookout positioned halfway up the mainmast. A cheer rose up from the crew, even as a chill went down Hoell's spine.

He gazed out over the water, and staring into the shifting mists, saw a glimpse of greenish brown, the rounded edge of the broad breast of the lowlands of Far Nearing. Saltwater splashed on his face, and he thought he heard someone singing. He looked over one shoulder, and then the other, but the sound persisted. *It's at dusk the goblins hunt.* Was that old nursery warning the reason for his fear? Another snatch of song intruded on his thoughts, and he looked up this time, expecting to see a sailor whistling in the rigging just above. But there was no one anywhere even within earshot, for the Commander was conferring with the Captain of the ship and the Admiral of the King's Navy. The sound came again, closer this time, and Hoell looked down.

And saw a face staring back at him. He gasped, and nearly fell back, as the sound came again, and he realized it was singing, it was the sound of many voices singing and he peered over the edge of the boat, and saw many faces now, smiling back at him, beckoning him to join them. He glanced over his shoulder and saw the Commander look at him and raise an eyebrow, saw the Captain nudge the Commander and the two exchange a glance. *They think I'm mad,* Hoell thought. *They think I'm mad. But I'm not. There are people under the water, and they're singing to me.*

The voices were distinct now, so that he could hear the blending of male and female, high and low, into a harmony more melodious than even the ghastly battle-song of the sidhe that had awakened him. The harmonies were subtle and fluid, reminded him of currents running through deeper water, blending so delicately and so precisely, one scarcely heard the shift. And they were singing to him.

There was no doubt of it at all, he thought as he put one knee up on the rail and leaned over to get a better look.

"Steady on, Your Grace, grip that line if you must lean so far!" It was the Captain.

Hoell turned, smiled and nodded and grabbed for a line as a sudden swell, caused by the number of faces clustering closer, crowding, really. They were beautiful and kind and they were smiling as they sang. He looked up, to the horizon, to Brynhyvar, and saw a black mass gathering. He raised his arm and pointed. "There's a storm out there. A storm over the land—"

But neither the Commander nor the Captain seemed to hear, although the faces beneath the water nodded faster as if they had understood and they agreed. They were singing to him, now, he could see, pointing at him, gesturing for him to join them, parting in a great swell so that he could see the dark blue light that was beginning to glow beneath the waves. They were waving to him now, raising their hands above the water so that little drops of water flung this way and that. They landed on his face and he leaned farther out, and farther down, reaching out to see if he could catch one of the singers by their fair, white hands.

"My lord!" It was the Commander and the Captain together.

But he nearly had one, a dark-eyed minx who winked at him before she dived again beneath the waves to join her sisters' song. He leaned out and looked toward Brynhyvar. The clouds were black now, a dark line massed across the horizon like a threatening wall. "Turn back," he cried to the Captain. "Turn back!"

But they only rushed forward and tried to wrestle him away from the side, even as his fingers brushed those of another of the glimmering creatures. "My lord, you'll be lost—"

"Can't you hear them?" he cried. The clouds were looming larger now, billowing up like a monstrous keep, and he pointed, desperate to make them understand. "Can't you see that?"

He flung them away and turned back to the side, to see the same dark-haired, dark-eyed woman rising up from the water's depths, music of such exquisite beauty pouring from her throat that tears ran down his eyes. *Come with us, poor Hoell, come with us. Leave the ones who are blind and cannot see, and sing with those of us who do.*

She understands, he thought. They understand. He looked at them and suddenly he knew exactly where he belonged, where he'd belonged all his life if only he'd understood. No wonder he'd always lived in houses perched over water. In one fast motion, he kicked off his boots and dived in.

It is recorded in the annals of the Kingdom of Humbria that the invasion of Brynhyvar in the thirty-fifth year of the reign of Fedarovahr the Fourth was thwarted by a great storm that rose up off the land as dusk was falling and drove the Humbrian vessels into the sea, during which the King of the Brynnish, Hoell, was lost. And so great a loss of men and ships and equipment was suffered by the Humbrians that it

tempered Fedarovahr's ambition at last to attempt to annex
the land of Brynhyvar.

But in the songs of the Druids of Brynhyvar, it is remembered as the first time the forces of King Finuviel of the sidhe
and Queen Cecily of the mortals joined together to repel an
invader from their land.

* * * * *

*The Caul is unMade—but the Making of it is a tale not
yet told. Soon the story will come to light—and we'll all
discover
SILVER'S LURE.*

THE TEARS OF LUNA

A shimmering crown grows and dims and is always reborn. Luna has the power and gift to brighten dark nights and lend mystery to the shadows. She will sometimes show up on the brightest of days, but her most powerful moments are when she fills the heaven with her light. Just as the moon comes each night to caress sleeping mortals, Luna takes a special interest in lovers. Her belief in the power of romance is so strong that it is said she cries gem-like tears which linger when her light moves on. Those lucky enough to find the Tears of Luna will be blessed with passion enduring, love fulfilled and the strength to find and fight for what is theirs.

A WORLD YOU CAN ONLY IMAGINE ™

LUNA™

www.LUNA-Books.com

THE TEARS OF LUNA MYTH COMES ALIVE IN

A WORLD AN ARTIST CAN IMAGINE ™

This year LUNA Books and Duirwaigh Gallery are proud to present the work of five magical artists.

This month, the art featured on our inside back cover has been created by:

MARK FISHMAN

If you would like to order a print of Mark's work, or learn more about him please visit Duirwaigh Gallery at www.DuirwaighGallery.com.

For details on how to enter for a chance to win this great prize:

- A print of Mark's art

- Prints from the four other artists that will be featured in LUNA novels

- A library of LUNA novels

Visit www.LUNA-Books.com

LBDG0605TR